ISAAC ASIMOV PRESENTS THE BEST
SCIENCE FICTION OF THE 19TH CENTURY

Also Edited by Isaac Asimov,
Charles G. Waugh,
and Martin H. Greenberg

The Science Fiction Solar System

The Thirteen Crimes of Science Fiction

ISAAC ASIMOV

PRESENTS THE BEST SCIENCE FICTION OF THE 19TH CENTURY

Edited by Isaac Asimov,
Charles G. Waugh,
and Martin Greenberg

BEAUFORT BOOKS, INC.

New York / Toronto

Copyright © 1981 by Nightfall, Inc., Charles G. Waugh,
and Martin H. Greenberg

Library of Congress Cataloging in Publication Data
Main entry under title:

Isaac Asimov presents the best science fiction of
the 19th century.

1. Science fiction. I. Asimov, Isaac, 1920-
II. Waugh, Charles. III. Greenberg, Martin Harry.
PN6120.95.S33I8 1981 808.83'876 80-27721
ISBN 0-8253-0038-X

Published in the United States by Beaufort Books, Inc., New York.
Published simultaneously in Canada by Nelson, Foster and Scott Ltd.

Printed in the U.S.A. First Edition
10 9 8 7 6 5 4 3 2

CONTENTS

Introduction: THE FIRST CENTURY OF SCIENCE FICTION
Isaac Asimov   9

THE SANDMAN (1817)
E.T.A. Hoffmann
   (translated from the German by J.T. Bealby)   13

THE MORTAL IMMORTAL (1834)
Mary Wollstonecraft Shelley   49

A DESCENT INTO THE MAELSTROM (1841)
Edgar Allan Poe   65

RAPPACCINI'S DAUGHTER (1844)
Nathaniel Hawthorne   83

THE CLOCK THAT WENT BACKWARD (1881)
Edward Page Mitchell   113

INTO THE SUN (1882)
Robert Duncan Milne   129

A TALE OF NEGATIVE GRAVITY (1884)
Frank R. Stockton   149

THE HORLA (1887)
Guy de Maupassant   171

THE SHAPES (1887)
J.-H. Rosny aîné
   (translated from the French by Damon Knight)   195

CONTENTS

To Whom This May Come (1888)
Edward Bellamy   221

The Great Keinplatz Experiment (1894)
Sir Arthur Conan Doyle   239

In the Abyss (1896)
H.G. Wells   257

The Thames valley Catastrophe (1897)
Grant Allen   275

The Lizard (1898)
C.J. Cutcliffe Hyne   295

A Thousand Deaths (1899)
Jack London   305

ISAAC ASIMOV PRESENTS THE BEST
SCIENCE FICTION OF THE 19TH CENTURY

Introduction:
THE FIRST CENTURY
OF SCIENCE FICTION

Isaac Asimov

Every enthusiasm aspires to respectability and one way of getting it is to demonstrate that it is old, even ancient. Respect automatically clings to anything that is hoary, and many an old fool is treated with reverence merely because of his white hairs and his talent for survival.

It may be that which has induced some to claim a background for science fiction that is as old as literature. To do so, it is only necessary to broaden the definition.

Suppose we consider science fiction as that branch of literature that deals with the imaginative and unfamiliar. In that case almost any fantasy, any legend, any traveler's tale, would be science fiction. When speech was first born there must have been lies told around the campfire concerning the great feats of the hunters of the tribe, and that would be science fiction, too.

Or, if we wish to stick to formal literature and deal with those portions of it more or less familiar to our culture, we might begin with Homer's *Odyssey,* written about 800 B.C. If we are willing to consider one-eyed giants and witches and monsters to be the stuff of science fiction, then the *Odyssey* is not only the first, but the most successful piece of s.f. ever written. After all, what other piece of s.f. writing can we be sure will still be hailed as an eternal classic after twenty-seven centuries?

On the other hand, if we want to be more restrictive, we might define science fiction as that branch of literature that deals with those aspects of the imaginative and unfamiliar that have come to be accepted as ''science-fictionish.''

In that case, the first science fiction tale we know of would be

Lucian of Samosata's *True History,* written somewhere about A.D. 150, nearly a thousand years after the *Odyssey*. In *True History,* we have a protagonist who is carried up to the moon by a waterspout. All sorts of imaginative monsters are described as living on the moon, and surely nothing could be as science-fictionish as a trip to the satellite that circles us.

Yet that's still not enough. Lucian, after all, was merely writing a travel-tale. He called the exotic land to which his hero had come the moon, but he might as well have called it Africa, or made up some name for an invented island in the sea.

Suppose, then, we wanted to define science fiction as that branch of literature that deals with things imaginative and unfamiliar but that attempts, nevertheless, to be realistic and to portray the universe as it is. In that case, we must look further than Lucian.

The German astronomer, Johann Kepler, wrote a tale called *Somnium,* published (posthumously) in 1634, about fifteen centuries after *True History*. Here, too, we have a protagonist who finds himself on the moon (carried there by spirits, this time). Again we have a world populated by strange and monstrous forms of life.

The crucial difference here, though, is that Kepler gave the moon a two-week-long day and a two-week-long night, which is an astronomical fact. It was the first intrusion of authentic observation into what would otherwise be a sheer work of fantasy.

That, too, is not enough. The advance and retreat of sunlight on the moon is something that is not human. It required neither science nor technology to be understood; merely sensibly directed eyesight.

True science fiction deals with human science, with the continuing advance of knowledge, with the continuing ability of human beings to make themselves better understand the universe and even to alter some parts of it for their own comfort and security by the ingenuity of their ideas. And if that is so, then science fiction becomes quite a modern phenomenon and cannot claim the respectability of age.

Why is that so? Have not human beings been learning new things and altering their environment since earliest times? Who knows when clothing was first used or when the first tree branch or thighbone was used as a club? As for the first use of fire, that antedates *Homo sapiens*, for it was the invention of small-brained *Homo erectus*.

And yet through almost all of human history, such advances were made so slowly and spread outward from their point or points of origin so gradually that individual human beings were not particularly aware of change in the course of their own lifetimes. At the most, they would assume that some god or some legendary ancestor had invented the technology they used and that was that. It came all at once and in a finished state.

It is characteristic of technology, however, that it is cumulative. The further it advances the faster it advances. In addition, the further it advances, the more it makes possible new and better ways of experimenting and of observing the universe. By the seventeenth century, technology, thanks to its telescopes, microscopes, clocks, and so on, had given rise to modern science. And the more science advances, the more easily it can guide technology to still further and speedier advances.

Eventually, this leapfrogging phenomenon brought the advance of technology to a stage of such rapidity that change became clearly visible in a human lifetime. Individual people became aware that the world was changing and that it was human thought and human ingenuity that was the agent of the change.

Once that happened, it became possible to write about a world that was changing and to try to forecast, or anticipate, or simply to depict plausibly, additional changes that had not yet taken place, but that might take place, and to describe how such changes would affect human beings.

We can then define science fiction as that branch of literature that deals with the human response to changes in the level of science and technology—it being understood that the changes involved would be rational ones in keeping with what was known about science, technology and people.

True science fiction, by its modern definition (or at least, *my* modern definition) could not have been written prior to the nineteenth century then, because it was only with the coming of the Industrial Revolution in the last few decades of the eighteenth century that the rate of technological change became great enough to notice in a single lifetime—in those areas of the globe affected by that revolution.

In fact, it has become fashionable to consider Mary Shelley's *Frankenstein,* published in 1818, nearly two centuries after *Somnium,* as the first true science-fiction tale.

This does not mean that science fiction has to hang its head in shame because it is only two centuries old. Rather it should glory in the fact that it is the literary response to humanity's crowning triumph—modern science and technology. It should trumpet forth the fact that it deals with the great truth of contemporary times—rapid change.

Science fiction is young because it is *today's* literature; and, more than that, *tomorrow's.*

Of course, since science fiction tends to go out of date with the science and technology upon which it is based, the tendency is to concentrate on contemporary science fiction, and the great writers of the first century of science fiction tend to be neglected.

The one great nineteenth-century science-fiction writer whom everyone knows is Jules Verne. To be sure, he was the first *professional* science-fiction writer. He was the first to make a good living out of a literary career that was devoted primarily to science fiction. His first great success was *Five Weeks in a Balloon,* published in 1863, half a century after *Frankenstein.*

Yet if Verne was by far the greatest science-fiction writer of the nineteenth century, he was not the only one. The advances of the Industrial Revolution fired the imagination of Europeans and Americans and many wrote with enthusiasm, and sometimes with dread, of the anticipated changes yet to come, and did so with varying degrees of insight.

In this anthology, Martin, Charles, and I have brought together the works of a number of these nineteenth-century science-fiction writers; first, because they are interesting social documents, presenting, as they do, the views of imaginative men and women facing a world which was just beginning to convert the winds of change into a whirlwind; second, because the tales are precursors of what is to come in twentieth-century science fiction; and third, because they are interesting in themselves.

Come back with us, then, to the first century of science fiction.

E.T.A. Hoffman (1776–1822)

E.T.A. Hoffmann was a very talented lawyer, artist, musician, critic, and writer. A romanticist and pioneer in psychological fiction, his music influenced Wagner, his criticism brought recognition to Bach and Beethoven, and his writings were adapted into several operas as well as inspiring Poe, Gogol, and Dostoevsky.

Enormously intelligent, he was born in Konigsberg, Germany, and grew up with relatives after his parents' divorce. His childhood was not particularly happy, but he did form an invaluable lifelong friendship with his study companion, Theodor Hippel. And as long as Hoffmann progressed toward the family's traditional legal career he was permitted time for music and art.

When admitted to the local university in 1792, he worked hard and did well. However, he became romantically involved with a married woman to whom he was giving piano lessons. So upon graduation in 1795, his relatives dispatched him to another city for additional studies. He completed advanced exams (*Referendar* and *Assessor*) in 1798 and 1800, but by now, perhaps because of his affair, music had become the major focus of his life. Still, he accepted a government appointment to Posen, distinguishing himself for two years. Then a series of Hoffmann's military caricatures created a scandal and, as a compromise, he received promotion to *Regierungsrat* (councillor) and immediate transfer to an obscure Polish village. He hated Plock but, freed from outside distractions, he studied music theory, composed, and sold both fiction and music criticism.

By 1804 Hippel had gained great influence and was able to shift Hoffmann to Warsaw. There Hoffmann became immersed in the musical society he founded. However, Napoleon captured the city, eventually forcing Hoffmann back to Berlin. Hoffmann found no legal openings, so he advertised for a position as conductor. The Bamberg Theater hired him in 1808, but he ended up making less than he needed and, under great financial pressure, he started contributing musical reviews and fiction to *Allgemeine musikalische Zeitung*. By 1810, his first collection of stories was published and he began working on his opera *Undine* (based on Fouque's fairy tale).

In 1814 Hippel secured Hoffmann's appointment to the Supreme Court. And by 1816 Hoffmann's life seemed set: chairman of the court, a famous author in great demand, and a successful operatic composer. But he drank excessively, experienced serious illnesses, and spent money faster than it came in. Finally, in 1818, King William made the disastrous mistake of appointing Hoffmann chairman of a committee to investigate "demagogic activities." Hoffmann, who was basically fair-minded and apolitical, blocked all attempts at a witch hunt and proceeded to satirize one of the king's friends for suggesting such tactics. This time even Hippel's influence might have failed except for the fact that a mysterious illness (possibly tabes dorsalis) had begun to paralyze Hoffmann. An official reprimand was issued, but Hoffmann was allowed to continue writing until the disease finished him.

Many of Hoffmann's stories are permeated with fantastic or science-fictional elements such as humanoid robots. He is a subtle writer who often uses experimental forms and synesthetic images. And as "The Sandman" demonstrates, his strengths include powerful narrative drive, vivid pathological characterizations, and convincingly realistic presentations of grotesque and supernatural elements.

THE SANDMAN
(translated from the German by J.T. Bealby)

NATHANAEL TO LOTHAIR

I know you are all very uneasy because I have not written for such a long, long time. Mother, to be sure, is angry, and Clara, I dare say, believes I am living here in riot and revelry, and quite forgetting my sweet angel, whose image is so deeply engraved upon my heart and mind. But that is not so; daily and hourly do I think of you all, and my lovely Clara's form comes to gladden me in my dreams, and smiles upon me with her bright eyes, as graciously as she used to do in the days when I went in and out amongst you. Oh! How could I write to you in the distracted state of mind in which I have been, and which, until now, has quite bewildered me! A terrible thing has happened to me. Dark forebodings of some awful fate threatening me are spreading themselves out over my head like black clouds, impenetrable to every friendly ray of sunlight. I must now tell you what has taken place; I must, that I see well enough, but only to think upon it makes the wild laughter burst from my lips. Oh! My dear, dear Lothair, what shall I say to make you feel, if only in an inadequate way, that that which happened to me a few days ago could thus really exercise such a hostile and disturbing influence upon my life? Oh that you were here to see for yourself! But now you will, I suppose, take me for a superstitious ghost-seer. In a word, the terrible thing which I have experienced, the fatal effect of which I in vain exert every effort to shake off, is simply that some days ago, namely on the 30th October, at twelve o'clock at noon, a dealer in weatherglasses came into my room and wanted to sell me one of his wares. I bought nothing, and threatened to kick him downstairs, whereupon he went away of his own accord.

You will conclude that it can only be very peculiar relations—

relations intimately intertwined with my life—that can give significance to this event, and that it must be the person of this unfortunate hawker which has had such a very inimical effect upon me. And so it really is. I will summon up all my faculties in order to narrate to you calmly and patiently as much of the early days of my youth as will suffice to put matters before you in such a way that your keen sharp intellect may grasp everything clearly and distinctly, in bright and living pictures. Just as I am beginning, I hear you laugh and Clara say, "What's all this childish nonsense about?" Well, laugh at me, laugh heartily at me, pray do. But, good God! My hair is standing on end, and I seem to be entreating you to laugh at me in the same sort of frantic despair in which Franz Moor entreated Daniel to laugh him to scorn.[1] But to my story.

Except at dinner we, that is, I and my brothers and sisters, saw but little of our father all day long. His business no doubt took up most of his time. After our evening meal, which, in accordance with an old custom, was served at seven o'clock, we all went, Mother with us, into Father's room, and took our places around a round table. My father smoked his pipe, drinking a large glass of beer to it. Often he told us many wonderful stories, and got so excited over them that his pipe always went out; I used then to light it for him with a spill, and this formed my chief amusement. Often, again, he would give us picture books to look at, whilst he sat silent and motionless in his easy chair, puffing out such dense clouds of smoke that we were all as it were enveloped in mist. On such evenings mother was very sad; and directly it struck nine she said, "Come, children! Off to bed! Come! The Sandman is come, I see." And I always did seem to hear something trampling upstairs with slow heavy steps; that must be the Sandman. Once in particular I was very much frightened at this dull trampling and knocking; as Mother was leading us out of the room I asked her, "O Mamma! But who is this nasty Sandman who always sends us away from Papa? What does he look like?" "There is no Sandman, my dear child," Mother answered; "when I say the Sandman is come, I only mean that you are sleepy and can't keep your eyes open, as if somebody had put sand in them." This answer of Mother's did not

---

[1] See Schiller's *Räuber*, Act V, Scene I. Franz Moor, seeing that the failure of all his villainous schemes is inevitable, and that his own ruin is close upon him, is at length overwhelmed with the madness of despair, and unburdens the terrors of his conscience to the old servant Daniel, bidding him laugh him to scorn.

satisfy me; nay, in my childish mind the thought clearly unfolded itself that Mother denied there was a Sandman only to prevent us being afraid—why, I always heard him come upstairs. Full of curiosity to learn something more about this Sandman and what he had to do with us children, I at length asked the old woman who acted as my youngest sister's attendant, what sort of a man was he—the Sandman? "Why, 'thanael, darling, don't you know?" she replied. "Oh! He's a wicked man, who comes to little children when they won't go to bed and throws handfuls of sand in their eyes, so that they jump out of their heads all bloody; and he puts them into a bag and takes them to the half-moon as food for his little ones; and they sit there in the nest and have hooked beaks like owls, and they pick naughty little boys' and girls' eyes out with them." After this I formed in my own mind a horrible picture of the cruel Sandman. When anything came blundering upstairs at night I trembled with fear and dismay; and all that my mother could get out of me were the stammered words "The Sandman! The Sandman!" whilst the tears coursed down my cheeks. Then I ran into my bedroom, and the whole night through tormented myself with the terrible apparition of the Sandman. I was quite old enough to perceive that the old woman's tale about the Sandman and his little ones' nest in the half-moon couldn't be altogether true; nevertheless the Sandman continued to be for me a fearful incubus, and I was always seized with terror—my blood always ran cold, not only when I heard anybody come up the stairs, but when I heard anybody noisily open my father's room door and go in. Often he stayed away for a long season altogether; then he would come several times in close succession.

This went on for years, without my being able to accustom myself to this fearful apparition, without the image of the horrible Sandman growing any fainter in my imagination. His intercourse with my father began to occupy my fancy ever more and more; I was restrained from asking my father about him by an unconquerable shyness; but as the years went on the desire waxed stronger and stronger within me to fathom the mystery myself and to see the fabulous Sandman. He had been the means of disclosing to me the path of the wonderful and the adventurous, which so easily find lodgment in the mind of the child. I liked nothing better than to hear or read horrible stories of goblins, witches, Tom Thumbs, and so on; but always at the head of them all stood the Sandman, whose picture I scribbled in the most extraordinary and repulsive forms with both chalk and coal everywhere, on the tables, and cupboard doors, and walls. When I was ten years old my mother removed me from the nursery into a little chamber off the corridor not far from my father's room. We still had to withdraw hastily whenever, on the stroke of nine, the mysterious unknown was heard in the house. As I lay in my little chamber I could hear him go into Father's room, and soon afterwards I fancied there was a fine and peculiar-smelling steam spreading itself through the house. As my curiosity waxed stronger, my resolve to make somehow or other the Sandman's acquaintance took deeper root. Often when my mother had gone past, I slipped quickly out of my room into the corridor, but I could never see anything, for always before I could reach the place where I could get sight of him, the Sandman was well inside the door. At last, unable to resist the impulse any longer, I determined to conceal myself in Father's room and there wait for the Sandman.

One evening I perceived from my father's silence and Mother's sadness that the Sandman would come; accordingly, pleading that I was excessively tired, I left the room before nine o'clock and concealed myself in a hiding place close beside the door. The street door creaked, and slow, heavy, echoing steps crossed the passage towards the stairs. Mother hurried past me with my brothers and sisters. Softly—softly—I opened Father's room door. He sat as usual, silent and motionless, with his back towards it; he did not hear me; and in a moment I was in and behind a curtain drawn before my father's open wardrobe, which stood just inside the room. Nearer and nearer and nearer came the echoing footsteps. There was a strange coughing and shuffling and mumbling outside. My heart beat with expectation and fear. A quick step now close, close beside the door, a noisy rattle of the handle, and the door flies open with a bang. Recovering my courage with an effort, I take a cautious peep out. In the middle of the room in front of my father stands the Sandman, the bright light of the lamp falling full upon his face. The Sandman, the terrible Sandman, is the old advocate Coppelius who often comes to dine with us.

But the most hideous figure could not have awakened greater trepidation in my heart than this Coppelius did. Picture to yourself a large broad-shouldered man, with an immensely big head, a face the color of yellow-ochre, grey bushy eyebrows, from beneath which two piercing, greenish, catlike eyes glittered, and a prominent Roman nose hanging over his upper lip. His distorted mouth was often screwed up into a malicious smile; then two dark-red spots appeared on his cheeks, and a strange hissing noise proceeded from between his tightly clenched teeth. He always wore an ash-grey coat of an old-fashioned cut, a waistcoat of the same, and nether extremeties to match, but black stockings and buckles set with stones on his shoes. His little wig scarcely extended beyond the crown of his head, his hair was curled round high up above his big red ears, and plastered to his temples with cosmetic, and a broad closed hair-bag stood out prominently from his neck, so that you could see the silver buckle that fastened his folded neck-cloth. Altogether he was a most disagreeable and horribly ugly figure; but what we children detested most of all was his big coarse hairy hands; we could never fancy anything that he once touched. This he had noticed; and so, whenever our good mother quietly placed a piece of cake or sweet fruit on our plates, he delighted to touch it under some pretext or other, until the bright tears stood in our eyes, and from disgust and loathing we lost the enjoyment of the tidbit that was intended to please us. And he did just the same thing when Father gave us a glass of sweet wine on holidays. Then he would quickly pass his hand over it, or even sometimes raise the glass to his blue lips, and he laughed quite sardonically when all we dared do was to express our vexation in stifled sobs. He habitually called us the ''little brutes''; and when he was present we might not utter a sound; and we cursed the ugly spiteful man who deliberately and intentionally spoilt all our little pleasures. Mother seemed to dislike this hateful Coppelius as much as we did; for as soon as he appeared her cheerfulness and bright and natural manner were transformed into sad, gloomy seriousness. Father treated him as if he were a being of some higher race, whose ill-manners were to be tolerated, whilst no effort ought to be spared to keep him in good humor. He had only to give a slight hint, and his favorite dishes were cooked for him and rare wine uncorked.

As soon as I saw this Coppelius, therefore, the fearful and hideous thought arose in my mind that he, and he alone, must be the Sandman; but I no longer conceived of the Sandman as the bugbear in the old nurse's fable, who fetched children's eyes and took them to the half-moon as food for his little ones—no!—but as an ugly spectre-like fiend bringing trouble and misery and ruin, both temporal and everlasting, everywhere wherever he appeared.

I was spellbound on the spot. At the risk of being discovered, and, as I well enough knew, of being severely punished, I remained as I was, with my head thrust through the curtains listening. My father received Coppelius in a ceremonious manner. "Come, to work!" cried the latter, in a hoarse, snarling voice, throwing off his coat. Gloomily and silently my father took off his dressing gown, and both put on long black smock frocks. Where they took them from I forgot to notice. Father opened the folding doors of a cupboard in the wall; but I saw that what I had so long taken to be a cupboard was really a dark recess, in which was a little hearth. Coppelius approached it, and a blue flame crackled upwards from it. Round about were all kinds of strange utensils. Good God! As my old father bent down over the fire how different he looked! His gentle and venerable features seemed to be drawn up by some dreadful convulsive pain into an ugly, repulsive, Satanic mask. He looked like Coppelius. Coppelius plied the red-hot tongs and drew bright glowing masses out of the thick smoke and began assiduously to hammer them. I fancied that there were men's faces visible round about, but without eyes, having ghastly deep black holes where the eyes should have been. "Eyes here! Eyes here!" cried Coppelius, in a hollow, sepulchral voice. My blood ran cold with horror; I screamed and tumbled out of my hiding place onto the floor. Coppelius immediately seized upon me. "You little brute! You little brute!" he bleated, grinding his teeth. Then, snatching me up, he threw me on the hearth, so that the flames began to singe my hair. "Now we've got eyes—eyes—a beautiful pair of children's eyes," he whispered, and, thrusting his hands into the flames, he took out some red-hot grains and was about to strew them into my eyes. Then my father clasped his hands and entreated him, saying, "Master, master, let my Nathanael keep his eyes—oh!—do let him keep them." Coppelius laughed shrilly and replied, "Well then, the boy may keep his eyes and whine and pule his way through the world; but we will now at any rate observe the mechanism of the hand and the foot." And therewith he roughly laid hold upon me, so that my joints cracked and twisted my hands and my feet, pulling them now this way, and now that. "That's not quite right altogether! It's better as it was! The old fellow knew what he was about." Thus lisped and hissed Coppelius; but all around me grew black and dark; a sudden convulsive pain shot through all my nerves and bones; I knew nothing more.

I felt a soft, warm breath fanning my cheek; I awakened as if out of the sleep of death; my mother was bending over me. "Is the Sandman still there?'' I stammered. ''No, my dear child; he's been gone a long, long time; he'll not hurt you.'' Thus spoke my mother, as she kissed her recovered darling and pressed him to her heart. But why should I tire you, my dear Lothair? Why do I dwell at such length on these details, when there's so much remains to be said? Enough—I was detected in my eavesdropping, and roughly handled by Coppelius. Fear and terror had brought on a violent fever, of which I lay ill several weeks. ''Is the Sandman still there?'' These were the first words I uttered on coming to myself again, the first sign of my recovery, of my safety. Thus, you see, I have only to relate to you the most terrible moment of my youth for you to thoroughly understand that it must not be ascribed to the weakness of my eyesight if all that I see is colorless, but to the fact that a mysterious destiny has hung a dark veil of clouds about my life, which I shall perhaps only break through when I die.

Coppelius did not show himself again; it was reported he had left the town.

It was about a year later when, in pursuance of the old unchanged custom, we sat around the round table in the evening. Father was in very good spirits, and was telling us amusing tales about his youthful travels. As it was striking nine we all at once heard the street door creak on its hinges, and slow ponderous steps echoed across the passage and up the stairs. ''That is Coppelius,'' said my mother, turning pale. ''Yes, it is Coppelius,'' replied my father in a faint broken voice. The tears started from my mother's eyes. ''But, Father, Father,'' she cried, ''must it be so?'' ''This is the last time,'' he replied; ''this is the last time he will come to me, I promise you. Go now, go and take the children. Go, go to bed—good night.''

As for me, I felt as if I were converted into cold, heavy stone; I could not get my breath. As I stood there immovable my mother seized me by the arm. ''Come, Nathanael! Do come along!'' I suffered myself to be led away; I went into my room. ''Be a good boy and keep quiet,'' Mother called after me; ''get into bed and go to sleep.'' But, tortured by indescribable fear and uneasiness, I could not close my eyes. That hateful, hideous Coppelius stood before me with his glittering eyes, smiling maliciously down upon me; in vain did I strive to banish the image. Somewhere about midnight there was a terrific crack, as if a cannon were being fired off. The whole house shook; something went rustling and clattering past my door; the house door was pulled to with a bang. "That is Coppelius," I cried, terror-struck, and leapt out of bed. Then I heard a wild, heartrending scream; I rushed into my father's room; the door stood open, and clouds of suffocating smoke came rolling towards me. The servant-maid shouted, "Oh! my master! my master!" On the floor in front of the smoking hearth lay my father, dead, his face burned black and fearfully distorted, my sisters weeping and moaning around him, and my mother lying near them in a swoon. "Coppelius, you atrocious fiend, you've killed my father," I shouted. My senses left me. Two days later, when my father was placed in his coffin, his features were mild and gentle again as they had been when he was alive. I found great consolation in the thought that his association with the diabolical Coppelius could not have ended in his everlasting ruin.

Our neighbors had been awakened by the explosion; the affair got talked about, and came before the magisterial authorities, who wished to cite Coppelius to clear himself. But he had disappeared from the place, leaving no traces behind him.

Now when I tell you, my dear friend, that the weatherglass hawker I spoke of was the villain Coppelius, you will not blame me for seeing impending mischief in his inauspicious reappearance. He was differently dressed; but Coppelius's figure and features are too deeply impressed upon my mind for me to be capable of making a mistake in the matter. Moreover, he has not even changed his name. He proclaims himself here, I learn, to be a Piedmontese mechanician, and styles himself Giuseppe Coppola.

I am resolved to enter the lists against him and revenge my father's death, let the consequences be what they may.

Don't say a word to Mother about the reappearance of this odious monster. Give my love to my darling Clara; I will write to her when I am in a somewhat calmer frame of mind. Adieu, &c.

CLARA TO NATHANAEL

You are right, you have not written to me for a very long time, but nevertheless I believe that I still retain a place in your mind and thoughts. It is a proof that you were thinking a good deal about me when you were sending off your last letter to brother Lothair, for instead of directing it to him you directed it to me. With joy I tore open the envelope, and did not perceive the mistake until I read the words, "Oh! My dear, dear Lothair." Now I know I ought not to have read any more of the letter, but ought to have given it to my brother. But as you have so often in innocent raillery made it a sort of reproach against me that I possessed such a calm, and, for a woman, cool-headed temperament that I should be like the woman we read of—if the house was threatening to tumble down, I should, before hastily fleeing, stop to smooth down a crumple in the window-curtains—I need hardly tell you that the beginning of your letter quite upset me. I could hardly breathe; there was a bright mist before my eyes. Oh! My darling Nathanael! What could this terrible thing be that had happened? Separation from you—never to see you again, the thought was like a sharp knife in my heart. I read on and on. Your description of that horrid Coppelius made my flesh creep. I now learnt for the first time what a terrible and violent death your good old father died. Brother Lothair, to whom I handed over his property, sought to comfort me, but with little success. That horrid weatherglass hawker Giuseppe Coppola followed me everywhere; and I am almost ashamed to confess it, but he was able to disturb my sound and in general calm sleep with all sorts of wonderful dream-shapes. But soon—the next day—I saw everything in a different light. Oh! Do not be angry with me, my best-beloved, if, despite your strange presentiment that Coppelius will do you some mischief, Lothair tells you I am in quite as good spirits, and just the same as ever.

I will frankly confess, it seems to me that all that was fearsome and terrible of which you speak, existed only in your own self, and that the real true outer world had but little to do with it. I can quite admit that old Coppelius may have been highly obnoxious to you children, but your real detestation of him arose from the fact that he hated children.

Naturally enough the gruesome Sandman of the old nurse's story was associated in your childish mind with old Coppelius, who, even though you had not believed in the Sandman, would have been to you a ghostly bugbear, especially dangerous to children. His mysterious labors along with your father at nighttime were, I daresay, nothing more than secret experiments in alchemy, with which your mother could not be over well pleased, owing to the large sums of money that most likely were thrown away upon them; and besides, your father, his mind full of the deceptive striving after higher knowledge, may probably have become rather indifferent to his family, as so often happens in the case of such experimentalists. So also it is equally probable that your father brought about his death by his own imprudence, and that Coppelius is not to blame for it. I must tell you that yesterday I asked our experienced neighbor, the chemist, whether in experiments of this kind an explosion could take place which would have a momentarily fatal effect. He said, "Oh, certainly!" and described to me in his prolix and circumstantial way how it could be occasioned, mentioning at the same time so many strange and funny words that I could not remember them at all. Now I know you will be angry at your Clara, and will say, "Of the Mysterious which often clasps man in its invisible arms there's not a ray can find its way into this cold heart. She sees only the varied surface of the things of the world, and, like the little child, is pleased with the golden glittering fruit, at the kernel of which lies the fatal poison."

Oh! My beloved Nathanael, do you believe then that the intuitive prescience of a dark power working within us to our own ruin cannot exist also in minds which are cheerful, natural, free from care? But please forgive me that I, a simple girl, presume in any way to indicate to you what I really think of such an inward strife. After all, I should not find the proper words, and you would only laugh at me, not because my thoughts were stupid, but because I was so foolish as to attempt to tell them to you.

If there is a dark and hostile power which traitorously fixes a thread in our hearts in order that, laying hold of it and drawing us by means of it along a dangerous road to ruin, which otherwise we should not have trod—if, I say, there is such a power, it must assume within us a form like ourselves, nay, it must be ourselves; for only in that way can we believe in it, and only so understood do we yield to it so far that it is able to accomplish its secret purpose. So long as we have sufficient firmness, fortified by cheerfulness, to always acknowledge foreign hostile influences for what they really are, whilst we quietly pursue the path pointed out to us by both inclination and calling, then this mysterious power perishes in its futile struggles to attain the form which is to be the reflected image of ourselves. It is also certain, Lothair adds, that if we have once voluntarily given ourselves up to this dark physical power, it often reproduces within us the strange forms which the outer world throws in our way, so that thus it is we ourselves who engender within ourselves the spirit which by some remarkable delusion we imagine to speak in that outer form. It is the phantom of our own self whose intimate relationship with, and whose powerful influence upon our soul either plunges us into hell or elevates us to heaven. Thus you will see, my beloved Nathanael, that I and brother Lothair have well talked over the subject of dark powers and forces; and now, after I have with some difficulty written down the principal results of our discussion, they seem to me to contain many really profound thoughts. Lothair's last words, however, I don't quite understand altogether; I only dimly guess what he means; and yet I cannot help thinking it is all very true. I beg you, dear, strive to forget the ugly advocate Coppelius as well as the weatherglass hawker Giuseppe Coppola. Try and convince yourself that these foreign influences can have no power over you, that it is only the belief in their hostile power which can in reality make them dangerous to you. If every line of your letter did not betray the violent excitement of your mind, and if I did not sympathize with your condition from the bottom of my heart, I could in truth jest about the advocate Sandman and weatherglass hawker Coppelius. Pluck up your spirits! Be cheerful! I have resolved to appear to you as your guardian angel if that ugly man Coppola should dare take it into his head to bother you in your dreams, and drive him away with a good hearty laugh. I'm not afraid of him and his nasty hands, not the least little bit; I won't let him either as advocate spoil any daintly tidbit I've taken, or as Sandman rob me of my eyes.

My darling, darling Nathanael
Eternally your, &c. &c.

NATHANAEL TO LOTHAIR

I am very sorry that Clara opened and read my last letter to you; of course the mistake is to be attributed to my own absence of mind. She has written me a very deep philosophical letter, proving conclusively that Coppelius and Coppola only exist in my own mind and are phantoms of my own self, which will at once be dissipated, as soon as I look upon them in that light. In very truth one can hardly believe that the mind which so often sparkled in those bright, beautifully smiling, childlike eyes of hers like a sweet lovely dream could draw such subtle and scholastic distinctions. She also mentions your name. You have been talking about me. I suppose you have been giving her lectures, since she sifts and refines everything so acutely. But enough of this! I must now tell you it is most certain that the weatherglass hawker Giuseppe Coppola is not the advocate Coppelius. I am attending the lectures of our recently appointed Professor of Physics, who, like the distinguished naturalist,[1] is called Spalanzani, and is of Italian origin. He has known Coppola for many years; and it is also easy to tell from his accent that he really is a Piedmontese. Coppelius was a German, though no honest German, I fancy. Nevertheless I am not quite satisfied. You and Clara will perhaps take me for a gloomy dreamer, but nohow can I get rid of the impression which Coppelius's cursed face made upon me. I am glad to learn from Spalanzani that he has left the town. This Professor Spalanzani is a very queer fish. He is a little fat man, with prominent cheekbones, thin nose, projecting lips, and small piercing eyes. You cannot get a better picture of him than by turning over one of the Berlin pocket almanacs[2] and looking at Cagliostro's[3] portrait engraved by Chodowiecki;[4] Spalanzani looks just like him.

Once lately, as I went up the steps to his house, I perceived that beside the curtain which generally covered a glass door there was a small chink. What it was that excited my curiosity I cannot explain; but I looked through. In the room I saw a female, tall, very slender, but of perfect proportions, and splendidly dressed, sitting at a little table, on which she had placed both her arms, her hands being folded together. She sat opposite the door, so that I could easily see her angelically beautiful face. She did not appear to notice me, and there was moreover a strangely fixed look about her eyes, I might almost say they appeared as if they had no power of vision; I thought she was sleeping with her eyes

---

[1]Lazaro Spallanzani, a celebrated anatomist and naturalist (1729–1799), filled for several years the chair of Natural History at Pavia, and traveled extensively for scientific purposes in Italy, Turkey, Sicily, Switzerland, et cetera.

[2]Or Almanacs of the Muses, as they were also sometimes called, were periodical, mostly yearly publications, containing all kinds of literary effusions; mostly, however, lyrical. They originated in the eighteenth century. Schiller, A.W. and F. Schlegel, Tieck, and Chamisso, amongst others, conducted undertakings of this nature.

[3]Joseph Balsamo, a Sicilian by birth, calling himself Count Cagliostro, one of the greatest impostors of modern times, lived during the latter part of the eighteenth century. See Carlyle's "Miscellanies" for an account of his life and character.

[4]Daniel Nikolas Chodowiecki, painter and engraver, of Polish descent, was born at Dantzic in 1726. For some years he was so popular an artist that few books were published in Prussia without plates or vignettes by him. The catalogue of his works is said to include 3000 items.

open. I felt quite uncomfortable, and so I slipped away quietly into the Professor's lecture room, which was close at hand. Afterwards I learnt that the figure which I had seen was Spalanzani's daughter, Olimpia, whom he keeps locked in a most wicked and unaccountable way, and no man is ever allowed to come near her. Perhaps, however, there is after all something peculiar about her; perhaps she's an idiot or something of that sort. But why am I telling you all this? I could have told you it all better and more in detail when I see you. For in a fortnight I shall be amongst you. I must see my dear sweet angel, my Clara, again. Then the little bit of ill-temper, which, I must confess, took possession of me after her fearfully sensible letter, will be blown away. And that is the reason why I am not writing to her as well today. With all best wishes, &c.

Nothing more strange and extraordinary can be imagined, gracious reader, than what happened to my poor friend, the young student Nathanael, and which I have undertaken to relate to you. Have you ever lived to experience anything that completely took possession of your heart and mind and thoughts to the utter exclusion of everything else? All was seething and boiling within you; your blood, heated to fever pitch, leapt through your veins and inflamed your cheeks. Your gaze was so peculiar, as if seeking to grasp in empty space forms not seen of any other eye, and all your words ended in sighs betokening some mystery. Then your friends asked you, "What is the matter with you, my dear friend? What do you see?" And, wishing to descirbe the inner pictures in all their vivid colors, with their lights and their shades, you in vain struggled to find words with which to express yourself. But you felt as if you must gather up all the events that had happened, wonderful, splendid, terrible, jocose, and awful, in the very first word, so that the whole might be revealed by a single electric discharge, so to speak. Yet every word and all that partook of the nature of communication by intelligible sounds seemed to be colorless, cold, and dead. Then you try and try again, and stutter and stammer, whilst your friends' prosy questions strike like icy winds upon your heart's hot fire until they extinguish it. But if, like a bold painter, you had first sketched in a few audacious strokes the outline of the picture you had in your soul, you would then easily have been able to deepen and intensify the colors one after the other, until the varied throng of living figures carried your friends away, and they, like you, saw themselves in the midst of the scene that had proceeded out of your own soul.

Strictly speaking, indulgent reader, I must indeed confess to you, nobody has asked me for the history of young Nathanael; but you are very well aware that I belong to that remarkable class of authors who, when they are bearing anything about in their minds in the manner I have just described, feel as if everybody who comes near them, and also the whole world to boot, were asking, "Oh! What is it? Oh! Do tell us, my good sir?" Hence I was most powerfully impelled to narrate to you Nathanael's ominous life. My soul was full of the elements of wonder and extraordinary peculiarity in it; but, for this very reason, and because it was necessary in the very beginning to dispose you, indulgent reader, to bear with what is fantastic—and that is not a little thing—I racked my brain to find a way of commencing the story in a significant and original manner, calculated to arrest your attention. To begin with "Once upon a time," the best beginning for a story, seemed to me too tame; with "In the small country town S——lived," rather better, at any rate allowing plenty of room to work up to the climax; or to plunge at once *in medias res*, " 'Go to the devil!' cried the student Nathanael, his eyes blazing wildly with rage and fear, when the weatherglass hawker Giuseppe Coppola"—well, that is what I really had written, when I thought I detected something of the ridiculous in Nathanael's wild glance; and the history is anything but laughable. I could not find any words which seemed fitted to reflect in even the feeblest degree the brightness of the colors of my mental vision. I determined not to begin at all. So I pray you, gracious reader, accept the three letters which my friend Lothair has been so kind as to communicate to me as the outline of the picture, into which I will endeavour to introduce more and more color as I proceed with my narrative. Perhaps, like a good portrait painter, I may succeed in depicting more than one figure in such wise that you will recognize it as a good likeness without being acquainted with the original, and feel as if you had very often seen the original with your own bodily eyes. Perhaps, too, you will then believe that nothing is more wonderful, nothing more fantastic than real life, and that all that a writer can do is to present it as a dark reflection from a dim-cut mirror.

In order to make the very commencement more intelligible, it is necessary to add to the letters that, soon after the death of Nathanael's father, Clara and Lothair, the children of a distant relative, who had likewise died, leaving them orphans, were taken by Nathanael's mother into her own house. Clara and Nathanael conceived a warm affection for each other, against which not the slightest objection in the world could be urged. When therefore Nathanael left home to prosecute his studies in G——, they were betrothed. It is from G——that his last letter is written, where he is attending the lectures of Spalanzani, the distinguished Professor of Physics.

I might now proceed comfortably with my narration, did not at this moment Clara's image rise up so vividly before my eyes that I cannot turn them away from it, just as I never could when she looked upon me and smiled so sweetly. Nowhere would she have passed for beautiful; that was the unanimous opinion of all who professed to have any technical knowledge of beauty. But whilst architects praised the pure proportions of her figure and form, painters averred that her neck, shoulders, and bosom were almost too chastely modeled, and yet, on the other hand, one and all were in love with her glorious Magdalene hair, and talked a good deal of nonsense about Battoni-like[1] coloring. One of them, a veritable romanticist, strangely enough likened her eyes to a lake by Ruisdael,[2] in which is reflected the pure azure of the cloudless sky, the beauty of woods and flowers, and all the bright and varied life of a living landscape. Poets and musicians went still further and said, "What's all this talk about seas and reflections? How can we look upon the girl without feeling that wonderful heavenly songs and melodies beam upon us from her eyes, penetrating deep down into our hearts, till all becomes awake and throbbing with emotion? And if we cannot sing anything at all passable then, why, we are not worth much; and this we can also plainly read in the rare smile which flits around her lips when we have the hardihood to squeak out something in her presence which we pretend to call singing, in spite of the fact that it is nothing more than a few single notes confusedly linked together." And it really was so. Clara had the powerful fancy of a bright, innocent, unaffected child, a woman's deep and sympathetic heart, and an understanding clear, sharp, and discriminating. Dreamers and visionaries had but a bad time of it with her; for without saying very much—she was not by nature of a

---

[1]Pompeo Girolamo Batoni, an Italian painter of the eighteenth century, whose works were at one time greatly overestimated.

[2]Jakob Ruysdael (c. 1625-1682), a painter of Haarlem, in Holland. His favorite subjects were remote farms, lonely stagnant water, deep-shaded woods with marshy paths, the seacost—subjects of a dark melancholy kind. His sea pieces are greatly admired.

talkative disposition—she plainly asked, by her calm steady look, and rare ironical smile, "How can you imagine, my dear friends, that I can take these fleeting shadowy images for true lving and breathing forms?" For this reason many found fault with her as being cold, prosaic, and devoid of feeling; others, however, who had reached a clearer and deeper conception of life, were extremely fond of the intelligent, child-like, largehearted girl. But none had such an affection for her as Nathanael, who was a zealous and cheerful cultivator of the fields of science and art. Clara clung to her lover with all her heart; the first clouds she encountered in life were when he had to separate from her. With what delight did she fly into his arms when, as he had promised in his last letter to Lothair, he really came back to his native town and entered his mother's room! And as Nathanael had foreseen, the moment he saw Clara again he no longer thought about either the advocate Coppelius or her sensible letter; his ill-humor had quite disappeared.

Nevertheless Nathanael was right when he told his friend Lothair that the repulsive vendor of weatherglasses, Coppola, had exercised a fatal and disturbing influence upon his life. It was quite patent to all; for even during the first few days he showed that he was completely and entirely changed. He gave himself up to gloomy reveries, and moreover acted so strangely; they had never observed anything at all like it in him before. Everything, even his own life, was to him but dreams and pesentiments. His constant theme was that every man who delusively imagined himself to be free was merely the plaything of the cruel sport of mysterious powers, and it was vain for man to resist them; he must humbly submit to whatever destiny had decreed for him. He went so far as to maintain that it was foolish to believe that a man could do anything in art or science of his own accord; for the inspiration in which alone any true artistic work could be done did not proceed from the spirit within outwards, but was the result of the operation directed inwards of some Higher Principle existing without and beyond ourselves.

This mystic extravagance was in the highest degree repugnant to Clara's clear intelligent mind, but it seemed vain to enter upon any attempt at refutation. Yet when Nathanael went on to prove that Coppelius was the Evil Principle which had entered into him and taken possession of him at the time he was listening behind the curtain, and that this hateful demon would in some terrible way ruin their happiness, then Clara grew grave and said, "Yes, Nathanael. You are right; Coppelius is an Evil Principle; he can do dreadful things, as bad as could a Satanic power which should assume a living physical form, but only—only if you do not banish him from your mind and thoughts. So long as you believe in him he exists and is at work; your belief in him is his only power.'' Whereupon Nathanael, quite angry because Clara would only grant the existence of the demon in his own mind, began to dilate at large upon the whole mystic doctrine of devils and awful powers, but Clara abruptly broke off the theme by making, to Nathanael's very great disgust, some quite commonplace remark. Such deep mysteries are sealed books to cold, unsusceptible characters, he thought, without being clearly conscious to himself that he counted Clara amongst these inferior natures, and accordingly he did not remit his efforts to initiate her into these mysteries. In the morning, when she was helping to prepare breakfast, he would take his stand beside her, and read all sorts of mystic books to her, until she begged him—''But, my dear Nathanael, I shall have to scold you as the Evil Principle which exercises a fatal influence upon my coffee. For if I do as you wish, and let things go their own way, and look into your eyes whilst you read, the coffee will all boil over into the fire, and you will none of you get any breakfast.'' Then Nathanael hastily banged the book to and ran away in great displeasure to his own room.

Formerly he had possessed a peculiar talent for writing pleasing, sparkling tales, which Clara took the greatest delight in listening to; but now his productions were gloomy, unintelligible, and wanting in form, so that, although Clara out of forbearance toward him did not say so, he nevertheless felt how very little interest she took in them. There was nothing that Clara disliked so much as what was tedious; at such times her intellectual sleepiness was not to be overcome; it was betrayed both in her glances and in her words. Nathanael's effusions were, in truth, exceedingly tedious. His ill-humour at Clara's cold prosaic temperament continued to increase; Clara could not conceal her distaste of his dark, gloomy, wearying mysticism; and thus both began to be more and more estranged from each other without exactly being aware of it themselves. The image of the ugly Coppelius had, as Nathanael was obliged to confess to himself, faded considerably in his fancy, and it often cost him great pains to present him in vivid colors in his literary efforts, in which he played the part of the ghoul of Destiny. At length it entered into his head to make his dismal presentiment that Coppelius would ruin his

31

happiness the subject of a poem. He made himself and Clara, united by true love, the central figures, but represented a black hand as being from time to time thrust into their life and plucking out a joy that had blossomed for them. At length, as they were standing at the altar, the terrible Coppelius appeared and touched Clara's lovely eyes, which leapt into Nathanael's own bosom, burning and hissing like bloody sparks. Then Coppelius laid hold upon him, and hurled him into a blazing circle of fire, which spun round with the speed of a whirlwind, and, storming and blustering, dashed away with him. The fearful noise it made was like a furious hurricane lashing the foaming sea-waves until they rise up like black, white-headed giants in the midst of the raging struggle. But through the midst of the savage fury of the tempest he heard Clara's voice calling, "Can you not see me, dear? Coppelius has deceived you; they were not my eyes which burned so in your bosom; they were fiery drops of your own heart's blood. Look at me, I have got my own eyes still." Nathanael thought, "Yes, that is Clara, and I am hers forever." Then this thought laid a powerful grasp upon the fiery circle so that it stood still, and the riotous turmoil died away rumbling down a dark abyss. Nathanael looked into Clara's eyes; but it was death whose gaze rested so kindly upon him.

Whilst Nathanael was writing this work he was very quiet and sober-minded; he filed and polished every line, and as he had chosen to submit himself to the limitations of metre, he did not rest until all was pure and musical. When, however, he had at length finished it and read it aloud to himself he was seized with horror and awful dread, and he screamed, "Whose hideous voice is this?" But he soon came to see in it again nothing beyond a very successful poem, and he confidently believed it would enkindle Clara's cold temperament, though to what end she would be thus aroused was not quite clear to his own mind, nor yet what would be the real purpose served by tormenting her with these dreadful pictures, which prophesied a terrible and ruinous end to her affection.

Nathanael and Clara sat in his mother's little garden. Clara was bright and cheerful, since for three entire days her lover, who had been busy writing his poem, had not teased her with his dreams or forebodings. Nathanael, too, spoke in a gay and vivacious way of things of merry import, as he formerly used to do, so that Clara said, "Ah! now I have you again. We have driven away that ugly Coppelius, you see."

Then it suddenly occurred to him that he had got the poem in his pocket which he wished to read to her. He at once took out the manuscript and began to read. Clara, anticipating something tedious as usual, prepared to submit to the infliction, and calmly resumed her knitting. But as the somber clouds rose up darker and darker she let her knitting fall on her lap and sat with her eyes fixed in a set stare upon Nathanael's face. He was quite carried away by his own work, the fire of enthusiasm colored his cheeks a deep red, and tears started from his eyes. At length he concluded, groaning and showing great lassitude; grasping Clara's hand, he sighed as if he were being utterly melted in inconsolable grief, "Oh! Clara! Clara!" She drew him softly to her heart and said in a low but very grave and impressive tone, "Nathanael, my darling Nathanael, throw that foolish, senseless, stupid thing into the fire." Then Nathanael leapt indignantly to his feet crying, as he pushed Clara from him, "You damned lifeless automaton!" and rushed away. Clara was cut to the heart, and wept bitterly. "Oh! he has never loved me, for he does not understand me," she sobbed.

Lothair entered the arbor. Clara was obliged to tell him all that had taken place. He was passionately fond of his sister; and every word of her complaint fell like a spark upon his heart, so that the displeasure which he had long entertained against his dreamy friend Nathanael was kindled into furious anger. He hastened to find Nathanael, and upbraided him in harsh words for his irrational behavior toward his beloved sister. The fiery Nathanael answered him in the same style. "A fantastic, crack-brained fool," was retaliated with, "A miserable, common, everyday sort of fellow." A meeting was the inevitable consequence. They agreed to meet on the following morning behind the garden-wall, and fight, according to the custom of the students of the place, with sharp rapiers. They went about silent and gloomy; Clara had both heard and seen the violent quarrel, and also observed the fencing master bring the rapiers in the dusk of the evening. She had a presentiment of what was to happen. They both appeared at the appointed place wrapped up in the same gloomy silence, and threw off their coats. Their eyes flaming with the bloodthirsty light of pugnacity, they were about to begin their contest when Clara burst through the garden door. Sobbing, she screamed, "You savage, terrible men! Cut me down before you attack each other; for how can I live when my lover has slain my brother, or my brother slain my lover?" Lothair let his weapon fall and gazed silently upon the ground, whilst Nathanael's heart was rent with sorrow, and all the affection which he had felt for his lovely Clara in the happiest days of her golden youth was awakened within him. His murderous weapon, too, fell from his hand; he threw himself at Clara's feet. "Oh! Can you ever forgive me, my only, my dearly loved Clara? Can you, my dear brother Lothair, also forgive me?" Lothair was touched by his friend's great distress; the three young people embraced each other amidst endless tears, and swore never again to break their bond of love and fidelity.

Nathanael felt as if a heavy burden that had been weighing him down to the earth was now rolled from off him, nay, as if by offering resistance to the dark power which had possessed him, he had rescued his own self from the ruin which had threatened him. Three happy days he now spent amidst the loved ones, and then returned to G——, where he had still a year to stay before settling down in his native town for life.

Everything having reference to Coppelius had been concealed from the mother, for they knew she could not think of him without horror, since she as well as Nathanael believed him to be guilty of causing her husband's death.

When Nathanael came to the house where he lived he was greatly astonished to find it burnt down to the ground, so that nothing but the outer walls were left standing amidst a heap of ruins. Although the fire had broken out in the laboratory of the chemist who lived on the ground floor, and had therefore spread upwards, some of Nathanael's bold, active friends had succeeded in time in forcing a way into his room in the upper story and saving his books and manuscripts and instruments. They had carried them all uninjured into another house, where they engaged a room for him; this he now at once took possession of. That he lived opposite Professor Spalanzani did not strike him particularly, nor did it occur to him as anything more singular that he could, as he observed, by looking out of his window, see straight into the room where Olimpia often sat alone. Her figure he could plainly distinguish, although her features were uncertain and confused. It did at length occur to him, however, that she remained for hours together in the same position in which he had first discovered her through the glass door, sitting at a little table without any occupation whatever, and it was evident that she was constantly gazing across in his direction. He could not but confess to himself that he had never seen a finer figure. However, with Clara mistress of his heart, he remained perfectly unaffected by Olimpia's stiffness and apathy; and it was only occasionally that he sent a fugitive glance over his compendium across to her—that was all.

He was writing to Clara; a light tap came at the door. At his summons to "Come in," Coppola's repulsive face appeared peeping in. Nathanael felt his heart beat with trepidation; but, recollecting what Spalanzani had told him about his fellow-countryman Coppola, and what he had himself so faithfully promised his beloved in respect to the Sandman Coppelius, he was ashamed at himself for this childish fear of specters. Accordingly, he controlled himself with an effort, and said, as quietly and as calmly as he possibly could, "I don't want to buy any weatherglasses, my good friend; you had better go elsewhere." Then Coppola came right into the room, and said in a hoarse voice, screwing up his wide mouth into a hideous smile, whilst his little eyes flashed keenly from beneath his long grey eyelashes, "What! Nee weathergless? Nee weathergless? 've got foine oyes as well—foine oyes!" Affrighted, Nathanael cried, "You stupid man, how can you have eyes—eyes—eyes?" But Coppola, laying aside his weatherglasses, thrust his hands into his big coat-pockets and brought out several spyglasses and spectacles, and put them on the table. "Theer! Theer! Spect'cles! Spect'cles to put 'n nose! Them's my oyes—foine oyes." And he continued to produce more and more spectacles from his pockets until the table began to gleam and flash all over. Thousands of eyes were looking and blinking convulsively, and staring up at Nathanael; he could not avert his gaze from the table. Coppola went on heaping up his spectacles, whilst wilder and ever wilder burning flashes crossed through and through each other and darted their bloodred rays into Nathanael's breast. Quite overcome, and frantic with terror, he souted, "Stop! Stop! You terrible man!" and he seized Coppola by the arm, which he had again thrust into his pocket in order to bring out still more spectacles, although the whole table was covered all over with them. With a harsh disagreeable laugh Coppola gently freed himself; and with the words "So! Went none! Well, here foine gless!" he swept all his spectacles together and put them back into his coat-pockets, whilst from a breast-pocket he produced a great number of large and small perspectives. As soon as the spectacles were gone Nathanael recovered his equanimity again; and, bending his thoughts upon Clara, he clearly discerned that the gruesome incubus had proceeded only from himself, as also that Coppola was a right honest mechanician and optician, and far from being Coppelius's dreaded double and ghost. And then, besides, none of the glasses which Coppola now placed on the table had anything at all singular about them, at least nothing so weird as the spectacles; so, in order to square accounts with himself, Nathanael now really determined to buy something of the man. He took up a small, very beautifully cut pocket perspective, and by way of proving it looked through the window. Never before in his life had he had a glass in his hands that brought out things so clearly and sharply and distinctly. Involuntarily he directed the glass upon Spalanzani's room; Olimpia sat at the little table as usual, her arms laid upon it and her hands folded. Now he saw for the first time the regular and exquisite beauty of her features. The eyes, however, seemed to him to have a singular look of fixity and lifelessness. But as he continued to look closer and more carefully through the glass he fancied a light like humid moonbeams came into them. It seemed as if their power of vision was now being enkindled; their glances shone with ever-increasing vivacity. Nathanael remained standing at the window as if glued to the spot by a wizard's spell, his gaze riveted unchangeably upon the divinely beautiful Olimpia. A coughing and shuffling of the feet awakened him out of his enchaining dream, as it were. Coppola stood behind him, ''Tre zechini'' (three ducats). Nathanael had completely forgotten the optician; he hastily paid the sum demanded. ''Ain't? Foine gless? Foine gless?'' asked Coppola in his harsh unpleasant voice, smiling sardonically. ''Yes, yes, yes,'' rejoined Nathanael impatiently; ''adieu, my good friend.'' But Coppola did not leave the room without casting many peculiar side-glances upon Nathanael; and the young student heard him laughing loudly on the stairs. ''Ah, well!'' thought he, ''he's laughing at me because I've paid him too much for this little perspective—because I've given him too much money—that's it.'' As he softly murmured these words he fancied he detected a gasping sign as of a dying man stealing awfully through the room; his heart stopped beating with fear. But to be sure he had heaved a deep sigh himself; it was quite plain. ''Clara is quite right,'' said he to himself, ''in holding me to be an incurable ghost-seer; and yet it's very ridiculous—ay, more than ridiculous, that the stupid thought of having paid Coppola too much for his glass should cause me this strange anxiety; I can't see any reason for it.''

Now he sat down to finish his letter to Clara; but a glance through the window showed him Olimpia still in her former posture. Urged by an irresistible impulse he jumped up and seized Coppola's perspective; nor could he tear himself away from the fascinating Olimpia until his friend and brother Siegmund called for him to go to Professor Spalanzani's lecture. The curtains before the door of the all-important room were closely drawn, so that he could not see Olimpia. Nor could he even see her from his own room during the two following days, notwithstanding that he scarcely ever left his window, and maintained a scarce-interrupted watch through Coppola's perspective upon her room. On the third day curtains even were drawn across the window. Plunged into the depths of despair, goaded by longing and ardent desire, he hurried outside the walls of the town. Olimpia's image hovered about his path in the air and stepped forth out of the bushes, and peeped up at him with large and lustrous eyes from the bright surface of the brook. Clara's image was completely faded from his mind; he had no thoughts except for Olimpia. He uttered his love-plaints aloud and in a lachrymose tone, "Oh! My glorious, noble star of love, have you only risen to vanish again, and leave me in the darkness and hopelessness of night?'

Returning home, he became aware that there was a good deal of noisy bustle going on in Spalanzani's house. All the doors stood wide open; men were taking in all kinds of gear and furniture; the windows of the first floor were all lifted off their hinges; busy maidservants with immense hair-brooms were driving backwards and forwards dusting and sweeping, whilst within could be heard the knocking and hammering of carpenters and upholsterers. Utterly astonished, Nathanael stood still in the street; then Siegmund joined him, laughing, and said, "Well, what do you say to our old Spalanzani?" Nathanael assured him that he could not say anything, since he knew not what it all meant; to his great astonishment, he could hear, however, that they were turning the quiet gloomy house almost inside out with their dusting and cleaning and making of alterations. Then he learned from Siegmund that Spalanzani intended giving a great concert and ball on the following day, and that half the university was invited. It was generally reported that Spalanzani was going to let his daughter Olimpia, whom he had so long so jealously guarded from every eye, make her first appearance.

Nathanael received an invitation. At the appointed hour, when the carriages were rolling up and the lights were gleaming brightly in the decorated halls, he went across to the Professor's, his heart beating high with expectation. The company was both numerous and brilliant. Olimpia was richly and tastefully dressed. One could not but admire her figure and the regular beauty of her features. The striking inward curve of her back, as well as the wasp-like smallness of her waist, appeared to be the result of too-tight lacing. There was something stiff and measured in her gait and bearing that made an unfavorable impression upon many; it was ascribed to the constraint imposed upon her by the company. The concert began. Olimpia played on the piano with great skill; and sang as skillfully an *aria di bravura,* in a voice which was, if anything, almost too sharp, but clear as glass bells. Nathanael was transported with delight; he stood in the background farthest from her, and owing to the blinding lights could not quite distinguish her features. So, without being observed, he took Coppola's glass out of his pocket, and directed it upon the beautiful Olimpia. Oh! Then he perceived how her yearning eyes sought him, how every note only reached its full purity in the loving glance which penetrated to and inflamed his heart. Her artificial *roulades* seemed to him to be the exultant cry towards heaven of the soul refined by love; and when at last, after the *cadenza,* the long trill rang shrilly and loudly through the hall, he felt as if he were suddenly grasped by burning arms and could no longer control himself, he could not help shouting aloud in his mingled pain and delight, "Olimpia!" All eyes were turned upon him; many people laughed. The face of the cathedral organist bore a still more gloomy look than it had done before, but all he said was, "Very well!"

The concert came to an end, and the ball began. Oh! To dance with her—with her—that was now the aim of all Nathanael's wishes, of all his desires. But how should he have courage to request her, the queen of the ball, to grant him the honor of a dance? And yet he couldn't tell how it came about, just as the dance began, he found himself standing close beside her, nobody having as yet asked her to be his partner; so, with some difficulty stammering out a few words, he grasped her hand. It was cold as ice; he shook with an awful, frosty shiver. But, fixing his eyes upon her face, he saw that her glance was beaming upon him with love and longing, and at the same moment he thought that the pulse began to beat in her cold hand, and the warm lifeblood to course through her veins. And passion burned more intensely in his own heart also; he threw his arm round her beautiful waist and whirled her round the hall. He had always thought that he kept good and accurate time in dancing, but from the perfectly rhythmical evenness with which Olimpia danced, and which frequently put him quite out, he perceived how very faulty his own time really was. Notwithstanding, he would not dance with any other lady; and everybody else who approached Olimpia to call upon her for a dance, he would have liked to kill on the spot. This, however, only happened twice; to his astonishment Olimpia remained after this without a partner, and he failed not on each occasion to take her out again. If Nathanael had been able to see anything else except the beautiful Olimpia, there would inevitably have been a good deal of unpleasant quarreling and strife; for it was evident that Olimpia was the object of the smothered laughter only with difficulty suppressed, which was heard in various corners amongst the young people; and they followed her with very curious looks, but nobody knew for what reason. Nathanael, excited by dancing and the plentiful supply of wine he had consumed, had laid aside the shyness which at other times characterized him. He sat beside Olimpia, her hand in his own, and declared his love enthusiastically and passionately in words which neither of them understood, neither he nor Olimpia. And yet she perhaps did, for she sat with her eyes fixed unchangeably upon his, sighing repeatedly, "Ach! Ach! Ach!" Upon this Nathanael would answer, "Oh, you glorious heavenly lady! You ray from the promised paradise of love! Oh! What a profound soul you have! My whole being is mirrored in it!" and a good deal more in the same strain. But Olimpia only continued to sigh "Ach! Ach!" again and again.

Professor Spalanzani passed by the two happy lovers once or twice, and smiled with a look of peculiar satisfaction. All at once it seemed to Nathanael, albeit he was far away in a different world, as if it were growing perceptibly darker down below at Professor Spalanzani's. He looked about him, and to his very great alarm became aware that there were only two lights left burning in the hall, and they were on the point of going out. The music and dancing had long ago ceased. "We must part—part!" he cried, wildly and despairingly; he kissed Olimpia's hand; he bent down to her mouth, but ice-cold lips met his burning ones. As he touched her cold hand, he felt his heart thrilled with awe; the legend of "The Dead Bride"[1] shot suddenly through his mind. But

---

[1]Phlegon, the freedman of Hadrian, relates that a young maiden, Philemium, the daughter of Philostratus and Charitas, became deeply enamored of a young man, named Machates, a guest in the house of her father. This did not meet with the approbation of her parents, and they turned Machates away. The young maiden took this so much to heart that she pined away and died. Some time afterwards Machates returned to his old lodgings, when he was visited at night by his beloved, who came from the grave to see him again. The story may be read in Heywood's (Thos.) "Hierarchie of Blessed Angels," Book vii., p. 479 (London, 1637). Goethe has made this story the foundation of his beautiful poem *Die Braut von Korinth*, with which form of it Hoffmann was most likely familiar.

Olimpia had drawn him closer to her, and the kiss appeared to warm her lips into vitality. Professor Spalanzani strode slowly through the empty apartment, his footsteps giving a hollow echo; and his figure had, as the flickering shadows played about him, a ghostly, awful appearance. "Do you love me? Do you love me, Olimpia? Only one little word—Do you love me?" whispered Nathanael, but she only sighed, "Ach! Ach!" as she rose to her feet. "Yes, you are my lovely, glorious star of love," said Nathanael, "and will shine forever, purifying and ennobling my heart." "Ach! Ach!" replied Olimpia, as she moved along. Nathanael followed her; they stood before the Professor. "You have had an extraordinarily animated conversation with my daughter," said he, smiling; "well, well, my dear Mr. Nathanael, if you find pleasure in talking to the stupid girl, I am sure I shall be glad for you to come and do so." Nathanael took his leave, his heart singing and leaping in a perfect delirium of happiness.

During the next few days Spalanzani's ball was the general topic of conversation. Although the Professor had done everything to make the thing a splendid success, yet certain gay spirits related more than one thing that had occurred which was quite irregular and out of order. They were especially keen in pulling Olimpia to pieces for her taciturnity and rigid stiffness; in spite of her beautiful form they alleged that she was hopelessly stupid, and in this fact they discerned the reason why Spalanzani had so long kept her concealed from publicity. Nathanael heard all this with inward wrath, but nevertheless he held his tongue; for, thought he, would it indeed be worthwhile to prove to these fellows that it is their own stupidity which prevents them from appreciating Olimpia's profound and brilliant parts? One day Siegmund said to him, "Pray, brother, have the kindness to tell me how you, a sensible fellow, came to lose your head over that Miss Wax-face—that wooden doll across there?" Nathanael was about to fly into a rage, but he recollected himself and replied, "Tell me, Siegmund, how came it that Olimpia's divine charms could escape your eye, so keenly alive as it always is to beauty, and your acute perception as well? But Heaven be thanked for it, otherwise I should have had you for a rival, and then the blood of one of us would have had to be spilled." Siegmund, perceiving how matters stood with his friend, skillfully interposed and said, after remarking that all argument with one in love about the object of his affections was out of place, "Yet it's very strange that several of us have formed pretty much the same opinion about Olimpia. We think she is—you won't take it ill, brother?—that she is singularly statuesque and soulless. Her figure is regular, and so are her features, that can't be gainsaid; and if her eyes were not so utterly devoid of life, I may say, of the power of vision, she might pass for a beauty. She is strangely measured in her movements, they all seem as if they were dependent upon some wound-up clock-work. Her playing and singing has the disagreeably perfect, but insensitive time of a singing machine, and her dancing is the same. We felt quite afraid of this Olimpia, and did not like to have anything to do with her; she seemed to us to be only acting *like* a living creature, and as if there was some secret at the bottom of it all.'' Nathanael did not give way to the bitter feelings which threatened to master him at these words of Siegmund's; he fought down and got the better of his displeasure, and merely said, very earnestly, ''You cold prosaic fellows may very well be afraid of her. It is only to its like that the poetically organized spirit unfolds itself. Upon me alone did her loving glances fall, and through my mind and thoughts alone did they radiate; and only in her love can I find my own self again. Perhaps, however, she doesn't do quite right not to jabber a lot of nonsense and stupid talk like other shallow people. It is true, she speaks but few words; but the few words she does speak are genuine hieroglyphs of the inner world of Love and of the higher cognition of the intellectual life revealed in the intuition of the Eternal beyond the grave. But you have no understanding for all these things, and I am only wasting words.'' ''God be with you, brother,'' said Siegmund very gently, almost sadly, ''but it seems to me that you are in a very bad way. You may rely upon me, if all—No, I can't say anymore.'' It all at once dawned upon Nathanael that his cold prosaic friend Siegmund really and sincerely wished him well, and so he warmly shook his proffered hand.

Nathanael had completely forgotten that there was a Clara in the world, whom he had once loved—and his mother and Lothair. They had all vanished from his mind; he lived for Olimpia alone. He sat beside her every day for hours together, rhapsodizing about his love and sympathy enkindled into life, and about psychic elective affinity[1]—all of which Olimpia listened to with great reverence. He fished up from the very

---

[1]This phrase (*Die Wahlverwandschaft* in German) has been made celebrated as the title of one of Goethe's works.

bottom of his desk all the things that he had ever written—poems, fancy sketches, visions, romances, tales, and the heap was increased daily with all kinds of aimless sonnets, stanzas, canzonets. All these he read to Olimpia hour after hour without growing tired; but then he had never had such an exemplary listener. She neither embroidered, nor knitted; she did not look out of the window, or feed a bird, or play with a little pet dog or a favorite cat, neither did she twist a piece of paper or anything of that kind round her finger; she did not forcibly convert a yawn into a low affected cough—in short, she sat hour after hour with her eyes bent unchangeably upon her lover's face, without moving or altering her position, and her gaze grew more ardent and more ardent still. And it was only when at last Nathanael rose and kissed her lips or her hand that she said, "Ach! Ach!" and then "Good-night, dear." Arrived in his own room, Nathanael would break out with, "Oh! What a brilliant—what a profound mind! Only you—you alone understand me." And his heart trembled with rapture when he reflected upon the wondrous harmony which daily revealed itself between his own and his Olimpia's character; for he fancied that she had expressed in respect to his works and his poetic genius the identical sentiments which he himself cherished deep down in his own heart in respect to the same, and even as if it was his own heart's voice speaking to him. And it must indeed have been so; for Olimpia never uttered any other words than those already mentioned. And when Nathanael himself in his clear and sober moments, as, for instance, directly after waking in a morning, thought about her utter passivity and taciturnity, he only said, "What are words—but words? The glance of her heavenly eyes says more than any tongue of earth. And how can, anyway, a child of heaven accustom herself to the narrow circle which the exigencies of a wretched mundane life demand?"

Professor Spalanzani appeared to be greatly pleased at the intimacy that had sprung up between his daughter Olimpia and Nathanael, and showed the young man many unmistakable proofs of his good feeling toward him; and when Nathanael ventured at length to hint very delicately at an alliance with Olimpia, the Professor smiled all over his face at once, and said he should allow his daughter to make a perfectly free choice. Encouraged by these words, and with the fire of desire burning in his heart, Nathanael resolved the very next day to implore Olimpia to tell him frankly, in plain words, what he had long read in her sweet loving glances—that she would be his forever. He looked for the ring which his mother had given him at parting; he would present it to Olimpia as a symbol of his devotion, and of the happy life he was to lead with her from that time onwards. Whilst looking for it he came across his letters from Clara and Lothair; he threw them carelessly aside, found the ring, put it in his pocket, and ran across to Olimpia. Whilst still on the stairs, in the entrance-passage, he heard an extraordinary hubbub; the noise seemed to proceed from Spalanzani's study. There was a stamping—a rattling—pushing—knocking against the door, with curses and oaths intermingled. "Leave hold—leave hold—you monster—you rascal—staked your life and honor upon it?—Ha! Ha! Ha! Ha!—That was not our wager—I, I made the eyes—I the clockwork—Go to the devil with your clockwork—you damned dog of a watchmaker—be off—Satan—stop—you paltry turner—you infernal beast!—Stop—Begone—Let me go." The voices which were thus making all this racket and rumpus were those of Spalanzani and the fearsome Coppelius. Nathanael rushed in, impelled by some nameless dread. The Professor was grasping a female figure by the shoulders, the Italian Coppola held her by the feet; and they were pulling and dragging each other backwards and forwards, fighting furiously to get possession of her. Nathanael recoiled with horror on recognizing that the figure was Olimpia. Boiling with rage, he was about to tear his beloved from the grasp of the madmen, when Coppola by an extraordinary exertion of strength twisted the figure out of the Professor's hands and gave him such a terrible blow with her, that he reeled backwards and fell over the table all amongst the phials and retorts, the bottles and glass cylinders, which covered it; all these things were smashed into a thousand pieces. But Coppola threw the figure across his shoulder, and, laughing shrilly and horribly, ran hastily down the stairs, the figure's ugly feet hanging down and banging and rattling like wood against the steps. Nathanael was stupefied—he had seen only too distinctly that in Olimpia's pallid waxed face there were no eyes, merely black holes in their stead; she was an inanimate puppet. Spalanzani was rolling on the floor; the pieces of glass had cut his head and breast and arm; the blood was escaping from him in streams. But he gathered his strength together by an effort.

"After him—after him! What do you stand staring there for? Coppelius—Coppelius—he's stolen my best automaton—at which I've worked for twenty years—staked my life upon it—the clockwork—speech—movement—mine—your eyes—stolen your eyes—

damn him—curse him—after him—fetch me back Olimpia—there are the eyes.'' And now Nathanael saw a pair of bloody eyes lying on the floor staring at him; Spalanzani seized them with his uninjured hand and threw them at him, so that they hit his breast. Then madness dug her burning talons into him and swept down into his heart, rending his mind and thoughts to shreds. ''Aha! Aha! Aha! Fire-wheel—fire-wheel! Spin round, fire-wheel! Merrily, Merrily! Aha! Wooden doll! Spin round, pretty wooden doll!'' And he threw himself upon the Professor, clutching him fast by the throat. He would certainly have strangled him had not several people, attracted by the noise, rushed in and torn away the madman; and so they saved the Professor, whose wounds were immediately dressed. Siegmund, with all his strength, was not able to subdue the frantic lunatic, who continued to scream in a dreadful way, ''Spin round, wooden doll!'' and to strike out right and left with his doubled fists. At length the united strength of several succeeded in overpowering him by throwing him on the floor and binding him. His cries passed into a brutish bellow that was awful to hear; and thus raging with the harrowing violence of madness, he was taken away to the madhouse.

Before continuing my narration of what happened further to the unfortunate Nathanael, I will tell you, indulgent reader, in case you take any interest in that skillful mechanician and fabricator of automata, Spalanzani, that he recovered completely from his wounds. He had, however, to leave the university, for Nathanael's fate had created a great sensation; and the opinion was pretty generally expressed that it was an imposture altogether unpardonable to have smuggled a wooden puppet instead of a living person into intelligent tea-circles—for Olimpia had been present at several with success. Lawyers called it a cunning piece of knavery, and all the harder to punish since it was directed against the public; and it had been so craftily contrived that it had escaped unobserved by all except a few preternaturally acute students, although everybody was very wise now and remembered to have thought of several facts which occurred to them as suspicious. But these latter could not succeed in making out any sort of a consistent tale. For was it, for instance, a thing likely to occur to anyone as suspicious that, according to the declaration of an elegant beau of these tea-parties, Olimpia had, contrary to all good manners, sneezed oftener than she had yawned? The former must have been, in the opinion of this elegant gentleman, the winding up of the concealed clock-work; it had always been accompanied by an observable creaking, and so on. The Professor of Poetry and Eloquence took a pinch of snuff, and, slapping the lid to and clearing his throat, said solemnly, "My most honorable ladies and gentlemen, don't you see then where the rub is? The whole thing is an allegory, a continuous metaphor. You understand me? *Sapienti sat.*" But several most honorable gentlemen did not rest satisfied with this explanation; the history of this automaton had sunk deeply into their souls, and an absurd mistrust of human figures began to prevail. Several lovers, in order to be fully convinced that they were not paying court to a wooden puppet, required that their mistress should sing and dance a little out of time, should embroider or knit or play with her little pug, et cetera, when being read to, but above all things else that she should do something more than merely listen—that she should frequently speak in such a way as to really show that her words presupposed as a condition some thinking and feeling. The bonds of love were in many cases drawn closer in consequence, and so of course became more engaging; in other instances they gradually relaxed and fell away. "I cannot really be made responsible for it," was the remark of more than one young gallant. At the tea-gatherings everybody, in order to ward off suspicion, yawned to an incredible extent and never sneezed. Spalanzani was obliged, as has been said, to leave the place in order to escape a criminal charge of having fraudulently imposed an automaton upon human society. Coppola, too, had also disappeared.

When Nathanael awoke he felt as if he had been oppressed by a terrible nightmare; he opened his eyes and experienced an indescribable sensation of mental comfort, whilst a soft and most beautiful sensation of warmth pervaded his body. He lay on his own bed in his own room at home; Clara was bending over him, and at a little distance stood his mother and Lothair. "At last, at last, O my darling Nathanael; now we have you again; now you are cured of your grievous illness, now you are mine again." And Clara's words came from the depths of her heart; and she clasped him in her arms. The bright scalding tears streamed from his eyes, he was so overcome with mingled feelings of sorrow and delight; and he gasped forth, "My Clara, my Clara!" Siegmund, who had staunchly stood by his friend in his hour of need, now came into the room. Nathanael gave him his hand—"My faithful brother, you have not deserted me." Every trace of insanity had left him, and in the tender

hands of his mother and his beloved, and his friends, he quickly recovered his strength again. Good fortune had in the meantime visited the
house; a niggardly old uncle, from whom they had never expected to get
anything, had died, and left Nathanael's mother not only a considerable
fortune, but also a small estate, pleasantly situated not far from the town.
There they resolved to go and live, Nathanael and his mother, and Clara,
to whom he was now to be marrried, and Lothair. Nathanael was become
gentler and more childlike than he had ever been before, and now began
really to understand Clara's supremely pure and noble character. None
of them ever reminded him, even in the remotest degree, of the past. But
when Siegmund took leave of him, he said, "By heaven, brother! I was
in a bad way, but an angel came just at the right moment and led me back
upon the path of light. Yes, it was Clara." Siegmund would not let him
speak further, fearing lest the painful recollections of the past might arise
too vividly and too intensely in his mind.

The time came for the four happy people to move to their little
property. At noon they were going through the streets. After making
several purchases they found that the lofty tower of the town-house was
throwing its giant shadows across the marketplace. "Come," said
Clara, "let us go up to the top once more and have a look at the distant
hills." No sooner said than done. Both of them, Nathanael and Clara,
went up the tower; their mother, however, went on with the servant-girl
to her new home, and Lothair, not feeling inclined to climb up all the
many steps, waited below. There the two lovers stood arm in arm on the
topmost gallery of the tower, and gazed out into the sweet-scented
wooded landscape, beyond which the blue hills rose up like a giant's
city.

"Oh! Do look at that strange little grey bush, it looks as if it were
actually walking towards us," said Clara. Mechanically he put his hand
into his side pocket; he found Coppola's perspective and looked for the
bush; Clara stood in front of the glass. Then a convulsive thrill shot
through his pulse and veins; pale as a corpse, he fixed his staring eyes
upon her; but soon they began to roll, and a fiery current flashed and
sparkled in them, and he yelled fearfully, like a hunted animal. Leaping
up high in the air and laughing horribly at the same time, he began to
shout, in a piercing voice, "Spin round, wooden doll! Spin round,
wooden doll!" With the strength of a giant he laid hold upon Clara and
tried to hurl her over, but in an agony of despair she clutched fast hold of

the railing that went round the gallery. Lothair heard the madman raging and Clara's scream of terror; a fearfull presentiment flashed across his mind. He ran up the steps; the door of the second flight was locked. Clara's scream for help rang out more loudly. Mad with rage and fear, he threw himself against the door, which at length gave way. Clara's cries were growing fainter and fainter—"Help! Save me! Save me!"—and her voice died away in the air. "She is killed—murdered by that madman," shouted Lothair. The door to the gallery was also locked. Despair gave him the strength of a giant; he burst the door off its hinges. Good God! There was Clara in the grasp of the madman Nathanael, hanging over the gallery in the air; she only held to the iron bar with one hand. Quick as lightning, Lothair seized his sister and pulled her back, at the same time dealing the madman a blow in the face with his doubled fist, which sent him reeling backwards, forcing him to let go his victim.

Lothair ran down with his insensible sister in his arms. She was saved. But Nathanael ran round and round the gallery, leaping up in the air and shouting, "Spin round, fire-wheel! Spin round, fire-wheel!" The people heard the wild shouting, and a crowd began to gather. In the midst of them towered the advocate Coppelius, like a giant; he had only just arrived in the town, and had gone straight to the marketplace. Some were going up to overpower and take charge of the madman, but Coppelius laughed and said, "Ha! Ha! Wait a bit; he'll come down of his own accord"; and he stood gazing upwards along with the rest. All at once Nathanael stopped as if spellbound; he bent down over the railing, and perceived Coppelius. With a piercing scream, "Ha! Foine oyes! Foine oyes!" he leapt over.

When Nathanael lay on the stone pavement with a broken head, Coppelius had disappeared in the crush and confusion.

Several years afterwards it was reported that, outside the door of a pretty country house in a remote district, Clara had been sitting hand in hand with a pleasant gentleman, whilst two bright boys were playing at her feet. From this it may be concluded that she eventually found that quiet domestic happiness which her cheerful, blithesome character required, and which Nathanael, with his tempest-tossed soul, could never have been able to give her.

Mary Wollstonecraft Shelley (1797–1851)

Ironically, the "father" of science fiction may actually have been a twenty-year-old woman. For a strong case can be made that Mary Shelley's *Frankenstein: or The Modern Prometheus* (1818) was the first modern science-fiction novel. It represents the initial fusion of the science story with the strange travel-tale, the utopian novel, and the gothic romance. And its central theme—man creating artificial life in an attempt to better God's work, but botching the job—has been called the quintessential myth of the industrial age.

The daughter of a pair of freethinking parents, Mary Shelley was born in London, England. Her mother, Mary Wollstonecraft Godwin, was a noted author and feminist whose unfortunate death by childbirth fever largely detemined the tragic tone of Mary Shelley's life. Childbirth infection was the result of doctors failing to wash their hands and instruments prior to delivery, but its etiology was then unknown and sometimes the parent's death was blamed on the child. Such was Mary Shelley's fate. Her father, William Godwin, treated her with psychological abuse and emotional neglect. And throughout her entire life she wrestled with this unnecessary burden of guilt.

Coldness, cruelty, and intolerance made her childhood very unhappy. One contemporary described her as a "sad-eyed little girl who would sit motionless for hours hardly daring to breathe." Even her favorite childhood memories were of withdrawn pastimes such as reading, writing, and daydreaming.

Then in the spring of her seventeenth year she returned from a two-year banishment to Scotland to discover the handsome young poet Percy Shelley a guest in her home. He was talented and nice to her, and she desperately craved attention. One thing led to another, and within three months they had become lovers and run off to Europe.

During the summer of 1816 while she, Percy Shelley, Byron, and Dr. Polidori were staying near Geneva they fell into the habit of reading ghost stories to each other. One day, as a result of a challenge by Byron, they all resolved to write novels of horror. But Mary Shelley could think of nothing until she overheard Byron and her lover talking about Erasmus Darwin's ideas about life. That evening the idea for *Frankenstein* came to her in a nightmare. When published, the novel met with great acclaim and by 1823 six versions of it were being staged.

By then, however, Shelley's life had changed dramatically. Three of her four children had died early. Percy's first wife had committed suicide in the winter of 1816 and while Mary became, shortly thereafter, Mrs. Shelley, her husband was lost at sea in 1822.

Shelley was famous, attractive, and intelligent. Throughout the rest of her life she received marriage offers from many prominent suitors (including Washington Irving). But she chose to cling to Percy Shelley's memory by remaining his widow. Living in near-poverty for much of her life, she pursued a literary career that eventually included another science-fiction novel, *The Last Man* (1826), a fantasy short story, "Transformation" (1831), and an excellent science-fiction short story about immortality, "The Mortal Immortal" (1834), which is included here.

THE MORTAL IMMORTAL

July 16, 1833—This is a memorable anniversary for me; on it I complete my three hundred and twenty-third year!

The Wandering Jew?—certainly not. More than eighteen centuries have passed over his head. In comparison with him, I am a very young Immortal.

Am I, then, immortal? This is a question which I have asked myself, by day and night, for now three hundred and three years, and yet cannot answer it. I detected a grey hair amidst my brown locks this very day—that surely signifies decay. Yet it may have remained concealed there for three hundred years—for some persons have become entirely whiteheaded before twenty years of age.

I will tell my story, and my reader shall judge for me. I will tell my story, and so contrive to pass some few hours of a long eternity, become so wearisome to me. Forever! Can it be? to live forever! I have heard of enchantments, in which the victims were plunged into a deep sleep, to awake, after a hundred years, as fresh as ever: I have heard of the Seven Sleepers—thus to be immortal would not be so burdensome: but, oh! the weight of never-ending time—the tedious passage of the still-succeeding hours! How happy was the fabled Nourjahad!—But to my task.

All the world has heard of Cornelius Agrippa. His memory is as immortal as his arts have made me. All the world has also heard of his scholar, who, unawares, raised the foul fiend during his master's absence, and was destroyed by him. The report, true or false, of this accident, was attended with many inconveniences to the renowned philosopher. All his scholars at once deserted him—his servants disappeared. He had no one near him to put coals on his ever-burning fires while he slept, or attend to the changeful colors of his medicines while he studied. Experiment after experiment failed, because one pair of hands was insufficient to complete them: the dark spirits laughed at him for not being able to retain a single mortal in his service.

I was then very young—very poor—and very much in love. I had been for about a year the pupil of Cornelius, though I was absent when this accident took place. On my return, my friends implored me not to return to the alchemist's abode. I trembled as I listened to the dire tale they told; I required no second warning; and when Cornelius came and offered me a purse of gold if I would remain under his roof, I felt as if Satan himself tempted me. My teeth chattered—my hair stood on end—I ran off as fast as my trembling knees would permit.

My failing steps were directed whither for two years they had every evening been attracted—a gently bubbling spring of pure living water, beside which lingered a dark-haired girl, whose beaming eyes were fixed on the path I was accustomed each night to tread. I cannot remember the hour I did not love Bertha; we had been neighbors and playmates from infancy—her parents, like mine, were of humble life, yet respectable— our attachment had been a source of pleasure to them. In an evil hour, a malignant fever carried off both her father and mother, and Bertha became an orphan. She would have found a home beneath my paternal roof, but, unfortunately, the old lady of the near castle, rich, childless, and solitary, declared her intention to adopt her. Henceforth Bertha was clad in silk—inhabited a marble palace—and was looked on as being highly favored by fortune. But in her new situation among her new associates, Bertha remained true to the friend of her humbler days; she often visited the cottage of my father, and when forbidden to go thither, she would stray towards the neighboring wood, and meet me beside its shady fountain.

She often declared that she owed no duty to her new protectress equal in sanctity to that which bound us. Yet still I was too poor to marry, and she grew weary of being tormented on my account. She had a haughty but an impatient spirit, and grew angry at the obstacles that prevented our union. We met now after an absence, and she had been sorely beset while I was away; she complained bitterly, and almost reproached me for being poor. I replied hastily,—

"I am honest, if I am poor!—were I not, I might soon become rich!"

This exclamation produced a thousand questions. I feared to shock

her by owning the truth, but she drew it from me; and then casting a look
of disdain on me, she said,—

"You pretend to love, and you fear to face the Devil for my sake!"

I protested that I had only dreaded to offend her;—while she dwelt
on the magnitude of the reward that I should receive. Thus encouraged—
shamed by her—led on by love and hope, laughing at my late fears, with
quick steps and a light heart, I returned to accept the offers of the
alchemist, and was instantly installed in my office.

A year passed away. I became possessed of no insignificant sum of
money. Custom had banished my fears. In spite of the most painful
vigilance, I had never detected the trace of a cloven foot; nor was the
studious silence of our abode ever disturbed by demoniac howls. I still
continued my stolen interviews with Bertha, and Hope dawned on
me—Hope—but not perfect joy: for Bertha fancied that love and security were enemies, and her pleasure was to divide them in my bosom.
Though true of heart, she was somewhat of a coquette in manner; and I
was jealous as a Turk. She slighted me in a thousand ways, yet would
never acknowledge herself to be in the wrong. She would drive me mad
with anger, and then force me to beg her pardon. Sometimes she fancied
that I was not sufficiently submissive, and then she had some story of a
rival, favored by her protectress. She was surrounded by silk-clad
youths—the rich and gay. What chance had the sad-robed scholar of
Cornelius compared with these?

On one occasion, the philosopher made such large demands upon
my time, that I was unable to meet her as I was wont. He was engaged in
some mighty work, and I was forced to remain, day and night, feeding
his furnaces and watching his chemical preparations. Bertha waited for
me in vain at the fountain. Her haughty spirit fired at this neglect; and
when at last I stole out during the few short minutes allotted to me for
slumber, and hoped to be consoled by her, she received me with disdain,
dismissed me in scorn, and vowed that any man should possess her hand
rather than he who could not be in two places at once for her sake. She
would be revenged! And truly she was. In my dingy retreat I heard that
she had been hunting, attended by Albert Hoffer. Albert Hoffer was
favored by her protectress, and the three passed in cavalcade before my
smoky window. Methought that they mentioned my name; it was followed by a laugh of derision, as her dark eyes glanced contemptuously
towards my abode.

Jealousy, with all its venom and all its misery, entered my breast.

Now I shed a torrent of tears, to think that I should never call her mine; and, anon, I imprecated a thousand curses on her inconstancy. Yet, still I must stir the fires of the alchemist, still attend on the changes of his unintelligible medicines.

Cornelius had watched for three days and nights, nor closed his eyes. The progress of his alembics was slower than he expected: in spite of his anxiety, sleep weighed upon his eyelids. Again and again he threw off drowsiness with more than human energy; again and again it stole away his senses. He eyed his crucibles wistfully. "Not ready yet," he murmured; "will another night pass before the work is accomplished? Winzy, you are vigilant—you are faithful—you have slept, my boy—you slept last night. Look at that glass vessel. The liquid it contains is of a soft rose-color: the moment it begins to change its hue, awaken me—till then I may close my eyes. First, it will turn white; and then emit golden flashes; but wait not till then; when the rose-color fades, rouse me." I scarcely heard the last words, muttered, as they were, in sleep. Even then he did not quite yield to nature. "Winzy, my boy," he again said, "do not touch the vessel—do not put it to your lips; it is a philter—a philter to cure love; you would not cease to love your Bertha—beware to drink!"

And he slept. His venerable head sunk on his breast, and I scarce heard his regular breathing. For a few minutes I watched the vessels—the rosy hue of the liquid remianed unchanged. Then my thoughts wandered—they visited the fountain, and dwelt on a thousand charming scenes never to be renewed—never! Serpents and adders were in my heart as the word "Never!" half formed itself on my lips. False girl! False and cruel! Nevermore would she smile on me as that evening she smiled on Albert. Worthless, detested woman! I would not remain unrevenged—she should see Albert expire at her feet—she should die beneath my vengeance. She had smiled in disdain and triumph—she knew my wretchedness and her power. Yet what power had she?—the power of exciting my hate—my utter scorn—my—oh, all but indifference! Could I attain that—could I regard her with careless eyes, transferring my rejected love to one fairer and more true, that were indeed a victory!

A bright flash darted before my eyes. I had forgotten the medicine of the adept; I gazed on it with wonder: flashes of admirable beauty, more bright than those which the diamond emits when the sun's rays are on it, glanced from the surface of the liquid; an odor the most fragrant and grateful stole over my sense; the vessel seemed one globe of living radiance, lovely to the eye, and most inviting to the taste. The first thought, instinctively inspired by the grosser sense, was, I will—I must drink. I raised the vessel to my lips. "It will cure me of love—of torture!" Already I had quaffed half of the most delicious liquor ever tasted by the palate of man, when the philosopher stirred. I started—I dropped the glass—the fluid flamed and glanced along the floor, while I felt Cornelius's grip at my throat, as he shrieked aloud, "Wretch! you have destroyed the labor of my life!"

The philosopher was totally unaware that I had drunk any portion of his drug. His idea was, and I gave a tacit assent to it, that I had raised the vessel from curiosity, and that, frightened at its brightness, and the flashes of intense light it gave forth, I had let it fall. I never undeceived him. The fire of the medicine was quenched—the fragrance died away—he grew calm, as a philosopher should under the heaviest trials, and dismissed me to rest.

I will not attempt to describe the sleep of glory and bliss which bathed my soul in paradise during the remaining hours of that memorable night. Words would be faint and shallow types of my enjoyment, or of the gladness that possessed my bosom when I woke. I trod air—my thoughts were in heaven. Earth appeared heaven, and my inheritance upon it was to be one trace of delight. "This is to be cured of love," I thought; "I will see Bertha this day, and she will find her lover cold and regardless; too happy to be disdainful, yet how utterly indifferent to her!"

The hours danced away. The philosopher, secure that he had once succeeded, and believing that he might again, began to concoct the same medicine once more. He was shut up with his books and drugs, and I had a holiday. I dressed myself with care; I looked in an old but polished shield, which served me for a mirror; methought my good looks had wonderfully improved. I hurried beyond the precincts of the town, joy in my soul, the beauty of heaven and earth around me. I turned my steps towards the castle—I could look on its lofty turrets with lightness of heart, for I was cured of love. My Bertha saw me afar off, as I came up the avenue. I know not what sudden impulse animated her bosom, but at the sight, she sprung with a light fawn-like bound down the marble steps, and was hastening toward me. But I had been perceived by another person. The old high-born hag, who called herself her protectress, and was her tyrant, had seen me also; she hobbled, panting, up the terrace; a page, as ugly as herself, held up her train, and fanned her as she hurried along, and stopped my fair girl with a "How, now, my bold mistress? Whither so fast? Back to your cage—hawks are abroad!"

Bertha clasped her hands—her eyes were still bent on my approaching figure. I saw the contest. How I abhorred the old crone who checked the kind impulses of my Bertha's softening heart. Hitherto, respect for her rank had caused me to avoid the lady of the castle; now I disdained such trivial consideration. I was cured of love, and lifted above all human fears; I hastened forwards, and soon reached the terrace. How lovely Bertha looked! Her eyes flashing fire, her cheeks glowing with impatience and anger, she was a thousand times more graceful and charming than ever. I no longer loved—oh no! I adored—worshiped—idolized her!

She had that morning been persecuted, with more than usual vehemence, to consent to an immediate marriage with my rival. She was reproached with the encouragement that she had shown him—she was threatened with being turned out of doors with disgrace and shame. Her proud spirit rose in arms at the threat; but when she remembered the scorn that she had heaped upon me, and how, perhaps, she had thus lost one whom she now regarded as her only friend, she wept with remorse and rage. At that moment I appeared. "Oh, Winzy!" she exclaimed, "take me to your mother's cot; swiftly let me leave the detested luxuries and wretchedness of this noble dwelling—take me to poverty and happiness."

I clasped her in my arms with transport. The old dame was speechless with fury, and broke forth into invective only when we were far on our road to my natal cottage. My mother received the fair fugitive, escaped from a gilt cage to nature and liberty, with tenderness and joy; my father, who loved her, welcomed her heartily; it was a day of rejoicing, which did not need the addition of the celestial potion of the alchemist to steep me in delight.

Soon after this eventful day, I became the husband of Bertha. I ceased to be the scholar of Cornelius, but I continued his friend. I always felt grateful to him for having, unawares, procured me that delicious draught of a divine elixir, which, instead of curing me of love (sad cure! solitary and joyless remedy for evils which seem blessings to the memory), had inspired me with courage and resolution, thus winning for me an inestimable treasure in my Bertha.

I often called to mind that period of trance-like inebriation with wonder. The drink of Cornelius had not fulfilled the task for which he affirmed that it had been prepared, but its effects were more potent and blissful than words can express. They had faded by degrees, yet they lingered long—and painted life in hues of splendor. Bertha often wondered at my lightness of heart and unaccustomed gaiety; for, before, I had been rather serious, or even sad, in my disposition. She loved me the better for my cheerful temper, and our days were winged by joy.

Five years afterwards I was suddenly summoned to the bedside of the dying Cornelius. He had sent for me in haste, conjuring my instant presence. I found him stretched on his pallet, enfeebled even to death; all of life that yet remained animated his piercing eyes, and they were fixed on a glass vessel, full of a roseate liquid.

"Behold," he said, in a broken and inward voice, "the vanity of human wishes! A second time my hopes are about to be crowned, a second time they are destroyed. Look at that liquor—you remember five years ago I prepared the same, with the same success—then, as now, my thirsting lips expected to taste the immortal elixir—you dashed it from me! And at present it is too late."

He spoke with difficulty, and fell back on his pillow. I could not help saying,—

"How, revered master, can a cure for love restore you to life?"

A faint smile gleamed across his face as I listened earnestly to his scarcely intelligible answer.

"A cure for love and for all things—the Elixir of Immortality. Ah! if now I might drink, I should live forever!"

As he spoke, a golden flash gleamed from the fluid; a well-remembered fragrance stole over the air; he raised himself, all weak as he was—strength seemed miraculously to reenter his frame—he stretched forth his hand—a loud explosion startled me—a ray of fire shot up from the elixir, and the glass vessel which contained it was shivered to atoms! I turned my eyes towards the philosopher; he had ballen back—his eyes were glassy—his features rigid—he was dead!

But I lived, and was to live forever! So said the unfortunate alchemist, and for a few days I believed his words. I remembered the glorious intoxication that had followed my stolen draught. I reflected on the change I had felt in my frame—in my soul. The bounding elasticity of the one—the buoyant lightness of the other. I surveyed myself in a mirror, and could perceive no change in my features during the space of the five years which had elapsed. I remembered the radiant hues and grateful scent of that delicious beverage—worthy the gift it was capable of bestowing—I was, then IMMORTAL!

A few days after I laughed at my credulity. The old proverb, that "a prophet is least regarded in his own country," was true with respect to me and my defunct master. I loved him as a man—I respected him as a sage—but I derided the notion that he could command the powers of darkness, and laughed at the superstitious fears with which he was regarded by the vulgar. He was a wise philosopher, but had no acquaintance with any spirits but those clad in flesh and blood. His science was simply human; and human science, I soon persuaded myself, could never conquer nature's laws so far as to imprison the soul forever within its carnal habitation. Cornelius had brewed a soul-refreshing drink—more inebriating than wine—sweeter and more fragrant than any fruit: it possessed probably strong medicinal powers, imparting gladness to the heart and vigor to the limbs; but its effects would wear out; already were they diminished in my frame. I was a lucky fellow to have quaffed health and joyous spirits, and perhaps long life, at my master's hands; but my good fortune ended there: longevity was far different from immortality.

I continued to entertain this belief for many years. Sometimes a thought stole across me—Was the alchemist indeed deceived? But my habitual credence was, that I should meet the fate of all the children of Adam at my appointed time—a little late, but still at a natural age. Yet it was certain that I retained a wonderfully youthful look. I was laughed at for my vanity in consulting the mirror so often, but I consulted it in vain—my brow was untrenched—my cheeks—my eyes—my whole person continued as untarnished as in my twentieth year.

I was troubled. I looked at the faded beauty of Bertha—I seemed more like her son. By degrees our neighbors began to make similar observations, and I found at last that I went by the name of the Scholar bewitched. Bertha herself grew uneasy. She became jealous and peevish, and at length she began to question me. We had no children; we were all in all to each other; and though, as she grew older, her vivacious spirit became a little allied to ill-temper, and her beauty sadly diminished, I cherished her in my heart as the mistress I had idolized, the wife I had sought and won with such perfect love.

At last our situation became intolerable: Bertha was fifty—I twenty years of age. I had, in very shame, in some measure adopted the habits of a more advanced age; I no longer mingled in the dance among the young and gay, but my heart bounded along with them while I restrained my feet; and a sorry figure I cut among the Nestors of our village. But before the time I mentioned, things were altered—we were universally shunned; we were—at least, I was—reported to have kept up an iniquitous acquaintance with some of my former master's supposed friends. Poor Bertha was pitied, but deserted. I was regarded with horror and detestation.

What was to be done? We sat by our winter fire—poverty had made itself felt, for none would buy the produce of my farm; and often I had been forced to journey twenty miles, to some place where I was not known, to dispose of our property. It is true, we had saved something for an evil day—that day was come.

We sat by our lone fireside—the old-hearted youth and his antiquated wife. Again Betha insisted on knowing the truth; she recapitulated all she had ever heard said about me, and added her own observations. She conjured me to cast off the spell; she described how much more comely grey hairs were than my chestnut locks; she descanted on the reverence and respect due to age—how preferable to the slight regard paid to mere children: could I imagine that the despicable gifts of youth and good looks outweighed disgrace, hatred, and scorn? Nay, in the end I should be burnt as a dealer in the black art, while she, to whom I had not deigned to communicate any portion of my good fortune, might be stoned as my accomplice. At length she insinuated that I must share my secret with her, and bestow on her like benefits to those I myself enjoyed, or she would denounce me—and then she burst into tears.

Thus beset, methought it was the best way to tell the truth. I revealed it as tenderly as I could, and spoke only of a *very long life*, not of immortality—which representation, indeed, coincided best with my own ideas. When I ended, I rose and said,—

"And now, my Bertha, will you denounce the lover of your youth? You will not, I know. But it is too hard, my poor wife, that you should suffer from my ill-luck and accursed arts of Cornelius. I will leave you—you have wealth enough, and friends will return in my absence. I will go; young as I seem, and strong as I am, I can work and gain my bread among strangers, unsuspected and unknown. I loved you in youth; God is my witness that I would not desert you in age, but that your safety and happiness require it.''

I took my cap and moved towards the door; in a moment Bertha's arms were round my neck, and her lips were pressed to mine. ''No, my husband, my Winzy,'' she said, ''you shall not go alone—take me with you; we will remove from this place, and, as you say, among strangers we shall be unsuspected and safe. I am not so very old as quite to shame you, my Wimzy; and I daresay the charm will soon wear off, and, with the blessing of God, you will become more elderly-looking, as is fitting; you shall not leave me.''

I returned the good soul's embrace heartily. ''I will not, my Bertha; but for your sake I had not thought of such a thing. I will be your true, faithful husband while you are spared to me, and do my duty by you to the last.''

The next day we prepared secretly for our emigration. We were obliged to make great pecuniary sacrifices—it could not be helped. We realized a sum sufficient, at least, to maintain us while Bertha lived; and, without saying adieu to any one, quitted our native country to take refuge in a remote part of western France.

It was a cruel thing to transport poor Bertha from her native village, and the friends of her youth, to a new country, new language, new customs. The strange secret of my destiny rendered this removal immaterial to me; but I compassioned her deeply, and was glad to perceive that she found compensation for her misfortunes in a variety of little ridiculous circumstances. Away from all telltale chroniclers, she sought to decrease the apparent disparity of our ages by a thousand feminine arts—rouge, youthful dress, and assumed juvenility of manner. I could not be angry. Did not I myself wear a mask? Why quarrel with hers, because it was less successful? I grieved deeply when I remembered that this was my Bertha, whom I had loved so fondly and won with such transport—the dark-eyed, dark-haired girl, with smiles of enchanting archness and a step like a fawn—this mincing, simpering, jealous old woman. I should have revered her grey locks and withered cheeks; but thus! It was my work, I knew; but I did not the less deplore this type of human weakness.

Her jealousy never slept. Her chief occupation was to discover that, in spite of outward appearances, I was myself growing old. I verily believe that the poor soul loved me truly in her heart, but never had woman so tormenting a mode of displaying fondness. She would discern wrinkles in my face and decrepitude in my walk, while I bounded along in youthful vigor, the youngest-looking of twenty youths. I never dared address another woman. On one occasion, fancying that the belle of the village regarded me with favoring eyes, she brought me a grey wig. Her constant discourse among her acquaintances was, that though I looked so young, there was ruin at work within my frame; and she affirmed that the worst symptom about me was my apparent health. My youth was a disease, she said, and I ought at all times to prepare, if not for a sudden and awful death, at least to awake some morning white-headed and bowed down with all the marks of advanced years. I let her talk—I often joined in her conjectures. Her warnings chimed in with my never-ceasing speculations concerning my state, and I took an earnest, though painful, interest in listening to all that her quick wit and excited imagination could say on the subject.

Why dwell on these minute circumstances? We lived on for many long years. Bertha became bedridden and paralytic; I nursed her as a mother might a child. She grew peevish, and still harped upon one string—of how long I should survive her. It has ever been a source of consolation to me, that I performed my duty scrupulously towards her. She had been mine in youth, she was mine in age; and at last, when I heaped the sod over her corpse, I wept to feel that I had lost all that really bound me to humanity.

Since then how many have been my cares and woes, how few and empty my enjoyments! I pause here in my history—I will pursue it no further. A sailor without rudder or compass, tossed on a stormy sea—a traveler lost on a widespread heath, without landmark or stone to guide him—such have I been: more lost, more hopeless than either. A nearing ship, a gleam from some far cot, may save them; but I have no beacon except the hope of death.

Death! Mysterious, ill-visaged friend of weak humanity! Why alone of all mortals have you cast me from your sheltering fold? Oh, for the peace of the grave! The deep silence of the iron-bound tomb! That thought would cease to work in my brain, and my heart beat no more with emotions varied only by new forms of sadness!

Am I immortal? I return to my first question. In the first place, is it not more probable that the beverage of the alchemist was fraught rather with longevity than eternal life? Such is my hope. And then be it remembered, that I only drank *half* of the potion prepared by him. Was not the whole necessary to complete the charm? To have drained half the Elixir of Immortality is but to be half-immortal—my Forever is thus truncated and null.

But again, who shall number the years of the half of eternity? I often try to imagine by what rule the infinite may be divided. Sometimes I fancy age advancing upon me. One grey hair I have found. Fool! Do I lament? Yes, the fear of age and death often creeps coldly into my heart; and the more I live, the more I dread death, even while I abhor life. Such an enigma is man—born to perish—when he wars, as I do, against the established laws of his nature.

But for this anomaly of feeling surely I might die: the medicine of the alchemicst would not be proof against fire—sword—and the strangling waters. I have gazed upon the blue depths of many a placid lake, and the tumultuous rushing of many a mighty river, and have said, peace inhabits those waters; yet I have turned my steps away, to live yet another day. I have asked myself, whether suicide would be a crime in one to whom thus only the portals of the other world could be opened. I have done all, except presenting myself as a soldier or duelist, an objection of destruction to my—no *not* my fellow-mortals, and therefore I have shrunk away. They are not my fellows. The inextinguishable power of life in my frame, and their ephemeral existence, places us wide as the poles asunder. I could not raise a hand against the meanest or the most powerful among them.

Thus I have lived on for many a year—alone, and weary of myself—desirous of death, yet never dying—a mortal immortal. Neither ambition nor avarice can enter my mind, and the ardent love that gnaws at my heart, never to be returned—never to find an equal on which to expend itself—lives there only to torment me.

This very day I conceived a design by which I may end all—without self-slaughter, without making another man a Cain—an expedition, which mortal frame can never survive, even endued with the youth and strength that inhabits mine. Thus I shall put my immortality to the test, and rest forever—or return, the wonder and benefactor of the human species.

Before I go, a miserable vanity has caused me to pen these pages. I would not die, and leave no name behind. Three centuries have passed since I quaffed the fatal beverage; another year shall not elapse before, encountering gigantic dangers—warring with the powers of frost in their home—beset by famine, toil, and tempest—I yield this body, too tenacious a cage for a soul which thirsts for freedom, to the destructive elements of air and water; or, if I survive, my name shall be recorded as one of the most famous among the sons of men; and, my task achieved, I shall adopt more resolute means; and, by scattering and annihilating the atoms that compose my frame, set at liberty the life imprisoned within, and so cruelly prevented from soaring from this dim earth to a sphere more congenial to its immortal essence.

Edgar Allan Poe (1809–1849)

Edgar Allan Poe was the seminal genre writer of the nineteenth century.
He popularized stories of science fiction and psychological terror in
England, America, and France. He invented stories of detection and he
influenced Arthur Conan Doyle, Jules Verne, and Guy de Maupassant.
Ironically, however, his life was filled with poverty, failure, and
tragedy.

Shortly after Poe's birth in Boston his father ran away; three years
later his mother died of consumption in Richmond, Virginia. Fortunately, Mrs. John Allan, the childless wife of a merchant, was attracted
to the boy and took him into her house. Poe was clever and loving, so at
first he brought great joy to his new family. But he showed no interest in
John Allan's business and Mr. Allan strongly disapproved of the young
man's literary bent. Eventually Poe was dispatched to the University of
Virginia, tried to increase his insufficient funds through gambling, and
lost everything. In disgrace, he made two abortive attempts at an army
career, then decided to try full-time writing. He entered the Baltimore
Saturday Visitor short-story contest of 1833, winning first prize for
"Ms. Found in a Bottle." That success led to his editing the *Southern
Literary Messenger*. Poe dramatically increased circulation of this and
subsequent journals he worked on, but was invariably fired because of
his strong views, his arrogance, and his penchant for self-destruction
through liquor and drugs.

After marrying his cousin he moved to New York, where he lived
for several years in abject poverty. He watched his child bride waste
away before his eyes and often ate only because of his mother-in-law's
successful begging. Great works such as "The Raven," "The Purloined

Letter,'' and ''Annabel Lee'' brought little money, were printed for copies, or were given away. And the moderate degree of fame he did achieve he handled badly.

Considering his short life and his many personal and financial difficulties, Poe was still quite prolific, having written a short science-fiction novel, *The Narrative of Arthur Gordon Pym of Nantucket* (1837), and enough short stories and poems to fill several volumes. His stories are usually written at a passionate pitch, often hallucinatory in nature, and filled with obsessive phobias. However, he is also capable of writing in a quasi-documentary method, as in ''The Great Balloon Hoax,'' or in a closely reasoned style, as in our selection, ''A Descent into the Maelstrom.'' This latter is one of his best tales and may be the first science-fiction ''problem'' story. However, in what seems typical for Poe, Harold Beaver suggests, in his thorough annotations of *The Science Fiction of Edgar Allan Poe* (1976), that the solution is an intentional fraud.

Finally, in 1849 it appeared that Poe might get his life straightened out. He had plans to marry his childhood sweetheart (now a rich widow) and had been offered a good deal of money to edit some poems. But he disappeared on a bender, was found days later in a Baltimore gutter, and died shortly thereafter.

A DESCENT INTO THE MAELSTROM

The ways of God in Nature, as in Providence, are not as *our* ways; nor are the models that we frame in any way commensurate to the vastness, profundity, and unsearchableness of His works, *which have a depth in them greater than the well of Democritus.*

—*Joseph Glanville*

We had now reached the summit of the loftiest crag. For some minutes the old man seemed too much exhausted to speak.

"Not long ago," said he at length, "and I could have guided you on this route as well as the youngest of my sons; but, about three years past, there happened to me an event such as never happened before to mortal man—or at least such as no man ever survived to tell of—and the six hours of deadly terror which I then endured have broken me up body and soul. You suppose me a *very* old man—but I am not. It took less than a single day to change these hairs from a jetty black to white, to weaken my limbs, and to unstring my nerves, so that I tremble at the least exertion, and am frightened at a shadow. Do you know I can scarcely look over this little cliff without getting giddy?"

The "little cliff," upon whose edge he had so carelessly thrown himself down to rest that the weightier portion of his body hung over it, while he was only kept from falling by the tenure of his elbow on its extreme and slippery edge—this "little cliff" arose, a sheer unobstructed precipice of black shining rock, some fifteen or sixteen hundred feet from the world of crags beneath us. Nothing would have tempted me

to be within half a dozen yards of its brink. In truth so deeply was I
excited by the perilous position of my companion, that I fell at full length
upon the ground, clung to the shrubs around me, and dared not even
glance upward at the sky—while I struggled in vain to divest myself of
the idea that the very foundations of the mountain were in danger from
the fury of the winds. It was long before I could reason myself into
sufficient courage to sit up and look out into the distance.

"You must get over these fancies," said the guide, "for I have
brought you here that you might have the best possible view of the scene
of that event I mentioned—and to tell you the whole story with the spot
just under your eye.

"We are now," he continued, in that particularizing manner which
distinguished him—"we are now close upon the Norwegian coast—in
the sixty-eighth degree of latitude—in the great province of Nordland—
and in the dreary district of Lofoden. The mountain upon whose top we
sit is Helseggen, the Cloudy. Now raise yourself up a little higher—hold
on to the grass if you feel giddy—so—and look out, beyond the belt of
vapor beneath us, into the sea."

I looked dizzily, and beheld a wide expanse of ocean, whose waters
wore so inky a hue as to bring at once to my mind the Nubian geogra-
pher's account of the *Mare Tenebrarum*. A panorama more deplorably
desolate no human imagination can conceive. To the right and left, as far
as the eye could reach, there lay outstretched, like ramparts of the world,
lines of horridly black and beetling cliff, whose character of gloom was
but the more forcibly illustrated by the surf which reared high up against
its white and ghastly crest, howling and shrieking forever. Just opposite
the promontory upon whose apex we were placed, and at a distance of
some five or six miles out at sea, there was visible a small, bleak-looking
island; or, more properly, its position was discernible through the wilderness of surge in which it was enveloped. About two miles nearer the
land, arose another of smaller size, hideously craggy and barren, and
encompassed at various intervals by a cluster of dark rocks.

The appearance of the ocean, in the space between the more distant
island and the shore, had something very unusual about it. Although, at
the time, so strong a gale was blowing landward that a brig in the remote
offing lay to under a double-reefed trysail, and constantly plunged her
whole hull out of sight, still there was here nothing like a regular swell,
but only a short, quick, angry cross-dashing of water in every direc-

tion—as well in the teeth of the wind as otherwise. Of foam there was little except in the immediate vicinity of the rocks.

"The island in the distance," resumed the old man, "is called by the Norwegians Vurrgh. The one midway is Moskoe. That a mile to the northward is Ambaaren. Yonder are Islesen, Hotholm, Keildhelm, Suarven, and Buckholm. Further off—between Moskoe and Vurrgh— are Otterholm, Flimen, Sandflesen, and Stockholm. These are the true names of the places—but why it has been thought necessary to name them at all, is more than either you or I can understand. Do you hear anything? Do you see any change in the water?''

We had now been about ten minutes upon the top of Helseggen, to which we had ascended from the interior of Lofoden, so that we had caught no glimpse of the sea until it had burst upon us from the summit. As the old man spoke, I became aware of a loud and gradually increasing sound, like the moaning of a vast herd of buffaloes upon an American prairie; and at the same moment I perceived that what seamen term the *chopping* character of the ocean beneath us, was rapidly changing into a current which set to the eastward. Even while I gazed, this current acquired a monstrous velocity. Each moment added to its speed—to its headlong impetuosity. In five minutes the whole sea, as far as Vurrgh, was lashed into ungovernable fury; but it was between Moskoe and the coast that the main uproar held its sway. Here the vast bed of the waters seamed and scarred into a thousand conflicting channels, burst suddenly into frenzied convulsion—heaving, boiling, hissing—gyrating in gigantic and innumerable vortices, and all whirling and plunging on to the eastward with a rapidity which water never elsewhere assumes, except in precipitous descents.

In a few minutes more, there came over the scene another radical alteration. The general surface grew somewhat more smooth, and the whirlpools, one by one, disappeared, while prodigious streaks of foam became apparent where none had been seen before. These streaks, at length, spreading out to a great distance, and entering into combination, took unto themselves the gyratory motion of the subsided vortices, and seemed to form the germ of another more vast. Suddenly—very suddenly—this assumed a distinct and definite existence, in a circle of more than a mile in diameter. The edge of the whirl was represented by a broad belt of gleaming spray; but no particle of this slipped into the mouth of the terrific funnel, whose interior, as far as the eye could fathom it, was a smooth, shining, and jet-black wall of water, inclined to the horizon at an angle of some forty-five degrees, speeding dizzily round and round with a swaying and sweltering motion, and sending forth to the winds an appalling voice, half shriek, half roar, such as not even the mighty cataract of Niagara ever lifts up in its agony to Heaven.

The mountain trembled to its very base, and the rock rocked. I threw myself upon my face, and clung to the scant herbage in an excess of nervous agitation.

"This," said I at length, to the old man—"this *can* be nothing else than the great whirlpool of the Maelström."

"So it is sometimes termed," said he. "We Norwegians call it the Moskoe-ström, from the island of Moskoe in the midway."

The ordinary account of this vortex had by no means prepared me for what I saw. That of Jonas Ramus, which is perhaps the most circumstantial of any, cannot impart the faintest conception either of the magnificence, or of the horror of the scene—or of the wild bewildering sense of *the novel* which confounds the beholder. I am not sure from what point of view the writer in question surveyed it, nor at what time; but it could neither have been from the summit of Helseggen, nor during a storm. There are some passages of his description, nevertheless, which may be quoted for their details, although their effect is exceedingly feeble in conveying an impression of the spectacle.

"Between Lofoden and Modkoe," he says, "the depth of the water is between thirty-six and forty fathoms; but on the other side, toward Ver (Vurrgh) this depth decreases so as not to afford a convenient passage for a vessel, without the risk of splitting on the rocks, which happens even in the calmest weather. When it is flood, the stream runs up the country between Lofoden and Moskoe with a boisterous rapidity; but the roar of its impetuous ebb to the sea is scarce equaled by the loudest and most dreadful cataracts; the noise being heard several leagues off, and the vortices or pits are of such an extent and depth, that if a ship comes within its attraction, it is inevitably absorbed and carried down to the bottom, and there beat to pieces against the rocks; and when the water relaxes, the fragments thereof are thrown up again. But these intervals of tranquillity are only at the turn of the ebb and flood, and in calm weather, and last but a quarter of an hour, its violence gradually returning. When the stream is most boisterous, and its fury heightened by a storm, it is dangerous to come within a Norway mile of it. Boats, yachts, and ships have been carried away by not guarding against it before they were carried within its reach. It likewise happens frequently, that whales come too near the stream, and are overpowered by its violence; and then it is impossible to describe their howlings and bellowings in their fruitless struggles to disengage themselves. A bear once, attempting to swim from Lofoden to Moskoe, was caught by the stream and borne down, while he roared terribly, so as to be heard on shore. Large stocks of firs and pine trees, after being absorbed by the current, rise again broken and torn to such a degree as if bristles grew upon them. This plainly shows the bottom to consist of craggy rocks, among which they are whirled to and fro. This stream is regulated by the flux and reflux of the sea—it being constantly high and low water every six hours. In the year 1645, early in the morning of Sexagesima Sunday, it raged with such noise and impetuosity that the very stones of the houses on the coast fell to the ground.''

In regard to the depth of the water, I could not see how this could have been ascertained at all in the immediate vicinity of the vortex. The ''forty fathoms'' must have reference only to portions of the channel close upon the shore either of Moskoe or Lofoden. The depth in the center of the Moskoe-ström must be unmeasurably greater; and no better proof of this fact is necessary than can be obtained from even the sidelong glance into the abyss of the whirl which may be had from the highest crag of Helseggen. Looking down from this pinnacle upon the howling Phlegethon below, I could not help smiling at the simplicity with which the honest Jonas Ramus records, as a matter difficult of believe, the anecdotes of the whales and the bears, for it appeared to me, in fact, a self-evident thing, that the largest ships of the line in existence, coming within the influence of that deadly attraction, could resist it as little as a feather the hurricane, and must disappear bodily and at once.

The attempts to account for the phenomenon—some of which I remember, seemed to me sufficiently plausible in perusal—now wore a very different 'and unsatisfactory aspect. The idea generally received is that this, as well as three smaller vortices among the Ferroe Islands, ''have no other cause than the collision of waves rising and falling, at flux and reflux, against a ridge of rocks and shelves, which confines the water so that it precipitates itself like a cataract; and thus the higher the flood rises, the deeper must the fall be, and the natural result of all is a whirlpool or vortex, the prodigious suction of which is sufficiently known by lesser experiments.''—These are the words of the Encyclopedia Britannica. Kircher and others imagine that in the center of the channel of the maelström is an abyss penetrating the globe, and issuing in some very remote part—the Gulf of Bothnia being somewhat decidedly named in one instance. This opinion, idle in itself, was the one to which, as I gazed, my imagination most readily assented; and, mentioning it to the guide, I was rather surprised to hear him say that, although it was the view almost universally entertained of the subject by the Norwegians, it nevertheless was not his own. As to the former notion he confessed his inability to comprehend it; and here I agreed with him—for, however conclusive on paper, it becomes altogether unintelligible, and even absurd, amid the thunder of the abyss.

"You have had a good look at the whirl now," said the old man, "and if you will creep round this crag, so as to get in its lee, and deaden the roar of the water, I will tell you a story that will convince you I ought to know something of the Moskoe-ström."

I placed myself as desired, and he proceeded.

"Myself and my two brothers once owned a schooner-rigged smack of about seventy tons burden, with which we were in the habit of fishing among the islands beyond Moskoe, nearly to Vurrgh. In all violent eddies at sea there is good fishing, at proper opportunities, if one has only the courage to attempt it; but among the whole of the Lofoden coastmen, we three were the only ones who made a regular business of going out to the islands, as I tell you. The usual grounds are a great way lower down to the southward. There fish can be got at all hours, without much risk, and therefore these places are preferred. The choice spots over here among the rocks, however, not only yield the finest variety, but in far greater abundance; so that we often got in a single day, what the more timid of the craft could not scrape together in a week. In fact, we made it a matter of desperate speculation—the risk of life standing instead of labor, and courage answering for capital.

"We kept the smack in a cove about five miles higher up the coast than this; and it was our practice, in fine weather, to take advantage of the fifteen minutes' slack to push across the main channel of the Moskoe-ström, far above the pool, and then drop down upon anchorage somewhere near Otterholm, or Sandflesen, where the eddies are not so violent as elsewhere. Here we used to remain until nearly time for slack water again, when we weighed and made for home. We never set out upon this expedition without a steady side wind for going and coming—one that we felt sure would not fail us before our return—and we seldom made a miscalculation upon this point. Twice, during six years, we were forced to stay all night at anchor on account of a dead calm, which is a rare thing indeed just about here; and once we had to remain on the grounds nearly a week, starving to death, owing to a gale which blew up shortly after our arrival, and made the channel too boisterous to be thought of. Upon this occasion we should have been driven out to sea in spite of everything (for the whirlpools threw us round and round so violently, that, at length, we fouled our anchor and dragged it), if it had not been that we drifted into one of the innumerable cross currents—here today and gone tomorrow—which drove us under the lee of Flimen, where, by good luck, we brought up.

"I could not tell you the twentieth part of the difficulties we encountered 'on the ground'—it is a bad spot to be in, even in good weather—but we made shift always to run the gauntlet of the Moskoeström itself without accident; although at times my heart has been in my mouth when we happened to be a minute or so behind or before the slack. The wind sometimes was not as strong as we thought it at starting, and then we made rather less way than we could wish, while the current rendered the smack unmanageable. My eldest brother had a son eighteen years old, and I had two stout boys of my own. These would have been of great assistance at such times, in using the sweeps as well as afterward in fishing—but, somehow, although we ran the risk ourselves, we had not the heart to let the young ones get into the danger—for, after all said and done, it *was* a horrible danger, and that is the truth.

"It is now within a few days of three years since what I am going to tell you occurred. It was on the tenth of July, 18—, a day which the people of this part of the world will never forget—for it was one in which blew the most terrible hurricane that ever came out of the heavens. And yet all the morning, and indeed until late in the afternoon, there was a gentle and steady breeze from the southwest, while the sun shone brightly, so that the oldest seaman among us could not have foreseen what was to follow.

"The three of us—my two brothers and myself—had crossed over to the islands about two o'clock P.M., and soon nearly loaded the smack with fine fish, which, we all remarked, were more plenty that day than we had ever known them. It was just seven, *by my watch*, when we weighed and started for home, so as to make the worst of the Ström at slack water, which we knew would be at eight.

"We set out with a fresh wind on our starboard quarter, and for

73

some time spanked along at a great rate, never dreaming of danger, for indeed we saw not the slightest reason to apprehend it. All at once we were taken aback by a breeze from over Helseggen. This was most unusual—something that had never happened to us before—and I began to feel a little uneasy, without exactly knowing why. We put the boat on the wind, but could make no headway at all for the eddies, and I was upon the point of proposing to return to the anchorage, when, looking astern, we saw the whole horizon covered with a singular copper-colored cloud that rose with the most amazing velocity.

"In the meantime the breeze that had headed us off fell away and we were dead becalmed, drifting about in every direction. This state of things, however, did not last long enough to give us time to think about it. In less than a minute the storm was upon us—in less than two the sky was entirely overcast—and what with this and the driving spray, it became suddenly so dark that we could not see each other in the smack.

"Such a hurricane as then blew it is folly to attempt describing. The oldest seaman in Norway never experienced anything like it. We had let our sails go by the run before it cleverly took us; but, at the first puff, both our masts went by the board as if they had been sawed off—the mainmast taking with it my youngest brother, who had lashed himself to it for safety.

"Our boat was the lightest feather of a thing that ever sat upon water. It had a complete flush deck, with only a small hatch near the bow, and this hatch it had always been our custom to batten down when about to cross the Ström, by way of precaution against the chopping seas. But for this circumstance we should have foundered at once—for we lay entirely buried for some moments. How my elder brother escaped destruction I cannot say, for I never had an opportunity of ascertaining. For my part as soon as I had let the foresail run, I threw myself flat on deck, with my feet against the narrow gunwale of the bow, and with my hands grasping a ring-bolt near the foot of the foremast. It was mere instinct that prompted me to do this—which was undoubtedly the very best thing I could have done—for I was too much flurried to think.

"For some moments we were completely deluged, as I say, and all this time I held my breath, and clung to the bolt. When I could stand it no longer I raised myself upon my knees, still keeping hold with my hands, and thus got my head clear. Presently our little boat gave herself a shake just as a dog does in coming out of the water, and thus rid herself, in some measure, of the seas. I was now trying to get the better of the stupor that had come over me, and to collect my senses to as to see what was to be done, when I felt somebody grasp my arm. It was my elder brother, and my heart leaped for joy, for I had made sure that he was overboard—but the next moment all this joy was turned into horror—for he put his mouth close to my ear, and screamed out the word '*Moskoe-ström.*'

"No one ever will know what my feelings were at that moment. I shook from head to foot as if I had had the most violent fit of the ague. I knew what he meant by that one word well enough—I knew what he wished to make me understand. With the wind that now drove us on, we were bound for the whirl of the Ström, and nothing could save us!

"You perceive that in crossing the Ström *channel,* we always went a long way up above the whirl, even in the calmest weather, and then had to wait and watch carefully for the slack—but now we were driving right upon the pool itself, and in such a hurricane as this! 'To be sure,' I thought, 'we shall get there just about the slack—there is some little hope in that'—but in the next moment I cursed myself for being so great a fool as to dream of hope at all. I knew very well that we were doomed, had we been ten times a ninety-gun ship.

"By this time the first fury of the tempest had spent iself, or perhaps we did not feel it so much, as we scudded before it, but at all events the seas, which at first had been kept down by the wind, and lay flat and frothing, now got up into absolute mountains. A singular change, too, had come over the heavens. Around in every direction it was still as black as pitch, but nearly overhead there burst out, all at once, a circular rift of clear sky—as clear as I ever saw—and of a deep bright blue—and through it there blazed forth the full moon with a lustre that I never before knew her to wear. She lit up everything about us with the greatest distinctness—but, oh God, what a scene it was to light up!

"I now made one or two attempts to speak to my brother—but in some manner which I could not understand, the din had so increased that I could not make him hear a single word, although I screamed at the top of my voice in his ear. Presently he shook his head, looking as pale as death, and held up one of his fingers, as if to say '*listen!*'

"At first I could not make out what he meant—but soon a hideous thought flashed upon me. I dragged my watch from its fob. It was not going. I glanced at its face by the moonlight, and then burst into tears as I flung it far away into the ocean. *It had run down at seven o'clock! We*

*were behind the time of the slack, and the whirl of the Ström was in full
fury!*

"When a boat is well built, properly trimmed, and not deep laden,
the waves in a strong gale, when she is going large, seem always to slip
from beneath her—which appears strange to a landsman—and this is
what is called *riding,* in sea phrase.

"Well, so far we had ridden the swells very cleverly; but presently a
gigantic sea happened to take us right under the counter, and bore us with
it as it rose—up—up—as if into the sky. I would not have believed that
any wave could rise so high. And then down we came with a sweep, a
slide, and a plunge that made me feel sick and dizzy, as if I was falling
from some lofty mountaintop in a dream. But while we were up I had
thrown a quick glance around—and that one glance was all-sufficient. I
saw our exact position in an instant. The Moskoe-ström whirlpool was
about a quarter of a mile dead ahead—but no more like the everyday
Moskoe-ström than the whirl, as you now see it, is like a mill-race. If I
had not known where we were, and what we had to expect, I should not
have recognized the place at all. As it was, I involuntarily closed my eyes
in horror. The lids clenched themselves together as if in a spasm.

"It could not have been more than two minutes afterwards until we
suddenly felt the waves subside, and were enveloped in foam. The boat
made a sharp half turn to larboard, and then shot off in its new direction
like a thunderbolt. At the same moment the roaring noise of the water
was completely drowned in a kind of shrill shriek—such a sound as you
might imagine given out by the water-pipes of many thousand steam-
vessels letting off their steam all together. We were now in the belt of
surf that always surrounds the whirl; and I thought, of course, that
another moment would plunge us into the abyss, down which we could
only see indistinctly on account of the amazing velocity with which we
were borne along. The boat did not seem to sink into the water at all, but
to skim like an air-bubble upon the surface of the surge. Her starboard
side was next the whirl, and on the larboard arose the world of ocean we
had left. It stood like a huge writhing wall between us and the horizon.

"It may appear strange, but now, when we were in the very jaws of
the gulf, I felt more composed than when we were only approaching it.
Having made up my mind to hope no more I got rid of a great deal of that
terror which unmanned me at first. I supposed it was despair that strung
my nerves.

"It may look like boasting—but what I tell you is truth—I began to reflect how magnificent a thing it was to die in such a manner and how foolish it was in me to think of so paltry a consideration as my own individual life, in view of so wonderful a manifestation of God's power. I do believe that I blushed with shame when this idea crossed my mind. After a little while I became possessed with the keenest curiosity about the whirl itself. I positively felt a *wish* to explore its depths, even at the sacrifice I was going to make; and my principal grief was that I should never be able to tell my old companions on shore about the mysteries I should see. These, no doubt, were singular fancies to occupy a man's mind in such extremity—and I have often thought since, that the revolutions of the boat around the pool might have rendered me a little light-headed.

"There was another circumstance which tended to restore my self-possession; and this was the cessation of the wind, which could not reach us in our present situation—for, as you saw for yourself, the belt of the surf is considerably lower than the general bed of the ocean, and this latter now towered above us, a high, black, mountainous ridge. If you have never been at sea in a heavy gale, you can form no idea of the confusion of mind occasioned by the wind and spray together. They blind, deafen, and strangle you, and take away all power of action or reflection. But we were now, in a great measure, rid of these annoyances—just as death-condemned felons in prison are allowed petty indulgences, forbidden them while their doom is yet uncertain.

"How often we made the circuit of the belt it is impossible to say. We careered round and round for perhaps an hour, flying rather than floating, getting gradually more and more into the middle of the surge, and then nearer and nearer to its horrible inner edge. All this time I had never let go of the ring-bolt. My brother was at the stern, holding on to a small empty water-cask which had been securely lashed under the coop of the counter, and was the only thing on deck that had not been swept overboard when the gale first took us. As we approached the brink of the pit he let go his hold upon this, and made for the ring, from which, in the agony of his terror, he endeavored to force my hands, as it was not large enough to afford us both a secure grasp. I never felt deeper grief than when I saw him attempt this act—although I knew he was a madman when he did it—a raving maniac through sheer fright. I did not care, however, to contest the point with him. I knew it could make no

77

difference whether either of us held on at all; so I let him have the bolt, and went astern to the cask. This there was no great difficulty in doing; for the smack flew round steadily enough, and upon an even keel—only swaying to and fro with the immense sweeps and swelters of the whirl. Scarcely had I secured myself in my new position, when we gave a wild lurch to starboard, and rushed headlong into the abyss. I muttered a hurried prayer to God, and thought all was over.

"As I felt the sickening sweep of the descent, I had instinctively tightened my hold upon the barrel, and closed my eyes. For some seconds I dared not open them—while I expected instant destruction, and wondered that I was not already in my death-struggles with the water. But moment after moment elapsed. I still lived. The sense of falling had ceased; and the motion of the vessel seemed much as it had been before, while in the belt of foam, with the exception that she now lay more along. I took courage and looked once again upon the scene.

"Never shall I forget the sensation of awe, horror, and admiration with which I gazed about me. The boat appeared to be hanging, as if by magic, midway down, upon the interior surface of a funnel vast in circumference, prodigious in depth, and whose perfectly smooth sides might have been mistaken for ebony, but for the bewildering rapidity with which they spun around, and for the gleaming and ghastly radiance they shot forth, as the rays of the full moon, from that circular rift amid the clouds which I have already described, streamed in a flood of golden glory along the black walls, and far away down into the inmost recesses of the abyss.

"At first I was too much confused to observe anything accurately. The general burst of terrific grandeur was all that I beheld. When I recovered myself a little, however, my gaze fell instinctively downward. In this direction I was able to obtain an unobstructed view, from the manner in which the smack hung on the inclined surface of the pool. She was quite upon an even keel—that is to say, her deck lay in a plane parallel with that of the water—but this latter sloped at an angle of more than forty-five degrees, so that we seemed to be lying upon our beam-ends. I could not help observing, nevertheless, that I had scarcely more difficulty in maintaining my hold and footing in this situation, than if we had been upon a dead level; and this, I suppose, was owing to the speed at which we revolved.

"The rays of the moon seemed to search the very bottom of the profound gulf; but still I could make out nothing distinctly on account of a thick mist in which every thing there was enveloped, and over which there hung a magnificent rainbow, like that narrow and tottering bridge which Mussulmen say is the only pathway between Time and Eternity. This mist, or spray, was no doubt occasioned by the clashing of the great walls of the funnel, as they all met together at the bottom—but the yell that went up to the Heavens from out of that mist I dare not attempt to describe.

"Our first slide into the abyss itself, from the belt of foam above, had carried us to a great distance down the slope; but our farther descent was by no means proportionate. Round and round we swept—not with any uniform movement—but in dizzying swings and jerks, that sent us sometimes only a few hundred yards—sometimes nearly the complete circuit of the whirl. Our progress downward, at each revolution, was slow, but very perceptible.

"Looking about me upon the wide waste of liquid ebony on which we were thus borne, I perceived that our boat was not the only object in the embrace of the whirl. Both above and below us were visible fragments of vessels, large masses of building-timber and trunks of trees, with many smaller articles, such as pieces of house furniture, broken boxes, barrels and staves. I have already described the unnatural curiosity which had taken the place of my original terrors. It appeared to grow upon me as I drew nearer and nearer to my dreadful doom. I now began to watch, with a strange interest, the numerous things that floated in our company. I *must* have been delirious, for I even sought *amusement* in speculating upon the relative velocities of their several descents toward the foam below. 'This fir-tree,' I found myself at one time saying, 'will certainly be the next thing that takes the awful plunge and disappears,'— and then I was disappointed to find that the wreck of a Dutch merchant ship overtook it and went down before. At length, after making several guesses of this nature, and being deceived in all—this fact—the fact of my invariable miscalculation, set me upon a train of reflection that made my limbs again tremble, and my heart beat heavily once more.

"It was not a new terror that thus affected me, but the dawn of a more exciting *hope*. This hope arose partly from memory, and partly from present observation. I called to mind the great variety of buoyant matter that strewed the coast of Lofoden, having been absorbed and then thrown forth by the Moskoe-ström. By far the greater number of the articles were shattered in the most extraordinary way—so chafed and roughened as to have the appearance of being stuck full of splinters—but then I distinctly recollected that there were *some* of them which were not disfigured at all. Now I could not account for this difference except by supposing that the roughened fragments were the only ones which had been *completely absorbed*—that the others had entered the whirl at so late a period of the tide, or, from some reason, had descended so slowly after entering, that they did not reach the bottom before the turn of the flood came, or of the ebb, as the case might be. I conceived it possible, in either instance, that they might thus be whirled up again to the level of the ocean, without undergoing the fate of those which had been drawn in more early or absorbed more rapidly. I made, also, three important observations. The first was, that as a general rule, the larger the bodies were, the more rapid their descent—the second, that, between two masses of equal extent, the one spherical, and the other *of any other shape*, the superiority in speed of descent was with the sphere—the third, that, between two masses of equal size, the one cylindrical, and the other of any other shape, the cylinder was absorbed the more slowly. Since my escape, I have had several conversations on this subject with an old school-master of the district; and it was from him that I learned the use of the words 'cylinder' and 'sphere.' He explained to me—although I have forgotten the explanation—how what I observed was, in fact, the natural consequence of the forms of the floating fragments—and showed me how it happened that a cylinder, swimming in a vortex, offered more resistance to its suction, and was drawn in with greater difficulty than an equally bulky body, of any form whatever.[1]

"There was one startling circumstance which went a great way in enforcing these observations, and rendering me anxious to turn them to account, and this was that, at every revolution, we passed something like a barrel, or else the yard or the mast of a vessel, while many of these things, which had been on our level when I first opened my eyes upon the wonders of the whirlpool, were now high up above us, and seemed to have moved but little from their original station.

"I no longer hesitated what to do. I resolved to lash myself securely to the water-cask upon which I now held, to cut it loose from the counter, and to throw myself with it into the water. I attracted my brother's attention by signs, pointed to the floating barrels that came near us, and

---

[1] See Archimedes, *"De Incidentibus in Fluido."*—lib. 2.

did everything in my power to make him understand what I was about to do. I thought at length that he comprehended my design—but, whether this was the case or not, he shook his head despairingly, and refused to move from his station by the ring-bolt. It was impossible to reach him; the emergency admitted of no delay; and so, with a bitter struggle, I resigned him to his fate, fastened myself to the cask by means of the lashings which secured it to the counter, and precipitated myself with it into the sea without another moment's hesitation.

"The result was precisely what I had hoped it might be. As it is myself who now tells you this tale—as you see that I *did* escape—and as you are already in possession of the mode in which this escape was effected, and must therefore anticipate all that I have farther to say—I will bring my story quickly to conclusion. It might have been an hour, or thereabout, after my quitting the smack, when, having descended to a vast distance beneath me, it made three or four wild gyrations in rapid succession, and, bearing my loved brother with it, plunged headlong, at once and forever into the chaos of foam below. The barrel to which I was attached sunk very little farther than half the distance between the bottom of the gulf and the spot at which I leaped overboard before a great change took place in the character of the whirlpool. The slope of the sides of the vast funnel became momently less and less steep. The gyrations of the whirl grew gradually, less and less violent. By degrees, the froth and the rainbow disappeared, and the bottom of the gulf seemed slowly to uprise. The sky was clear, the winds had gone down, and the full moon was setting radiantly in the west, when I found myself on the surface of the ocean, in full view of the shores of Lofoden, and above the spot where the pool of the Moskoe-ström *had been*. It was the hour of the slack—but the sea still heaved in mountainous waves from the effects of the hurricane. I was borne violently into the channel of the Ström, and in a few minutes, was hurried down the coast into the 'grounds' of the fishermen. A boat picked me up—exhausted from the fatigue—and (now that the danger was removed) speechless from the memory of its horror. Those who drew me on board were my old mates and daily companions—but they knew me no more than they would have known a traveller from the spirit-land. My hair, which had been raven black the day before, was as white as you see it now. They say too that the whole expression of my countenance had changed. I told them my story—they did not believe it. I now tell it to *you*—and I can scarcely expect you to put more faith in it than did the merry fisherman of Lofoden.''

Nathaniel Hawthorne (1804–1864)

One of the best-known American writers of the nineteenth century, Nathaniel Hawthorne was also a major producer of fantasy and science-fiction short stories, many of which can be found in *Twice-Told Tales* (1837) and *Mosses from an Old Manse* (1846). Most of his work is strongly allegorical and a warning against pride, particularly intellectual pride, which causes a person to stand alone, taking, at best, a merely speculative or scientific interest in others.

Born in Salem, Massachusetts, Hawthorne came from a long line of Puritans. His father died when Hawthorne was four, so the boy spent most of his childhood with his mother's family. At the age of nine he severely injured a foot, and during his three-year recovery he developed avid reading habits. Then in 1818 his mother moved to Maine, and he got in the habit of taking long walks in the woods, which he later described as the origin of his lifelong taste for solitude. In 1819 his mother returned to Salem, and shortly thereafter he departed to Bowdoin College, where he studied literature and made many influential friends.

Three years after graduation, Hawthorne published a vanity novel, *Fanshawe* (1828), which he came to detest almost immediately. He found that American publishers, given the existing copyright laws, were not willing to take a chance on him when they could simply reprint famous British authors. So for the next eleven years he lived in his mother's house and concentrated on short stories. Goodrich's annual story collection, *The Token*, published dozens of his stories, but did so anonymously so that many pieces could be used in the same volume. And it wasn't until an old Bowdoin friend, Horatio Bridge, paid Goodrich two hundred and fifty dollars to bring out a collection of

Hawthorne's stories, *Twice-Told Tales* (1837), that the author's name appeared on them.

In 1839 Hawthorne began contemplating marriage. He sought out a political appointment as measurer of coal and salt at the Boston Custom House, resigning two years later when his love moved to Brook Farm. After marrying in 1842 he obtained another political appointment, but was ousted when his side lost the next election. Then his mother died, and the shock of that plus the strain of supporting his family by writing sent him into nervous depression.

Fortunately, Boston publisher James T. Fields came to visit Hawthorne, pointed to a massive chest, and demanded to know what manuscript was in there. It was the incomplete first draft of *The Scarlet Letter*, a novel whose appearance in 1850 brought Hawthorne great fame. *The House of the Seven Gables*, which followed in 1851, was an even bigger success.

In 1852 old college chum Franklin Pierce was elected president and Hawthorne was given a consulship in Liverpool, England. This five years of service, combined with royalties from literary works, finally provided Hawthorne with financial security. And after two years' stay in Italy, he returned home in 1860, continuing to write until his death four years later.

RAPPACCINI'S DAUGHTER

A young man, named Giovanni Guasconti, came, very long ago, from the more southern region of Italy, to pursue his studies at the University of Padua. Giovanni, who had but a scanty supply of gold ducats in his pocket, took lodgings in a high and gloomy chamber of an old edifice which looked not unworthy to have been the palace of a Paduan noble, and which, in fact, exhibited over its entrance the armorial bearings of a family long since extinct. The younger stranger, who was not unstudied in the great poem of his country, recollected that one of the ancestors of this family, and perhaps an occupant of this very mansion, had been pictured by Dante as a partaker of the immortal agonies of his Inferno. These reminiscences and associations, together with the tendency to heartbreak natural to a young man for the first time out of his native sphere, caused Giovanni to sigh heavily as he looked around the desolate and ill-furnished apartment.

"Holy Virgin, signor!" cried old Dame Lisabetta, who, won by the youth's remarkable beauty of person, was kindly endeavoring to give the chamber a habitable air, "what a sigh was that to come out of a young man's heart! Do you find this old mansion gloomy? For the love of Heaven, then, put your head out of the window, and you will see as bright sunshine as you have left in Naples."

Guasconti mechanically did as the old woman advised, but could not quite agree with her that the Paduan sunshine was as cheerful as that of southern Italy. Such as it was, however, it fell upon a garden beneath the window and expended its fostering influences on a variety of plants, which seemed to have been cultivated with exceeding care.

"Does this garden belong to the house?" asked Giovanni.

"Heaven forbid, signor, unless it were fruitful of better pot herbs than any that grow there now," answered old Lisabetta. "No; that garden is cultivated by the own hands of Signor Giacomo Rappaccini, the famous doctor, who, I warrant you, has been heard of as far as Naples. It is said that he distills these plants into medicines that are as potent as a charm. Oftentimes you may see the signor doctor at work, and perchance the signora, his daughter, too, gathering the strange flowers that grow in the garden."

The old woman had now done what she could for the aspect of the chamber; and, commending the young man to the protection of the saints, took her departure.

Giovanni still found no better occupation than to look down into the garden beneath his window. From its appearance, he judged it to be one of those botanic gardens which were of earlier date in Padua than elsewhere in Italy or in the world. Or, not improbably, it might once have been the pleasure-place of an opulent family; for there was the ruin of a marble fountain in the center, sculptured with rare art, but so woefully shattered that it was impossible to trace the original design from the chaos of remaining fragments. The water, however, continued to gush and sparkle into the sunbeams as cheerfully as ever. A little gurgling sound ascended to the young man's window, and made him feel as if the fountain were an immortal spirit that sung its song unceasingly and without heeding the vicissitudes around it, while one century imbodied it in marble and another scattered the perishable garniture on the soil. All about the pool into which the water subsided grew various plants, that seemed to require a plentiful supply of moisture for the nourishment of gigantic leaves, and, in some instances, flowers gorgeously magnificent. There was one shrub in particular, set in a marble vase in the midst of the pool, that bore a profusion of purple blossoms, each of which had the luster and richness of a gem; and the whole together made a show so resplendent that it seemed enough to illuminate the garden, even had there been no sunshine. Every portion of the soil was peopled with plants and herbs, which, if less beautiful, still bore tokens of assiduous care, as if all had their individual virtues, known to the scientific mind that fostered them. Some were placed in urns, rich with old carving, and others in common garden pots; some crept serpent-like along the ground or climbed on high, using whatever means of ascent was offered them. One plant had wreathed itself around a statue of Vertumnus, which was thus quite veiled and shrouded in a drapery of hanging foliage, so happily arranged that it might have served a sculptor for a study.

While Giovanni stood at the window he heard a rustling behind a screen of leaves, and became aware that a person was at work in the garden. His figure soon emerged into view, and showed itself to be that of no common laborer, but a tall, emaciated, sallow and sickly-looking man, dressed in a scholar's garb of black. He was beyond the middle term of life, with gray hair, a thin, gray beard, and a face singularly marked with intellect and cultivation, but which could never, even in his more youthful days, have expressed much warmth of heart.

Nothing could exceed the intentness with which this scientific gardener examined every shrub which grew in his path: it seemed as if he was looking into their inmost nature, making observations in regard to their creative essence, and discovering why one leaf grew in this shape and another in that, and wherefore such and such flowers differed among themselves in hue and perfume. Nevertheless, in spite of this deep intelligence on his part, there was no approach to intimacy between himself and these vegetable existences. On the contrary, he avoided their actual touch or the direct inhaling of their odors with a caution that impressed Giovanni most disagreeably; for the man's demeanor was that of one walking among malignant influences, such as savage beasts, or deadly snakes, or evil spirits, which, should he allow them one moment of license, would wreak upon him some terrible fatality. It was strangely frightful to the young man's imagination to see this air of insecurity in a person cultivating a garden, that most simple and innocent of human toils, and which had been alike the joy and labor of the unfallen parents of the race. Was this garden, then, the Eden of the present world? And this man, with such a perception of harm in what his own hands caused to grow—was he the Adam?

The distrustful gardener, while plucking away the dead leaves or pruning the too-luxuriant growth of the shrubs, defended his hands with a pair of thick gloves. Nor were these his only armor. When, in his walk through the garden, he came to the magnificent plant that hung its purple gems beside the marble fountain, he placed a kind of mask over his mouth and nostrils, as if all this beauty did not conceal a deadlier malice; but, finding his task still too dangerous, he drew back, removed the mask, and called loudly, but in the infirm voice of a person affected with inward disease:

"Beatrice! Beatrice!"

"Here am I, my father. What would you?" cried a rich and youthful voice from the window of the opposite house—a voice as rich as a tropical sunset, and which made Giovanni, though he knew not why, think of deep hues of purple or crimson and of perfumes heavily delectable. "Are you in the garden?"

"Yes, Beatrice," answered the gardener, "and I need your help."

Soon there emerged from under a sculptured portal the figure of a young girl, arrayed with as much richness of taste as the most splendid of the flowers, beautiful as the day, and with a bloom so deep and vivid that one shade more would have been too much. She looked redundant with life, health, and energy; all of which attributes were bound down and compressed, as it were, and girdled tensely, in their luxuriance, by her virgin zone. Yet Giovanni's fancy must have grown morbid while he looked down into the garden; for the impression which the fair stranger made upon him was as if here were another flower, the human sister of those vegetable ones, as beautiful as they, more beautiful than the richest of them, but still to be touched only with a glove, nor to be approached without a mask. As Beatrice came down the garden path, it was observable that she handled and inhaled the odor of several of the plants which her father had most sedulously avoided.

"Here, Beatrice," said the latter, "see how many needful offices require to be done to our chief treasure. Yet, shattered as I am, my life might pay the penalty of approaching it so closely as circumstances demand. Henceforth, I fear, this plant must be consigned to your sole charge."

"And gladly will I undertake it," cried again the rich tones of the young lady, as she bent toward the magnificent plant and opened her arms as if to embrace it. "Yes, my sister, my splendor, it shall be Beatrice's task to nurse and serve thee; and thou shalt reward her with thy kisses and perfumed breath, which to her is as the breath of life."

Then, with all the tenderness in her manner that was so strikingly expressed in her words, she busied herself with such attentions as the plant seemed to require; and Giovanni, at his lofty window, rubbed his eyes and almost doubted whether it were a girl tending her favorite flower, or one sister performing the duties of affection to another. The scene soon terminated. Whether Dr. Rappaccini had finished his labors in the garden, or that his watchful eye had caught the stranger's face, he now took his daughter's arm and retired. Night was already closing in; oppressive exhalations seemed to proceed from the plants and steal upward past the open window; and Giovanni, closing the lattice went to his couch and dreamed of a rich flower and beautiful girl. Flower and maiden were different, and yet the same, and fraught with some strange peril in either shape.

But there is an influence in the light of morning that tends to rectify whatever errors of fancy, or even of judgment, we may have incurred during the sun's decline, or among the shadows of the night, or in the less wholesome glow of moonshine. Giovanni's first movement, on starting from sleep, was to throw open the window and gaze down into the garden which his dreams had made so fertile of mysteries. He was surprised and a little ashamed to find how real and matter-of-fact an affair it proved to be, in the first rays of the sun which gilded the dewdrops that hung upon leaf and blossom, and, while giving a brighter beauty to each rare flower, brought everything within the limits of ordinary experience. The young man rejoiced that, in the heart of the barren city, he had the privilege of overlooking this spot of lovely and luxuriant vegetation. It would serve, he said to himself, as a symbolic language to keep him in communion with Nature. Neither the sickly and thought-worn Dr. Giacomo Rappaccini, it is true, nor his brilliant daughter, were now visible; so that Giovanni could not determine how much of the singularity which he attributed to both was due to their own qualities and how much to his wonder-working fancy; but he was inclined to take a most rational view of the whole matter. In the course of the day he paid his respects to Signor Pietro Baglioni, professor of medicine in the university, a physician of eminent repute, to whom Giovanni had brought a letter of introduction. The professor was an elderly personage, apparently of genial nature, and habits that might almost be called jovial. He kept the young man to dinner, and made himself very agreeable by the freedom and liveliness of his conversation, especially when warmed by a flask or two of Tuscan wine. Giovanni, conceiving that men of science, inhabitants of the same city, must needs be on familiar terms with one another, took an opportunity to mention the name of Dr. Rappaccini. But the professor did not respond with so much cordiality as he had anticipated.

"Ill would it become a teacher of the divine art of medicine," said Professor Pietro Baglioni, in answer to a question of Giovanni, "to

89

withhold due and well-considered praise of a physician so eminently skilled as Rappaccini; but, on the other hand, I should answer it but scantily to my conscience were I to permit a worthy youth like yourself, Signor Giovanni, the son of an ancient friend, to imbibe erroneous ideas respecting a man who might hereafter chance to hold your life and death in his hands. The truth is, our worshipful Dr. Rappaccini has as much science as any member of the faculty—with perhaps one single exception—in Padua, or all Italy; but there are certain grave objections to his professional character.''

"And what are they?'' asked the young man.

"Has my friend Giovanni any disease of body or heart, that he is so inquisitive about physicians?'' said the professor, with a smile. "But as for Rappaccini, it is said of him—and I, who know the man well, can answer for its truth—that he cares infinitely more for science than for mankind. His patients are interesting to him only as subject for some new experiment. He would sacrifice human life, his own among the rest, or whatever else was dearest to him, for the sake of adding so much as a grain of mustard seed to the great heap of his accumulated knowledge.''

"Methinks he is an awful man indeed,'' remarked Guasconti, mentally recalling the cold and purely intellectual aspect of Rappaccini. "And yet, worshipful professor, is it not a noble spirit? Are there many men capable of so spiritual a love of science?''

"God forbid,'' answered the professor, somewhat testily; "at least, unless they take sounder views of the healing art than those adopted by Rappaccini. It is his theory that all medicinal virtues are comprised within those substances which we term vegetable poisons. These he cultivates with his own hands, and is said even to have produced new varieties of poison, more horribly deleterious than Nature, without the assistance of this learned person, would ever have plagued the world withal. That the signor doctor does less mischief than might be expected with such dangerous substances is undeniable. Now and then, it must be owned, he has effected, or seemed to effect, a marvelous cure; but, to tell you my private mind, Signor Giovanni, he should receive little credit for such instances of success—they being probably the work of chance—but should be held strictly accountable for his failures, which may justly be considered his own work.''

The youth might have taken Baglioni's opinions with many grains of allowance had he known that there was a professional warfare of long continuance between him and Dr. Rappaccini, in which the latter was generally thought to have gained the advantage. If the reader be inclined to judge for himself, we refer him to certain black-letter tracts on both sides, preserved in the medical department of the University of Padua.

"I know not, most learned professor," returned Giovanni, after musing on what had been said of Rappaccini's exclusive zeal for science, "I know not how dearly this physician may love his art; but surely there is one object more dear to him. He has a daughter."

"Aha!" cried the professor, with a laugh. "So now our friend Giovanni's secret is out. You have heard of this daughter, whom all the young men in Padua are wild about, though not half a dozen have ever had the good hap to see her face. I know little of the Signora Beatrice save that Rappaccini is said to have instructed her deeply in his science, and that, young and beautiful as fame reports her, she is already qualified to fill a professor's chair. Perchance her father destines her for mine! Other absurd rumors there be, not worth talking about or listening to. So now, Signor Giovanni, drink off your glass of lachryma."

Guasconti returned to his lodgings somewhat heated with the wine he had quaffed, and which caused his brain to swim with strange fantasies in reference to Dr. Rappaccini and the beautiful Beatrice. On his way, happening to pass by a florist's, he bought a fresh bouquet of flowers.

Ascending to his chamber, he seated himself near the window, but within the shadow thrown by the depth of the wall, so that he could look down into the garden with little risk of being discovered. All beneath his eye was a solitude. The strange plants were basking in the sunshine, and now and then nodding gently to one another, as if in acknowledgement of sympathy and kindred. In the midst, by the shattered fountain, grew the magnificent shrub, with its purple gems clustering all over it; they glowed in the air, and gleamed back again out of the depths of the pool, which thus seemed to overflow with colored radiance from the rich reflection that was steeped in it. At first, as we have said, the garden was a solitude. Soon, however—as Giovanni had half hoped, half feared, would be the case—a figure appeared beneath the antique sculptured portal, and came down between the rows of plants, inhaling their various perfumes as if she were one of those beings of old classic fables that lived upon sweet odors. On again beholding Beatrice, the young man was even startled to perceive how much her beauty exceeded his recollection of it; so brilliant, so vivid, was its character, that she glowed amid the sunlight, and, as Giovanni whispered to himself, positively illuminated the more shadowy intervals of the garden path. Her face being now more revealed than on the former occasion, he was struck by its expression of simplicity and sweetness—qualities that had not entered into his idea of her character, and which made him ask anew what manner of mortal she might be. Nor did he fail again to observe, or imagine, an analogy between the beautiful girl and the gorgeous shrub that hung its gemlike flowers over the fountain—a resemblance which Beatrice seemed to have indulged a fantastic humor in heightening, both by the arrangement of her dress and the selection of its hues.

Approaching the shurb, she threw open her arms, as with a passionate ardor, and drew its branches into an intimate embrace—so intimate that her features were hidden in its leafy bosom and her glistening ringlets all intermingled with the flowers.

"Give me thy breath, my sister," exclaimed Beatrice; "for I am faint with common air. And give me this flower of thine, which I separate with gentlest fingers from the stem and place it close beside my heart."

With these words the beautiful daughter of Rappaccini plucked one of the richest blossoms of the shrub, and was about to fasten it in her bosom. But now, unless Giovanni's draughts of wine had bewildered his senses, a singular incident occurred. A small orange-colored reptile, of the lizard or chameleon species, chanced to be creeping along the path, just at the feet of Beatrice. It appeared to Giovanni—but, at the distance from which he gazed, he could scarcely have seen anything so minute—it appeared to him, however, that a drop or two of moisture from the broken stem of the flower descended upon the lizard's head. For an instant the reptile contorted itself violently, and then lay motionless in the sunshine. Beatrice observed this remarkable phenomenon, and crossed herself, sadly, but without surprise; nor did she therefore hesitate to arrange the fatal flower in her bosom. There it blushed, and almost glimmered with the dazzling effect of a precious stone, adding to her dress and aspect the one appropriate charm which nothing else in the world could have supplied. But Giovanni, out of the shadow of his window, bent forward and shrank back, and murmured and trembled.

"Am I awake? Have I my senses?" said he to himself. "What is this being? Beautiful shall I call her, or inexpressibly terrible?"

Beatrice now strayed carelessly through the garden, approaching closer beneath Giovanni's window, so that he was compelled to thrust his head quite out of its concealment in order to gratify the intense and painful curiosity which she excited. At this moment there came a beautiful insect over the garden wall; it had, perhaps, wandered through the city, and found no flowers or verdure among those antique haunts of men until the heavy perfumes of Dr. Rappaccini's shrubs had lured it from afar. Without alighting on the flowers, this winged brightness seemed to be attracted by Beatrice, and lingered in the air and fluttered about her head. Now, here it could not be but that Giovanni Guasconti's eyes deceived him. Be that as it might, he fancied that, while Beatrice was gazing at the insect with childish delight, it grew faint and fell at her feet; its bright wings shivered; it was dead—from no cause that he could discern, unless it were the atmosphere of her breath. Again Beatrice crossed herself and sighed heavily as she bent over the dead insect.

An impulsive movement of Giovanni drew her eyes to the window. There she beheld the beautiful head of the young man—rather a Grecian than an Italian head, with fair, regular features, and a glistening of gold among his ringlets—gazing down upon her like a being that hovered in midair. Scarcely knowing what he did, Giovanni threw down the bouquet which he had hitherto held in his hand.

"Signora," said he, "there are pure and healthful flowers. Wear them for the sake of Giovanni Guasconti."

"Thanks, signor," replied Beatrice, with her rich voice, that came forth as it were like a gush of music, and with a mirthful expression half childish and half woman-like. "I accept your gift, and would fain recompense it with this precious purple flower; but if I toss it into the air it will not reach you. So Signor Guasconti must even content himself with my thanks."

She lifted the bouquet from the ground, and then, as if inwardly ashamed at having stepped aside from her maidenly reserve to respond to a stranger's greeting, passed swiftly homeward through the garden. But few as the moments were, it seemed to Giovanni, when she was on the point of vanishing beneath the sculptured portal, that his beautiful bouquet was already beginning to wither in her grasp. It was an idle thought; there could be no possibility of distinguishing a faded flower from a fresh one at so great a distance.

For many days after this incident the young man avoided the

window that looked into Dr. Rappaccini's garden, as if something ugly and monstrous would have blasted his eyesight had he been betrayed into a glance. He felt conscious of having put himself, to a certain extent, within the influence of an unintelligible power by the communication which he had opened with Beatrice. The wisest course would have been, if his heart were in any real danger, to quit his lodgings and Padua itself at once; the next wiser, to have accustomed himself, as far as possible, to the familiar and daylight view of Beatrice—thus bringing her rigidly and systematically within the limits of ordinary experience. Least of all, while avoiding her sight, ought Giovanni to have remained so near this extraordinary being that the proximity and possibility even of intercourse should give a kind of substance and reality to the wild vagaries which his imagination ran riot continually in producing. Guasconti had not a deep heart—or, at all events, its depths were not sounded now; but he had a quick fancy, and an ardent southern temperament, which rose every instant to a higher fever pitch. Whether or not Beatrice possessed those terrible attributes, that fatal breath, the affinity with those so beautiful and deadly flowers which were indicated by what Giovanni had witnessed, she had at least instilled a fierce and subtle poison into his system. It was not love, although her rich beauty was a madness to him; nor horror, even while he fancied her spirit to be imbued with the same baneful essence that seemed to pervade her physical frame; but a wild offspring of both love and horror that had each parent in it, and burned like one and shivered like the other. Giovanni knew not what to dread; still less did he know what to hope; yet hope and dread kept a continual warfare in his breast, alternately vanquishing one another and starting up afresh to renew the contest. Blessed are all simple emotions, be they dark or bright! It is the lurid intermixture of the two that produces the illuminating blaze of the infernal regions.

Sometimes he endeavored to assuage the fever of his spirit by a rapid walk through the streets of Padua or beyond its gates: his footsteps kept time with the throbbings of his brain, so that the walk was apt to accelerate itself to a race. One day he found himself arrested; his arm was seized by a portly personage, who had turned back on recognizing the young man and expending much breath in overtaking him.

"Signor Giovanni! Stay, my young friend!" cried he. "Have you forgotten me? That might well be the case if I were as much altered as yourself."

It was Baglioni, whom Giovanni had avoided ever since their first meeting, from a doubt that the professor's sagacity would look too deeply into his secrets. Endeavoring to recover himself, he stared forth wildly from his inner world to the outer one and spoke like a man in a dream.

"Yes; I am Giovanni Guasconti. You are Professor Pietro Baglioni. Now let me pass!"

"Not yet, not yet, Signor Giovanni Guasconti," said the professor, smiling, but at the same time scrutinizing the youth with an earnest glance. "What! Did I grow up side by side with your father? And shall his son pass me like a stranger in these old streets of Padua? Stand still, Signor Giovanni, for we must have a word or two before we part."

"Speedily, then, most worshipful professor, speedily," said Giovanni, with feverish impatience. "Does not your worship see I am in haste?"

Now, while he was speaking there came a man in black along the street, stooping and moving feebly like a person in inferior health. His face was all overspread with a most sickly and sallow hue, but yet so pervaded with an expression of piercing and active intellect that an observer might easily have overlooked the merely physical attributes and have seen only this wonderful energy. As he passed, this person exchanged a cold and distant salutation with Baglioni, but fixed his eyes on Giovanni with an intentness that seemed to bring out whatever was within him worthy of notice. Nevertheless, there was a peculiar quietness in the look, as if taking merely a speculative, not a human, interest in the young man.

"It is Dr. Rappaccini!" whispered the professor when the stranger had passed. "Has he ever seen your face before?"

"Not that I know," answered Giovanni, starting at the name.

"He *has* seen you! He must have seen you!" said Baglioni, hastily. "For some purpose or other, this man of science is making a study of you. I know that look of his! It is the same that coldly illuminates his face as he bends over a bird, a mouse, or a butterfly, which, in pursuance of some experiment, he has killed by the perfume of a flower; a look as deep as Nature itself, but without Nature's warmth of love. Signor Giovanni, I will stake my life upon it, you are the subject of one of Rappaccini's experiments!"

"Will you make a fool of me?" cried Giovanni, passionately. "*That*, signor professor, were an untoward experiment."

"Patience! Patience!" replied the imperturbable professor. "I tell thee, my poor Giovanni, that Rappaccini has a scientific interest in thee. Thou hast fallen into fearful hands! And the Signora Beatrice—what part does she act in this mystery?''

But Guasconti, finding Baglioni's pertinacity intolerable, here broke away, and was gone before the professor could again seize his arm. He looked after the young man intently and shook his head.

''This must not be,'' said Baglioni to himself. ''The youth is the son of my old friend, and shall not come to any harm from which the arcana of medical science can preserve him. Besides, it is too insufferable an impertinence in Rappaccini, thus to snatch the lad out of my own hands, as I may say, and make use of him for his infernal experiments. This daughter of his! It shall be looked into. Perchance, most learned Rappaccini, I may foil you where you little dream of it!''

Meanwhile Giovanni himself had pursued a circuitous route, and at length found himself at the door of his lodgings. As he crossed the threshold he was met by old Lisabetta, who smirked and smiled, and was evidently desirous to attract his attention; vainly, however, as the ebullition of his feelings had momentarily subdued into a cold vacuity. He turned his eyes full upon the withered face that was puckering itself into a smile, but seemed to behold it not. The old dame, therefore, laid her grasp upon his cloak.

''Signor! Signor!'' whispered she, still with a smile over the whole breadth of her visage, so that it looked not unlike a grotesque carving in wood, darkened by centuries. ''Listen, signor! There is a private entrance into the garden!''

''What do you say?'' exclaimed Giovanni, turning quickly about, as if an inanimate thing should start into feverish life. ''A private entrance into Dr. Rappaccini's garden?''

''Hush! Hush! Not so loud!'' whispered Lisabetta, putting her hand over his mouth. ''Yes; into the worshipful doctor's garden, where you may see all his fine shrubbery. Many a young man in Padua would give gold to be admitted among those flowers.''

Giovanni put a piece of gold into her hand.

''Show me the way,'' said he.

A surmise, probably excited by his conversation with Baglioni, crossed his mind, that this interposition of old Lisabetta might perchance be connected with the intrigue, whatever were its nature, in which the professor seemed to suppose that Dr. Rappaccini was involving him. But such a suspicion, though it disturbed Giovanni, was inadequate to restrain him. The instant that he was aware of the possibility of approaching Beatrice, it seemed an absolute necessity of his existence to do so. It mattered not whether she were angel or demon; he was irrevocably within her sphere, and must obey the law that whirled him onward, in ever-lessening circles towards a result which he did not attempt to foreshadow; and yet, strange to say, there came across him a sudden doubt whether this intense interest on his part were not delusory; whether it were really of so deep and positive a nature as to justify him in now thrusting himself into an incalculable position; whether it were not merely the fantasy of a young man's brain, only slightly or not at all connected with his heart.

He paused, hesitated, turned half about, but again went on. His withered guide led him along several obscure passages, and finally undid a door, through which, as it was opened, there came the sight and sound of rustling leaves, with the broken sunshine glimmering among them. Giovanni stepped forth, and, forcing himself through the entanglement of a shrub that wreathed its tendrils over the hidden entrance, stood beneath his own window in the open area of Dr. Rappaccini's garden.

How often is it the case that, when impossibilities have come to pass and dreams have condensed their misty substance into tangible realities, we find ourselves calm, and even coldly self-possessed, amid circumstances which it would have been a delirium of joy or agony to anticipate! Fate delights to thwart us thus. Passion will choose his own time to rush upon the scene, and lingers sluggishly behind when an appropriate adjustment of events would seem to summon his appearance. So was it now with Giovanni. Day after day his pulses had throbbed with feverish blood at the improbable idea of an interview with Beatrice, and of standing with her, face to face, in this very garden, basking in the Oriental sunshine of her beauty, and snatching from her full gaze the mystery which he deemed the riddle of his own existence. But now there was a singular and untimely equanimity within his breast. He threw a glance around the garden to discover if Beatrice or her father were present, and, perceiving that he was alone, began a critical observation of the plants.

The aspect of one and all of them dissatisfied him; their gorgeousness seemed fierce, passionate, and even unnatural. There was hardly an individual shrub which a wanderer, straying by himself through a forest, would not have been startled to find growing wild, as if an unearthly face had glared at him out of the thicket. Several also would have shocked a delicate instinct by an appearance of artificialness indicating that there had been such commixture, and, as it were, adultery, of various vegetable species, that the production was no longer of God's making, but the monstrous offspring of man's depraved fancy, glowing with only an evil mockery of beauty. They were probably the result of experiment, which in one or two cases had succeeded in mingling plants individually lovely into a compound possessing the questionable and ominous character that distinguished the whole growth of the garden. In fine, Giovanni recognized but two or three plants in the collection, and those of a kind that he well knew to be poisonous. While busy with these contemplations he heard the rustling of a silken garment, and, turning, beheld Beatrice emerging from beneath the sculptured portal.

Giovanni had not considered with himself what should be his deportment; whether he should apologize for his intrusion into the garden, or assume that he was there with the privity at least, if not by the desire, of Dr. Rappaccini or his daughter; but Beatrice's manner placed him at his ease, though leaving him still no doubt by what agency he had gained admittance. She came lightly along the path and met him near the broken fountain. There was surprise in her face, but brightened by a simple and kind expression of pleasure.

"You are a connoisseur in flowers, signor," said Beatrice, with a smile, alluding to the bouquet which he had flung her from the window. "It is no marvel, therefore, if the sight of my father's rare collection has tempted you to take a nearer view. If he were here, he could tell you many strange and interesting facts as to the nature and habits of these shrubs; for he has spent a lifetime in such studies, and this garden is his world."

"And yourself, lady," observed Giovanni, "if fame says true, you likewise are deeply skilled in the virtues indicated by these rich blossoms and these spicy perfumes. Would you deign to be my instructress, I should prove an apter scholar than if taught by Signor Rappaccini himself."

"Are there such idle rumors?" asked Beatrice, with the music of a pleasant laugh. "Do people say that I am skilled in my father's science of plants? What a jest is there! No; though I have grown up among these flowers, I know no more of them than their hues and perfume; and sometimes methinks I would fain rid myself of even that small knowledge. There are many flowers here, and those not the least brilliant, that shock and offend me when they meet my eye. But pray, signor, do not believe these stories about my science. Believe nothing of me save what you see with your own eyes.''

"And must I believe all that I have seen with my own eyes?" asked Giovanni, pointedly, while the recollection of former scenes made him shrink. "No, signora; you demand too little of me. Bid me believe nothing save what comes from your own lips."

It would appear that Beatrice understood him. There came a deep flush to her cheek; but she looked full into Giovanni's eyes, and responded to his gaze of uneasy suspicion with a queenlike haughtiness.

"I do so bid you, signor," she replied. "Forget whatever you may have fancied in regard to me. If true to the outward senses, still it may be false in its essence; but the words of Beatrice Rappaccini's lips are true from the depths of the heart outward. Those you may believe."

A fervor glowed in her whole aspect and beamed upon Giovanni's consciousness like the light of truth itself; but while she spoke there was a fragrance in the atmosphere around her, rich and delightful, though evanescent, yet which the young man, from an indefinable reluctance, scarcely dared to draw into his lungs. It might be the odor of the flowers. Could it be Beatrice's breath which thus embalmed her words with a strange richness, as if by steeping them in her heart? A faintness passed like a shadow over Giovanni and flitted away; he seemed to gaze through the beautiful girl's eyes into her transparent soul, and felt no more doubt or fear.

The tinge of passion that had colored Beatrice's manner vanished; she became gay, and appeared to derive a pure delight from her communion with the youth not unlike what the maiden of a lonely island might have felt conversing with a voyager from the civilized world. Evidently her experience of life had been confined within the limits of that garden. She talked now about matters as simple as the daylight or summer clouds, and now asked questions in reference to the city; or Giovanni's distant home, his friends his mother, and his sisters—questions indicating such seclusion, and such lack of familiarity with modes and forms, that Giovanni responded as if to an infant. Her spirit gushed out before him like a fresh rill that was just catching its first glimpse of the sunlight and wondering at the reflections of earth and sky which were flung into its bosom. There came thoughts, too, from a deep source, and fantasies of a gemlike brilliancy, as if diamonds and rubies sparkled upward among the bubbles of the fountain. Ever and anon there gleamed across the young man's mind a sense of wonder that he should be walking side by side with the being who had so wrought upon his imagination, whom he had idealized in such hues of terror, in whom he had positively witnessed such manifestations of dreadful attributes—that he should be conversing with Beatrice like a brother, and should find her so human and so maidenlike. But such reflections were only momentary; the effect of her character was too real not to make itself familiar at once.

In this free intercourse they had strayed through the garden, and now, after many turns among its avenues, were come to the shattered fountain, beside which grew the magnificent shrub, with its treasury of glowing blossoms. A fragrance was diffused from it which Giovanni recognized as identical with that which he had attributed to Beatrice's breath, but incomparably more powerful. As her eyes fell upon it, Giovanni beheld her press her hand to her bosom as if her heart were throbbing suddenly and painfully.

"For the first time in my life," murmured she, addressing the shrub, "I had forgotten thee."

"I remember, signora," said Giovanni, "that you once promised to reward me with one of these living gems for the bouquet which I had the happy boldness to fling at your feet. Permit me now to pluck it as a memorial of this interview."

He made a step towards the shrub with extended hand; but Beatrice darted forward, uttering a shriek that went through his heart like a dagger. She caught his hand and drew it back with the whole force of her slender figure. Giovanni felt her touch thrilling through his fibers.

"Touch it not!" exclaimed she, in a voice of agony. "Not for thy life! It is fatal!"

Then, hiding her face, she fled from him and vanished beneath the sculptured portal. As Giovanni followed her with his eyes, he beheld the emaciated figure and pale intelligence of Dr. Rappaccini, who had been watching the scene, he knew not how long, within the shadow of the entrance.

No sooner was Guasconti alone in his chamber than the image of Beatrice came back to his passionate musings, invested with all the witchery that had been gathering around it ever since his first glimpse of

her, and now likewise imbued with a tender warmth of girlish woman-
hood. She was human; her nature was endowed with all gentle and
feminine qualities; she was worthiest to be worshiped; she was capable,
surely, on her part, of the height and heroism of love. Those tokens
which he had hitherto considered as proofs of a frightful peculiarity in
her physical and moral system were now either forgotten, or, by the
subtle sophistry of passion transmitted into a golden crown of enchant-
ment, rendering Beatrice the more admirable by so much as she was the
more unique. Whatever had looked ugly was now beautiful; or, if
incapable of such a change, it stole away and hid itself among those
shapeless half ideas which throng the dim region beyond the daylight of
our perfect consciousness. Thus did he spend the night, nor fell asleep
until the dawn had begun to awake the slumbering flowers in Dr.
Rappaccini's garden, whither Giovanni's dreams doubtless led him. Up
rose the sun in his due season, and, flinging his beams upon the young
man's eyelids, awoke him to a sense of pain. When thoroughly aroused,
he became sensible of a burning and tingling agony in his hand—in his
right hand—the very hand which Beatrice had grasped in her own when
he was on the point of plucking one of the gemlike flowers. On the back
of that hand there was now a purple print like that of four small fingers,
and the likeness of a slender thumb upon his wrist.

Oh, how stubbornly does love—or even that cunning semblance of
love which flourishes in the imagination, but strikes no depth of root into
the heart—how stubbornly does it hold its faith until the moment comes
when it is doomed to vanish into thin mist! Giovanni wrapped a handkerchief about his hand and wondered what evil thing had stung him, and
soon forgot his pain in a reverie of Beatrice.

After the first interview, a second was in the inevitable course of
what we call fate. A third; a fourth; and a meeting with Beatrice in the
garden was no longer an incident in Giovanni's daily life, but the whole
space in which he might be said to live; for the anticipation and memory
of that ecstatic hour made up the remainder. Nor was it otherwise with
the daughter of Rappaccini. She watched for the youth's appearance,
and flew to his side with confidence as unreserved as if they had been
playmates from early infancy—as if they were such playmates still. If,
by any unwonted chance, he failed to come at the appointed moment, she
stood beneath the window and sent up the rich sweetness of her tones to
float around him in his chamber and echo and reverberate throughout his

heart: "Giovanni! Giovanni! Why tarriest thou? Come down!" And down he hastened into that Eden of poisonous flowers.

But, with all this intimate familiarity, there was still a reserve in Beatrice's demeanor, so rigidly and invariably sustained that the idea of infringing it scarcely occurred to his imagination. By all appreciable signs, they loved; they had looked love with eyes that conveyed the holy secret from the depths of one soul into the depths of the other, as if it were too sacred to be whispered by the way; they had even spoken love in those gushes of passion when their spirits darted forth in articulated breath like tongues of long-hidden flame; and yet there had been no seal of lips, no clasp of hands, nor any slightest caress such as love claims and hallows. He had never touched one of the gleaming ringlets of her hair; her garment—so marked was the physical barrier between them—had never been waved against him by a breeze. On the few occasions when Giovanni had seemed tempted to overstep the limit, Beatrice grew so sad, so stern, and withal wore such a look of desolate separation, shuddering at itself, that not a spoken word was requisite to repel him. At such times he was startled at the horrible suspicions that rose, monster-like, out of the caverns of his heart and stared him in the face; his love grew thin and faint as the morning mist, his doubts alone had substance. But, when Beatrice's face brightened again after the momentary shadow, she was transformed at once from the mysterious, questionable being whom he had watched with so much awe and horror; she was now the beautiful and unsophisticated girl whom he felt that his spirit knew with a certainty beyond all other knowledge.

A considerable time had now passed since Giovanni's last meeting with Baglioni. One morning, however, he was disagreebly surprised by a visit from the professor, whom he had scarcely thought of for whole weeks, and would willingly have forgotten still longer. Given up as he had long been to a pervading excitement, he could tolerate no companions except upon condition of their perfect sympathy with his present state of feeling. Such sympathy was not to be expected from Professor Baglioni.

The visitor chatted carelessly for a few moments about the gossip of the city and the university, and then took up another topic.

"I have been reading an old classic author lately," said he, "and met with a story that strangely interested me. Possibly you may remember it. It is of an Indian prince, who sent a beautiful woman as a present to Alexander the Great. She was as lovely as the dawn and gorgeous as the sunset; but what especially distinguished her was a certain rich perfume in her breath—richer than a garden of Persian roses. Alexander, as was natural to a youthful conqueror, fell in love at first sight with this magnificent stranger; but a certain sage physician, happening to be present, discovered a terrible secret in regard to her."

"And what was that?" asked Giovanni, turning his eyes downward to avoid those of the professor.

"That this lovely woman," continued Baglioni, with emphasis, "had been nourished with poisons from her birth upward, until her whole nature was so imbued with them that she herself had become the deadliest poison in existence. Poison was her element of life. With that rich perfume of her breath she blasted the very air. Her love would have been poison—her embrace death. Is not this a marvelous tale?"

"A childish fable," answered Giovanni, nervously starting from his chair. "I marvel how your worship finds time to read such nonsense among your graver studies."

"By the by," said the professor, looking uneasily about him, "what singular fragrance is this in your apartment? Is it the perfume of your gloves? It is faint, but delicious; and yet, after all, by no means agreeable. Were I to breathe it long, methinks it would make me ill. It is like the breath of a flower; but I see no flowers in the chamber."

"Nor are there any," replied Giovanni, who had turned pale as the professor spoke; "nor, I think, is there any fragrance except in your worship's imagination. Odors, being a sort of element combined of the sensual and the spiritual, are apt to deceive us in this manner. The recollection of a perfume, the bare idea of it, may easily be mistaken for a present reality."

"Aye; but my sober imagination does not often play such tricks," said Baglioni; "and, were I to fancy any kind of odor, it would be that of some vile apothecary drug, wherewith my fingers are likely enough to be imbued. Our worshipful friend Rappaccini, as I have heard, tinctures his medicaments with odors richer than those of Araby. Doubtless, likewise, the fair and learned Signora Beatrice would minister to her patients with draughts as sweet as a maiden's breath; but woe to him that sips them!"

Giovanni's face evinced many contending emotions. The tone in which the professor alluded to the pure and lovely daughter of Rappaccini was a torture to his soul; and yet the intimation of a view of her character, opposite to his own, gave instantaneous distinctness to a thousand dim suspicions, which now grinned at him like so many demons. But he strove hard to quell them and to respond to Baglioni with a true lover's perfect faith.

"Signor professor," said he, "you were my father's friend; perchance, too, it is your purpose to act a friendly part towards his son. I would fain feel nothing towards you save respect and deference; but I pray you to observe, signor, that there is one subject on which we must not speak. You know not the Signora Beatrice. You cannot, therefore, estimate the wrong—the blasphemy, I may even say—that is offered to her character by a light or injurious word."

"Giovanni! My poor Giovanni!" answered the professor, with a calm expression of pity, "I know this wretched girl far better than yourself. You shall hear the truth in respect to the poisoner Rappaccini and his poisonous daughter; yes, poisonous as she is beautiful. Listen; for, even should you do violence to my gray hairs, it shall not silence me. That old fable of the Indian woman has become a truth by the deep and deadly science of Rappaccini and in the person of the lovely Beatrice."

Giovanni groaned and hid his face.

"Her father," continued Baglioni, "was not restrained by natural affection from offering up his child in this horrible manner as the victim of his insane zeal for science; for, let us do him justice, he is as true a man of science as ever distilled his own heart in an alembic. What, then, will be your fate? Beyond a doubt you are selected as the material of some new experiment. Perhaps the result is to be death; perhaps a fate more awful still. Rappaccini, with what he calls the interest of science before his eyes, will hesitate at nothing."

"It is a dream," muttered Giovanni to himself; "surely it is a dream."

"But," resumed the professor, "be of good cheer, son of my friend. It is not yet too late for the rescue. Possibly we may even succeed in bringing back this miserable child within the limits of ordinary nature, from which her father's madness has estranged her. Behold this little silver vase! It was wrought by the hands of the renowned Benvenuto Cellini, and is well worthy to be a love gift to the fairest dame in Italy. But its contents are invaluable. One little sip of this antidote would have rendered the most virulent poisons of the Borgias innocuous. Doubt not that it will be as efficacious against those of Rappaccini. Bestow the vase, and the precious liquid within it, on your Beatrice, and hopefully await the result."

Baglioni laid a small, exquisitely wrought silver vial on the table and withdrew, leaving what he had said to produce its effect upon the young man's mind.

"We will thwart Rappaccini yet," thought he, chuckling to himself, as he descended the stairs; "but, let us confess the truth of him, he is a wonderful man—a wonderful man indeed; a vile empiric, however, in his practice, and therefore not to be tolerated by those who respect the good old rules of the medical profession."

Throughout Giovanni's whole acquaintance with Beatrice, he had occasionally, as we have said, been haunted by dark surmises as to her character; yet so thoroughly had she made herself felt by him as a simple, natural, most affectionate, and guileless creature, that the image now held up by Professor Baglioni looked as strange and incredible as if it were not in accordance with his own original conception. True, there were ugly recollections connected with his first glimpses of the beautiful girl; he could not quite forget the bouquet that withered in her grasp, and the insect that perished amid the sunny air, by no ostensible agency save the fragrance of her breath. These incidents, however, dissolving in the pure light of her character, had no longer the efficacy of facts, but were acknowledged as mistaken fantasies, by whatever testimony of the senses they might appear to be substantiated. There is something truer and more real than what we can see with the eyes and touch with the finger. On such better evidence had Giovanni founded his confidence in Beatrice, though rather by the necessary force of her high attributes than by any deep and generous faith on his part. But now his spirit was incapable of sustaining itself at the height to which the early enthusiasm of passion had exalted it; he fell down, groveling among earthly doubts, and defiled therewith the pure whiteness of Beatrice's image. Not that he gave her up; he did but distrust. He resolved to institute some decisive test that should satisfy him, once for all, whether there were those dreadful peculiarities in her physical nature which could not be supposed to exist without some corresponding monstrosity of soul. His eyes, gazing down afar, might have deceived him as to the lizard, the insect, and the flowers; but if he could witness, at the distance of a few paces, the sudden blight of one fresh and healthful flower in Beatrice's hand, there would be room for no further question. With this idea he hastened to the florist's and purchased a bouquet that was still gemmed with the morning dewdrops.

It was now the customary hour of his daily interview with Beatrice. Before descending into the garden, Giovanni failed not to look at his figure in the mirror—a vanity to be expected in a beautiful young man, yet, as displaying itself at that troubled and feverish moment, the token of a certain shallowness of feeling and insincerity of character. He did gaze, however, and said to himself that his features had never before possessed so rich a grace, nor his eyes such vivacity, nor his cheeks so warm a hue of superabundant life.

"At least," thought he, "her poison has not yet insinuated itself into my system. I am no flower to perish in her grasp."

With that thought he turned his eyes on the bouquet, which he had never once laid aside from his hand. A thrill of indefinable horror shot through his frame on perceiving that those dewy flowers were already beginning to droop; they wore the aspect of things that had been fresh and lovely yesterday. Giovanni grew white as marble, and stood motionless before the mirror, staring at his own reflection there as at the likeness of something frightful. He remembered Baglioni's remark about the fragrance that seemed to pervade the chamber. It must have been the poison in his breath! Then he shuddered—shuddered at himself. Recovering from his stupor, he began to watch with curious eye a spider that was busily at work hanging its web from the antique cornice of the apartment, crossing and recrossing the artful system of interwoven lines—as vigorous and active a spider as ever dangled from an old ceiling. Giovanni bent towards the insect, and emitted a deep, long breath. The spider suddenly ceased its toil; the web vibrated with a tremor originating in the body of the small artisan. Again Giovanni sent forth a breath, deeper, longer, and imbued with a venomous feeling out of his heart: he knew not whether he were wicked, or only desperate. The spider made a convulsive gripe with his limbs and hung dead across the window.

"Accursed! Accursed!" muttered Giovanni, addressing himself. "Hast thou grown so poisonous that this deadly insect perishes by thy breath?"

At that moment a rich, sweet voice came floating up from the garden.

"Giovanni! Giovanni! It is past the hour! Why tarriest thou? Come down!"

"Yes," muttered Giovanni again. "She is the only being whom my breath may not slay! Would that it might!"

He rushed down, and in an instant was standing before the bright and loving eyes of Beatrice. A moment ago his wrath and despair had been so fierce that he could have desired nothing so much as to wither her by a glance; but with her actual presence there came influences which had too real an existence to be at once shaken off: recollections of the delicate and benign power of her feminine nature, which had so often enveloped him in a religious calm; recollections of many a holy and passionate outgush of her heart, when the pure fountain had been unsealed from its depths and made visible in its transparency to his mental eye; recollections which, had Giovanni known how to estimate them, would have assured him that all this ugly mystery was but an earthly illusion, and that, whatever mist of evil might seem to have gathered over her, the real Beatrice was a heavenly angel. Incapable as he was of such high faith, still her presence had not utterly lost its magic. Giovanni's rage was quelled into an aspect of sullen insensibility. Beatrice, with a quick spiritual sense, immediately felt that there was a gulf of blackness between them which neither he nor she could pass. They walked on together, sad and silent, and came thus to the marble fountain and to its pool of water on the ground, in the midst of which grew the shrub that bore gem-like blossoms. Giovanni was affrighted at the eager enjoyment—the appetite, as it were—with which he found himself inhaling the fragrance of the flowers.

"Beatrice," asked he, abruptly, "whence came this shrub?"

"My father created it," answered she, with simplicity.

"Created it! Created it!" repeated Giovanni. "What mean you, Beatrice?"

"He is a man fearfully acquainted with the secrets of Nature," replied Beatrice; "and, at the hour when I first drew breath, this plant sprang from the soil, the offspring of his science, of his intellect, while I was but his earthly child. Approach it not!" continued she, observing with terror that Giovanni was drawing nearer to the shrub. "It has qualities that you little dream of. But I, dearest Giovanni—I grew up and blossomed with the plant and was nourished with its breath. It was my sister, and I loved it with a human affection; for, alas!—hast thou not suspected it?—there was an awful doom."

Here Giovanni frowned so darkly upon her that Beatrice paused and trembled. But her faith in his tenderness reassured her, and made her blush that she had doubted for an instant.

"There was an awful doom," she continued, "the effect of my father's fatal love of science, which estranged me from all society of my kind. Until Heaven sent thee, dearest Giovanni, oh, how lonely was thy poor Beatrice!"

"Was it a hard doom?" asked Giovanni, fixing his eyes upon her.

"Only of late have I known how hard it was," answered she, tenderly. "Oh, yes; but my heart was torpid, and therefore quiet."

Giovanni's rage broke forth from his sullen gloom like a lightning flash out of a dark cloud.

"Accursed one!" cried he, with venomous scorn and anger. "And, finding thy solitude wearisome, thou hast severed me likewise from all the warmth of life and enticed me into thy region of unspeakable horror!"

"Giovanni!" exclaimed Beatrice, turning her large bright eyes upon his face. The force of his words had not found its way into her mind; she was merely thunderstruck.

"Yes, poisonous thing!" repeated Giovanni, beside himself with passion. "Thou hast done it! Thou hast blasted me! Thou hast filled my veins with poison! Thou hast made me as hateful, as ugly, as loathsome and deadly a creature as thyself—a world's wonder of hideous monstrosity! Now, if our breath be happily as fatal to ourselves as to all others, let us join our lips in one kiss of unutterable hatred, and so die!"

"What has befallen me?" murmured Beatrice, with a low moan out of her heart. "Holy Virgin, pity me, a poor heartbroken child!"

"Thou—dost thou pray?" cried Giovanni, still with the same fiendish scorn. "Thy very prayers, as they come from thy lips, taint the atmosphere with death. Yes, yes; let us pray! Let us to church and dip our fingers in the holy water at the portal! They that come after us will perish as by a pestilence! Let us sign crosses in the air! It will be scattering curses abroad in the likeness of holy symbols!"

"Giovanni," said Beatrice, calmly, for her grief was beyond passion, "why dost thou join thyself with me thus in those terrible words? I, it is true, am the horrible thing thou namest me. But thou— what hast thou to do, save with one other shudder at my hideous misery to go forth out of the garden and mingle with thy race, and forget that there ever crawled on earth such a monster as poor Beatrice?"

"Dost thou pretend ignorance?" asked Giovanni, scowling upon her. "Behold! this power have I gained from the pure daughter of Rappaccini."

There was a swarm of summer insects flitting through the air in search of the food promised by the flower odors of the fatal garden. They circled round Giovanni's head, and were evidently attracted towards him by the same influence which had drawn them for an instant within the sphere of several of the shrubs. He sent forth a breath among them, and smiled bitterly at Beatrice as at least a score of the insects fell dead upon the ground.

"I see it! I see it!" shrieked Beatrice. "It is my father's fatal science! No, no, Giovanni; it was not I! Never! Never! I dreamed only to love thee and be with thee a little time, and so to let thee pass away, leaving but thine image in mine heart; for, Giovanni, believe it, though my body be nourished with poison, my spirit is God's creature, and craves love as its daily food. But my father—he has united us in this fearful sympathy. Yes; spurn me, tread upon me, kill me! Oh, what is death after such words as thine? But it was not I. Not for a world of bliss would I have done it."

Giovanni's passion had exhausted itself in its outburst from his lips. There now came across him a sense, mournful, and not without tenderness, of the intimate and peculiar relationship between Beatrice and himself. They stood, as it were, in an utter solitude, which would be made none the less solitary by the densest throng of human life. Ought not, then, the desert of humanity around them to press this insulated pair closer together? If they should be cruel to one another, who was there to be kind to them? Besides, thought Giovanni, might there not still be a hope of his returning within the limits of ordinary nature, and leading Beatrice, the redeemed Beatrice, by the hand? O, weak, and selfish, and unworthy spirit, that could dream of an earthly union and earthly happiness as possible, after such deep love had been so bitterly wronged as was Beatrice's love by Giovanni's blighting words! No, no; there could be no such hope. She must pass heavily, with that broken heart, across the borders of Time—she must bathe her hurts in some fount of paradise, and forget her grief in the light of immortality, and *there* be well.

But Giovanni did not know it.

"Dear Beatrice," said he, approaching her, while she shrank away as always at his approach, but now with a different impulse, "dearest

Beatrice, our fate is not yet so desperate. Behold! There is a medicine, potent, as a wise physician has assured me, and almost divine in its efficacy. It is composed of ingredients the most opposite to those by which thy awful father has brought this calamity upon thee and me. It is distilled of blessed herbs. Shall we not quaff it together, and thus be purified from evil?''

"Give it to me!'' said Beatrice, extending her hand to receive the little silver vial which Giovanni took from his bosom. She added, with a peculiar emphasis, ''I will drink; but do thou await the result.''

She put Baglioni's antidote to her lips; and, at the same moment, the figure of Rappaccini emerged from the portal and came slowly towards the marble fountain. As he drew near, the pale man of science seemed to gaze with a triumphant expression at the beautiful youth and maiden, as might an artist who should spend his life in achieving a picture or a group of statuary and finally be satisfied with his success. He paused; his bent form grew erect with conscious power; he spread out his hands over them in the attitude of a father imploring a blessing upon his children; but those were the same hands that had thrown poison into the stream of their lives. Giovanni trembled. Beatrice shuddered nervously, and pressed her hand upon her heart.

"My daughter,'' said Rappaccini, ''thou art no longer lonely in the world. Pluck one of those precious gems from thy sister shrub and bid thy bridegroom wear it in his bosom. It will not harm him now. My science and the sympathy between thee and him have so wrought within his system that he now stands apart from common men as thou dost, daughter of my pride and triumph, from ordinary women. Pass on, then, through the world, most dear to one another and dreadful to all besides!''

"My father,'' said Beatrice, feebly—and still as she spoke she kept her hand upon her heart—''wherefore didst thou inflict this miserable doom upon thy child?''

"Miserable!'' exclaimed Rappaccini. ''What mean you, foolish girl? Dost thou deem it misery to be endowed with marvelous gifts against which no power nor strength could avail an enemy—misery, to be able to quell the mightiest with a breath—misery, to be as terrible as thou art beautiful? Wouldst thou, then, have preferred the condition of a weak woman, exposed to all evil and capable of none?''

"I would fain have been loved, not feared,'' murmured Beatrice, sinking down upon the ground. ''But now it matters not. I am going,

Father, where the evil which thou hast striven to mingle with my being will pass away like a dream—like the fragrance of these poisonous flowers, which will no longer taint my breath among the flowers of Eden. Farewell, Giovanni! Thy words of hatred are like lead within my heart; but they, too, will fall away as I ascend. Oh, was there not, from the first, more poison in thy nature than in mine?''

To Beatrice—so radically had her earthly part been wrought upon by Rappaccini's skill—as poison had been life, so the powerful antidote was death; and thus the poor victim of man's ingenuity and of thwarted nature, and of the fatality that attends all such efforts of perverted wisdom, perished there, at the feet of her father and Giovanni. Just at that moment Professor Pietro Baglioni looked forth from the window, and called loudly, in a tone of triumph mixed with horror, to the thunderstricken man of science:

"Rappaccini! Rappaccini! and is *this* the upshot of your experiment!''

Edward Page Mitchell (1852–1927)

Edward Page Mitchell was a talented nineteenth-century science-fiction writer whose works were recently rediscovered and collected in *The Crystal Man* (1973).

He was born in Bath, Maine and after childhood sojourns in New York City and North Carolina he returned to Brunswick, Maine, to attend Bowdoin College. But even before graduating in 1874, he was appointed editor of *The Lewiston Journal*, the still-flourishing newspaper of a nearby town.

Shortly after assuming his job a fluke train accident blinded him in one eye. During convalescence he began to write science fiction, sending his first effort, "The Tachypomp," off to *Scribner's Monthly* where it was promptly accepted and published anonymously in the spring of 1874.

However, Mitchell soon became fascinated by New York City's lively newspaper, the *New York Sun*. He submitted short features and then two story hoaxes, "Back From That Bourne" (1874) and "The Story of the Deluge" (1875), which were so successful the *Sun*'s editor, Charles A. Dana, offered the young journalist a job at a generous increase in salary. Mitchell accepted, and on October 1, 1875, he began a forty-seven year association that lasted until his retirement in 1922.

During Mitchell's first eleven years with the *Sun*, it published two dozen more of his science-fiction and fantasy stories—at least four of which were remarkable.

"The Ablest Man in the World" (1879) introduced the theme of replacing man's brain with a small computer. A powerful tale that seemingly foreshadows Asimov's belief in the superiority of intelligent machines, it is weakened only by Mitchell's unsympathetic portrayal of the resulting creature.

"The Crystal Man" (1881) first suggested a scientific means of achieving invisibility. Strangely paralleling Wells's later novel, it features a detailed consideration of the disadvantages of such a state.

"The Clock That Went Backward" (1881) is our selection for this anthology. It is both the earliest time-machine story and the pioneer version of the time-paradox story. Furthermore, it is a delightful romance that highlights an interesting slice of Dutch history.

Finally, "The Balloon Tree" (1883) deals with an intelligent plant that flies. Sam Moskowitz calls it "the closest thing to the initial story of a friendly alien yet found."

As an author Mitchell is somewhat reminiscent of L. Sprague de Camp—intelligent, erudite, and witty. Had he continued to produce he might today be known as the American H.G. Wells, but unfortunately his increasing editorial responsibility forced him to stop writing by 1886. And since his work appeared in a newspaper only (with one exception) and was anonymous (with one exception), it lay forgotten for more than eighty years.

As a man, however, Edward Page Mitchell led a successful life. He was an acquaintance of Edward Everett Hale and Edward Bellamy and a friend of Madame Blavatsky, Frank R. Stockton, Garrett P. Serviss, and Frank A. Munsey. When Dana died in 1903, Mitchell became the *Sun*'s editor, serving in that capacity until his retirement in 1922. In 1927 he died a contented man.

THE CLOCK THAT WENT BACKWARD

A row of Lombardy poplars stood in front of my Great-Aunt Gertrude's house, on the bank of the Sheepscot River. In personal appearance my aunt was surprisingly like one of those trees. She had the look of hopeless anemia that distinguishes them from fuller-blooded sorts. She was tall, severe in outline, and extremely thin. Her habiliments clung to her. I am sure that had the gods found occasion to impose upon her the fate of Daphne she would have taken her place easily and naturally in the dismal row, as melancholy a poplar as the rest.

Some of my earliest recollections are of this venerable relative. Alive and dead she bore an important part in the events I am about to recount: events which I believe to be without parallel in the experience of mankind.

During our periodical visits of duty to Aunt Gertrude in Maine, my cousin Harry and myself were accustomed to speculate much on her age. Was she sixty, or was she six score? We had no precise information; she might have been either. The old lady was surrounded by old-fashioned things. She seemed to live altogether in the past. In her short half-hours of communicativeness over her second cup of tea, or on the piazza where the poplars sent slim shadows directly toward the east, she used to tell us stories of her alleged ancestors. I say alleged, because we never fully believed that she had ancestors.

A genealogy is a stupid thing. Here is Aunt Gertrude's, reduced to its simplest forms:

Her great-great-grandmother (1599–1642) was a woman of Holland who married a Puritan refugee, and sailed from Leyden to Plymouth in the ship *Ann* in the year of our Lord 1632. This Pilgrim mother had a daughter, Aunt Gertrude's great-grandmother (1640–1718). She came to the Eastern District of Massachusetts in the early part of the last century, and was carried off by the Indians in the Penobscot wars. Her daughter (1680–1776) lived to see these colonies free and independent, and contributed to the population of the coming republic not less than nineteen stalwart sons and comely daughters. One of the latter (1735–1802) married a Wiscasset skipper engaged in the West India trade, with whom she sailed. She was twice wrecked at sea—once on what is now Seguin Island and once on San Salvador. It was on San Salvador that Aunt Gertrude was born.

We got to be very tired of hearing this family history. Perhaps it was the constant repetition and the merciless persistency with which the above dates were driven into our young ears that made us skeptics. As I have said, we took little stock in Aunt Gertrude's ancestors. They seemed highly improbable. In our private opinion the great-grandmothers and grandmothers and so forth were pure myths, and Aunt Gertrude herself was the principal in all the adventures attributed to them, having lasted from century to century while generations of contemporaries went the way of all flesh.

On the first landing of the square stairway of the mansion loomed a tall Dutch clock. The case was more than eight feet high, of a dark red wood, not mahogany, and it was curiously inlaid with silver. No common piece of furniture was this. About a hundred years ago there flourished in the town of Brunswick a horologist named Cary, an industrious and accomplished workman. Few well-to-do houses on that part of the coast lacked a Cary timepiece. But Aunt Gertrude's clock had marked the hours and minutes of two full centuries before the Brunswick artisan was born. It was running when William the Taciturn pierced the dikes to relieve Leyden. The name of the maker, Jan Lipperdam, and the date, 1572, were still legible in broad black letters and figures reaching quite across the dial. Cary's masterpieces were plebeian and recent beside this ancient aristocrat. The jolly Dutch moon, made to exhibit the phases over a landscape of windmills and polders, was cunningly painted. A skilled hand had carved the grim ornament at the top, a death's-head transfixed by a two-edged sword. Like all timepieces of the sixteenth century, it had no pendulum. A simple Van Wyck escapement governed the descent of the weights to the bottom of the tall case.

But these weights never moved. Year after year, when Harry and I returned to Maine, we found the hands of the old clock pointing to the quarter past three, as they had pointed when we first saw them. The fat moon hung perpetually in the third quarter, as motionless as the death's-head above. There was a mystery about the silenced movement and the paralyzed hands. Aunt Gertrude told us that the works had never performed their functions since a bolt of lightning entered the clock; and she showed us a black hole in the side of the case near the top, with a yawning rift that extended downward for several feet. This explanation failed to satisfy us. It did not account for the sharpness of her refusal when we proposed to bring over the watchmaker from the village, or for her singular agitation once when she found Harry on a stepladder, with a borrowed key in his hand, about to test for himself the clock's suspended vitality.

One August night, after we had grown out of boyhood, I was awakened by a noise in the hallway. I shook my cousin. "Somebody's in the house," I whispered.

We crept out of our room and onto the stairs. A dim light came from below. We held our breath and noiselessly descended to the second landing. Harry clutched my arm. He pointed down over the banisters, at the same time drawing me back into the shadow.

We saw a strange thing.

Aunt Gertrude stood on a chair in front of the old clock, as spectral in her white nightgown and white nightcap as one of the poplars when covered with snow. It chanced that the floor creaked slightly under our feet. She turned with a sudden movement, peering intently into the darkness, and holding a candle high toward us, so that the light was full upon her pale face. She looked many years older than when I bade her good night. For a few minutes she was motionless, except in the trembling arm that held aloft the candle. Then, evidently reassured, she placed the light upon a shelf and turned again to the clock.

We now saw the old lady take a key from behind the face and proceed to wind up the weights. We could hear her breath, quick and short. She rested a hand on either side of the case and held her face close to the dial, as if subjecting it to anxious scrutiny. In this attitude she remained for a long time. We heard her utter a sigh of relief, and she half turned toward us for a moment. I shall never forget the expression of wild joy that transfigured her features then.

The hands of the clock were moving; they were moving backward.

Aunt Gertrude put both arms around the clock and pressed her withered cheek against it. She kissed it repeatedly. She caressed it in a hundred ways, as if it had been a living and beloved thing. She fondled it and talked to it, using words which we could hear but could not understand. The hands continued to move backward.

Then she started back with a sudden cry. The clock had stopped. We saw her tall body swaying for an instant on the chair. She stretched out her arms in a convulsive gesture of terror and despair, wrenched the minute hand to its old place at a quarter past three, and fell heavily to the floor.

II

Aunt Gertrude's will left me her bank and gas stocks, real estate, railroad bonds, and city sevens, and gave Harry the clock. We thought at the time that this was a very unequal division, the more surprising because my cousin had always seemed to be the favorite. Half in seriousness we made a thorough examination of the ancient timepiece, sounding its wooden case for secret drawers, and even probing the not complicated works with a knitting needle to ascertain if our whimsical relative had bestowed there some codicil or other document changing the aspect of affairs. We discovered nothing.

There was testamentary provision for our education at the University of Leyden. We left the military school in which we had learned a little of the theory of war, and a good deal of the art of standing with our noses over our heels, and took ship without delay. The clock went with us. Before many months it was established in a corner of a room in the Breede Straat.

The fabric of Jan Lipperdam's ingenuity, thus restored to its native air, continued to tell the hour of quarter past three with its old fidelity. The author of the clock had been under the sod for nearly three hundred years. The combined skill of his successors in the craft at Leyden could make it go neither forward nor backward.

We readily picked up enough Dutch to make ourselves understood by the townspeople, the professors, and such of our eight hundred and odd fellow students as came into intercourse. This language, which looks so hard at first, is only a sort of polarized English. Puzzle over it a little while and it jumps into your comprehension like one of those simple

118

cryptograms made by running together all the words of a sentence and then dividing in the wrong places.

The language acquired and the newness of our surroundings worn off, we settled into tolerably regular pursuits. Harry devoted himself with some assiduity to the study of sociology, with especial reference to the round-faced and not unkind maidens of Leyden. I went in for the higher metaphysics.

Outside of our respective studies, we had a common ground of unfailing interest. To our astonishment, we found that not one in twenty of the faculty or students knew or cared a stiver about the glorious history of the town, or even about the circumstances under which the university itself was founded by the Prince of Orange. In marked contrast with the general indifference was the enthusiasm of Professor Van Stopp, my chosen guide through the cloudiness of speculative philosophy.

This distinguished Hegelian was a tobacco-dried little old man, with a skullcap over features that reminded me strangely of Aunt Gertrude's. Had he been her own brother the facial resemblance could not have been closer. I told him so once, when we were together in the Stadthuis looking at the portrait of the hero of the siege, the Burgomaster Van der Werf. The professor laughed. "I will show you what is even a more extraordinary coincidence," said he; and, leading the way across the hall to the great picture of the siege, by Wanners, he pointed out the figure of a burgher participating in the defense. It was true. Van Stopp might have been the burgher's son; the burgher might have been Aunt Gertrude's father.

The professor seemed to be fond of us. We often went to his rooms in an old house in the Rapenburg Straat, one of the few houses remaining that antedate 1574. He would walk with us through the beautiful suburbs of the city, over straight roads lined with poplars that carried us back to the bank of the Sheepscot in our minds. He took us to the top of the ruined Roman tower in the center of the town, and from the same battlements from which anxious eyes three centuries ago had watched the slow approach of Admiral Boisot's fleet over the submerged polders, he pointed out the great dike of the Landscheiding, which was cut that the oceans might bring Boisot's Zealanders to raise the leaguer and feed the starving. He showed us the headquarters of the Spaniard Valdez at Leyderdorp, and told us how heaven sent a violent northwest wind on the night of the first of October, piling up the water deep where it had been shallow and sweeping the fleet on between Zoeterwoude and Zwieten up to the very walls of the fort at Lammen, the last stronghold of the besiegers and the last obstacle in the way of succor to the famishing inhabitants. Then he showed us where, on the very night before the retreat of the besieging army, a huge breach was made in the wall of Leyden, near the Cow Gate, by the Walloons from Lammen.

"Why!" cried Harry, catching fire from the eloquence of the professor's narrative, "that was the decisive moment of the siege."

The professor said nothing. He stood with his arms folded, looking intently into my cousin's eyes.

"For," continued Harry, "had that point not been watched, or had defense failed and the breach been carried by the night assault from Lammen, the town would have been burned and the people massacred under the eyes of Admiral Boisot and the fleet of relief. Who defended the breach?"

Van Stopp replied very slowly, as if weighing every word:

"History records the explosion of the mine under the city wall on the last night of the siege; it does not tell the story of the defense or give the defender's name. Yet no man that ever lived had a more tremendous charge than fate entrusted to this unknown hero. Was it chance that sent him to meet that unexpected danger? Consider some of the consequences had he failed. The fall of Leyden would have destroyed the last hope of the Prince of Orange and of the free states. The tyranny of Philip would have been reestablished. The birth of religious liberty and of self-government by the people would have been postponed, who knows for how many centuries? Who knows that there would or could have been a republic of the United States of America had there been no United Netherlands? Our University, which has given to the world Grotius, Scaliger, Arminius, and Descartes, was founded upon this hero's successful defense of the breach. We owe to him our presence here today. Nay, you owe to him your very existence. Your ancestors were of Leyden; between their lives and the butchers outside the walls he stood that night."

The little professor towered before us, a giant of enthusiasm and patriotism. Harry's eyes glistened and his cheeks reddened.

"Go home, boys," said Van Stopp, "and thank God that while the burghers of Leyden were straining their gaze toward Zoeterwoude and the fleet, there was one pair of vigilant eyes and one stout heart at the town wall just beyond the Cow Gate!"

III

The rain was splashing against the windows one evening in the autumn of our third year at Leyden, when Professor Van Stopp honored us with a visit in the Breede Straat. Never had I seen the old gentleman in such spirits. He talked incessantly. The gossip of the town, the news of Europe, science, poetry, philosophy, were in turn touched upon and treated with the same high and good humor. I sought to draw him out on Hegel, with whose chapter on the complexity and interdependency of things I was just then struggling.

"You do not grasp the return of the Itself into Itself through its Otherself?" he said smiling. "Well, you will, sometime."

Harry was silent and preoccupied. His taciturnity gradually affected even the professor. The conversation flagged, and we sat a long while without a word. Now and then there was a flash of lightning succeeded by distant thunder.

"Your clock does not go," suddenly remarked the professor. "Does it ever go?"

"Never since we can remember," I replied. "That is, only once, and then it went backward. It was when Aunt Gertrude—"

Here I caught a warning glance from Harry. I laughed and stammered, "The clock is old and useless. It cannot be made to go."

"Only backward?" said the professor, calmly, and not appearing to notice my embarrassment. "Well, and why should not a clock go backward? Why should not Time itself turn and retrace its course?"

He seemed to be waiting for an answer. I had none to give.

"I thought you Hegelian enough," he continued, "to admit that every condition includes its own contradiction. Time is a condition, not an essential. Viewed from the Absolute, the sequence by which future follows present and present follows past is purely arbitrary. Yesterday, today, tomorrow; there is no reason in the nature of things why the order should not be tomorrow, today, yesterday."

A sharper peal of thunder interrupted the professor's speculations.

"The day is made by the planet's revolution on its axis from west to east. I fancy you can conceive conditions under which it might turn from east to west, unwinding, as it were, the revolutions of past ages. Is it so much more difficult to imagine Time unwinding itself; Time on the ebb, instead of on the flow; the past unfolding as the future recedes; the centuries countermarching; the course of events proceeding toward the Beginning and not, as now, toward the End?''

"But," I interposed, "we know that as far as we are concerned the—''

"We know!'' exclaimed Van Stopp, with growing scorn. "Your intelligence has no wings. You follow in the trail of Compte and his slimy brood of creepers and crawlers. You speak with amazing assurance of your position in the universe. You seem to think that your wretched little individuality has a firm foothold in the Absolute. Yet you go to bed tonight and dream into existence men, women, children, beasts of the past or the future. How do you know that at this moment you yourself, with all your conceit of nineteenth-century thought, are anything more than a creature of a dream of the future, dreamed, let us say, by some philosopher of the sixteenth century? How do you know that you are anything more than a creature of a dream of the past, dreamed by some Hegelian of the twenty-sixth century? How do you know, boy, that you will not vanish into the sixteenth century or 2060 the moment the dreamer awakes?''

There was no replying to this, for it was sound metaphysics. Harry yawned. I got up and went to the window. Profesor Van Stopp approached the clock.

"Ah, my children,'' said he, "there is no fixed progress of human events. Past, present, and future are woven together in one inextricable mesh. Who shall say that this old clock is not right to go backward?''

A crash of thunder shook the house. The storm was over our heads.

When the blinding glare had passed away, Professor Van Stopp was standing upon a chair before the tall timepiece. His face looked more than ever like Aunt Gertrude's. He stood as she had stood in that last quarter of an hour when we saw her wind the clock.

The same thought struck Harry and myself.

"Hold!'' we cried, as he began to wind the works. "It may be death if you—''

The professor's sallow features shone with the strange enthusiasm that had transformed Aunt Gerturde's.

"True,'' he said, "it may be death; but it may be the awakening. Past, present, future; all woven together! The shuttle goes to and fro, forward and back—''

He had wound the clock. The hands were whirling around the dial from right to left with inconceivable rapidity. In this whirl we ourselves seemed to be borne along. Eternities seemed to contract into minutes while lifetimes were thrown off at every tick. Van Stopp, both arms outstretched, was reeling in his chair. The house shook again under a tremendous peal of thunder. At the same instant a ball of fire, leaving a wake of sulphurous vapor and filling the room with dazzling light, passed over our heads and smote the clock. Van Stopp was prostrated. The hands ceased to revolve.

IV

The roar of the thunder sounded like heavy cannonading. The lightning's blaze appeared as the steady light of a conflagration. With our hands over our eyes, Harry and I rushed into the night.

Under a red sky people were hurrying toward the Stadthius. Flames in the direction of the Roman tower told us that the heart of the town was afire. The faces of those we saw were haggard and emaciated. From every side we caught disjointed phrases of complaint or despair. "Horse-flesh at ten schillings the pound," said one, "and bread at sixteen schillings." "Bread indeed!" an old woman retorted: "It's eight weeks gone since I have seen a crumb." "My little grandchild, the lame one, went last night." Do you know what Gekke Betje, the washerwoman did? She was starving. Her babe died, and she and her man—"

A louder cannon burst cut short this revelation. We made our way on toward the citadel of the town, passing a few soldiers here and there and many burghers with grim faces under their broad-brimmed felt hats.

"There is bread plenty yonder where the gunpowder is, and full pardon, too. Valdez shot another amnesty over the walls this morning."

An excited crowd immediately surrounded the speaker. "But the fleet!" they cried.

"The fleet is grounded fast on the Greenway polder. Boisot may turn his one eye seaward for a wind till famine and pestilence have carried off every mother's son of ye, and his ark will not be a rope's length nearer. Death by plague, death by starvation, death by fire and musketry—that is what the burgomaster offers us in return for glory for himself and kingdom for Orange."

"He asks us," said a sturdy citizen, "to hold out only twenty-four hours longer, and to pray meanwhile for an ocean wind."

"Ah, yes!" sneered the first speaker. "Pray on. There is bread enough locked in Pieter Adriaanszoon van der Werf's cellar. I warrant you that is what gives him so wonderful a stomach for resisting the Most Catholic King."

A young girl, with braided yellow hair, pressed through the crowd and confronted the malcontent. "Good people," said the maiden, "do not listen to him. He is a traitor with a Spanish heart. I am Pieter's daughter. We have no bread. We ate malt cakes and rapeseed like the rest of you till it was gone. Then we stripped the green leaves from the lime trees and willows in our garden and ate them. We have eaten even the thistles and weeds that grew between the stones by the canal. The coward lies."

Nevertheless, the insinuation had its effect. The throng, now become a mob, surged off in the direction of the burgomaster's house. One ruffian raised his hand to strike the girl out of the way. In a wink the cur was under the feet of his fellows, and Harry panting and glowing, stood at the maiden's side, shouting defiance in good English at the backs of the rapidly retreating crowd.

With the utmost frankness she put both her arms around Harry's neck and kissed him.

"Thank you," she said. "You are a hearty lad. My name is Gertruyd van der Werf."

Harry was fumbling in his vocabulary for the proper Dutch phrases, but the girl would not stay for compliments. "They mean mischief to my father"; and she hurried us through several exceedingly narrow streets into a three-cornered marketplace dominated by a church with two spires. "There he is," she exclaimed, "on the steps of St. Pancras."

There was a tumult in the marketplace. The conflagration raging beyond the church and the voices of the Spanish and Walloon cannon outside of the walls were less angry than the roar of this multitude of desperate men clamoring for the bread that a single word from their leader's lips would bring them. "Surrender to the King!" they cried, "or we will send your dead body to Lammen as Leyden's token of submission."

One tall man, taller by half a head than any of the burghers confronting him, and so dark of complexion that we wondered how he could be the father of Gertruyd, heard the threat in silence. When the burgomaster spoke, the mob listened in spite of themselves.

"What is it you ask, my friends? That we break our vow and surrender Leyden to the Spaniards? That is to devote ourselves to a fate far more horrible than starvation. I have to keep the oath! Kill me, if you will have it so. I can die only once, whether by your hands, by the enemy's, or by the hand of God. Let us starve, if we must, welcoming starvation because it comes before dishonor. Your menaces do not move me; my life is at your disposal. Here, take my sword, thrust it into my breast, and divide my flesh among you to appease your hunger. So long as I remain alive expect no surrender."

There was silence again while the mob wavered. Then there were mutterings around us. Above these rang out the clear voice of the girl whose hand Harry still held—unnecessarily, it seemed to me.

"Do you not feel the sea wind? It has come at last. To the tower! And the first man there will see by moonlight the full white sails of the prince's ships."

For several hours I scoured the streets of the town, seeking in vain my cousin and his companion; the sudden movement of the crowd toward the Roman tower had separated us. On every side I saw evidences of the terrible chastisement that had brought this stout-hearted people to the verge of despair. A man with hungry eyes chased a lean rat along the bank of the canal. A young mother, with two dead babes in her arms, sat in a doorway to which they bore the bodies of her husband and father, just killed at the walls. In the middle of a deserted street I passed unburied corpses in a pile twice as high as my head. The pestilence had been there—kinder than the Spaniard, because it held out no treacherous promises while it dealt its blows.

Toward morning the wind increased to a gale. There was no sleep in Leyden, no more talk of surrender, no longer any thought or care about defense. These words were on the lips of everybody I met: "Daylight will bring the fleet!"

Did daylight bring the fleet? History says so, but I was not a witness. I know only that before dawn the gale culminated in a violent thunderstorm, and that at the same time a muffled explosion, heavier than the thunder, shook the town. I was in the crowd that watched from the Roman Mound for the first signs of the approaching relief. The concussion shook hope out of every face. "Their mine has reached the wall!" But where? I pressed forward until I found the burgomaster, who was standing among the rest. "Quick!" I whispered. "It is beyond the

Cow Gate, and this side of the Tower of Burgundy.'' He gave me a searching glance, and then strode away, without making any attempt to quiet the general panic. I followed close at his heels.

It was a tight run of nearly half a mile to the rampart in question. When we reached the Cow Gate this is what we saw:

A great gap, where the wall had been, opening to the swampy fields beyond: in the moat, outside and below, a confusion of upturned faces, belonging to men who struggled like demons to achieve the breach, and who now gained a few feet and now were forced back; on the shattered rampart a handful of soldiers and burghers forming a living wall where masonry had failed; perhaps a double handful of women and girls, serving stones to the defenders and boiling water in buckets, besides pitch and oil and unslaked lime, and some of them quoiting tarred and burning hoops over the necks of the Spaniards in the moat; my cousin Harry leading and directing the men; the burgomaster's daughter Gertruyd encouraging and inspiring the women.

But what attracted my attention more than anything else was the frantic activity of a little figure in black, who, with a huge ladle, was showering molten lead on the heads of the assailing party. As he turned to the bonfire and kettle which supplied him with ammunition, his features came into the full light. I gave a cry of surprise: the ladler of molten lead was Professor Van Stopp.

The burgomaster Van der Werf turned at my sudden exclamation. ''Who is that?'' I said. ''The man at the kettle?''

''That,'' replied Van der Werf, ''is the brother of my wife, the clockmaker Jan Lipperdam.''

The affair at the breach was over almost before we had had time to grasp the situation. The Spaniards, who had overthrown the wall of brick and stone, found the living wall impregnable. They could not even maintain their position in the moat; they were driven off into the darkness. Now I felt a sharp pain in my left arm. Some stray missile must have hit me while we watched the fight.

''Who has done this thing?'' demanded the burgomaster. ''Who is it that has kept watch on today while the rest of us were straining fools' eyes toward tomorrow?''

Gertruyd van der Werf came forward proudly, leading my cousin. ''My father,'' said the girl, ''he has saved my life.''

''That is much to me,'' said the burgomaster, ''but it is not all. He has saved Leyden and he has saved Holland.''

I was becoming dizzy. The faces around me seemed unreal. Why were we here with these people? Why did the thunder and lightning forever continue? Why did the clockmaker, Jan Lipperdam, turn always toward me the face of Professor Van Stopp? "Harry!" I said, "come back to our rooms."

But though he grasped my hand warmly his other hand still held that of the girl, and he did not move. Then nausea overcame me. My head swam, and the breach and its defenders faded from sight.

V

Three days later I sat with one arm bandaged in my accustomed seat in Van Stopp's lecture room. The place beside me was vacant.

"We hear much," said the Hegelian professor, reading from a notebook in his usual dry, hurried tone, "of the influence of the sixteenth century upon the nineteenth. No philosopher, as far as I am aware, has studied the influence of the nineteenth century upon the sixteenth. If cause produces effect, does effect never induce cause? Does the law of heredity, unlike all other laws of this universe of mind and matter, operate in one direction only? Does the descendant owe everything to the ancestor, and the ancestor nothing to the descendant? Does destiny, which may seize upon our existence, and for its own purposes bear us far into the future, never carry us back into the past?"

I went back to my rooms in the Breede Straat, where my only companion was the silent clock.

Robert Duncan Milne (1844–1899)

A close friend of Ambrose Bierce and Robert Louis Stevenson, Robert Duncan Milne was the nineteenth century's most prolific writer of science-fiction short stories, with over sixty to his credit. He was a "hard" science-fiction writer in the vein of Arthur Clarke and Larry Niven and should have been a major influence on the field. Unfortunately, however, his work only appeared in San Francisco newspapers and magazines and lay forgotten until recently collected by Sam Moskowitz (*Into the Sun and Other Stories,* 1980).

Milne was born in Cupar Fifeshire, Scotland, attended Trinity College, and was a graduate of Oxford University. Though he had been an excellent scholar and an outstanding athlete, he was a problem drinker and it appears as if his family may have paid him to leave the country. For years he earned his living by taking odd jobs while wandering around California and Mexico. Then in the late 1870's he began writing for the San Francisco press.

Beginning with his first story ("A Modern Robe of Nessus") Milne received popular acclaim and had no difficulty placing work. One reason for his success is that his stories are imbued with a great deal of scientific verisimilitude. He seemed to keep abreast of scientific development and he had a mechanically oriented mind—obtaining a patent for a rotary steam engine and providing the earliest literary description of a helicopter yet found. Secondly, he dealt with a wide variety of themes such as genetic manipulation, wireless transmission, the fourth dimension, baseball, interplanetary exploration, television, and prehistoric monsters. Third, he was a credible stylist whose stories still remain easy to read.

129

Indeed, when William Randolph Hearst gained control of the *San Francisco Examiner* in 1887, Milne had become so popular on the West Coast that he was hired for special features despite his notorious reputation as a drinker. But ultimately Milne was fired because he had fallen into an almost perpetual state of inebriation. Finally, just two weeks before the new century, he staggered in front of one of the cable cars and was fatally injured.

For this anthology we have selected Milne's excellent cosmic disaster story, "Into the Sun" (1882), which vividly describes the impact a sudden solar temperature rise would have on earth. Told through the first-person account of a young balloonist, it also features a Poe-like ending.

INTO THE SUN

"**A**nd so you think, doctor, that the comet which has just been reported from South Africa is the same as last year's comet—the one discovered first by Cruls at Rio Janeiro, I mean, and which was afterward so plainly visible to us here all through the month of October?"

"Judging from the statement in the papers regarding its general appearance, and the course in which it is traveling, I do not see to what other conclusion we can come. It is approaching the sun from the same quarter as last year's comet; it resembles it in appearance; its rate of motion is as great, if not greater; all these things are very strong arguments of identity."

"But, then, how do you account for so speedy a return? This is only the end of August, and last year's comet was computed to have passed its perihelion about the eighteenth of September—scarcely a year ago. Even Encke's and Biela's comets, which are denizens of our solar system, so to speak, have longer periods than that."

"I account for it simply on the hypothesis that this comet passes so close to the sun that its motion is retarded, and its course consequently changed after every such approach. I believe, with Mr. Proctor and Professor Boss, that this is the comet of 1843 and 1880; that it is moving in a succession of eccentric spirals, the curvatures of which have reduced its periods of revolution from perhaps many hundreds of years to—at its last recorded return—thirty-seven years, then to two and a fraction, and now to less than one; and that its ultimate destination is to be precipitated into the sun."

"This is certainly startling, supposing your hypothesis to be cor-

rect; and should such a casualty happen, what result would you anticipate?''

"That demands some consideration. Take another cigar, and we
shall look into the matter.''

The foregoing conversation took place in the rooms of my friend
Doctor Arkwright, upon Market Street; the time was about eleven
o'clock at night; the date, the twenty-seventh of August; the interroga-
tions had been mine and the answers the doctor's. I may add that the
doctor was a chemist of no mean attainments, and took great interest in
all scientific discussions and experiments.

"The effect of the collision of a comet with the sun,'' observed the
doctor, as he lit his cigar, "would depend upon a good many conditions.
It would depend primarily upon the mass, momentum, and velocity of
the comet—something, too, upon its constitution. Let me see that
paragraph again. Ah, here it is,'' and the doctor proceeded to read from
the paper:

" 'RIO JANEIRO, August 18th. The comet was again visible last
evening, before and after sunset, about thirty degrees from the sun. Mr.
Cruls pronounces it identical with the comet of last year. It is approaching the sun at the rate of two and a half degrees a day. R.A., at noon,
yesterday, 178 degrees, 24 minutes; Dec. 83 degrees, 40 minutes, S.'

"Now this,'' he went on, "corresponds exactly with the position
and motion of last year's comet. It came from a point nearly due south of
the sun, consequently was invisible to the northern hemisphere before
perihelion.''

"Pardon me,'' I interrupted, "but you remember the newspaper
predictions regarding last year's comet were to the effect that it would
speedily become invisible to us here, whereas it continued to adorn the
morning skies for weeks, till it faded away in the remote distance.''

"That was because the nature of its orbit was not distinctly understood. The plane of the comet's orbit cut the plane of the earth's orbit
nearly at right angles, but the major axis or general direction of this orbit
in space, was also inclined some fifty degrees to our plane; and so it came
about that while the approach of the comet was from a point somewhat
east of south, its return journey into space was along a line some twenty
degrees south of west, which threw its course nearly along the line of the
celestial equator; consequently, last year's comet was visible in the early
morning, not only to us, but to every inhabitant of the earth between the

sixtieth parallel north and the south pole, until the vast distance caused it to disappear. But, as I was going to say when you interrupted me, if the distance of the comet from the sun was only thirty degrees when observed at Rio Janeiro, nine days ago, and its speed was then two and a half degrees a day, it can not be far from perihelion now, especially as its speed increases as it approaches the sun.''

"Suppose it should strike the sun this time," said I. "What results would you predict?"

"A solid globe," replied the doctor, "of the size of our earth, if falling upon the sun with the momentum resulting from direct attraction from its present position in space, would engender sufficient heat to maintain the solar fires at their existing standard, without further supply, for about ninety years. This calculation does not involve great scientific or mathematical knowledge, but, on the contrary, is as simple as it is reliable, because we have positive data to go upon in the mass and momentum of our planet. But with a comet the case is different. We do not know what elements its nucleus is composed of. It is true we know the value of its momentum; but what does that tell us if we do not know its density or its mass? A momentum of four hundred miles a second— the estimated rate of speed of the present comet at perihelion—would undoubtedly engender fierce combustion were the comet a ponderable body. On the other hand, large bodies composed of fluid matter highly volatilized might collide with the sun without an appreciable effect.''

"Have we any data to go upon in this matter?" I inquired.

"With regard to our own sun," replied the doctor, "we have not; but several suggestive circumstances have occurred in the case of other suns which lead us to infer that something similar might happen to our own. Some years ago, a star in the constellation Cygnus was observed to suddenly blaze out with extraordinary brilliancy, its luster increasing from that of a star of the sixth magnitude—but faintly distinguishable to the unaided eye—to that of a star of the first. This brilliancy was maintained for several days, when it resumed its original condition. Now, it is fair to infer that this great increase of light may have been caused by the precipitation of some large solid body—a planet, a comet, or perhaps another sun—upon the sun in question; and, as light and heat are now understood to be merely different modes or expressions of the same quality of motion, it is fair to infer further that the increment of heat corresponded to that of light.''

"What, then, do you suppose would be the natural effect upon ourselves here, on this planet, by some such catastrophe as you have just imagined happening to our own sun!" I asked.

"The light and heat of our luminary might be increased a hundredfold, or a thousandfold, according to the nature of the collision. One can conceive of cumbustion so fierce as to evaporate all of our oceans in one short minute, or even to volatilize the solid matter of our planet in less than that time, like a globule of mercury in a hot-air chamber. 'Large' and 'small' are not absolute, but relative, terms in Nature's vocabulary; both are equally amenable to her laws," sententiously observed the doctor.

"A comforting reflection, certainly," I remarked. "Let us hope we shall not be favored with any such experience."

"Who can tell?" rejoined the doctor, as he rose from his seat. "Excuse me for a minute. You know there is a balloon ascension from Woodward's Gardens tomorrow, and there is a new ingredient I am going to introduce at the inflation. The stuff wants a little more mixing. Take another cigar. I won't be a minute."

I sat back and meditated as I listened to the retreating footsteps of the doctor, as he passed into an adjoining room. I looked at the clock. It was half past eleven. It was a warm night for San Francisco in August— remarkably so, in fact. I got up to open the window, and as I did so the doctor entered the room again.

"What is that?" I exclaimed involuntarily, as I threw up the sash. And the spectacle which met my gaze as I did so, certainly warranted the exclamation.

Doctor Arkwright's rooms were on the north side of Market Street, and the inferior height of the buildings opposite afforded an uninterrupted view of the horizon to the south and east. Over the tops of the houses to the east could be seen a thin, livid line, marking the waters of the bay, and beyond it the serrated outline of the Alameda hills. All this was normal and just as I had seen it a hundred times before, but in the northeast the sky was lit up with a lurid, dull-red glow, which extended northward along the horizon in a broadening arc, till the view was shut out by the street line to our left. This light resembled in all respects the *aurora borealis,* except that of color. Instead of the cold, clear radiance of the northern light, we were confronted by an angry, blood-red glare which ever and anon shot forks, and tongues, and streamers of fire upward toward the zenith. It was as if some vast conflagration were in progress to our north. But what, I asked myself, could produce so extensive, so powerful an illumination? Vast forest fires, or the burning of large cities, make themselves manifest by a sky-reflected glare for great distances, but they do not display the regularity—or the harmony, so to speak—which was apparent in the present instance. The conclusion was inevitable that the phenomenon was not local in its source.

As we looked out at the window we could see that the scene had arrested the attention of others besides ourselves. Little knots of people had collected on the sidewalk; larger knots at the street corners; and the passersby kept turning their heads to gaze at the strange spectacle. At the same time the air was growing heavier and more sultry every minute. There was not a breath stirring, but an ominous and preternatural calm seemed to brood over the city, like that which in some climates is the precursor of a storm, and which here is frequently known as "earthquake weather."

The doctor broke the silence.

"This is something quite out of the common run of events," he exclaimed. "That light in the north must have a cause. All the Sonoma and Mendocino redwoods, with the pineries of Oregon and Washington Territory thrown in, would not make such a blaze as that. Besides, that is not the sort of sky-reflection a forest fire would cause."

"Just my own idea," I asserted.

"Let us see if we can not connect it with a wider origin. It is now nearly midnight. That light is in the north. The sun's rays are now illuminating the other side of the globe. It is, therefore, sunrise on the Atlantic, noon in eastern Europe, and sunset in Western Asia. When you came here, scarcely an hour ago, the heavens were clear, and the temperature normal. Whatever has given rise to this extraordinary phenomenon has done so within the last hour. Even since we began to look I see that the extremity of the illuminated arc has shifted further to the east. That light has its origin in the sun, but it altogether passes the bounds of experience."

"Might we not connect it with the comet we have just been speaking about?" I suggested. "It should now be near its perihelion point."

"That must be it," acquiesced the doctor. "Who knows but that the fiery wanderer has actually come in contact with the sun? Let us go out."

We put on our hats, and left the building. All along the sidewalks we came upon excited groups staring at the strange light, and speculating upon its cause. The general expression of opinion referred it to some vast forest fire, though there were not wanting religions enthusiasts who saw in it a manifestation of all things; for in the uninformed human mind there is no middle ground between the grossly practical and the purely fanatical. We hurried along Market Street and turned down Kearny, where the crowds were even denser and more anxious-looking. Arrived at the *Chronicle* office, I noticed that a succession of messengers from the various telegraph offices were encountering each other on the stairs of the building.

"If you will wait a minute," I said to the doctor, "I will run upstairs and find out what is the matter."

"Strange news from the East," said the telegraphic editor, hurriedly, in answer to my question, at the same time pointing to a little pile of dispatches. "These have been coming in for the last half hour from all points of the Union."

I took up one, and read the contents:

NEW YORK, 3:15 A.M. EXTRAORDINARY LIGHT JUST BROKE OUT OVER THE EASTERN HORIZON. VERY RED AND THREATENING. SEEMS TO PROCEED FROM A GREAT DISTANCE OUT AT SEA. PEOPLE UNABLE TO ASSIGN CAUSE.

Another ran as follows:

NEW ORLEANS, 4:10 A.M. VIVID CONFLAGRATION REFLECTED IN THE SKY, A LITTLE NORTH OF EAST. GENERAL SENTIMENT THAT VAST FIRES HAVE SPRUNG UP IN THE CANE-BRAKES. POPULATION ABROAD AND ANXIOUS.

"There are a score more," remarked the editor, "from Chicago, Memphis, Canada—everywhere, in fact—all to the same purpose. What do you make of it?"

"The phenomenon is evidently universal," I said. "It must have its origin in the sun. Do you notice how hot and stifling the air is getting? Have you any dispatches from Europe?"

"None yet. Ah, here is a cablegram repeated from New York,"

said the editor, taking a dispatch from the hand of a messenger who just then entered. "This may tell us something. Listen:

" 'LONDON, 7:45 A.M. Five minutes ago sun's heat became overpowering. Business stopped. People falling dead in streets. Thermometer risen from 52 degrees to 113. Still rising. Message from Greenwich Observatory says—'

"The dispatch stops abruptly there," interpolated the editor, "and the New York operator goes on thus: 'Message cut short. Nothing more through cable. Intense alarm everywhere. Light and heat increasing.' "

"Well," said I, "it must be as Doctor Arkwright suggested. The comet observed again at Rio Janeiro, ten days ago, has fallen into the sun. Heaven only knows what we had better do."

"I shall edit these dispatches and get the paper out, at any rate," said the editor with determination. "Ah, here comes the ice for the printers," as half a dozen men filed past the door, each with a sack upon his shoulder. "The paper must come out if the earth burns for it. I fancy we can hold out until sunrise, and before then the worst may be over."

I left the office, rejoined the doctor in the street, and told him the news.

"There is no doubt about it," he remarked at once. "The comet of last year has fallen into the sun. All the telegraphic messages were nearly identical in time, as it is now just midnight here, and consequently about four o'clock in New York, and eight o'clock in England."

"What had we better do?" queried I.

"I do not think there is any cause for immediate alarm," replied the doctor. "We shall see whether the heat increases materially between now and sunrise, and take measures accordingly. Meanwhile, let us look about us."

The scenes of alarm were intensified in the streets as we passed along. It seemed as if half the population of the city had left their houses, and gathered in the most public places. Thousands of people were pushing and jostling each other in the neighborhood of the various newspaper offices in frantic endeavors to get a glimpse of the bulletin boards, where the substance of the various telegrams was posted up as fast as they came in. Multitudes of hacks and express wagons were driving hither and thither, crowded with family parties seemingly intent upon leaving the city, and probably without any definite aim or accurate comprehension of what they were doing or whither they were going.

As the hours wore on toward morning the angry red arch moved farther along the horizon, its outlines grew bolder and brighter, and its flaming crest towered higher in the heavens. Nothing could be conceived more ominous or ghastly, more calculated to produce feelings of brutish terror, and to convince the spectator of his utter powerlessness to cope with an inevitable and inexorable event, than this blood-red arch of flame which spread over one fourth of the apparent horizon. The air, too, was momentarily growing heavier and more stifling. A glance at a thermometer in one of the hotels gave a temperature of 114 degrees.

Between two and three o'clock four successive alarms of fire were sounded from the lower quarters of the city. Two large wholesale houses and a liquor store, in three contiguous blocks, caught fire, evidently the work of incendiaries. Multitudes of the worst rabble collected, as if by concert, in the business quarters. Shops and warehouses were broken into and looted—the police force, though working vigorously, not being strong enough to arrest the work of pillage, backed as it was by the moral terrors of the night, and the general paralysis which unnerved the better class of citizens. Strange scenes were being enacted at every corner and on every street. Groups of women kneeling upon sidewalks, and rending the air with prayers and lamentations, were jostled aside by ruffians wild and furious with liquor. A procession of religious fanatics, chanting shrill and discordant hymns, and bearing lanterns in their hands, passed unheeded through the crowded streets, and we could afterward watch them threading their way up the steep side of Telegraph Hill. In short, the terrible and bizarre effects of that fearful night would overtax the pen of a Dante to describe, or the pencil of a Dore to portray.

"Let us go home," said the doctor, looking at his watch. "It is now half past three. The temperature of the atmosphere is evidently rising. The chances are that it will become unbearable after sunrise. We must consider what is best to do."

We pushed our way back through the crowded streets, past despairing and terror-stricken men and wailing women; but as we passed the bulletin boards at the corner of Bush and Kearny streets, it was encouraging to mark that at least one earthly industry would continue to go on till the mechanism could run no longer, and that the world would, at any rate, get full particulars of its approaching doom, so long as wires could transmit them, compositors set them in type, and pressmen print them. I felt that the power and grandeur of the press had never been more fully exemplified than in the regular and ceaseless pulsations of its machinery as the daily issue was being thrown off, with the news that the other hemisphere was in conflagration, and that a few short hours would in all probability witness the same catastrophe in our own.

The last two wagons which had driven up with ice for the employees had been boarded and sacked by the thirsty mob, and, looking down into the pressroom as I entered the building, I could see the pressmen stripped to the waist in that terrible hot-air bath, while upstairs the telegraphic editor was in similar *deshabille,* with the additional feature of a wet towel bound round his temples. He motioned to the last dispatch from New York as I entered. I took it up and read as follows:

NEW YORK, 6 A.M. SUN JUST RISEN. HEAT TERRIBLE. AIR SUFFOCATING. PEOPLE SEEKING SHADE. THOUSANDS BATHING OFF THE DOCKS. THOUSANDS KILLED BY SUNSTROKE.

"Almost a recapitulation of the London message of three hours ago," I said, as I hurried out. "Three hours hence we may expect the same here."

I rejoined the doctor in the street, and together we proceeded to his apartments.

"Now," said he, as I told him the purport of the last message, "there is only one thing to be done if we wish to save our lives. It is a chance if even this plan will succeed, but at all events there *is* a chance."

"What is it?" I asked eagerly.

"I take it," answered he, "that the increase of heat and light which will accrue as soon as the sun rises above the horizon must prove fatal to all animal life beneath the influence of his beams. The population of Europe, and by this time, I doubt not, of all this country east of the Mississippi, is next to annihilated. With us it is but a question of time unless—"

"Unless what?" I exlaimed excitedly, as he paused meditatively.

"Unless we are willing to run a great risk," he added. "You are a philosopher enough to know that heat and light are simply modes of motion—expressions, so to speak, of the same molecular action of the elements they pass through or agitate. They have no intrinsic being in themselves, no entity, no existence, as it were, independent of outside matter. In their case the two forms of outside matter affected by them are the ether pervading space and the atmosphere of our planet. Do you follow?''

"Certainly,'' I replied, impatiently, for I dreaded one of the doctor's disquisitions at such a critical moment as this. "But my dear sir, what is the practical application of your theorem? How can we apply it to the case in point?''

"In this wise,'' he went on: "heat—that is, the heat we have to do with now—is caused by the action of the sun's rays upon our atmosphere. If we get beyond the limits of that atmosphere, what then? Simply, we have no heat. Ascend to a sufficient altitude, even under the cloudless rays of the vertical sun, and you will freeze to death. The limit of perpetual snow is not an extreme one.''

"I catch your idea perfectly,'' I assented. "I concede the accuracy of your premises. But what does it avail us? The Sierra Nevada mountains are practically as far off as the peaks of the Himalayas.''

"There are other means,'' rejoined the doctor, "of attaining the necessary altitude. A balloon ascension, as you are aware, was to have taken place today from Woodward's Gardens. I was going to assist at the inflation, to test a new method of generating gas. I now propose that we endeavor to gain possession of the balloon and make the ascension. I do not think we shall be anticipated or thwarted in doing so.

"We must remember that the risk of the balloon bursting, through the expansion of the gas, is great; for we shall be exposed, not only to its normal expansion, should we penetrate the upper atmospheric strata, but to its abnormal expansion through heat, should we fail to do so in time.''

"It is shaking the dice with Death in any case,'' I answered, and proceeded to assist the doctor in packing the apparatus and chemicals he had prepared overnight; and, having done so, we left the building and hastened southward along Market Street. The cars were not running, and the carriages we saw paid no heed to our importunities; so the precious time seemed to fly past, while we swiftly covered the mile which separated us from the gardens. The gates were luckily open, and none of the employees visible, so we made for the spot where the balloon, half-inflated, lay like some slimy antediluvian monster in its lair. We adjusted the apparatus and arranged the ropes as speedily as possible, and waited anxiously while the great bag slowly swelled and shook, rearing itself and falling back by turns, but gradually assuming more and more spherical proportions.

Meanwhile, we had again opportunity to observe the condition of the atmosphere and the heavens. It was already half past four, and in less than an hour the sun would spring up in the east. The pale, bluish tints of daybreak were beginning to assert themselves beside the lurid semicircle which flamed above them. This latter changed to a hard, coppery hue as daylight became stronger, but preserved its contour unchanged. The heat became more oppressive, the thermometer we had brought with us now registering 133 degrees. Strange sounds were wafted in from the city—meaningless, indeed, but rendered fearfully suggestive by the circumstances of the morning. The animals howled unceasingly from their cages, and we could hear their frantic struggles for liberty. One catlike form that had made good its escape shot past us in the gloom. Had the whole menagerie been set free at that moment, we should have had nothing to fear from them, so great is the influence elemental crises exert over the brute creation.

We had at last the satisfaciton of seeing the great globe swing clear of the ground, though not yet full inflated, and tug at the ropes which moored it. We had already placed the ballast-bags and other necessary articles in the car, when, perspiring at every pore, we simultaneously cut the last ropes, and rose heavily into the air. There was not a breath of wind stirring, but our course was guided slightly east in the direction of the bay.

It was now broad daylight, and the upper limb of the sun appeared above the horizon as we estimated our altitude from surrounding objects at about a thousand feet. As the full orb appeared the heat became more intense, and by the doctor's direction we swathed our heads in flannel, sprinkled sparingly with a preparation of ether and alcohol, the swift evaporation of which imparted coolness for a short time. The sky had now assumed the appearance of a vast brazen dome, and the waters of the ocean to the west and the bay beneath us reflected the dull, dead, pitiless glare with horrible fidelity. We had taken the precaution to hang heavy blankets upon the ropes sustaining the car, and these we kept sparingly moistened with water. Our own thirst was as intense as our perspiration was profuse, and we had divested ourselves of everything but our woolen underclothing—wool being a nonconductor, and therefore as effective in excluding heat as retaining it. We were provided with a powerful ship telescope, and also a large binocular glass of long range, and so far as the discomforts of the situation would permit us we took observations of the prospect beneath. To the unaided eye the city simply presented a patch of little rectangles at the end of a brown peninsula, but through our glasses the streets and houses became surprisingly plain. Little squat black forms were to be seen moving, falling down, and lying in the streets. Down by the city front the wharves were seen to be lined with nude, or seminude bodies, which dived into the water and remained submerged, with the exception of their heads, though these disappeared at short intervals below the surface. Thousands upon thousands of people were thus engaged. The spectacle would have been utterly absurd and ludicrous had it not been tremendous in its awful suggestiveness.

"The mortality will be terrible, I fear," said the doctor, "if things do not change for the better soon, and I see no prospect of that. Our thermometer already marks 147 degrees even at this altitude. We are in the *tepidarium* of a thrice-heated Turkish bath. And if this is the case at a barometric altitude of eleven thousand feet—nearly two perpendicular miles—what must it be down there? It is too terrible to contemplate!"

"It is only seven o'clock yet," I remarked, looking at my watch. "The sun is scarcely an hour high."

"We must throw out more ballast," said the doctor, "and reach the higher strata at all hazards." He threw out a forty-pound bag of sand.

We shot upward with tremendous velocity for several minutes, when our ascent again became regular. We now remarked, with intense relief, that the thermometer did not rise—that, in fact, it had fallen about two degrees; though this relief was counterbalanced by the extreme difficulty of breathing the rarefied air at this immense altitude, which we estimated by the barometer at twenty-five thousand feet, or nearly five perpendicular miles. We therefore opened the valve and discharged a quantity of gas, and presently descended into a stratum of dense fog. This fog reminded me of the steam which rises from tropical vegetation during the rainy season, and I mentioned the fact to the doctor.

"If these fogs," replied he, "would only rest upon the city, they might shield it from destruction, but in a case of this kind we have no meteorological data to go on. No one can estimate either the amount of heat or the meteorological results it is now producing on the surface of the earth five miles below us."

The stratum of fog in which we now were was dense and impenetrable. We lay in it as in a steam bath, the balloon not seeming to drift, but swaying sluggishly from side to side, like a sail flapping idly against a mast in a calm.

Hour after hour passed like this, the temperature still ranging from 130 to 140 degrees Fahrenheit. The doctor preserved his wonted equanimity.

"I have grave apprehensions," he remarked impressively, as if in answer to my thoughts, "that the final fiery cataclysm, a foreboding of which has run through all systems of philosophies and religions through all ages, and which seems to be, as it were, ingrained in the inner consciousness of man, is now upon us. I am determined, however, not to fall a victim to the fiery energy that has been evoked, and shall anticipate such a fate by an easier and less disagreeable one," and as he spoke he motioned significantly toward his right hip.

"Do you think, then," said I, "that an act under such circumstances"—designedly employing a vague periphrasis on such an unpleasant topic—"is morally defensible?"

"What can it matter?" returned the doctor, with a shrug. "Of two alternatives, both leading to the same end, common sense accepts the easier. A refusal to touch the hemlock would not have saved Socrates."

In spite of the terrible forebodings which filled me, the exigencies of the situation seemed to render my brain preternaturally concentrated and abnormally active. The surrounding stillness, the lack of sound of any description, the dreamy warmth of the dense mist in which we lay, exercised a sedative influence, and rendered the mind peculiarly impressionable to action from within.

"We have no means, then, of calculating the probable intensity of the heat at the earth's surface?" I asked.

"None whatever," replied the doctor. "We are now at an indicated elevation, by barometrical pressure, of twenty-two thousand feet. We are probably actually much higher, as the steam in which we lie is acting on the barometer. Atmospheric conditions like the present, at such an altitude, are totally beyond the experience of science. They might be, and probably are, caused by the action of intense heat upon hotter surfaces below us. To the fact of their presence, however, we owe our existence. This atmosphere, though peculiarly favorable to the passage of heat rays through it, is incapable of retaining them.''

''Supposing,'' I went on, in a wildly speculative mood, engendered by the excitement of the occasion, ''supposing that the heat of the surface of the earth were sufficiently intense to melt metals—iron, for instance—the most refractory substances, in fact. Take a further flight: supposing that such heat were ten times intensified, what would be its effect upon our planet?''

''The solid portions—the crust with everything upon it—would be the first to experience the effects of such a catastrophe. Then the oceans would boil, and their surface waters, at any rate, be converted into steam.''

''What then?'' I continued.

''This steam would ascend to the upper regions of the atmosphere till it reached an equilibrium of rarefaction, when its expansion would cool it, upon which rapid condensation would follow, and it would descend to earth in the form of rain. The more sudden and energetic the heat, the sooner would this result be accomplished, and the more copious the precipitation of the succeeding rain. After the first terrible crisis, the grand compensation of natural law would come into play, and the face of the planet would be protected from further harm by the shield of humid vapor—the *vis medicatrix naturae,* so to speak. Equilibrium would be restored, but most organisms would meanwhile have perished.''

''Most organisms, you say?'' I repeated, inquiringly.

''It is possible,'' said the doctor, ''that ocean infusoria, and even some of the comparatively higher forms of ocean life, might survive. It is also possible that terrestrial animals occupying high altitudes—mountaineers for example, whose homes are deep snows and glaciers, denizens of the frozen zone, and beings similarly situated—might escape. This would altogether depend upon the intensity and duration of the heat. We must remember that *size,* looked at from a universal point of view, is merely relative. If we consider our planet as a six-inch ball, our oceans, with their insignificant average depth of a few miles, would be aptly represented by a film of the finest writing paper. How long, think you, would a watery film, such as that, last a few feet from a suddenly stirred fire?''

I bowed acquiescence to the conclusion drawn from the simile, and the doctor proceeded:

"There can be no longer any doubt that the present elemental convulsion is due to the collision of the comet with the sun. Knowing what we do of its orbit from last year's computation, its precipitation upon the solar surface has taken place on the side farthest from our own position in space. We do not, therefore, experience so sudden and so fierce atmospherical excitement as would otherwise have followed. It now remains to be seen what the duration of the effect will be."

During the latter portion of our conversation a low moaning sound, which had been heard for the past few minutes, was growing more pronounced and seemingly coming nearer. At the same time the barometer was observed to be falling rapidly.

"That is the sound of wind," I exclaimed. "I have heard it on tropical deserts and on tropical seas. I can not be mistaken. It comes from the east."

"The hot air from the parched continent is approaching," said the doctor. "Scientifically speaking, atmospheric convection is taking place, and we shall bear the brunt of it."

As he spoke the balloon was seized with a violent tremor. It vibrated from apex to car, and the next moment was struck by the most terrific tornado it is possible to imagine. The blast was like the torrid breath of a furnace, and we involuntarily covered our heads with our blankets, and clutched convulsively to the frail bulwarks of the car, which was being dragged on at a tremendous velocity, and at a horribly acute angle, by the distended gas-bag which towered ahead of us. Luckily we had both clutched mechanically at the railing on the side whence the wind came, to let go which hold would have meant instant precipitation over the opposite side of the car into the yawning gulf beneath. For less than a minute, so far as my stricken and scattered senses could compute, we were borne on by this terrific simoom, when, suddenly, we found ourselves as before, in the midst of a preternatural calm. We had evidently drifted into an eddy of the cyclone; for I could hear its sullen and awful roar at some distance to our right. Hardly had we composed ourselves when the blast struck us again; this time on the opposite side of the car. Again we were hurled forward by the resistless elemental fury; but this time in a sensibly downward direction. The blast had struck us from above, and was hurling us before it—down, down, to inevitable destruction. Fortunately the comparative bulk of the balloon offered more resistance than the car to this downward progress. Down, down we sped, till, of a sudden, we emerged from the cloud-strata and obtained a brief and abrupt glimpse of the scene below. The counterblasts of the past few minutes had apparently compensated each other's action, for we found ourselves just over the city.

The city? There was no city. I recognized, indeed, the contour of the peninsula, and the well-known outlines of the bay and islands, through casual rifts in the dense clouds of steam which rose in volumes from below. Well-nigh stupefied and maddened as I was by the intense heat, a horrible curiosity seized me to peer into the dread mystery beneath, and while with one scorched and writhing hand I held the blankets, which had not yet parted with the moisture gathered from the clouds above, to my aching head and temples, with the other I raised the powerful binocular to my eyes, I caught glimpses which filled me with unutterable and nameless horror. Neither streets nor buildings were decipherable where the city once had been. The eye rested upon nothing but irregular and misshapen piles of vitrified slag and calcined ashes. Everything was as scarred in a ruinous silence as the ruined surface of the moon. There was neither flame nor fire to be seen. Things seemed to have long passed the stage of active combustion, as though all the elements necessary to sustain flame had already been abstracted from them. Here and there an ominous dark-red glow showed, however, that the lava into which the fair city had been transformed was still incandescent. The sand dunes to the west shone like glaciers or dull mirrors through the steam fissures, and long shapeless masses of what resembled charred wood were strewn here and there over the surface of the bay. Less than five seconds served to reveal all that I have taken so long to describe. The binocular, too hot to hold, dropped from my hand. At the same moment the balloon was again struck by the cyclone, and dashed eastward with the same fury as before. The doctor caught convulsively at the railing of the car, missed his hold, and with a wild, despairing shriek, outstretched arms, and starting eyes fixed upon mine, disappeared headlong in the abyss.

I am alone in the balloon—perhaps alone in the world. My companion has been hurled to a fiery death below. His awful shriek still rings in my ears. It sounds over the sullen roar of the cyclone. I am whirled resistlessly onward.

The blast shifts. Again the balloon pauses in one of the strange eddies formed by this strange simoom. The wind dies away to a moan. It rises again. It writhes around the car like the convulsive struggles of some gigantic reptile in the throes of death. It seizes me again in its resistless clutch. The balloon is being whirled toward the earth.

I am falling. But no—it seemed to me that the earth—the plutonic, igneous earth—is rising toward me. With lightning-like rapidity it seems to hurl itself up through the air to meet me. I hear the roar of flames mingling with the roar of the blast. I see the seething, bubbling waste of waters through rifts in the clouds of steam.

I am nearing the molten surface. My feeling has changed. I am conscious that it has ceased to seem to rise. I feel that I am falling now—falling into the fiery depths below. Nearer—nearer yet; scorched and blackened by the awful heat as I approach—I fall-down—down—down—

Frank R. Stockton (1834–1902)

During his lifetime Frank R. Stockton was such a popular writer that a twenty-three volume edition of his collected writings was published between 1899 and 1904. And much of what he wrote was science fiction or fantasy. Today, however, he is remembered primarily for his classic short story "The Lady or the Tiger?" (1882).

Born and educated in Philadelphia, Stockton's family expected him to pursue a medical career after graduating from high school. Instead, he spent fourteen years, from 1852 to 1866, working as a wood engraver. But as time went on literature increasingly absorbed his attention, and in 1859 he began selling stories to magazines such as the *Southern Literary Messenger,* the *Riverside Magazine for Young People,* and *Hearth and Home,* eventually specializing in humorous short fantasies for children.

When *St. Nicholas Magazine* for children started in 1873, Stockton became assistant editor and worked there for eight years before deciding, probably because of *Rudder Grange's* popular reception in 1879, to become a full-time writer.

For a number of years thereafter he lived in the quiet rural settings of Nutley and Convent Station, New Jersey, where he often dictated first drafts from the depths of a comfortable hammock. Still, he enjoyed traveling and the smashing success of such works as "The Lady or the Tiger?" and *The Casting Away of Mrs. Lecks and Mrs. Aleshine* (1886) allowed him to do so extensively.

Stockton's writings exude his personal characteristics—raconteur and ironic, witty, whimsical, gentle companion. Entertainment is primary and rarely disturbed by any message he chooses to present. Indeed, modern science-fiction fans may find him somewhat of a cross between Clifford D. Simak and Eric Frank Russell.

Although Stockton wrote four science-fiction novels—*The Great War Syndicate* (1889), *The Vizier of the Two-Horned Alexander* (1889), *The Adventures of Captain Horn* (1895), and *The Great Stone of Sardis* (1898)—his strength lay in short stories, some of which have been recently collected in *The Science Fiction of Frank R. Stockton* (1976). Always a meticulous craftsman, he sometimes labored an hour to revise just one word. But his shorter works wear better because in them he was also able to highlight on personal reactions to science and to generate humor that did not have to be sustained.

In the late 1890's Stockton bought a house near Harper's Ferry, West Virginia, where he lived for a few years until his death in Washington, D.C., in 1902.

A TALE OF NEGATIVE GRAVITY

M y wife and I were staying at a small town in northern Italy; and on a certain pleasant afternoon in spring we had taken a walk of six or seven miles to see the sun set behind some low mountains to the west of the town. Most of our walk had been along a hard, smooth highway, and then we turned into a series of narrower roads, sometimes bordered by walls, and sometimes by light fences of reed or cane. Nearing the mountain, to a low spur of which we intended to ascend, we easily scaled a wall about four feet high, and found ourselves upon pastureland, which led, sometimes by gradual ascents, and sometimes by bits of rough climbing, to the spot we wished to reach. We were afraid we were a little late, and therefore hurried on, running up the grassy hills, and bounding briskly over the rough and rocky places. I carried a knapsack strapped firmly to my shoulders, and under my wife's arm was a large, soft basket of a kind much used by tourists. Her arm was passed through the handles and around the bottom of the basket, which she pressed closely to her side. This was the way she always carried it. The basket contained two bottles of wine, one sweet for my wife, and another a little acid for myself. Sweet wines give me a headache.

When we reached the grassy bluff, well known thereabouts to lovers of sunset views, I stepped immediately to the edge to gaze upon the scene, but my wife sat down to take a sip of wine, for she was very thirsty; and then, leaving her basket, she came to my side. The scene was indeed one of great beauty. Beneath us stretched a wide valley of many shades of green, with a little river running through it, and red-tiled houses here and there. Beyond rose a range of mountains, pink, pale green, and purple where their tips caught the reflection of the setting sun,

151

and of a rich gray-green in shadows. Beyond all was the blue Italian sky, illumined by an especially fine sunset.

My wife and I are Americans, and at the time of this story were middle-aged people and very fond of seeing in each other's company whatever there was of interest or beauty around us. We had a son about twenty-two years old, of whom we were also very fond; but he was not with us, being at that time a student in Germany. Although we had good health, we were not very robust people, and, under ordinary circumstances, not much given to long country tramps. I was of medium size, without much muscular development, while my wife was quite stout, and growing stouter.

The reader may, perhaps, be somewhat surprised that a middle-aged couple, not very strong, or very good walkers, the lady loaded with a basket containing two bottles of wine and a metal drinking-cup, and the gentleman carrying a heavy knapsack, filled with all sorts of odds and ends, strapped to his shoulders, should set off on a seven-mile walk, jump over a wall, run up a hillside, and yet feel in very good trim to enjoy a sunset view. This peculiar state of things I will proceed to explain.

I had been a professional man, but some years before had retired upon a very comfortable income. I had always been very fond of scientific pursuits, and now made these the occupation and pleasure of much of my leisure time. Our home was in a small town; and in a corner of my grounds I built a laboratory, where I carried on my work and my experiments. I had long been anxious to discover the means not only of producing, but of retaining and controlling, a natural force, really the same as centrifugal force, but which I called negative gravity. This name I adopted because it indicated better than any other the action of the force in question, as I produced it. Positive gravity attracts everything toward the center of the earth. Negative gravity, therefore, would be that power which repels everything from the center of the earth, just as the negative pole of a magnet repels the needle, while the positive pole attracts it. My object was, in fact, to store centrifugal force and to render it constant, controllable, and available for use. The advantages of such a discovery could scarcely be described. In a word, it would lighten the burdens of the world.

I will not touch upon the labors and disappointments of several years. It is enough to say that at last I discovered a method of producing, storing, and controlling negative gravity.

The mechanism of my invention was rather complicated, but the method of operating it was very simple. A strong metallic case, about eight inches long, and half as wide, contained the machinery for producing the force; and this was put into action by means of the pressure of a screw worked from the outside. As soon as this pressure was produced, negative gravity began to be evolved and stored, and the greater the pressure the greater the force. As the screw was moved outward, and the pressure diminished, the force decreased, and when the screw was withdrawn to its fullest extent, the action of negative gravity entirely ceased. Thus this force could be produced or dissipated at will to such degrees as might be desired, and its action, so long as the requisite pressure was maintained, was constant.

When this little apparatus worked to my satisfaction I called my wife into my laboratory and explained to her my invention and its value. She had known that I had been at work with an important object, but I had never told her what it was. I had said that if I succeeded I would tell her all, but if I failed she need not be troubled with the matter at all. Being a very sensible woman, this satisfied her perfectly. Now I explained everything to her—the construction of the machine, and the wonderful uses to which this invention could be applied. I told her that it could diminish, or entirely dissipate, the weight of objects of any kind. A heavily loaded wagon, with two of these instruments fastened to its sides, and each screwed to a proper force, would be so lifted and supported that it would press upon the ground as lightly as an empty cart, and a small horse could draw it with ease. A bale of cotton, with one of these machines attached, could be handled and carried by a boy. A car, with a number of these machines, could be made to rise in the air like a balloon. Everything, in fact, that was heavy could be made light; and as a great part of labor, all over the world, is caused by the attraction of gravitation, so this repellent force, wherever applied, would make weight less and work easier. I told her of many, many ways in which the invention might be used, and would have told her of many more if she had not suddenly burst into tears.

"The world has gained something wonderful," she exclaimed, between her sobs, "but I have lost a husband!"

"What do you mean by that?" I asked, in surprise.

"I haven't minded so far," she said, "because it gave you something to do, and it pleased you, and it never interfered with our home pleasures and our home life. But now that is all over. You will never be your own master again. It will succeed, I am sure, and you may make a great deal of money, but we don't need money. What we need is the happiness which we have always had until now. Now there will be companies, and patents, and lawsuits, and experiments, and people calling you a humbug, and other people saying they discovered it long ago, and all sorts of persons coming to see you, and you'll be obliged to go to all sorts of places, and you will be an altered man, and we shall never be happy again. Millions of money will not repay us for the happiness we have lost."

These words of my wife struck me with much force. Before I had called her my mind had begun to be filled and perplexed with ideas of what I ought to do now that the great invention was perfected. Until now the matter had not troubled me at all. Sometimes I had gone backward and sometimes forward, but, on the whole, I had always felt encouraged. I had taken great pleasure in the work, but I had never allowed myself to be too much absorbed by it. But now everything was different. I began to feel that it was due to myself and to my fellow-beings that I should properly put this invention before the world. And how should I set about it? What steps should I take? I must make no mistakes. When the matter should become known hundreds of scientific people might set themselves to work; how could I tell but that they might discover other methods of producing the same effect? I must guard myself against a great many things. I must get patents in all parts of the world. Already, as I have said, my mind began to be troubled and perplexed with these things. I could not but agree with my wife that the joys of a quiet and contented life were now about to be broken into.

"My dear," said I, "I believe, with you, that the thing will do us more harm than good. If it were not for depriving the world of the invention I would throw the whole thing to the winds. And yet," I added, regretfully, "I had expected a great deal of personal gratification from the use of this invention."

"Now listen," said my wife, eagerly; "don't you think it would be best to do this: use the thing as much as you please for your own amusement and satisfction, but let the world wait? It has waited a long time, and let it wait a little longer. When we are dead let Herbert have the invention. He will then be old enough to judge for himself whether it will be better to take advantage of it for his own profit, or simply to give it to the public for nothing. It would be cheating him if we were to do the latter, but it would also be doing him a great wrong if we were, at his age, to load him with such a heavy responsibility. Besides, if he took it up, you could not help going into it, too.''

I took my wife's advice. I wrote a careful and complete account of the invention, and sealing it up, I gave it to my lawyers to be handed to my son after my death. If he died first, I would make other arrangements. Then I determined to get all the good and fun out of the thing that was possible without telling anyone anything about it. Even Herbert, who was away from home, was not to be told of the invention.

The first thing I did was to buy a strong leathern knapsack, and inside of this I fastened my little machine, with a screw so arranged that it could be worked from the outside. Strapping this firmly to my shoulders, my wife gently turned the screw at the back until the upward tendency of the knapsack began to lift and sustain me. When I felt myself so gently supported and upheld that I seemed to weigh about thirty or forty pounds, I would set out for a walk. The knapsack did not raise me from the ground, but it gave me a very buoyant step. It was no labor at all to walk; it was a delight, an ecstasy. With the strength of a man and the weight of a child, I gaily strode along. The first day I walked half a dozen miles at a very brisk pace, and came back without feeling in the least degree tired. These walks now became one of the greatest joys of my life. When nobody was looking, I would bound over a fence, sometimes just touching it with one hand, and sometimes not touching it at all. I delighted in rough places. I sprang over streams. I jumped and I ran. I felt like Mercury himself.

I now set about making another machine, so that my wife could accompany me in my walks; but when it was finished she positively refused to use it. ''I can't wear a knapsack,'' she said, ''and there is no other good way of fastening it to me. Besides, everybody about here knows I am no walker, and it would only set them talking.''

I occasionally made use of this second machine, but I will give only one instance of its application. Some repairs were needed to the foundation-walls of my barn, and a two-horse wagon, loaded with building-stone, had been brought into my yard and left there. In the evening, when the men had gone away, I took my two machines and fastened them, with strong chains, one on each side of the loaded wagon. Then, gradually turning the screws, the wagon was so lifted that its weight became very greatly diminished. We had an old donkey which used to belong to Herbert, and which was now occasionally used with a small cart to bring packages from the station. I went into the barn and put the harness on the little fellow, and, bringing him out to the wagon, I attached him to it. In this position he looked very funny with a long pole sticking out in front of him and the great wagon behind him. When all was ready I touched him up; and, to my great delight, he moved off with the two-horse load of stone as easily as if he were drawing his own cart. I led him out into the public road, along which he proceeded without difficulty. He was an opinionated little beast, and sometimes stopped, not liking the peculiar manner in which he was harnessed; but a touch of the switch made him move on, and I soon turned him and brought the wagon back into the yard. This determined the success of my invention in one of its most important uses, and with a satisfied heart I put the donkey into the stable and went into the house.

Our trip to Europe was made a few months after this, and was mainly on our son Herbert's account. He, poor fellow, was in great trouble, and so, therefore, were we. He had become engaged, with our full consent, to a young lady in our town, the daughter of a gentleman whom we esteemed very highly. Herbert was young to be engaged to be married, but as we felt that he would never find a girl to make him so good a wife, we were entirely satisfied, especially as it was agreed on all hands that the marriage was not to take place for some time. It seemed to us that, in marrying Janet Gilbert, Herbert would secure for himself, in the very beginning of his career, the most important element of a happy life. But suddenly, without any reason that seemed to us justifiable, Mr. Gilbert, the only surviving parent of Janet, broke off the match; and he and his daughter soon after left the town for a trip to the West.

This blow nearly broke poor Herbert's heart. He gave up his professional studies and came home to us, and for a time we thought he would be seriously ill. Then we took him to Europe, and after a Continental tour of a month or two we left him, at his own request, in Göttingen, where he thought it would do him good to go to work again. Then we went down to the little town in Italy where my story first finds us. My wife had suffered much in mind and body on her son's account, and for this reason I was anxious that she should take outdoor exercise, and enjoy as much as possible the bracing air of the country. I had brought with me both my little machines. One was still in my knapsack, and the other I had fastened to the inside of an enormous family trunk. As one is obliged to pay for nearly every pound of his baggage on the Continent, this saved me a great deal of money. Everything heavy was packed into this great trunk—books, papers, the bronze, iron, and marble relics we had picked up, and all the articles that usually weigh down a tourist's baggage. I screwed up the negative-gravity apparatus until the trunk could be handled with great ease by an ordinary porter. I could have made it weigh nothing at all, but this, of course, I did not wish to do. The lightness of my baggage, however, had occasioned some comment, and I had overheard remarks which were not altogether complimentary about people traveling around with empty trunks; but this only amused me.

Desirous that my wife should have the advantage of negative gravity while taking our walks, I had removed the machine from the trunk and fastened it inside of the basket, which she could carry under her arm. This assisted her wonderfully. When one arm was tired she put the basket under the other, and thus, with one hand on my arm, she could easily keep up with the free and buoyant steps my knapsack enabled me to take. She did not object to long tramps here, because nobody knew that she was not a walker, and she always carried some wine or other refreshment in the basket, not only because it was pleasant to have it with us, but because it seemed ridiculous to go about carrying an empty basket.

There were English-speaking people staying at the hotel where we were, but they seemed more fond of driving than walking, and none of them offered to accompany us on our rambles, for which we were very glad. There was one man there, however, who was a great walker. He was an Englishman, a member of an Alpine Club, and generally went about dressed in a knickerbocker suit, with gray woolen stockings covering an enormous pair of calves. One evening this gentleman was talking to me and some others about the ascent of the Matterhorn, and I took occasion to deliver in pretty strong language my opinion upon such exploits. I declared them to be useless, foolhardy, and, if the climber had any one who loved him, wicked.

"Even if the weather should permit a view," I said, "what is that compared to the terrible risk to life? Under certain circumstances," I added (thinking of a kind of waistcoat I had some idea of making, which, set about with little negative-gravity machines, all connected with a conveniently handled screw, would enable the wearer at times to dispense with his weight altogether), "such ascents might be divested of danger, and be quite admissible; but ordinarily they should be frowned upon by the intelligent public."

The Alpine Club man looked at me, especially regarding my somewhat slight figure and thinnish legs.

"It's all very well for you to talk that way," he said, "because it is easy to see that you are not up to that sort of thing."

"In conversations of this kind," I replied, "I never make personal allusions; but since you have chosen to do so, I feel inclined to invite you to walk with me tomorrow to the top of the mountain to the north of this town."

"I'll do it," he said, "at any time you choose to name." And as I left the room soon afterward I heard him laugh.

The next afternoon, about two o'clock, the Alpine Club man and myself set out for the mountain.

"What have you got in your knapsack?" he said.

"A hammer to use if I come across geological specimens, a field glass, a flask of wine, and some other things."

"I wouldn't carry any weight, if I were you," he said.

"Oh, I don't mind it," I answered, and off we started.

The mountain to which we were bound was about two miles from the town. Its nearest side was steep, and in places almost precipitous, but it sloped away more gradually toward the north, and up that side a road led by devious windings to a village near the summit. It was not a very high mountain, but it would do for an afternoon's climb.

"I suppose you want to go up by the road," said my companion.

"Oh no," I answered, "we won't go so far around as that. There is a path up this side, along which I have seen men driving their goats. I prefer to take that."

"All right, if you say so," he answered, with a smile; "but you'll find it pretty tough."

After a time he remarked:

"I wouldn't walk so fast, if I were you."

"Oh, I like to step along briskly," I said. And briskly on we went.

My wife had screwed up the machine in the knapsack more than usual, and walking seemed scarcely any affort at all. I carried a long alpenstock, and when we reached the mountain and began the ascent, I found that with the help of this and my knapsack I could go uphill at a wonderful rate. My companion had taken the lead, so as to show me how to climb. Making a detour over some rocks, I quickly passed him and went ahead. After that it was impossible for him to keep up with me. I ran up steep places, I cut off the windings of the path by lightly clambering over rocks, and even when I followed the beaten track my step was as rapid as if I had been walking on level ground.

"Look here!" shouted the Alpine Club man from below, "you'll kill yourself if you go at that rate! That's no way to climb mountains."

"It's my way!" I cried. And on I skipped.

Twenty minutes after I arrived at the summit my companion joined me, puffing, and wiping his red face with his handkerchief.

"Confound it!" he cried, "I never came up a mountain so fast in my life."

"You need not have hurried," I said, coolly.

"I was afraid something would happen to you," he growled, "and I wanted to stop you. I never saw a person climb in such an utterly absurd way."

"I don't see why you should call it absurd," I said, smiling with an air of superiority. "I arrived her in a perfectly comfortable condition, neither heated nor wearied."

He made no answer, but walked off to a little distance, fanning himself with his hat and growling words which I did not catch. After a time I proposed to descend.

"You must be careful as you go down," he said. "It is much more dangerous to go down steep places than to climb up."

"I am always prudent," I answered, and started in advance. I found the descent of the mountain much more pleasant than the ascent. It was positively exhilarating. I jumped from rocks and bluffs eight and ten feet in height, and touched the ground as gently as if I had stepped down but two feet. I ran down steep paths, and, with the aid of my alpenstock, stopped myself in an instant. I was careful to avoid dangerous places, but the runs and jumps I made were such as no man had ever made before upon that mountainside. Once only I heard my companion's voice.

"You'll break your——neck!" he yelled.

"Never fear!" I called back, and soon left him far above.

When I reached the bottom I would have waited for him, but my activity had warmed me up, and as a cool evening breeze was beginning to blow I thought it better not to stop and take cold. Half an hour after my arrival at the hotel I came down to the court, cool, fresh, and dressed for dinner, and just in time to meet the Alpine man as he entered, hot, dusty, and growling.

"Excuse me for not waiting for you," I said; but without stopping to hear my reason, he muttered something about waiting in a place where no one would care to stay, and passed into the house.

There was no doubt that what I had done gratified my pique and tickled my vanity.

"I think now," I said, when I related the matter to my wife, "that he will scarcely say that I am not up to that sort of thing."

"I am not sure," she answered, "that it was exactly fair. He did not know how you were assisted."

"I was fair enough," I said. "He is enabled to climb well by the inherited vigor of his constitution and by his training. He did not tell me what methods of exercise he used to get those great muscles upon his legs. I am enabled to climb by the exercise of my intellect. My method is my business and his method is his business. It is all perfectly fair."

Still she persisted:

"He *thought* that you climbed with your legs, and not with your head."

And now, after this long digression, necessary to explain how a middle-aged couple of slight pedestrian ability, and loaded with a heavy knapsack and basket, should have started out on a rough walk and climb, fourteen miles in all, we will return to ourselves, standing on the little bluff and gazing out upon the sunset view. When the sky began to fade a little we turned from it and prepared to go back to the town.

'Where is the basket?" I said.

"I left it right here," answered my wife. "I unscrewed the machine and it lay perfectly flat."

"Did you afterward take out the bottles?" I asked, seeing them lying on the grass.

"Yes, I believe I did. I had to take out yours in order to get at mine."

"Then," said I, after looking all about the grassy patch on which we stood, "I am afraid you did not entirely unscrew the instrument, and that when the weight of the bottles was removed the basket gently rose into the air."

"It may be so," she said, lugubriously. "The basket was behind me as I drank my wine."

"I believe that is just what has happened," I said. "Look up there! I vow that is our basket!"

I pulled out my field glass and directed it at a little speck high above our heads. It was the basket floating high in the air. I gave the glass to my wife to look, but she did not want to use it.

"What shall I do?" she cried. "I can't walk home without that basket. It's perfectly dreadful!" And she looked as if she was going to cry.

"Do not distress yourself," I said, although I was a good deal disturbed myself. "We shall get home very well. You shall put your hand on my shoulder, while I put my arm around you, then you can screw up my machine a good deal higher, and it will support us both. In this way I am sure that we shall get on very well."

We carried out this plan, and managed to walk on with moderate comfort. To be sure, with the knapsack pulling me upward, and the weight of my wife pulling me down, the straps hurt me somewhat, which they had not done before. We did not spring lightly over the wall into the road, but, still clinging to each other, we clambered awkwardly over it. The road for the most part declined gently toward the town, and with moderate ease we made our way along it. But we walked much more slowly than we had done before, and it was quite dark when we reached our hotel. If it had not been for the light inside the court it would have been difficult for us to find it. A traveling-carriage was standing before the entrance, and my wife went first. I attempted to follow her, but, strange to say, there was nothing under my feet. I stepped vigorously, but only wagged my legs in the air. To my horror I found that I was rising in the air! I soon saw, by the light below me, that I was some fifteen feet from the ground. The carriage drove away, and in the darkness I was not noticed. Of course I knew what had happened. The instrument in my knapsack had been screwed up to such an intensity, in order to support both myself and my wife, that when her weight was removed the force of the negative gravity was sufficient to raise me from the ground. But I was glad to find that when I had risen to the height I have mentioned I did not go up any higher, but hung in the air, about on a level with the second tier of windows of the hotel.

I now began to try to reach the screw in my knapsack in order to reduce the force of the negative gravity; but, do what I would, I could not get my hand to it. The machine in the knapsack had been placed so as to support me in a well-balanced and comfortable way; and in doing this it had been impossible to set the screw so that I could reach it. But in a temporary arrangement of this kind this had not been considered necessary, as my wife always turned the screw for me until sufficient lifting power had been attained. I had intended, as I have said before, to construct a negative-gravity waistcoat, in which the screw should be in front, and entirely under the wearer's control; but this was a thing of the future.

When I found that I could not turn the screw I began to be much alarmed. Here I was, dangling in the air, without any means of reaching the ground. I could not expect my wife to return to look for me, as she would naturally suppose I had stopped to speak to someone. I thought of loosening myself from the knapsack, but this would not do, for I should fall heavily, and either kill myself or break some of my bones. I did not dare to call for assistance, for if any of the simpleminded inhabitants of the town had discovered me floating in the air they would have taken me for a demon, and would probably have shot at me. A moderate breeze was blowing, and it wafted me gently down the street. If it had blown me against a tree I would have seized it, and have endeavored, so to speak, to climb down it; but there were no trees. There was a dim streetlamp here and there, but reflectors above them threw their light upon the pavement, and none up to me. On many accounts I was glad that the night was so dark, for, much as I desired to get down, I wanted no one to see me in my strange position, which, to anyone but myself and wife, would be utterly unaccountable. If I could rise as high as the roofs I might get on one of them, and, tearing off an armful of tiles, so load myself that I would be heavy enough to descend. But I did not rise to the eaves of any of the houses. If there had been a telegraph pole, or anything of the kind that I could have clung to, I would have taken off the knapsack, and would have endeavored to scramble down as well as I could. But there was nothing I could cling to. Even the waterspouts, if I could have reached the face of the houses, were embedded in the walls. At an open window, near which I was slowly blown, I saw two little boys going to bed by the light of a dim candle. I was dreadfully afraid that they would see me and raise an alarm. I actually came so near to the window that I threw out one foot and pushed against the wall with such force that I went nearly across the street. I thought I caught sight of a frightened look on the face of one of the boys; but of this I am not sure, and I heard no cries. I still floated, dangling, down the street. What was to be done? Should I call out? In that case, if I were not shot or stoned, my strange predicament, and the secret of my invention, would be exposed to the world. If I did not do this, I must either drop and be killed or mangled, or hang there and die. When, during the course of the night, the air became more rarefied, I might rise higher and higher, perhaps to an altitude of one or two hundred feet. It would then be impossible for the people to reach me and get me down, even if they were convinced that I was not a demon. I should then expire, and when the birds of the air had eaten all of me that they could devour, I should forever hang above the unlucky town, a dangling skeleton with a knapsack on its back.

Such thoughts were not reassuring, and I determined that if I could find no means of getting down without assistance, I would call out and run all risks; but so long as I could endure the tension of the straps I would hold out, and hope for a tree or a pole. Perhaps it might rain, and my wet clothes would then become so heavy that I would descend as low as the top of a lamppost.

As this thought was passing through my mind I saw a spark of light upon the street approaching me. I rightly imagined that it came from a tobacco pipe, and presently I heard a voice. It was that of the Alpine Club man. Of all people in the world I did not want him to discover me, and I hung as motionless as possible. The man was speaking to another person who was walking with him.

"He is crazy beyond a doubt," said the Alpine man. "Nobody but a maniac could have gone up and down that mountain as he did! He hasn't any muscles, and one need only look at him to know that he couldn't do any climbing in a natural way. It is only the excitement of insanity that gives him strength."

The two now stopped almost under me, and the speaker continued:

"Such things are very common with maniacs. At times they acquire an unnatural strength which is perfectly wonderful. I have seen a little fellow struggle and fight so that four strong men could not hold him."

Then the other person spoke.

"I am afraid what you say is too true," he remarked. "Indeed, I have known it for some time."

At these words my breath almost stopped. It was the voice of Mr. Gilbert, my townsman, and the father of Janet. It must have been he who had arrived in the traveling-carriage. He was acquainted with the Alpine Club man, and they were talking of me. Proper or improper, I listened with all my ears.

"It is a very sad case," Mr. Gilbert continued. "My daughter was engaged to marry his son, but I broke off the match. I could not have her marry the son of a lunatic, and there could be no doubt of his condition. He has been seen—a man of his age, and the head of a family—to load himself up with a heavy knapsack, which there was no earthly necessity for him to carry, and go skipping along the road for miles, vaulting over fences and jumping over rocks and ditches like a young calf or a colt. I myself saw a most heartrending instance of how a kindly man's nature can be changed by the derangement of his intellect. I was at some distance from his house, but I plainly saw him harness a little donkey which he owns to a large two-horse wagon loaded with stone, and beat and lash the poor little beast until it drew the heavy load some distance along the public road. I would have remonstrated with him on this horrible cruelty, but he had the wagon back in his yard before I could reach him."

"Oh, there can be no doubt of his insanity," said the Alpine Club man, "and he oughtn't to be allowed to travel about in this way. Some day he will pitch his wife over a precipice just for the fun of seeing her shoot through the air."

"I am sorry he is here," said Mr. Gilbert, "for it would be very painful to meet him. My daughter and I will retire very soon, and go away as early tomorrow morning as possible, so as to avoid seeing him."

And then they walked back to the hotel.

For a few moments I hung, utterly forgetful of my condition, and absorbed in the consideration of these revelations. One idea now filled my mind. Everything must be explained to Mr. Gilbert, even if it should be necessary to have him called to me, and for me to speak to him from the upper air.

Just then I saw something white approaching me along the road. My eyes had become accustomed to the darkness, and I perceived that it was an upturned face. I recognized the hurried gait, the form; it was my wife. As she came near me, I called her name, and in the same breath entreated her not to scream. It must have been an effort for her to restrain herself, but she did it.

"You must help me to get down," I said, "without anybody seeing us."

"What shall I do?" she whispered.

"Try to catch hold of this string."

Taking a piece of twine from my pocket, I lowered one end to her. But it was too short; she could not reach it. I then tied my handkerchief to it, but still it was not long enough.

"I can get more string, or handkerchiefs," she whispered, hurriedly.

"No," I said; "you could not get them up to me. But, leaning against the hotel wall, on this side, in the corner, just inside of the garden gate, are some fishing poles. I have seen them there every day. You can easily find them in the dark. Go, please, and bring me one of those."

The hotel was not far away, and in a few minutes my wife returned with a fishing pole. She stood on tiptoe, and reached it high in the air; but all she could do was to strike my feet and legs with it. My most frantic exertions did not enable me to get my hands low enough to touch it.

"Wait a minute," she said; and the rod was withdrawn.

I knew what she was doing. There was a hook and line attached to the pole and with womanly dexterity she was fastening the hook to the extreme end of the rod. Soon she reached up, and gently struck at my legs. After a few attempts the hook caught in my trousers, a little below my right knee. Then there was a slight pull, a long scratch down my leg, and the hook was stopped by the top of my boot. Then came a steady downward pull, and I felt myself descending. Gently and firmly the rod was drawn down; carefully the lower end was kept free from the ground; and in a few moments my ankle was seized with a vigorous grasp. Then someone seemed to climb up me, my feet touched the ground, an arm was thrown around my neck, the hand of another arm was busy at the back of my knapsack, and I soon stood firmly in the road, entirely divested of my negative gravity.

"Oh that I should have forgotten," sobbed my wife, "and that I should have dropped your arms and let you go up into the air! At first I thought that you had stayed below, and it was only a little while ago that the truth flashed upon me. Then I rushed out and began looking up for you. I knew that you had wax matches in your pocket, and hoped that you would keep on striking them, so that you would be seen."

"But I did not wish to be seen," I said, as we hurried to the hotel; "and I can never be sufficiently thankful that it was you who found me and brought me down. Do you know that it is Mr. Gilbert and his daughter who have just arrived? I must see him instantly. I will explain it all to you when I come upstairs."

I took off my knapsack and gave it to my wife, who carried it to our room, while I went to look for Mr. Gilbert. Fortunately I found him just as he was about to go up to his chamber. He took my offered hand, but looked at me sadly and gravely.

"Mr. Gilbert," I said, "I must speak to you in private. Let us step into this room. There is no one here."

"My friend," said Mr. Gilbert, "it will be much better to avoid discussing this subject. It is very painful to both of us, and no good can come from talking of it."

"You cannot now comprehend what it is I want to say to you," I replied. "Come in here, and in a few minutes you will be very glad that you listened to me."

My manner was so earnest and impressive that Mr. Gilbert was constrained to follow me, and we went into a small room called the smoking-room, but in which people seldom smoked, and closed the door. I immediately began my statement. I told my old friend that I had discovered, by means that I need not explain at present, that he had considered me crazy, and that now the most important object of my life was to set myself right in his eyes. I thereupon gave him the whole history of my invention, and explained the reason of the actions that had appeared to him those of a lunatic. I said nothing about the little incident of that evening. That was a mere accident, and I did not care now to speak of it.

Mr. Gilbert listened to me very attentively.

"Your wife is here?" he asked, when I had finished.

"Yes," I said; "and she will corroborate my story in every item, and no one could ever suspect her of being crazy. I will go and bring her to you."

In a few minutes my wife was in the room, had shaken hands with Mr. Gilbert, and had been told of my suspected madness. She turned pale, but smiled.

"He did act like a crazy man," she said, "but I never supposed that anybody would think him one." And tears came into her eyes.

"And now, my dear," said I, "perhaps you will tell Mr. Gilbert how I did all this."

And then she told him the story that I had told.

Mr. Gilbert looked from the one to the other of us with a troubled air.

"Of course I do not doubt either of you, or rather I do not doubt that you believe what you say. All would be right if I could bring myself to credit that such a force as that you speak of can possibly exist."

"That is a matter," said I, "which I can easily prove to you by actual demonstration. If you can wait a short time, until my wife and I have had something to eat—for I am nearly famished, and I am sure she must be—I will set your mind at rest upon that point."

"I will wait here," said Mr. Gilbert, "and smoke a cigar. Don't hurry yourselves. I shall be glad to have some time to think about what you have told me."

When we had finished the dinner, which had been set aside for us, I went upstairs and got my knapsack, and we both joined Mr. Gilbert in the smoking room. I showed him the little machine, and explained, very briefly, the principle of its construction. I did not give any practical demonstration of its action, because there were people walking about the corridor who might at any moment come into the room; but, looking out of the window, I saw that the night was much clearer. The wind had dissipated the clouds, and the stars were shining brightly.

"If you will come up the street with me," said I to Mr. Gilbert, "I will show you how this thing works."

"That is just what I want to see," he answered.

"I will go with you," said my wife, throwing a shawl over her head. And we started up the street.

When we were outside the little town I found the starlight was quite sufficient for my purpose. The white roadway, the low walls, and objects about us, could easily be distinguished.

"Now," said I to Mr. Gilbert, "I want you to put this knapsack on you, and let you see how it feels, and how it will help you to walk." To this he assented with some eagerness, and I strapped it firmly on him. "I will now turn this screw," said I, "until you shall become lighter and lighter."

"Be very careful not to turn it too much," said my wife, earnestly.

"Oh, you may depend on me for that," said I, turning the screw very gradually.

Mr. Gilbert was a stout man, and I was obliged to give the screw a good many turns.

"There seems to be considerable hoist in it," he said directly. And then I put my arms around him, and found that I could raise him from the ground.

"Are you lifting me?" he exclaimed, in surprise.

"Yes; I did it with ease," I answered.

"Upon—my—word!" ejaculated Mr. Gilbert.

I then gave the screw a half-turn more, and told him to walk and run. He started off, at first slowly, then he made long strides, then he began to run, and then to skip and jump. It had been many years since Mr. Gilbert had skipped and jumped. No one was in sight, and he was free to gambol as much as he pleased. "Could you give it another turn?" said he, bounding up to me. "I want to try that wall." I put on a little more negative gravity, and he vaulted over a five-foot wall with great ease. In an instant he had leaped back into the road, and in two bounds was at my side. "I came down as light as a cat," he said. "There was never anything like it." And away he went up the road, taking steps at least eight feet long, leaving my wife and me laughing heartily at the preternatural agility of our stout friend. In a few minutes he was with us again. "Take it off," he said. "If I wear it any longer I shall want one myself, and then I shall be taken for a crazy man, and perhaps clapped into an asylum."

"Now," said I, as I turned back the screw before unstrapping the knapsack, "do you understand how I took long walks, and leaped and jumped; how I ran uphill and downhill, and how the little donkey drew the loaded wagon?"

"I understand it all," cried he. "I take back all I ever said or thought about you, my friend."

"And Herbert may marry Janet?" cried my wife.

"*May* marry her!" cried Mr. Gilbert. "Indeed, he *shall* marry her, if I have anything to say about it! My poor girl has been drooping ever since I told her it could not be."

My wife rushed at him, but whether she embraced him or only shook his hands I cannot say; for I had the knapsack in one hand and was rubbing my eyes with the other.

"But, my dear fellow," said Mr. Gilbert, directly, "if you still consider it in your interest to keep your invention a secret, I wish you had never made it. No one having a machine like that can help using it, and it is often quite as bad to be considered a maniac as to be one."

"My friend," I cried, with some excitement, "I have made up my mind on this subject. The little machine in this knapsack, which is the only one I now possess, has been a great pleasure to me. But I now know it has also been of the greatest injury indireclty to me and mine, not to mention some direct inconvenience and danger, which I will speak of another time. The secret lies with us three, and we will keep it. But the invention itself is too full of temptation and danger for any of us.''

As I said this I held the knapsack with one hand while I quickly turned the screw with the other. In a few moments it was high above my head, while I with difficulty held it down by the straps. "Look!" I cried. And then I released my hold, and the knapsack shot into the air and disappeared into the upper gloom.

I was about to make a remark, but had no chance, for my wife threw herself upon my bosom, sobbing with joy.

"Oh, I am so glad—so glad!" she said. "And you will never make another?"

"Never another!" I answered.

"And now let us hurry and see Janet," said my wife.

"You don't know how heavy and clumsy I feel," said Mr. Gilbert, striving to keep up with us as we walked back. "If I had worn that thing much longer, I should never have been willing to take it off!"

Janet had retired, but my wife went up to her room.

"I think she has felt it as much as our boy," she said, when she rejoined me. "But I tell you, my dear, I left a very happy girl in that little bedchamber over the garden."

And there were three very happy elderly people talking together until quite late that evening. "I shall write to Herbert tonight," I said, when we separated, "and tell him to meet us all in Geneva. It will do the young man no harm if we interrupt his studies just now."

"You must let me add a postscript to the letter," said Mr. Gilbert, "and I am sure it will require no knapsack with a screw in the back to bring him quickly to us."

And it did not.

There is a wonderful pleasure in tripping over the earth like a winged Mercury, and in feeling one's self relieved of much of that attraction of gravitation which drags us down to earth and gradually makes the movement of our bodies but weariness and labor. But this pleasure is not to be compared, I think, to that given by the buoyancy and lightness of two young and loving hearts, reunited after a separation which they had supposed would last forever.

What became of the basket and the knapsack, or whether they ever met in upper air, I do not know. If they but float away and stay away from ken of mortal man, I shall be satisfied.

And whether or not the world will ever know more of the power of negative gravity depends entirely upon the disposition of my son Herbert, when—after a good many years, I hope—he shall open the packet my lawyers have in keeping.

[Note.—It would be quite useless for anyone to interview my wife on this subject, for she has entirely forgotten how my machine was made. And as for Mr. Gilbert, he never knew.]

Guy de Maupassant (1850–1893)

One of the world's finest short-story writers, Guy de Maupassant evinced little interest in science or science fiction. He was, however, fascinated with the supernatural and bizarre, and many of these stories are collected in *Allouma and Other Tales* (1895) and *Tales of Supernatural Terror* (1972). His birth was in Normandy, France—though perhaps not in the Chateau de Miromesmil as is claimed. Though of noble heritage, he spent much of his childhood in Etretat among the children of sailors and peasants because of the separation of his parents. In 1867 he sought help from the poet Bouilhet and enrolled in Caen University. Two years later he obtained a bachelor of letters degree and joined his father in Paris to read law. Bouilhet had died, but the poet's close friend (and maternal relative of de Maupassant) Gustave Flaubert assumed the role of writing instructor. From 1870 to 1880, with the exception of one year's service in the Franco-German War, de Maupassant supported himself as a clerk and persevered as a literary apprentice. Flaubert wondered if his protégé possessed the capacity to become a first-rate writer, but by 1880 de Maupassant felt ready. *Des Vers*, a book of poems, made no appreciable impact, but later that year the powerful "Ball of Fat" brought raves when it appeared in an anthology edited by Emile Zola. And though de Maupassant produced several novels during the next thirteen years, it was for the approximately two hundred short stories that he was to achieve world fame. These feature the precision of imagery, simplicity of style, conciseness and strength of a good news photo. De Maupassant presents people as he finds them, warts and all. Still, he is no realist, for his characters—much like those of Cornell Woolrich—seem players in a Greek tragedy, trying to deny fate, yet being crushed in the end.

Perhaps this pessimistic view was a response to de Maupassant's progressively worsening headaches—probably from syphilis—which convinced him there was no escape from his family's long history of mental problems. So more and more he turned to drugs and wine as a temporary means of relief. However, "The Horla" does not seem to be—as some have suggested—the work of a deranged mind. First, insanity and obsession were themes present in his work from the beginnng. Second, this particular story was suggested to de Maupassant by J. M. Charcot's theories of psychological disorder and hysteria. Third, it is well-crafted, gaining power from its presentation as a Janus story in which the reader must decide between two interpretations—the protagonist is being harassed by an invisible mutant or is simply descending into paranoid psychosis.

But in any case, "The Horla" proved prophetic. Five years later de Maupassant's once-athletic constitution had been ravaged by debauchery and pain. He attempted suicide, was confined to a Parisian nursing home, lapsed into complete insanity, and died at the age of forty-three.

THE HORLA

May 8. What a lovely day! I have spent all the morning lying in the grass in front of my house, under the enormous plane tree that shades the whole of it. I like this part of the country and I like to live here because I am attached to it by old associations, by those deep and delicate roots which attach a man to the soil on which his ancestors were born and died, which attach him to the ideas and usages of the place as well as to the food, to local expressions, to the peculiar twang of the peasants, to the smell of the soil, of the villages and of the atmosphere itself.

I love my house in which I grew up. From my windows I can see the Seine which flows alongside my garden, on the other side of the high road, almost through my grounds, the great and wide Seine, which goes to Rouen and Havre, and is covered with boats passing to and fro.

On the left, down yonder, lies Rouen, that large town, with its blue roofs, under its pointed Gothic towers. These are innumerable, slender or broad, dominated by the spire of the cathedral, and full of bells which sound through the blue air on fine mornings, sending their sweet and distant iron clang even as far as my home, that song of the metal, which the breeze wafts in my direction, now stronger and now weaker, according as the wind is stronger or lighter.

What a delicious morning it was!

About eleven o'clock, a long line of boats drawn by a steam tug as big as a fly, and which scarcely puffed while emitting its thick smoke, passed my gate.

After two English schooners, whose red flat fluttered in space, there came a magnificent Brazilian three-master; it was perfectly white, and wonderfully clean and shining. I saluted it, hardly knew why, except that the sight of the vessel gave me great pleasure.

May 12. I have had a slight feverish attack for the last few days, and I feel ill, or rather I feel low-spirited.

Whence come those mysterious influences which change our happiness into discouragement, and our self-confidence into diffidence? One might almost say that the air, the invisible air, is full of unknowable Powers whose mysterious presence we have to endure. I wake up in the best spirits, with an inclination to sing. Why? I go down to the edge of the water, and suddenly, after walking a short distance, I return home wretched, as if some misfortune were awaiting me there. Why? Is it a cold shiver which, passing over my skin, has upset my nerves and given me low spirits? Is it the form of the clouds, the color of the sky, or the color of the surrounding objects which is so changeable, that has troubled my thoughts as they passed before my eyes? Who can tell? Everything that surrounds us, everything that we see, without looking at it, everything that we touch, without knowing it, everything that we handle, without feeling it, all that we meet, without clearly distinguishing it, has a rapid, surprising and inexplicable effect upon us and upon our senses, and, through them, on our ideas and on our heart itself.

How profound that mystery of the Invisible is! We cannot fathom it with our miserable senses, with our eyes which are unable to perceive what is either too small or too great, too near to us, or too far from us—neither the inhabitants of a star nor of a drop of water; nor with our ears that deceive us, for they transmit to us the vibrations of the air in sonorous notes. They are fairies who work the miracle of changing these vibrations into sounds, and by that metamorphosis give birth to music, which makes the silent motion of nature musical . . . with our sense of smell which is less keen than that of a dog . . . with our sense of taste which can scarcely distinguish the age of wine!

Oh! If we only had other organs which would work other miracles in our favor, what a number of fresh things we might discover around us!

May 16. I am ill, decidedly! I was so well last month! I am feverish, horribly feverish, or rather I am in a state of feverish enervation, which makes my mind suffer as much as my body. I have, continually, that horrible sensation of some impending danger, that apprehension of some coming misfortune, or of approaching death; that presentiment which is, no doubt, an attack of some illness which is still unknown, which germinates in the flesh and in the blood.

May 17. I have just come from consulting my physician, for I could no longer get any sleep. He said my pulse was rapid, my eyes dilated, my nerves highly strung, but there were no alarming symptoms. I must take a course of shower baths and of bromide of potassium.

May 25. No change! My condition is really very peculiar. As the evening comes on, an incomprehensible feeling of disquietude seizes me, just as if night concealed some threatening disaster. I dine hurriedly, and then try to read, but I do not understand the words, and can scarcely distinguish the letters. Then I walk up and down my drawing-room, oppressed by a feeling of confused and irresistible fear, the fear of sleep and fear of my bed.

About ten o'clock I go up to my room. As soon as I enter it I double-lock and bolt the door; I am afraid . . . of what? Up to the present time I have been afraid of nothing. . . . I open my cupboards, and look under my bed; I listen . . . to what? How strange it is that a simple feeling of discomfort, impeded or heightened circulation, perhaps the irritation of a nerve filament, a slight congestion, a small disturbance in the imperfect delicate functioning of our living machinery, may turn the most lighthearted of men into a melancholy one, and make a coward of the bravest? Then, I go to bed, and wait for sleep as a man might wait for the executioner. I wait for its coming with dread, and my heart beats and my legs tremble, while my whole body shivers beneath the warmth of the bedclothes, until all at once I fall asleep, as though one should plunge into a pool of stagnant water in order to drown. I do not feel it coming on as I did formerly, this perfidious sleep which is close to me and watching me, which is going to seize me by the head, to close my eyes and annihilate me.

I sleep—a long time—two or three hours perhaps—then a dream—no—a nightmare lays hold on me. I feel that I am in bed and asleep . . . I feel it and I know it . . . and I feel also that somebody is coming close to me, is looking at me, touching me, is getting on to my bed, is kneeling on my chest, is taking my neck between his hands and squeezing it . . . squeezing it with all his might in order to strangle me.

I struggle, bound by that terrible sense of powerlessness which paralyzes us in our dreams; I try to cry out—but I cannot; I want to move—I cannot do so; I try, with the most violent efforts and breathing hard, to turn over and throw off this being who is crushing and suffocating me—I cannot!

And then, suddenly, I wake up, trembling and bathed in perspiration; I light a candle and find that I am alone, and after that crisis, which occurs every night, I at length fall asleep and slumber tranquilly till morning.

June 2. My condition has grown worse. What is the matter with me? The bromide does me no good, and the shower baths have no effect. Sometimes, in order to tire myself thoroughly, though I am fatigued enough already, I go for a walk in the forest of Roumare. I used to think at first that the fresh light and soft air, impregnated with the odor of herbs and leaves, would instill new blood into my veins and impart fresh energy to my heart. I turned into a broad hunting road, and then turned toward La Bouille, through a narrow path, between two rows of exceedingly tall trees, which placed a thick green, almost black, roof between the sky and me.

A sudden shiver ran through me, not a cold shiver, but a strange shiver of agony, and I hastened my steps, uneasy at being alone in the forest, afraid, stupidly and without reason, of the profound solitude. Suddenly it seemed to me as if I were being followed, that somebody was walking at my heels, close, quite close to me, near enough to touch me.

I turned round suddenly, but I was alone. I saw nothing behind me except the straight, broad path, empty and bordered by high trees, horribly empty; before me it also extended until it was lost in the distance, and looked just the same, terrible.

I closed my eyes. Why? And then I began to turn round on one heel very quickly, just like a top. I nearly fell down, and opened my eyes; the trees were dancing round me and the earth heaved; I was obliged to sit down. Then, ah! What a strange, strange idea! I did not in the least know. I started off to the right, and got back into the avenue which had led me into the middle of the forest.

June 2. I have had a terrible night. I shall go away for a few weeks, for no doubt a journey will set me up again.

July 2. I have come back, quite cured, and have had a most delightful trip into the bargain. I have been to Mont Saint-Michel, which I had not seen before.

What a sight, when one arrives, as I did, at Avranches, toward the end of the day! The town stands on a hill, and I was taken into the public garden at the extremity of the town. I uttered a cry of astonishment. An extraordinarily large bay lay extended before me, as far as my eyes could reach, between two hills which were lost to sight in the mist; and in the middle of this immense yellow bay, under a clear, golden sky, a peculiar hill rose up, somber and pointed in the midst of the sand. The sun had just disappeared, and under the still-flaming sky appeared the outline of that fantastic rock which bears on its summit a fantastic monument.

At daybreak I went out to it. The tide was low, as it had been the night before, and I saw that wonderful abbey rise up before me as I approached it. After several hours' walking, I reached the enormous mass of rocks which supports the little town, dominated by the great church. Having climbed the steep and narrow street, I entered the most wonderful Gothic building that has ever been built to God on earth, as large as a town, full of low rooms which seem buried beneath vaulted roofs, and lofty galleries supported by delicate columns.

I entered this gigantic granite gem, which is as light as a bit of lace, covered with towers, with slender belfries with spiral staircases, which raise their strange heads that bristle with chimeras, with devils, with fantastic animals, with monstrous flowers, to the blue sky by day, and to the black sky by night, and are connected by finely carved arches.

When I had reached the summit I said to the monk who accompanied me: "Father, how happy you must be here!" And he replied: "It is very windy here, monsieur"; and so we began to talk while watching the rising tide, which ran over the sand and covered it as with a steel cuirass.

And then the monk told me stories, all the old stories belonging to the place, legends, nothing but legends.

One of them struck me forcibly. The country people, those belonging to the Mount, declare that at night one can hear voices talking on the sands, and then that one hears two goats bleating, one with a strong, the other with a weak voice. Incredulous people declare that it is nothing but the cry of the seabirds, which occasionally resembles bleatings, and occasionally, human lamentations; but belated fishermen swear that they have met an old shepherd wandering between tides on the sands around the little town. His head is completely concealed by his cloak and he is followed by a billy goat with a man's face, and a nanny goat with a woman's face, both having long, white hair and talking incessantly and quarreling in an unknown tongue. Then suddenly they cease and begin to bleat with all their might.

"Do you believe it?" I asked the monk. "I scarcely know," he replied, and I continued: "If there are other beings beside ourselves on this earth, how comes it that we have not known it long since, or why

have *you* not seen them? How is that *I* have not seen them?'' He replied:
''Do we see the hundred-thousandth part of what exists? Look here; there
is the wind, which is the strongest force in nature, which knocks down
men, and blows down buildings, destroys cliffs and casts great ships on
the rocks; the wind which kills, which whistles, which sighs, which
roars—have you ever seen it, and can you see it? It exists for all that,
however.''

I was silent before this simple reasoning. That man was a philosopher, or perhaps a fool; I could not say which exactly, so I held my
tongue. What he had said had often been in my own thoughts.

July 3. I have slept badly; certainly there is some feverish influence
here, for my coachman is suffering in the same way as I am. When I went
back home yesterday, I noticed his singular paleness, and I asked him:
''What is the matter with you, Jean?'' ''The matter is that I never get any
rest, and my nights devour my days. Since your departure, monsieur,
there has been a spell over me.''

However, the other servants are all well, but I am very much afraid
of having another attack myself.

July 4. I am decidedly ill again; for my old nightmares have
returned. Last night I felt somebody leaning on me and sucking my life
from between my lips. Yes, he was sucking it out of my throat, like a
leech. Then he got up, satiated, and I woke up, so exhausted, crushed
and weak that I could not move. If this continues for a few days, I shall
certainly go away again.

July 5. Have I lost my reason? What happened last night is so
strange that my head wanders when I think of it!

I had locked my door, as I do now every evening, and then, being
thirsty, I drank half a glass of water, and accidentally noticed that the
water bottle was full up to the cut-glass stopper.

Then I went to bed and fell into one of my terrible sleeps, from
which I was aroused in about two hours by a still more frightful shock.

Picture to yourself a sleeping man who is being murdered and who
wakes up with a knife in his lung, and whose breath rattles, who is
covered with blood, and who can no longer breathe and is about to die,
and does not understand—there you have it.

Having recovered my senses, I was thirsty again, so I lit a candle
and went to the table on which stood my water bottle. I lifted it up and
tilted it over my glass, but nothing came out. It was empty! It was

completely empty! At first I could not understand it at all, and then suddenly I was seized by such a terrible feeling that I had to sit down, or rather I fell into a chair! Then I sprang up suddenly to look about me; then I sat down again, overcome by astonishment and fear, in front of the transparent glass bottle! I looked at it with fixed eyes, trying to conjure, and my hands trembled! Somebody had drunk the water, but who? I? I without any doubt. It could surely only be I. In that case I was a somnambulist; I lived, without knowing it, that mysterious double life which makes us doubt whether there are not two beings in us, or whether a strange, unknowable and invisible being does not at such moments, when our soul is in a state of torpor, animate our captive body, which obeys this other being, as it obeys us, and more than it obeys ourselves.

Oh! Who will understand my horrible agony? Who will understand the emotion of a man who is sound in mind, wide awake, full of common sense, who looks in horror through the glass of a water bottle for a little water that disappeared while he was asleep? I remained thus until it was daylight, without venturing to go to bed again.

July 6. I am going mad. Again all the contents of my water bottle have been drunk during the night—or rather, I have drunk it!

But is it I? Is it I? Who could it be? Who? Oh! God! Am I going mad? Who will save me?

July 10. I have just been through some surprising ordeals. Decidedly I am mad! And yet! . . .

On July 6, before going to bed, I put some wine, milk, water, bread and strawberries on my table. Somebody drank—I drank—all the water and a little of the milk, but neither the wine, bread, nor the strawberries were touched.

On the seventh of July I renewed the same experiment, with the same results, and on July 8, I left out the water and the milk, and nothing was touched.

Lastly, on July 9, I put only water and milk on my table, taking care to wrap up the bottles in white muslin and to tie down the stoppers. Then I rubbed my lips, my beard and my hands with pencil lead, and went to bed.

Irresistible sleep seized me, which was soon followed by a terrible awakening. I had not moved, and there was no mark of lead on the sheets. I rushed to the table. The muslin round the bottles remained intact; I undid the string, trembling with fear. All the water had been drunk, and so had the milk! Ah! Great God! . . .

I must start for Paris immediately.

July 2. Paris. I must have lost my head during the last few days. I must be the plaything of my enervated imagination, unless I am really a somnambulist, or that I have been under the power of one of those hitherto unexplained influences which are called suggestions. In any case, my mental state bordered on madness, and twenty-four hours of Paris sufficed to restore my equilibrium.

Yesterday, after doing some business and paying some visits which instilled fresh and invigorating air into my soul, I wound up the evening at the *Théâtre-Français*. A play by Alexandre Dumas the younger was being acted, and his active and powerful imagination completed my cure. Certainly solitude is dangerous for active minds. We require around us men who can think and talk. When we are alone for a long time, we people space with phantoms.

I returned along the boulevards to my hotel in excellent spirits. Amid the jostling of the crowd I thought, not without irony, of my terrors and surmises of the previous week, because I had believed—yes, I had believed—that an invisible being lived beneath my roof. How weak our brains are, and how quickly they are terrified and led into error by a small incomprehensible fact.

Instead of saying simply: "I do not understand because I do not know the cause," we immediately imagine terrible mysteries and supernatural powers.

July 14. Fête of the Republic. I walked through the streets, amused as a child at the firecrackers and flags. Still it is very foolish to be merry on a fixed date, by Government decree. The populace is an imbecile flock of sheep, now stupidly patient, and now in ferocious revolt. Say to it: "Amuse yourself," and it amuses itself. Say to it: "Go and fight with your neighbor," and it goes and fights. Say to it: "Vote for the Emperor," and it votes for the Emperor, and then say to it: "Vote for the Republic," and it votes for the Republic.

Those who direct it are also stupid; only, instead of obeying men, they obey principles which can only be stupid, sterile, and false, for the very reason that they are principles, that is to say, ideas which are considered as certain and unchangeable, in this world where one is certain of nothing, since light is an illusion and noise is an illusion.

July 16. I saw some things yesterday that troubled me very much.

I was dining at the house of my cousin, Madame Sable, whose husband is colonel of the 76th Chasseurs at Limoges. There were two young women there, one of whom had married a medical man, Dr. Parent, who devotes much attention to nervous diseases and to the remarkable manifestations taking place at this moment under the influence of hypnotism and suggestion.

He related to us at some length the wonderful results obtained by English scientists and by the doctors of the Nancy school; and the facts which he adduced appeared to me so strange that I declared that I was altogether incredulous.

"We are," he declared, "on the point of discovering one of the most important secrets of nature; I mean to say, one of its most important secrets on this earth, for there are certainly others of a different kind of importance up in the stars, yonder. Ever since man has thought, ever since he has been able to express and write down his thoughts, he has felt himself close to a mystery which is impenetrable to his gross and imperfect senses, and he endeavors to supplement through his intellect the inefficiency of his senses. As long as that intellect remained in its elementary stage, these apparitions of invisible spirits assumed forms that were commonplace, though terrifying. Thence sprang the popular belief in the supernatural, the legends of wandering spirits, of fairies, of gnomes, ghosts, I might even say the legend of God; for our conceptions of the workman-creator, from whatever religion they may have come down to us, are certainly the most mediocre, the most stupid and the most incredible inventions that ever sprang from the terrified brain of any human beings. Nothing is truer than what Voltaire says: 'God made man in His own image, but man has certainly paid Him back in his own coin.'

"However, for rather more than a century men seem to have had a presentiment of something new. Mesmer and some others have put us on an unexpected track, and, especially within the last two or three years, we have arrived at really surprising results."

My cousin, who is also very incredulous, smiled, and Dr. Parent said to her: "Would you like me to try and send you to sleep, madame?"
"Yes, certainly."

She sat down in an easy chair, and he began to look at her fixedly, so as to fascinate her. I suddenly felt myself growing uncomfortable, my heart beating rapidly and a choking sensation in my throat. I saw

Madame Sable's eyes becoming heavy, her mouth twitching and her bosom heaving, and at the end of ten minutes she was asleep.

"Go behind her," the doctor said to me, and I took a seat behind her. He put a visiting card into her hands, and said to her: "This is a looking glass; what do you see in it?" And she replied: "I see my cousin." "What is he doing?" "He is twisting his mustache." "And now?" "He is taking a photograph out of his pocket." "Whose photograph is it?" "His own."

That was true, and the photograph had been given me that same evening at the hotel.

"What is his attitude in this portrait?" "He is standing up with his hat in his hand."

She saw, therefore, on that card, on that piece of white pasteboard, as if she had seen it in a mirror.

The young women were frightened, and exclaimed: "That is enough! Quite, quite enough!"

But the doctor said to Madame Sable authoritatively: "You will rise at eight o'clock tomorrow morning; then you will go and call on your cousin at his hotel and ask him to lend you five thousand francs which your husband demands of you, and which he will ask for when he sets out on his coming journey."

Then he woke her up.

On returning to my hotel, I thought over this curious séance, and I was assailed by doubts, not as to my cousin's absolute and undoubted good faith, for I had known her as well as if she were my own sister ever since she was a child, but as to a possible trick on the doctor's part. Had he not, perhaps, kept a glass hidden in his hand, which he showed to the young woman in her sleep, at the same time as he did the card? Professional conjurors do things that are just as singular.

So I went home and to bed, and this morning, at about half past eight, I was awakened by my valet, who said to me: "Madame Sable has asked to see you immediately, monsieur." I dressed hastily and went to her.

She sat down in some agitation, with her eyes on the floor, and without raising her veil she said to me: "My dear cousin, I am going to ask a great favor of you." "What is it, cousin?" "I do not like to tell you, and yet I must. I am in absolute need of five thousand francs." "What, you?" "Yes, I, or rather my husband, who has asked me to procure them for him."

I was so thunderstruck that I stammered out my answers. I asked myself whether she had not really been making fun of me with Dr. Parent, if it was not merely a very well-acted farce which had been rehearsed beforehand. On looking at her attentively, however, all my doubts disappeared. She was trembling with grief, so painful was this step to her, and I was convinced that her throat was full of sobs.

I knew that she was very rich and I continued: "What! Has not your husband five thousand francs at his disposal? Come, think. Are you sure that he commissioned you to ask me for them?"

She hesitated for a few seconds, as if she were making a great effort to search her memory, and then she replied; "Yes . . . yes, I am quite sure of it." "He has written to you?"

She hesitated again and reflected, and I guessed the torture of her thoughts. She did not know. She only knew that she was to borrow five thousand francs of me for her husband. So she told a lie. "Yes, he had written to me." "When, pray? You did not mention it to me yesterday." "I received his letter this morning." "Can you show it me?" "No; no . . . no . . . it contained private matters . . . things too personal to ourselves . . . I burned it." "So your husband runs into debt?"

She hesitated again, and then murmured: "I do not know." Thereupon I said bluntly: "I have not five thousand francs at my disposal at this moment, my dear cousin."

She uttered a kind of cry as if she were in pain and said: "Oh! Oh! I beseech you, I beseech you to get them for me. . . . "

She got excited and clasped her hands as if she were praying to me! I heard her voice change its tone; she wept and stammered, harassed and dominated by the irresistible order that she had received.

"Oh! Oh! I beg you to . . . if you knew what I am suffering . . . I want them today."

I had pity on her: "You shall have them by and by, I swear to you." "Oh! Thank you! Thank you! How kind you are."

I continued: "Do you remember what took place at your house last night?" "Yes." "Do you remember that Dr. Parent sent you to sleep?" "Yes." "Oh! Very well then; he ordered you to come to me this morning to borrow five thousand francs, and at this moment you are obeying that suggestion."

She considered for a few moments, and then replied: "But as it is my husband who wants them—"

For a whole hour I tried to convince her, but could not succeed, and when she had gone I went to the doctor. He was just going out, and he listened to me with a smile, and said: "Do you believe now?" "Yes, I cannot help it." "Let us go to your cousin's."

She was already half asleep on a reclining chair, overcome with fatigue. The doctor felt her pulse, looked at her for some time with one hand raised toward her eyes, which she closed by degrees under the irresistible power of his magnetic influence, and when she was asleep, he said:

"Your husband does not require the five thousand francs any longer! You must, therefore, forget that you asked your cousin to lend them to you, and, if he speaks to you about it, you will not understand him."

Then he woke her up, and I took out a pocketbook and said: "Here is what you asked me for this morning, my dear cousin." But she was so surprised that I did not venture to persist; nevertheless, I tried to recall the circumstance to her, but she denied it vigorously, thought I was making fun of her, and, in the end, very nearly lost her temper.

There! I have just come back, and I have not been able to eat any lunch, for this experiment has altogether upset me.

July 19. Many people to whom I told the adventure laughed at me. I no longer know what to think. The wise man says: "It may be!"

July 21. I dined at Bougival, and then spent the evening at a boatmen's ball. Decidedly everything depends on place and surroundings. It would be the height of folly to believe in the supernatural on the Ile de la Grenouillière . . . but on top of Mont Saint-Michel? . . . and in India? We are terribly influenced by our surroundings. I shall return home next week.

July 30. I came back to my own house yesterday. Everything is going on well.

August 2. Nothing new; it is splendid weather, and I spend my days in watching the Seine flowing past.

August 4. Quarrels among my servants. They declare that the glasses are broken in the cupboards at night. the footman accuses the cook, who accuses the seamstress, who accuses the other two. Who is the culprit? It is a clever person who can tell.

August 6. This time I am not mad. I have seen . . . I have seen! . . . I can doubt no longer . . . I have seen it! . . .

I was walking at two o'clock among my rose trees, in the full sunlight . . . in the walk bordered by autumn roses, which are beginning to fall. As I stopped to look at a Géant de Bataille, which had three splendid blossoms, I distinctly saw the stalk of one of the roses near me bend, as if an invisible hand had bent it, and then break, as if that hand had picked it! Then the flower raised itself, following the curve which a hand would have described in carrying it toward a mouth, and it remained suspended in the transparent air, all alone and motionless, a terrible red spot, three yards from my eyes. In desperation I rushed at it to take it! I found nothing; it had disappeared. Then I was seized with furious rage against myself, for a reasonable and serious man should not have such hallucinations.

But was it a hallucination? I turned round to look for the stalk, and I found it at once, on the bush, freshly broken, between two other roses which remained on the branch. I returned home then, my mind greatly disturbed; for I am certain now, as certain as I am of the alternation of day and night, that there exists close to me an invisible being that lives on milk and water, that can touch objects, take them and change their places; that is, consequently, endowed with a material nature, although it is imperceptible to our senses, and that lives as I do, under my roof—

August 7. I slept tranquilly. He drank the water out of my decanter, but did not disturb my sleep. I wonder if I am mad. As I was walking just now in the sun by the riverside, doubts as to my sanity arose in me; not vague doubts such as I have had hitherto, but definite, absolute doubts. I have seen mad people, and I have known some who have been quite intelligent, lucid, even clear-sighted in every concern of life, except on one point. They spoke readily, clearly, profoundly on everything, when suddenly their mind struck upon the shoals of their madness and broke to pieces there, and scattered and floundered in that furious and terrible sea, full of rolling waves, fogs and squalls, which is called *madness*.

I certainly should think that I was mad, absolutely mad, if I were not conscious, did not perfectly know my condition, did not fathom it by analyzing it with the most complete lucidity. I should, in fact, be only a rational man who was laboring under a hallucination. Some unknown disturbance must have arisen in my brain, one of those disturbances which physiologists of the present day try to note and to verify; and that disturbance must have caused a deep gap in my mind and in the sequence and logic of my ideas. Similar phenomena occur in dreams which lead us among the most unlikely phantasmagoria, without causing us any surprise, because our verifying apparatus and our organ of control are asleep, while our imaginative faculty is awake and active. Is it not possible that one of the imperceptible notes of the cerebral keyboard had been paralyzed in me? Some men lose the recollection of proper names, of verbs, or of numbers, or merely of dates, in consequence of an accident. The localization of all the variations of thought has been established nowadays; why, then, should it be surprising if my faculty of controlling the unreality of certain hallucinations were dormant in me for the time being?

I thought of all this as I walked by the side of the water. The sun shone brightly on the river and made earth delightful, while it filled me with a love for life, for the swallows, whose agility always delights my eye, for the plants by the riverside, the rustle of whose leaves is a pleasure to my ears.

By degrees, however, an inexplicable feeling of discomfort seized me. It seemed as if some unknown force were numbing and stopping me, were preventing me from going further, and were calling me back. I felt that painful wish to return which oppresses you when you have left a beloved invalid at home, and when you are seized with a presentiment that he is worse.

I, therefore, returned in spite of myself, feeling certain that I should find some bad news awaiting me, a letter or a telegram. There was nothing, however, and I was more surprised and uneasy than if I had had another fantastic vision.

August 8. I spent a terrible evening yesterday. He does not show himself any more, but I feel that he is near me, watching me, looking at me, penetrating me, dominating me, and more redoubtable when he hides himself thus than if he were to manifest his constant and invisible presence by supernatural phenomena. However, I slept.

August 9. Nothing, but I am afraid.

August 10. Nothing; what will happen tomorrow?

August 11. Still nothing; I cannot stay at home with this fear hanging over me and these thoughts in my mind; I shall go away.

August 12. Ten o'clock at night. All day long I have been trying to get away, and have not been able. I wished to accomplish this simple and easy act of freedom—to go out—to get into my carriage in order to go to Rouen—and I have not been able to do it. What is the reason?

August 13. When one is attacked by certain maladies, all the springs of our physical being appear to be broken, all our energies destroyed, all our muscles relaxed; our bones, too, have become as soft as flesh, and our blood as liquid as water. I am experiencing these sensations in my moral being in a strange and distressing manner. I have no longer any strength, any courage, any self-control, not even any power to set my own will in motion. I have no power left to will anything; but someone does it for me and I obey.

August 14. I am lost. Somebody possesses my soul and dominates it. Somebody orders all my acts, all my movements, all my thoughts. I am no longer anything in myself, nothing except an enslaved and terrified spectator of all the things I do. I wish to go out; I cannot. He does not wish to, and so I remain, trembling and distracted, in the armchair in which he keeps me sitting. I merely wish to get up and to rouse myself; I cannot! I am riveted to my chair, and my chair adheres to the ground in such a manner that no power could move us.

Then, suddenly, I must, I must go to the bottom of my garden to pick some strawberries and eat them, and I go there. I pick the strawberries and eat them! Oh, my God! My God! Is there a God? If there be one, deliver me! Save me! Succor me! Pardon! Pity! Mercy! Save me! Oh, what sufferings! What torture! What horror!

August 15. This is certainly the way in which my poor cousin was possessed and controlled when she came to borrow five thousand francs of me. She was under the power of a strange will which had entered into her, like another soul, like another parasitic and dominating soul. Is the world coming to an end?

But who is he, this invisible being that rules me? This unknowable being, this rover of a supernatural race?

Invisible beings exist, then! How is it, then, that since the beginning of the world they have never manifested themselves precisely as they do to me? I have never read of anything that resembles what goes on in my house. Oh, if I could only leave it, if I could only go away, escape, and never return! I should be saved, but I cannot.

August 16. I managed to escape today for two hours, like a prisoner who finds the door of his dungeon accidentally open. I suddenly felt that I was free and that he was far away, and so I gave orders to harness the horses as quickly as possible, and I drove to Rouen. Oh, how delightful to be able to say to a man who obeys you: "Go to Rouen!"

I made him pull up before the library, and I begged them to lend me Dr. Herrmann Herestauss' treatise on the unknown inhabitants of the ancient and modern world.

Then, as I was getting into my carriage, I intended to say: "To the railway station!" but instead of this I shouted—I did not say, but I shouted—in such a loud voice that all the passersby turned round: "Home!" and I fell back on the cushion of my carriage, overcome by mental agony. He had found me again and regained possession of me.

August 17. Oh, what a night! What a night! And yet it seems to me that I ought to rejoice. I read until one o'clock in the morning! Herestauss, doctor of philosophy and theogony, wrote the history of the manifestation of all those invisible beings which hover round man, or of whom he dreams. He describes their origin, their domain, their power; but none of them resembles the one which haunts me. One might say that man, ever since he began to think, has had a foreboding fear of a new being, stronger than himself, his successor in this new world, and that, feeling his presence, and not being able to foresee the nature of that master, he has, in his terror, created the whole race of occult beings, of vague phantoms born of fear.

Having, therefore, read until one o'clock in the morning, I went and sat down at the open window, in order to cool my forehead and my thoughts, in the calm night air. It was very pleasant and warm! How I should have enjoyed such a night formerly!

There was no moon, but the stars darted out their rays in the dark heavens. Who inhabits those worlds? What forms, what living beings, what animals are there yonder? What do the thinkers in those distant worlds know more than we do? What can they do more than we can? What do they see which we do not know? Will not one of them, some day or other, traversing space, appear on our earth to conquer it, just as the Norsemen formerly crossed the sea in order to subjugate nations more feeble than themselves?

We are so weak, so defenseless, so ignorant, so small, we who live on this particle of mud which revolves in a drop of water.

I fell asleep, dreaming thus in the cool night air, and when I had slept for about three-quarters of an hour, I opened my eyes without moving, awakened by I know not what confused and strange sensation. At first I saw nothing, and then suddenly it appeared to me as if a page of a book which had remained open on my table turned over of its own accord. Not a breath of air had come in at my window, and I was surprised, and waited. In about four minutes, I saw, I saw, yes, I saw with my own eyes, another page lift itself up and fall down on the others, as if a finger had turned it over. My armchair was empty, appeared empty, but I knew that he was there, he, and sitting in my place, and that he was reading. With a furious bound, the bound of an enraged wild beast that springs at its tamer, I crossed my room to seize him, to strangle him, to kill him! But before I could reach it, the chair fell over as if somebody had run away from me—my table rocked, my lamp fell and went out, and my window closed as if some thief had been surprised and had fled out into the night, shutting it behind him.

So he had run away; he had been afraid; he, afraid of me!

But—but—tomorrow—or later—some day or other—I should be able to hold him in my clutches and crush him against the ground! Do not dogs occasionally bite and strangle their masters?

August 18. I have been thinking the whole day long. Oh, yes, I will obey him, follow his impulses, fulfill all his wishes, show myself humble, submissive, a coward. He is the stronger; but the hour will come—

August 19. I know—I know—I know all! I have just read the following in the *Revue du Monde Scientifique:* ''A curious piece of news comes to us from Rio de Janeiro. Madness, an epidemic of madness, which may be compared to that contagious madness which attacked the people of Europe in the Middle Ages, is at this moment raging in the Province of San-Paolo. The terrified inhabitants are leaving their houses, saying that they are pursued, possessed, dominated like human cattle by invisible, though tangible beings, a species of vampire, which feed on their life while they are asleep, and who, besides, drink water and milk without appearing to touch any other nourishment.

''Professor Don Pedro Henriquez, accompanied by several medical savants, has gone to the Province of San-Paolo, in order to study the origin and the manifestations of this surprising madness on the spot, and to propose such measures to the Emperor as may appear to him to be most fitted to restore the mad population to reason.''

Ah! Ah! I remember now that fine Brazilian three-master which passed in front of my windows as it was going up the Seine, on the eighth day of last May! I thought it looked so pretty, so white and bright! That Being was on board of her, coming from there, where its race originated.

And it saw me! It saw my house which was also white, and it sprang from the ship on to the land. Oh, merciful heaven!

Now I know, I can divine. The reign of man is over, and he has come. He who was feared by primitive man; whom disquieted priests exorcised; whom sorcerers evoked on dark nights, without having seen him appear, to whom the imagination of the transient masters of the world lent all the monstrous or graceful forms of gnomes, spirits, genii, fairies and familiar spirits. After the coarse conceptions of primitive fear, more clear-sighted men foresaw it more clearly. Mesmer divined it, and ten years ago physicians accurately discovered the nature of his power, even before he exercised it himself. They played with this new weapon of the Lord, the sway of a mysterious will over the human soul, which had become a slave. They called it magnetism, hypnotism, suggestion—what do I know? I have seen them amusing themselves like rash children with this horrible power! Woe to us! Woe to man! He has come, the—the—what does he call himself—the—I fancy that he is shouting out his name to me and I do not hear him—the—yes—he is shouting it out—I am listening—I cannot—he repeats it—the— Horla—I hear—the Horla—it is he—the Horla—he has come!

Ah! The vulture has eaten the pigeon; the wolf has eaten the lamb; the lion has devoured the sharp-horned buffalo; man has killed the lion with an arrow, with a sword, with gunpowder; but the Horla will make of man what we have made of the horse and of the ox; his chattel, his slave and his food, by the mere power of his will. Woe to us!

But, nevertheless, the animal sometimes revolts and kills the man who has subjugated it. I should also like—I shall be able to—but I must know him, touch him, see him! Scientists say that animals' eyes, being different from ours, do not distinguish objects as ours do. And my eye cannot distinguish this newcomer who is oppressing me.

Why? Oh, now I remember the words of the monk at Mont Saint-Michel: "Can we see the hundred-thousandth part of what exists? See here; there is the wind, which is the strongest force in nature, which knocks men, and bowls down buidings, uproots trees, raises the sea into mountains of water, destroys cliffs and casts great ships on the breakers; the wind which kills, which whistles, which sighs, which roars—have you ever seen it, and can you see it? It exists for all that, however!"

And I went on thinking; my eyes are so weak, so imperfect, that they do not even distinguish hard bodies, if they are as transparent as glass! If a glass without tinfoil behind it were to bar my way, I should run into it, just as a bird which has flown into a room breaks its head against the windowpanes. A thousand things, moreover, deceive man and lead him astray. Why should it then be surprising that he cannot perceive an unknown body through which the light passes?

A new being! Why not? It was assuredly bound to come! Why should we be the last? We do not distinguish it any more than all the others created before us! The reason is, that its nature is more perfect, its body finer and more finished than ours, that ours is so weak, so awkwardly constructed, encumbered with organs that are always tired, always on the strain like machinery that is too complicated, which lives like a plant and like a beast, nourishing itself with difficulty on air, herbs and flesh, an animal machine which is a prey to maladies, to malformations, to decay; broken-winded, badly regulated, simple and eccentric, ingeniously badly made, at once a coarse and a delicate piece of workmanship, the rough sketch of a being that might become intelligent and grand.

We are only a few, so few in this world, from the oyster up to man. Why should there not be one more, once that period is passed which separates the successive apparitions from all the different species?

Why not one more? Why not, also, other trees with immense, splendid flowers, perfuming whole regions? Why not other elements besides fire, air, earth and water? There are four, only four, those nursing fathers of various beings! What a pity! Why are there not forty, four hundred, four thousand? How poor everything is, how mean and wretched! Grudgingly produced, roughly constructed, clumsily made! Ah, the elephant and the hippopotamus, what grace! And the camel, what elegance!

But the butterfly, you will say, a flying flower? I dream of one that should be as large as a hundred worlds, with wings whose shape, beauty, colors and motion I cannot even express. But I see it—it flutters from star to star, refreshing them and perfuming them with the light and harmonious breath of its flight! And the people up there look at it as it passes in an ecstasy of delight!

What is the matter with me? It is he, the Horla, who haunts me, and who makes me think of these foolish things! He is within me, he is becoming my soul; I shall kill him!

August 19. I shall kill him. I have seen him! Yesterday I sat down at my table and pretended to write very assiduously. I knew quite well that he would come prowling round me, quite close to me, so close that I might perhaps be able to touch him, to seize him. And then—then I should have the strength of desperation; I should have my hands, my knees, my chest, my forehead, my teeth to strangle him, to crush him, to bite him, to tear him to pieces. And I watched for him with all my over-excited senses.

I had lighted my two lamps and the eight wax candles on my mantelpiece, as if with this light I could discover him.

My bedstead, my old oak-post bedstead, stood opposite to me; on my right was the fireplace; on my left, the door which was carefully closed, after I had left it open for some time in order to attract him; behind me was a very high wardrobe with a looking glass in it, before which I stood to shave and dress every day, and in which I was in the habit of glancing at myself from head to foot every time I passed it.

I pretended to be writing in order to deceive him, for he also was watching me, and suddenly I felt—I was certain that he was reading over my shoulder, that he was there, touching my ear.

I got up, my hands extended, and turned round so quickly that I almost fell. Eh! Well? It was as bright as at midday, but I did not see my reflection in the mirror! It was empty, clear, profound, full of light! But my figure was not reflected in it—and I, I was opposite to it! I saw the large clear glass from top to bottom, and I looked at it with unsteady eyes; and I did not dare to advance; I did not venture to make a movement, feeling that he was there, but that he would escape me again, he whose imperceptible body had absorbed my reflection.

How frightened I was! And then, suddenly, I began to see myself in a mist in the depths of the looking glass, in a mist as it were a sheet of water; and it seemed to me as if this water were flowing clearer every moment. It was like the end of an eclipse. Whatever it was that hid me did not appear to possess any clearly defined outlines, but a sort of opaque transparency which gradually grew clearer.

At last I was able to distinguish myself completely, as I do every day when I look at myself.

I had seen it! And the horror of it remained with me, and makes me shudder even now.

August 20. How could I kill it, as I could not get hold of it? Poison?

But it would see me mix it with the water; and then, would our poisons have any effect on its impalpable body? No—no—no doubt about the matter—Then—then?—

August 21. I sent for a blacksmith from Rouen, and ordered iron shutters for my room, such as some private hotels in Paris have on the ground floor, for fear of burglars, and he is going to make me an iron door as well. I have made myself out a coward, but I do not care about that!

September 10. Rouen, Hôtel Continental. It is done—it is done— but is he dead? My mind thoroughly upset by what I have seen.

Well then, yesterday, the locksmith having put on the iron shutters and door, I left everything open until midnight, although it was getting cold.

Suddenly I felt that he was there, and joy, mad joy, took possession of me. I got up softly, and walked up and down for some time, so that he might not suspect anything; then I took off my boots and put on my slippers carelessly; then I fastened the iron shutters, and, going back to the door, quickly double-locked it with a padlock, putting the key into my pocket.

Suddenly I noticed that he was moving restlessly round me, that in his turn he was frightened and was ordering me to let him out. I nearly yielded; I did not, however, but, putting my back to the door, I half opened it, just enough to allow me to go out backward, and as I am very tall my head touched the casing. I was sure that he had not been able to escape, and I shut him up alone, quite alone. What happiness! I had him fast. Then I ran downstairs; in the drawing-room, which was under my bedroom, I took the two lamps and I poured all the oil on the carpet, the furniture, everywhere; then I set fire to it and made my escape, after having carefully double-locked the door.

I went and hid myself at the bottom of the garden, in a clump of laurel bushes. How long it seemed! How long it seemed! Everything was dark, silent, motionless, not a breath of air and not a star, but heavy banks of clouds which one could not see, but which weighed, oh, so heavily on my soul.

I looked at my house and waited. How long it was! I already began to think that the fire had gone out of its own accord, or that he had extinguished it, when one of the lower windows gave way under the violence of the flames, and a long, soft, caressing sheet of red flame mounted up the white wall, and enveloped it as far as the roof. The light fell on the trees, the branches, and the leaves, and a shiver of fear pervaded them also! The birds awoke, a dog began to howl, and it seemed to me as if the day were breaking! Almost immediately two other windows flew into fragments, and I saw that the whole of the lower part of my house was nothing but a terrible furnace. But a cry, a horrible, shrill, heartrending cry, a woman's cry, sounded through the night, and two garret windows were opened! I had forgotten the servants! I saw their terror-stricken faces, and their arms waving franticaly.

Then, overwhelmed with horror, I set off to run to the village, shouting: "Help! Help! Fire! Fire!" I met some people who were already coming to the scene, and I returned with them.

By this time the house was nothing but a horrible and magnificent funeral pile, a monstrous funeral pile which lit up the whole country, a funeral pile where men were burning, and where he was burning also, He, He, my prisoner, that new Being, the new master, the Horla!

Suddenly the whole roof fell in between the walls, and a volcano of flames darted up to the sky. Through all the windows which opened on that furnace, I saw the flames darting, and I thought that he was there, in that kiln, dead.

Dead? Perhaps?—His body? was not his body, which was transparent, indestructible by such means as would kill ours?

If he were not dead?—Perhaps time alone has power over that Invisible and Redoubtable Being. Why this transparent, unrecognizable body, this body belonging to a spirit, if it also has to fear ills, infirmities and premature destruction?

Premature destruction? All human terror springs from that! After man, the Horla. After him who can die every day, at any hour, at any moment, by any accident, came the one who would die only at his own proper hour, day, and minute, because he had touched the limits of his existence!

No—no—without any doubt—he is not dead—Then—then—I suppose I must kill myself! . . .

J.-H. Rosny aîné (1856–1940)

Under the pen name of J.-H. Rosny aîné, Joseph-Henri Boex produced about two dozen works of science fiction. Long a favorite in Russia, he has been shamefully neglected by the English-speaking world even though he was an important European writer whose short stories are clearly superior to those of Jules Verne, his contemporary.

A French-speaking Belgian who was born in Brussels, Boex spent some time in England and then finished his education in Paris, where he was to remain for the rest of his life. Though Zola influenced Boex's early writings, in 1887 Boex repudiated Zola shortly before turning to science fiction. "The Shapes" (1887) is Boex's first effort in this field. It is a remarkable story, illustrating most of his themes and interests. There is the prehistoric setting, which is seen as strongly Edenic because mankind is more vigorous and accepting of nature's opposite and contradictory elements. There is the confrontation between the nomadic tribesmen and the cone-shaped silicon aliens who demonstrate Boex's interest in the hard sciences and who symbolize the widespread diversity of existence. Finally, there is the scientist whose anthropological studies of the problem—highlighting Boex's concern with the social sciences— lead to the discovery of principles needed for a solution, thus demonstrating through science that the universe's apparent diversity contains underlying similarities, which are a manifestation of a fundamental unity.

Between 1893 and 1907 Joseph-Henri and his younger brother, Seraphin Justin, who was also a writer, shared the Rosny pseudonym on six science-fiction works, among others. However, a textual analysis of these collaborations suggests that Joseph-Henri probably did much of the writing. After 1907 the brothers went their separate ways, but both continued using the pseudonym: Joseph-Henri adding *aîné* (the elder) and Seraphin Justin adding *jeune* (the younger).

During his life Joseph-Henri served as president of the Goncourt Academy and was one of its ten original members. He was a very popular author and a leading figure in French literature. However, he was an uneven writer, perhaps because he was too prolific. The strengths of his imagination, his vision, and his wide-ranging knowledge make his short science fiction and prehistoric novels still exciting. Yet the weaknesses of "prolixity, maudlin sentimentality and awkward stylistic mannerisms" render many of his later works and much of his realistic fiction virtually unreadable. And since realism had become the preeminent literary force by the time Boex died, his reputation suffered dreadfully. But with the growing ascendancy of science fiction in the 1970's, a publisher has brought out the first collection of these shorter works (*Recits de Science-Fiction,* 1973) and recognition of Boex's importance is growing.

THE SHAPES

(translated from the French by Damon Knight)

I t was a thousand years before the beginning of that center of civilization from which Nineveh, Babylon and Ecbatana were later to spring.

The nomadic tribe of Pjehu, with its horses, asses and cattle, was crossing the wild forest of Kzur toward the west, through a slanting curtain of light. The edge of the setting sun swelled, hovered, dropped from its graceful perches.

Everyone being weary, they were all silent, searching for a good clearing where the tribe might kindle the sacred fire, prepare the evening meal, and sleep in safety from wild animals, behind a double line of red-hot coals.

The clouds turned opalescent; illusory countrysides trailed away to the four horizons; the gods of night breathed their cradle song, and the tribe was still on the move. A scout came galloping back with word of a clearing and water, a pure spring.

The tribe gave three long shouts; everyone moved faster. Childish laughter rippled out; the very horses and asses, trained to recognize the nearness of a stopping-place by the return of the scouts and the nomads' cheers, raised their necks proudly.

The clearing came into view. Here, where the delightful spring had hollowed out its bed among mosses and shrubs, a phantasmagoria met the nomads' eyes.

It was, first, a great circle of translucent bluish cones, point uppermost, each nearly half the bulk of a man. A few clear streaks, a few dark convolutions were scattered across their surfaces; each one had a dazzling star near its base.

Farther distant, equally strange slabs stood on end, looking rather like birch bark, and spotted with varicolored elipses. Other Shapes, here and there, were almost cylindrical—some tall and thin, others low and squat, all of a bronzed color, tipped with green; and all, like the slabs, having the characteristic point of light.

The tribe stared in amazement. Even the bravest were frozen with superstitious fear, increasing still more when the Shapes began to sway in the twilight of the clearing. And suddenly, their stars wavering, flickering, the cones stretched higher, the cylinders and the slabs hissed like water thrown upon a flame, all of them moving toward the nomads with mounting speed.

Spellbound by the sight, the tribe did not move, but kept on watching. The Shapes fell upon them. The shock was terrible. Warriors, women and children fell in heaps, mysteriously struck down as if by lightning. Then the terrified survivors found strength to flee. And the Shapes, breaking their closed ranks, spread out around the tribe, implacably pursuing those who fled. Nevertheless, the frightful attack was not infallible: it killed some, stunned others, wounded none. A few red drops spurted from the nostrils, eyes and ears of the dying; but others, unhurt, soon arose and rejoined the fantastic rout.

Whatever might be the nature of the Shapes, they behaved like living creatures, not like elements of nature, having, like living creatures, an inconstancy and diversity of motion, evidently choosing their victims, not confounding the nomads with trees or shrubs, or even with animals.

In a short time the swiftest of the tribe noticed that no one was pursuing them any longer. Exhausted and in tatters, at last they dared retrace their steps toward the Mystery. Far away, between the tree trunks flooded with shadow, the resplendent chase went on. And the Shapes, seemingly by choice, ran down and massacred the warriors, often disdaining to attack the feeble, or the women and children.

Seen thus at a distance, in the night which had now fallen, the scene was more supernatural, move overwhelming to barbarian minds. About to take up their flight once more, the warriors made a vital discovery. It was this: whatever the fugitives did, *the Shapes abandoned the pursuit at a fixed boundary*. However weary and powerless the victim might be, even if he were unconscious, once he had crossed that invisible frontier, he was out of danger.

This reassuring discovery, soon confirmed by fifty observations, calmed the fugitives' frantic nerves. They dared to wait for their companions, their wives and their children who had escaped the butchery. One of them, indeed, their hero, who had been stunned at first, regained his spirit and lit a fire, blew on a buffalo horn to guide the fugitives.

Then one by one the pitiful survivors came. Many, cripples, dragged themselves by their hands.

The mothers, with indomitable maternal strength, had protected, gathered, and carried their children through the wild melee. And many asses, horses and cattle reappeared, less frightened than their masters.

A dismal night followed, passed in sleepless silence, while the warriors felt shivers run up and down their spines. But the dawn came, stealing pale through the heavy foliage; then the auroral fanfare of colors, of echoing bird cries, exhorted them to live, to cast off the terrors of darkness.

The hero, the natural leader, formed the crowd into groups and began counting the tribe. Half the warriors, two hundred, were missing. The loss of women was much less; of children, almost none.

When the counting was finished and the beasts of burden had been reassembled (few were missing, due to the superiority of instinct over reason during a crisis), the hero formed up the tribe as usual. Then, ordering everyone to wait for him, he walked, pale and alone, toward the clearing. No one dared follow him, even at a distance.

He went to where the trees were spaced out widely, a little inside the limit observed yesterday, and looked.

Far across the clearing, in the cool transparency of morning, flowed the pretty spring. Around the edges, reunited, the fantastic troop of Shapes shone resplendently. Their colors had changed. The Cones were more compact, their turquoise tint having turned greenish; the Cylinders were streaked with violet, and the Slabs looked like virgin copper. But each had its blazing star, dazzling even in daylight.

The outlines of these phantasmagorical Entities had also changed. The Cones tended to enlarge into Cylinders, the Cylinders to flatten and spread, while the Slabs curled slightly.

But suddenly, as on the night before, the Shapes swayed, their stars began to flicker; the hero, slowly, retreated beyond the borderline of safety.

The tribe of Pjehu halted at the doorway of the great nomad Tabernacle, where only chiefs might enter. In the starry depths, under the virile image of the Sun, sat the three high priests. Below them on the gilded steps, the dozen underpriests.

The hero stepped forward and recounted at length the fearful journey through the forest of Kzur; the priests listened very gravely, astonished, feeling their power dwindle before that inconceivable adventure.

The supreme high priest demanded that the tribe sacrifice to the Sun twelve bulls, seven onagers, three stallions. He recognized divine attributes in the Shapes, and, after the sacrifices, he resolved upon a hieratic expedition.

All the priests, all the chiefs of the Zahelal nation, were to take part. And messengers were sent out over the mountains and the plains, for a hundred leagues around the place where later would rise Ecbatana of the magi. Everywhere the dark tale made men's hair stand on end; everywhere the chiefs responded quickly to the priestly call.

One autumn morning, the Male pierced the clouds, flooded the Tabernacle, reached the altar where the bleeding heart of a bull lay smoking hot. The high priests, the under-priests, fifty tribal chiefs raised a cry of triumph. A hundred thousand nomads, standing in the dew outside, took up the clamor, turning their tanned faces toward the miraculous forest of Kzur and shivering a little. The omen was favorable.

Thus, with the priests at their head, a whole people marched through the trees. In the afternoon, at about the third hour, the hero of the Pjehu halted the throng. The great clearing lay spread out in its majesty, glowing with autumn, a torrent of dead leaves covering its mosses. On the banks of the spring, the priests saw the Shapes which they had come to worship and appease. They were pleasant to the eye, under the shade of the trees, with their trembling color changes, the pure flames of their stars, their tranquil movements at the edge of the spring.

"We must make the offering here," said the supreme high priests. "that they may know we submit to their power!"

All the graybeards nodded. One voice was raised, nevertheless. It was Yushik, of the tribe of Nim, the young star-counter, the pale prophetic watchman, of recent fame, who boldly demanded to go nearer the Shapes.

But the old men, white-haired in their wisdom, prevailed: the altar was built, the victim led forward—a dazzling white stallion. Then, in the silence of the prostrate people, the bronze knife found the animal's noble heart. A great moan went up. And the high priest intoned:

"Art thou appeased, O gods?"

Over there, among the silent trunks, the Shapes still moved in a ring, brightening themselves, preferring places where the sunbeams were thickest.

"Yea," cried the enthusiast, "they are appeased!"

And snatching up the stallion's warm heart, before the high priest could say a word, he flung himself into the clearing. Shouting, other fanatics followed him. The Shapes gently swayed, crowding together, skimming the grass, then suddenly hurled themselves on the daring ones, in a massacre that stunned the fifty tribes.

Six or seven fugitives, hotly pursued, managed to reach the boundary. The rest were dead, Yushik among them.

"These are relentless gods!" solemnly spoke the supreme high priest.

Then a council was held, the venerable council of priests, elders and chiefs. They decided to put up a row of stakes round the boundary line. In order to determine this line, they would force slaves to expose themselves to attack by the Shapes at one part of the perimeter after another.

And this was done. Under the threat of death, slaves entered the ring. So careful were the precautions taken, that few of them perished. The boundary was firmly established, made visible to all by its line of stakes.

Thus the hieratic expedition ended successfully, and the Zahelals believed themselves safe from the enemy.

But the preventive system advocated by the council was not long in showing its flaws. The following spring, the tribes of Hertoth and Nazzum, carelessly passing near the ring of stakes, suspecting nothing, were cruelly assaulted and decimated by the Shapes.

The chiefs who escaped the massacre told the great Zahelal council that the Shapes were now much more numerous than they had been the preceding autumn. Their pursuit was still limited, but the boundary had been enlarged.

This news dismayed the people; there was great mourning and many sacrifices. Then the council resolved to destroy the forest of Kzur by fire.

In spite of all their efforts, they could burn no more than the borders of the forest.

Then the priests, in despair, consecrated the forest and forebade anyone to enter it. And many summers passed.

One October night, the sleeping encampment of the tribe of Zulf, ten bowshots from the forbidden forest, was invaded by the Shapes. Three hundred more warriors lost their lives.

From this day a dark, mysterious tale went from tribe to tribe, a thing whispered by night, under the wide starry skies of Mesopotamia. *Man was going to perish.* The *others,* constantly expanding, in the forest, across the plains, indestructible, day by day would swallow up the overthrown race of man. And this dark, fearful secret haunted the brains of men, sapped their fighting strength and the confidence of their youth. The nomad, thinking such thoughts, no longer dared take pleasure in the lush pastures of his fathers. He turned his weary eyes upward, waiting for the stars to halt in their courses. It was the millennial year of this childlike people, the world's knell.

And in their distress, these thinkers turned to a bitter cult, a cult of death preached by pale prophets, the cult of Darknesses more powerful than the Stars, the Darknesses which would engulf and devour the holy Light, the resplendent fire.

Everywhere at the edge of the wilderness were seen the emaciated, immobile figures of the inspired ones, the men of silence, who, passing from time to time among the tribes, told of their terrible dreams, the Twilight of the great Night to come, of the dying Sun.

Now in those days there lived an extraordinary man called Bakhun, a member of the tribe of Ptuh and brother to the supreme high priest of the Zahelals. In his youth he had abandoned the nomadic life, had chosen a place in the wilderness, between four hills, in a narrow green valley where a spring poured out its pure song. He had built a fixed tent of stones, a cyclopean habitation. With patience and with the careful management of his horses and oxen, he had achieved the opulence of regular harvests. His four wives and thirty children lived the life of Eden there.

Bakhun professed unusual beliefs, for which he might have been stoned, save for the respect of the Zahelals for his elder brother, the supreme high priest.

First, he declared that the sedentary life was better than the life of the nomads, conserving man's strength to the profit of his spirit.

Second, he believed that the Sun, the Moon, and the Stars were not gods, but luminous masses.

Third, he said that men should really believe only in those things tested by measurement.

The Zahelals credited him with magical powers, and the most daring of them sometimes risked consulting him. They never repented it. It was said that he had often helped unfortunate tribes by distributing food to them.

Now, in this dark hour, when men were faced with the melancholy choice of giving up their green lands or being destroyed by the inexorable gods, the tribes thought of Bakhun, and the priests themselves, after a struggle with their pride, sent to him a deputation made up of three of the greatest among them.

Bakhun listened with close attention to their accounts, asking them to repeat certain parts, asking many detailed questions. He asked for two days to meditate. When the time was up, he announced simply that he would dedicate his life to the study of the Shapes.

The tribes were a little disappointed, for they had hoped Bakhun might be able to deliver the land by sorcery. Nevertheless, the chiefs expressed their happiness at his decision, and hoped that great things would come of it.

Then Bakhun took up his station at the edge of the forest of Kzur, leaving it only when night fell, and all day long, mounted on the swiftest stallion in Chaldea, he watched. Soon, convinced of the splendid animal's superiority over the most agile of the Shapes, he was able to begin his bold and painstaking study to which we owe the great ante-cuneiform book of sixty tablets, the finest stone book bequeathed by the nomadic age to modern civilization.

In this book, admirable for its restraint and its patient observation, is the description of a form of life absolutely distinct from our animal and vegetable kingdoms, a form which Bakhun humbly admitted he had been able to analyze only in its grossest and most superficial features. It is impossible for a man to read without shuddering, this monograph on the beings Bakhun called the Xipehuz; these dispassionate notes, never forced to fit into any system, of their actions, their modes of locomotion, of combat, of procreation—these notes which demonstrate that the human race was once on the brink of nothingness, that the Earth nearly became the patrimony of a *Kingdom* every trace of which has been lost.

The book should be read in Dessault's marvelous translation, full of unlooked-for discoveries in pre-Assyrian linguistics—discoveries unfortunately more admired in foreign countries, in England, in Germany, than in the author's native land. The eminent scholar has graciously made available the salient passages of this precious work, which are given in the following pages, and it is hoped that these passages will inspire the reader to look further into Dessault's superb translation.[1]

The Xipehuz are evidently living beings. All their motions reveal the free will, impulsiveness, cooperation and partial independence which distinguish the animal from the plant and from nonliving matter. Although their mode of progression is impossible to describe in comparative terms—being a simple gliding motion across the ground—it is plain that it is under voluntary control. We see them stop suddenly, turn, pursue one another, stroll together by twos and threes; they display preferences which will make them leave one companion to join another at a distance. They are incapable of climbing trees, but they succeed in killing birds after *attracting them* by undiscoverable means. They are frequently seen to surround forest animals or to lie in wait for them behind a bush; these they invariably kill and consume. It may be stated as a rule that they kill *all animals without distinction*, whenever they can catch them, and this without any apparent motive, for they do not devour them, but merely reduce them to ashes.

In doing so they make use of no funeral pyre; the incandescent point which each has at its base suffices them for this purpose. They form a circle of ten or twenty around the carcass of a large animal, and cause their rays to converge upon it. For small animals, birds for example, the rays of a single Xipehuz are sufficient to cause incineration. It should be noted that the heat they produce is not instantaneous in its effect. I have often received the irradiation of a Xipehuz upon my hand, and the skin began to feel warm only after a certain time.

---

[1]*The Precursors of Nineveh*, by B. Dessault (Calmann-Levy). In the interests of clarity, I have converted the extract from the *Book of Bakhun* into modern scientific language.

I do not know if it is correct to say that the Xipehuz have different forms, for any one of them can successively transform itself into a cone, a cylinder and a slab, and this in the course of a single day. Their colors vary constantly, a fact which I believe can be attributed in general to the changes in the quality of the light from morning to evening and from evening to morning. Nevertheless certain variations seem to be due to the impulses of individuals, and in particular to their *passions*, if I may be permitted this term, and thus constitue genuine expressions of physiognomy, of which, in spite of ardent study, I have been utterly unable to identify any except by hypothesis. Thus, I have never been able to distinguish between an angry tint and a calm one, which surely would be the primary discovery in this field.

I have spoken of their *passions*. I have also remarked earlier upon their preferences, which I might term their *friendships*. They also have their *hatreds*. One Xipehuz continually keeps his distance from another, and vice versa. They seem to experience violent rages. They hurl themselves upon one another with movements identical to those observed when they attack men or large animals, and in fact it was these combats which taught me they are not immortal, as I had been at first disposed to believe, for two or three times I have seen Xipehuz succumb in these encounters, that is to say *fall, shrink,* and *petrify*. I have carefully preserved some of these bizarre cadavers, [1] and perhaps at some future time they may serve to reveal the nature of the Xipehuz. They are yellowish crystals, arranged irregularly, and streaked with blue filaments.

From the fact that the Xipehuz are not immortal, I was able to deduce that it should be possible to attack and defeat them, and at that point I began the series of martial experiments of which I shall have to speak later.

Since the Xipehuz's radiance is always sufficient to make them visible through underbrush and even behind large tree trunks—a wide halo emanates from them in all directions and warns of their approach—I was able to venture often into the forest, trusting myself to the speed of my stallion.

There, I tried to find out if they built shelters, but I confess to having

---

[1] The Kensington Museum in London, and Professor Dessault himself, have in their possession certain mineral fragments, similar in every way to those described by Bakhun, which under chemical analysis have been found impossible to *decompose* or to *combine* with other substances, and which, in consequence, cannot be assigned a place in any conventional nomenclature.

failed in that research. They move neither stones nor plants, and appear to be strangers to any form of *tangible* and *visible* industry, the only sort which can be distinguished by human observation. Consequently they have no weapons, in the usual sense of that word. It is certain that they cannot kill at a distance: every animal which has been able to flee without coming inte *direct* contact with a Xipehuz, has invariably escaped, and I have witnessed this many times.

As the unfortunate tribe of Pjehu has already observed, they cannot cross certain intangible barriers; thus their movements are limited. But these limits continually expand from year to year, from month to month. I had to try to discover the cause of this.

Well, this cause appears to be nothing other than a phenomenon of *collective growth*, and like most Xipehuzian things, it is incomprehensible to the human mind. In brief, the governing principle is this: the limits of Xipehuzian movement enlarge in proportion to the number of living individuals, that is to say that when new beings are propagated, the frontiers are extended; but so long as their number does not increase, each individual is totally incapable of leaving the habitat determined— by natural forces?—for the race as a whole. This principle suggests a closer correlation between the individual and the group than that observed among other animals and men. Later we saw the reciprocal of this principle in operation, for when the numbers of Xipehuz began to diminish, their frontiers shrank in proportion.

Concerning the phenomenon of propagation itself, I have little to say, but this little is characteristic. To begin with, this propagation takes place four times a year, a little before the equinoxes and solstices, and only on very clear nights. The Xipehuz join in groups of three, and these groups draw together little by little until there is only one, tightly amalgamated and arranged in a very long ellipse. They remain so all night long, and until the Sun reaches the zenith on the following day. When they separate, vague forms arise, vaporous and *enormous*.

These forms slowly condense, dwindle, and transform themselves at the end of ten days into amber-tinted cones, considerably larger still than adult Xipehuz. It takes them two months and several days to reach their maximum development, which is to say diminution. At the end of this time, they become similar to other members of their race, their shapes and colors variable according to the weather, the time and the

mood of the individual. A few days after their development of diminution is complete, the boundaries enlarge. Needless to say, it was shortly
before this redoubtable moment that I kicked the flanks of my noble
Kuath, in order to establish my camp farther away.

It is impossible to say whether the Xipehuz have senses as we
understand the term. They certainly have organs which serve the same
purpose.

The ease with which they detect the presence of animals, men
above all, over great distances, makes it evident that their organs of
perception are at least as efficient as our eyes. I have never seen them
mistake a plant for an animal, even under circumstances in which I might
well have fallen into this error, deceived by the light filtering through
leaves, the color of the object, or its position. Their use of twenty to
consume a large animal, whereas one alone incinerates a bird, indicates a
correct understanding of proportions, and this understanding seems even
more perfect when one considers that they make use of ten, twelve,
fifteen, always in keeping with the relative size of the carcass. Still a
better argument, either for the existence of sense organs analogous to
ours, or for their intelligence, is their manner of attacking our tribes, for
they give little or no attention to women and children, while they
mercilessly pursue the warriors.

Now, the most important question—do they have a language? I am
able to reply without the slightest hesitation, "Yes, they have a language." And this language is composed of signs, some of which I have
even been able to decipher.

Suppose, for example, that a Xipehuz wishes to speak to another.
For this, it suffices for him to direct the radiation from his star toward the
other, a thing which is always perceived instantly. The one who is
hailed, if he is in motion, stops and waits. The speaker then traces rapidly
on the very skin of the listener—and it makes no difference on which
side—a series of short luminous characters made by directing the radiation from his base, and these characters remain fixed a moment, then
fade away.

The listener, after a short pause, responds.

As a preliminary to any action of combat or ambuscade, I have
always seen the Xipehuz employ the following characters:

When I myself am in question—and this happens frequently, for they have done everything possible to exterminate us, my noble Kuath and me—the signs

have invariably been exchanged—among others, such as the word or phrase

above. The usual calling sign is

and this makes the receiving individual hasten up. When the Xipehuz are invited to a general meeting, I have never failed to observe a signal of this form

representing the triple appearance of these beings.

In addition, the Xipehuz have more complicated signs, not relating to actions similar to ours, but to a completely extraordinary order of things, and these I have been unable to decipher. One can hardly entertain any doubt of their ability to exchange *ideas* of an abstract order, probably the equivalents of human ideas, for they are capable of standing motionless for long periods, doing nothing but conversing, which indicates real accumulations of thoughts.

In spite of their metamorphoses (whose laws differ for each, only very slightly, but characteristically enough for a determined observer), during my long sojourn among them I learned to know a number of Xipehuz rather intimately by recognizing the peculiarities among their individual differences . . . should I say among their characters? I have known taciturn ones, who almost never traced a word; voluble ones who wrote veritable discourses; attentive ones, gossips who spoke at the same time, one interrupting the other. Some were of a retiring nature and preferred a solitary life; others obviously sought company; some were fierce, constantly hunting birds and beasts, and some merciful, often sparing animals and letting them live in peace. Does not all this open an enormous avenue to the imagination? Does it not lead us to imagine diversities of aptitude, strength, intellignece, analogous to those of the human race?

They practice education. How many times have I not seen an old Xipehuz, seated in the midst of many young ones, irradiating them with signs which they then repeated one after another, and which he made them do over when their repetition was imperfect!

These lessons were indeed marvelous to my eyes, and in all that concerns the Xipehuz, there is nothing that has more often fixed my attention, nothing that has preoccupied me more during my nights of insomnia. It seemed to me that here, in the morning of the race, the veil of mystery might open, that some simple, primitive idea might spring forth and illuminate for me a corner of this profound darkness. No, nothing discouraged me; year after year I watched that education, and I tried innumerable interpretations. How many times have I thought to grasp a fugitive glimmer of the essential nature of the Xipehuz, an invisible light, a pure abstraction, which, alas! my poor flesh-burdened faculties could never follow!

I have said previously that for a long time I believed the Xipehuz to be immortal. Having abandoned this belief, after seeing the violent deaths which followed some encounters between Xipehuz, I was naturally led to seek their vulnerable points, and devoted all my days from that time forward to the search for means of destruction; for the Xipehuz were growing in numbers, to such a point that, having emerged from the forest of Kzur in the south, west and north, they were beginning to encroach upon the plains in the direction of the levant. Alas! in a few cycles they would have dispossessed man from his earthly abode.

Accordingly, I armed myself with a sling, and whenever a Xipehuz emerged from the forest within my range, I took aim and hurled my stone at him. I obtained no result in this way, although I had struck my targets on every part of their surface, even including the luminous point. They appeared entirely insensible to my blows, and none ever turned aside to avoid one of my projectiles. After a month's trial I could only conclude that nothing could be done against them with the sling, and I abandoned that weapon.

I took up the bow. With the first arrows I shot, the Xipehuz betrayed an intense fear, for they turned aside, stayed out of range, and avoided me as much as possible. For a week I did not succeed in striking one. On the eighth day, a party of Xipehuz, carried away I suppose by their enthusiasm for the hunt, passed fairly close to me in pursuit of a fine gazelle. I quickly shot several arrows, *without any apparent effect*, and the party dispersed, I pursuing them and using up my ammunition. I had barely shot my last arrow when they all turned back at full speed, from different directions, surrounding me on three sides, and I would have lost my life if not for the prodigious speed of my valiant Kuath.

This adventure left me full of hope and uncertainty; for a week I did nothing, lost in the oceanic depths of my meditations, in a subtle, absorbing, sleep-dispelling problem which filled me with joy and anguish. Why did the Xipehuz fear my arrows? Why, again, among the great number of projectiles with which I had struck the hunters, had none produced any effect? My knowledge of my enemy's intelligence ruled out the hypothesis of a terror without cause. On the contrary, everything I knew compelled me to believe that the *arrow*, under the proper conditions, must be a formidable weapon against them. But what were these conditions? What was the vulnerable point of the Xipehuz? And suddenly the thought came to me that it was the *star* that I must strike. For a moment I held this as a certainty, a blind, impassioned certainty. Then I was seized by doubt.

With the sling, had I not aimed at and struck this point many times? Why should the arrow be luckier than the stone . . .?

Now the night had come, the measureless abyss, with its marvelous lamps strewn above the earth. And I sat lost in thought, my head in my hands, my spirit darker than the night.

A lion began to roar, jackals were running across the plain, and once a gain a spark of hope was born. It had just come to my mind that the single stone was relatively large, and the Xipehuz' star so tiny! Perhaps it was necessary to penetrate deeply, to pierce with a sharp point, and then their fear of the bow was understandable!

But Vega was turning slowly around the Pole, dawn was near, and for a few hours weariness conquered my thoughts with sleep.

In the days that followed, armed with the bow, I was in constant pursuit of the Xipehuz, as deep in their territory as prudence would permit. But they all avoided my assault, keeping at a distance, out of range. Lying in ambush was not to be considered; their mode of perception enabled them to detect my presence behind obstacles.

Toward the end of the fifth day, an event occurred which in itself proved that the Xipehuz, like men, are fallible and perfectible creatures. That evening, at twilight, a Xipehuz deliberately approached me, with that constantly accelerating speed which they use in the attack. Surprised, my heart beating fast, I drew my bow. He, steadily advancing, like a column of turquoise in the growing dusk, came almost within bowshot. Then, as I made ready to loose my arrow, I was stunned to see him turn his body, hiding his star, while he continued to hurtle toward me. I had barely time to put Kuath into a gallop, and retreat out of the reach of this formidable adversary.

Now this simple maneuver, which no Xipehuz appeared to have thought of before, in addition to demonstrating once more the individuality and personal inventiveness of the enemy, suggested two ideas: the first, that it was probable that I had reasoned correctly about the vulnerability of the Xipehuz star; the second, less encouraging, that the same tactic, if adopted by all, would render my task extraordinarily difficult, perhaps impossible.

Nevertheless, having labored so long to learn the truth, I felt my courage grow in the face of this obstacle, and I dared to hope that my ingenuity would be great enough to surmount it. [1]

I returned to my wilderness. Anakhre, the third son of my wife Tepai, was a potent maker of weapons. I ordered him to carve a bow of extraordinary size. He took a branch of the tree Waham, hard as iron, and the bow he made of it was four times stronger than that of the shepherd Zankann, the mightiest archer of the thousand tribes. No man living could have bent it. But I had thought of an artifice, and Anakhre having wrought according to my plan, it came about that the immense bow could be bent and loosed by a woman.

Now I had always been skilled in casting darts and arrows, and in a few days I learned so perfectly the use of the weapon made by my son Anakhre that I never missed a target, be it as small as a fly or moving as swiftly as a falcon.

Having done all this, I returned to Kzur, mounted on my flame-eyed Kuath, and once more began to prowl around the enemies of man.

In order to give them confidence, I loosed many arrows with my customary bow, each time one of their parties approached the frontier, and my arrows fell far short of them. Thus they learned to know the exact range of the weapon, and from this to believe themselves absolutely out

---

[1]In the following chapters, of a narrative character, I have adhered closely to the literal translation of Professor Dessault, without, however, feeling bound to follow the tiresome division into verses or the needless repetitions.

of danger at a certain distance. Nevertheless they remained mistrustful; this caused them to be mobile and agitated when they were not sheltered by the forest, and to hide their stars from my view.

By dint of patience I wore out their suspicions, and on the morning of the sixth day, a troop of them took up a position facing me, beneath a great chestnut tree, at a distance of three ordinary bowshots.

At once I loosed a cloud of useless arrows. Then their vigilance lessened more and more, and their movements became as free as in the earliest days of my sojourn.

It was the decisive moment. My heart beat so loudly that at first I felt myself strengthless. I waited for the future, hung upon a single arrow. If it failed to strike its target, never again, perhaps, would the Xipehuz offer themselves to my experiments, and then how would it be possible to know whether they were vulnerable to the blows of men?

Nevertheless, little by little my will triumphed, quieted my heart, made my limbs supple and strong and my eye steady. Then, slowly, I raised the bow of Anakhre. There, in the distance, a great cone of emerald stood motionless in the shade of the tree; its sparkling star turned toward me. The enormous bow bent; the arrow flew whistling across space . . . and the Xipehuz *fell, shrank and petrified.*

A resounding cry of triumph burst from my lips. Stretching out my arms in ecstasy, I gave thanks to the One.

So, then, they were vulnerable to humans weapons, these terrible Xipehuz! We could hope to destroy them!

Now, without fear, I let my heart murmur, I gave myself up to the beating of the music of gladness, I who had so greatly despaired of the future of my race, I who beneath the stars in their courses, beneath the blue crystal of the abyss, had so often calculated that in two centuries the vast world's limits would have burst before the Xipehuz invasion.

And yet when it came again, the well-beloved night, the pensive night, a shadow fell over my happiness, the sorrow that man and Xipehuz could not exist together, that the annihilation of one was the grim condition of the other's survival.

The priests, the elders and the chiefs had listened marveling to my story; couriers had carried the good news into the depths of the wilderness. The great Council had ordered the warriors to gather in the sixth moon of the year 22,649, in the plain of Mehur-Asar, and the prophets had preached a holy war. More than a hundred thousand Zahelal warriors came, and many members of foreign races, Dzums, Sahrs, Khaldes, came to offer themselves to the great nation.

Kzur was surrounded by a tenfold ring of archers, but all their arrows failed against the tactics of the Xipehuz, and incautious warriors perished in great numbers.

Then for several weeks great fear prevailed among men. . . .

On the third day of the eighth moon, armed with a sharp-pointed knife, I announced to the multitudes that I would go to fight the Xipehuz alone, in the hope of laying to rest the doubts which had begun to arise concerning the truth of my story.

My sons Lum, Demja and Anakhre were violently opposed to this project, and offered to go in my place. And Lum said, "You cannot go, for once you are dead, all will believe the Xipehuz are invulnerable, and the human race will perish."

Demja, Anakhre and many of the chiefs having echoed these words, I found their reasons good, and withdrew.

Then Lum, taking my horn-handled knife, crossed the frontier. The Xipehuz hastened up. One swifter by far than the rest, was about to rush upon him, but Lum, more agile than a leopard, sprang aside, circled the Xipehuz, then with a giant bound closed in again and stabbed with his sharp point.

The waiting throng saw his adversary *collapse, dwindle and petrify*. A hundred thousand voices rose to the blue dawn, and already Lum was returning, crossing the frontier. The glory of his name spread throughout the armies.

The year 22,649 of the world, the seventh day of the eighth moon.

At daybreak the horns sounded; hammers beat brazen bells for the great battle. A hundred black buffalo and two hundred stallions were sacrificed by the priests, and my fifteen sons and I prayed to the One.

The globe of the sun was engulfed in the red dawn, the chiefs galloped in the forefront of their armies, the clamor of the attack swelled in the headlong rush of a hundred thousand warriors.

The tribe of Nazzum was first to encounter the enemy in bitter combat. Powerless at first, mowed down by invisible lightning bolts the warriors soon learned the art of striking the Xipehuz and destroying them. Then all the nations, Zahelals, Dzums, Sahrs, Khaldes, Xisoastres, Pjarvanns, roaring like oceans, invaded the plain and the forest, everywhere surrounding the silent enemy.

For a long time the battle was in chaos; messengers came continually to tell the priests that men were dying by hundreds, but that their deaths were being avenged.

In the heat of midday my swift-footed son Surdar, sent by Lum, came to tell me that for each Xipehuz destroyed, a dozen of ours had perished. My spirit was dark and my heart weak, but my lips murmured, "Let it be as the Father wills!"

In recalling to my mind the numbers of the armies, which added together gave a sum of a hundred and forty thousand, and knowing that the numbers of Xipehuz amounted to about four thousand, I told myself that more than a third of the vast army would perish, but that the earth would belong to man.

"It is a victory, then!" I murmured sadly.

But as I pondered on these things, the clamor of the battle shook the forest more violently; then great masses of warriors reappeared, all, with cries of distress, fleeing toward the frontier.

Then I saw the Xipehuz emerge at the border, not separate from one another as they had been in the morning, but in groups of twenty formed into circles, with their stars turned inward. In this array, invulnerable, they advanced on our helpless warriors and massacred them.

It was defeat.

The boldest warriors thought of nothing but flight. Nevertheless, in spite of the sorrow that weighed down my spirit, I patiently observed the fatal encounters, in the hope of finding some remedy in the very heart of misfortune, for often the venom and the antidote are found side by side.

For this confidence in power of thought, destiny repaid me with two discoveries. I remarked, first, that in places where our tribes were massed in multitudes and the Xipehuz were in small numbers, the slaughter, immeasurable at first, lessened by degrees, that the strength of the enemy's blows grew less and less, many of the victims rising again after a moment's dizziness. The strongest resisted the shock completely, continuing to flee after repeated blows. The same phenomenon being in evidence at various parts of the field of battle, I dared to conclude that the Xipehuz were growing weary, that their powers of destruction were not unlimited.

The second observation, which aptly complemented the first, was furnished to me by a group of Khaldes. These unfortunate men, surrounded on all sides by Xipehuz, and losing confidence in their short knives, pulled up bushes and made clubs of them, with which they tried to beat their way to freedom. To my great surprise, their attempt succeeded. I saw the Xipehuz topple by the dozen under these blows, and about half the Khaldes escaped through the hole they had opened in this way; but, curiously, those who made use of bronze implements instead of bushes (as in the case of several chiefs) killed themselves in striking the enemy. I must point out further that the blows from these clubs gave no apparent hurt to the Xipehuz, for those who fell rose again promptly and took up the pursuit. Nevertheless, I considered my double discovery of the greatest importance for future battles.

Meanwhile, the rout continued. The earth resounded to the flight of the vanquished; by nightfall, only our dead remained within the Xipehuz boundaries, and a few hundred warriors who had taken refuge in trees. The fate of these latter was terrible, for the Xipehuz burned them alive, concentrating a thousand fires in the branches which sheltered them. Their frightful cries echoed for hours under the vast firmament.

The next day, the tribes counted their survivors. The battle had cost nine thousand human lives or thereabout; a moderate estimate put the loss of Xipehuz at six hundred. Thus the death of each enemy had cost us fifteen men.

Despair settled in the hearts of the tribesmen, many crying out against the chiefs and talking of giving up the terrible enterprise. Then, under these complaints, I strode into the middle of the camp and loudly reproached the warriors for their faintheartedness. I asked them if it were better to let all men perish, or to sacrifice a part; I showed them that in ten years the Zahelal country would be invaded by the Shapes, and in twenty the country of the Khaldes, the Sahrs, the Pjarvanns and the Xisoastres; then, having reawakened their conscience in this way, I reminded them that already a sixth of the disputed territory had been reconquered, that on three sides the enemy had been driven back into the forest. Finally I told them of my observations, and made them understand that the Xipehuz were not tireless, that clubs of wood could topple them and force them to expose their vulnerable points.

Silence fell across the plain; hope returned to the hearts of the multitude who heard me. And to strenthen their confidence, I described the contrivances of wood which I had thought of, suited both for attack and defense. With renewed enthusiasm, the people applauded my words, and the chiefs laid their scepters of command at my feet.

In the days that followed, I had a great number of trees cut down, and displayed a model of a light, portable barrier, of which a brief description follows: a framework six cubits long and two cubits wide, fastened by crossbars to an interior framework one cubit wide and five long. Six men (two porters, two warriors armed with heavy, blunt wooden spears, two others also armed with wooden spears having sharp metal points, and furnished in addition with bows and arrows) could stand within it comfortably and could roam the forest, protected from the direct attack of the Xipehuz. Once within range of the enemy, the warriors armed with blunt spears were to strike and overturn them, force them to expose themselves, and the archer-spearmen were to aim at the stars, with bow or spear according to circumstance. Since the average height of the Xipehuz was a little more than a cubit and a half, I had arranged the crossbars in such a way that the exterior framework, while being carried, would reach a height above the ground of no more than a cubit and a quarter, and for this it sufficed to incline somewhat the supports by which it was attached to the interior framework. In addition, since the Xipehuz were unable to surmount any steep obstacle, nor to move in any way except upright, the barrier thus devised was sufficient to give shelter against their direct assaults. Undoubtedly they would attempt to burn these new weapons, and in some cases they would succeed; but since their fires were almost ineffective out of bowshot, they would be forced to expose themselves in order to do so. Besides, since these fires did not take effect instantaneously, it would be possible to avoid them in many cases by rapid movement.

The year 22,649 of the world, the eleventh day of the eighth moon. On this day the second battle with the Xipehuz took place, and the chiefs gave me the supreme command. Then I divided the people into three armies. Shortly before dawn, I sent against Kzur forty thousand warriors armed with the barrier devices. This attack was less confused than that of the seventh day. The tribes entered the forest slowly, in small bands disposed in a good order, and the encounter began. During the first hour the advantage was entirely ours, the Xipehuz being caught off guard by the new tactics; more than a hundred Shapes were slain, while only a dozen of our warriors perished. But, once over their surprise, the Xipehuz applied themselves to burning the barriers. In some circumstances they were able to do so. A more dangerous maneuver was the one they adopted toward the fourth hour of the day: taking advantage of their swiftness, groups of Xipehuz, tightly pressed together, hurled themselves at the barriers and succeeded in overturning them. In this fashion great numbers of men perished; so many that, the enemy having regained the advantage, a part of our army fell into despair.

Toward the fifth hour, the Zahelal tribes of Khemar, Djoh, and part of the Xisoastres and Sahrs began to flee. Wishing to avert a catastrophe, I sent messengers protected by strong barriers to promise reinforcements. At the same time, I disposed the second army for the attack; but first I gave new orders: the barriers were to cluster in groups, as thickly as movement in the forest would permit, and to arrange themselves in compact squares whenever a large band of Xipehuz approached. This was to be done without giving up the offensive.

After this, I gave the signal, and in a short time I had the pleasure of seeing the battle turn in our favor. At length, toward the middle of the day, an approximate reckoning, which brought the number of our losses to two thousand men, and of the Xipehuz to three hundred, decisively showed the progress we had accomplished, and strengthened the hearts of all.

Nevertheless, the proportion changed somewhat to our disadvantage during the fourth hour, the tribes then having lost four thousand warriors, and the Xipehuz five hundred.

It was then that I sent in the third army. The battle reached its greatest intensity; the warriors' enthusiasm rose from minute to minute, until the hour when the sun was about to sink into the West.

At that moment, the Xipehuz took the offensive again to the north of Kzur; a retreat of the Dzums and Pjarvanns gave me uneasiness. Judging that in any case the darkness would be more favorable to the enemy than to us, I signaled the end of the battle. The troops returned calm and victorious; much of the night was passed in celebrating our successes. These were considerable: eight hundred Xipehus had succumbed; their sphere of action was reduced to two thirds of Kzur. It is true that we had left seven thousand slain in the forest, but these losses were much smaller, in proportion to the result, than in the first battle. Thus, filled with hope, I dared to conceive the plan of a more decisive attack against the two thousand six hundred Sipehuz still living.

The year 22,649 of the world, the fifteenth day of the eighth moon.

When the red star rose over the eastern hills, the tribes were in battle array before Kzur.

With my heart full of hope, I gave my last instructions to the chiefs; the horns sounded, the bells set up their brazen clangor, and the first army marched against the forest.

Their barriers now were stronger and somewhat larger, enclosing twelve men instead of six, except for about a third which were constructed according to the old design. Thus they were more difficult either to set on fire or to overturn.

The beginning of the battle was promising; after the third hour, four hundred Xipehuz had been exterminated, and only two thousand men. Encouraged by the good news, I sent in the second army. The fury of the battle on both sides grew appalling, our warriors being flushed with triumph, their adversaries resisting with the stubbornness of a noble kingdom. From the fourth to the eighth hour, we sacrificed no less than ten thousand lives; but the Xipehuz paid with a thousand of theirs, so that only a thousand remained in the depths of Kzur.

From this moment, I knew that man would possess the world; my last misgivings faded.

Nevertheless, at the ninth hour, a great shadow fell over our victory. At this time, the Xipehuz appeared only in enormous masses in the clearings, concealing their stars, and it became almost impossible to overthrow them. In the heat of the battle, many of our warriors hurled themselves upon these masses. Then, with a rapid movement, a party of Xipehuz would detach itself, overthrowing and slaughtering these men.

A thousand perished thus, without any perceptible loss to the enemy; seeing which, the Pjarvanns cried that all was lost; a panic began which put more than ten thousand men to flight, many being so imprudent as to abandon their barriers in order to run faster. It cost them dear. A hundred Xipehuz, pursuing them, cut down more than two thousand Pjarvanns and Zahelals: terror was beginning to spread throughout our lines.

When the messengers brought me this dismal news, I knew that the day was lost unless by some swift maneuver I succeeded in retaking the abandoned positions. At once I gave the chiefs of the third army the order to attack, and I announced that I would assume command. Then I quickly brought these reserves to the place from which the others had fled. Shortly we found ourselves face to face with the pursuing Xipehuz.

Carried away by the passion of their slaughter, they did not regroup quickly enough, and in a few moments we had surrounded them: few escaped; the great acclamation for our victory went far to restore the courage of our men.

From that time on, I had no trouble in re-forming the attack; our methods were limited to detaching segments of the enemy groups, then surrounding these segments and annihilating them.

Soon, realizing how greatly these tactics worked to their disfavor, the Xipehuz once more took up the assault in small groups, and the massacre of the two kingdoms, neither of which could survive except by the annihilation of the other, redoubled dreadfully. But all doubt of the final issue had vanished from the faintest hearts. By the fourteenth hour, there remained hardly five hundred Xipehuz against more than a hundred thousand men, and this small number of the enemy was more and more hemmed in by narrow frontiers, about a sixth of the forest of Kzur, which greatly facilitated our movements.

Meanwhile, the red light of sunset streamed through the trees, and I broke off the battle.

The immensity of our victory swelled every heart; the chiefs talked of offering me the kingship of the nations. I counseled them never to confide the destinies of so many men to one poor fallible creature, and to take *Wisdom* for their earthly master.

The Earth belongs to Man. Two days of combat have annihilated the Xipehuz; the whole domain occupied by the last two hundred of them has been razed, every tree, every plant, every blade of grass has been cut down. And I, aided by my sons Lum, Azah and Simho, have finished inscribing this history upon tablets of granite for the instruction of future nations.

And now I am alone, at the edge of Kzur, in the pale night. A coppery half-moon hangs over the West. Lions are roaring at the stars. The brook wanders slowly among the willows; its eternal voice speaks of time passing, of the melancholy of perishable things. And I have buried my face in my hands, and my heart mourns. For, now that the Xipehuz are no more, my soul laments for them, and I ask the One what Fatality demanded that the splendor of Life be tarnished by the Shadow of Murder!

Edward Bellamy (1850–1898)

As the result of one novel, Looking Backward, 2000–1887 (1888), Edward Bellamy had more influence on society than any other nineteenth-century science-fiction writer. The book sold several million copies, was translated into over twenty languages, led to the founding of more than one hundred and sixty-five Bellamy clubs in the United States, and deeply affected such prominent social figures as Eugene V. Debs, John Dewey, Norman Thomas, Thorstein Veblen, and William Allen White. Hundreds of books were written in response, including William Morris's *News from Nowhere* (1891), H. G. Wells's *When the Sleeper Wakes* (1899) and Mack Reynolds's contemporary *Looking Backward, From the Year 2000* (1973). And even today Bellamy's *Looking Backward* retains much charm, selling several thousand copies a year.

Bellamy himself was born in Chicopee Falls, Massachusetts, where his father had served as a Baptist minister for many years. After spending a few months at Union College as a special literature student, Bellamy traveled to Germany in 1868. There he encountered urban slums that shocked him deeply and raised his consciousness about the plight of the economically dispossessed.

Returning home after a year, Bellamy studied law and was admitted to the bar, but never practiced. Instead, he became a journalist, working as associate editor of the Springfield *Union* and editorial writer for the New York *Evening Post* before founding the Springfield *Daily News* in 1880. However, his heart was in writing, not journalism, and after marrying Emma Sanderson in 1882 he withdrew to become a full-time author.

Then, in late 1886, perhaps triggered by the ongoing Haymarket strike, he sat down to begin reasoning out a method of economic organization that would reflect enlightened self-interest and wholesale common sense.[1] What he ended up with in *Looking Backward* was a system of state capitalism that was intensely democratic and very reflective of a village or small-town orientation. But equally appealing to the general public was Bellamy's belief that this ideal society would *evolve* naturally from capitalism without a class struggle.

A modest, reticent, and taciturn person, Bellamy forced himself to actively campaign for his ideas. As a result his already fragile health suffered, and while working on a sequel (*Equality*, 1897) he was discovered to have tuberculosis. Still, he refused to move to Colorado's healthier climate until he finished the book. By then it was too late and he returned from Colorado to die in his hometown at the age of forty-eight.

Bellamy also produced other, less well-known works of science fiction. There is an earlier novel, *Mrs. Ludington's Sister* (1884), which deals with immortality, and several short stories, such as the powerful "To Whom This May Come" (1888), which explores the implications of a telepathic society.

---

[1] Ironically, eighty-two years later Jack Finney wrote a novel *Time and Again* (1970) in which the protagonist finally escapes the turbulent 1960's and returns to what are described as idyllic times, the 1880's.

TO WHOM THIS MAY COME

I t is now about a year since I took passage at Calcultta in the ship *Adelaide* for New York. We had baffling weather till New Amsterdam Island was sighted, where we took a new point of departure. Three days later, a terrible gale struck us. Four days we flew before it, whither, no one knew, for neither sun, moon, nor stars were at any time visible, and we could take no observation. Toward midnight of the fourth day, the glare of lightning revealed the *Adelaide* in a hopeless position, close in upon a low-lying shore, and driving straight toward it. All around and astern far out to sea was such a maze of rocks and shoals that it was a miracle we had come so far. Presently the ship struck, and almost instantly went to pieces, so great was the violence of the sea. I gave myself up for lost, and was indeed already past the worst of drowning, when I was recalled to consciousness by being thrown with a tremendous shock upon the beach. I had just strength enough to drag myself above the reach of the waves, and then I fell down and knew no more.

When I awoke, the storm was over. The sun, already halfway up the sky, had dried my clothing, and renewed the vigor of my bruised and aching limbs. On sea or shore I saw no vestige of my ship or my companions, of whom I appeared the sole survivor. I was not, however, alone. A group of persons, apparently the inhabitants of the country, stood near, observing me with looks of friendliness which at once freed me from apprehension as to my treatment at their hands. They were a white and handsome people, evidently of a high order of civilization, though I recognized in them the traits of no race with which I was familiar.

Seeing that it was evidently their idea of etiquette to leave it to strangers to open conversation, I addressed them in English, but failed to elicit any response beyond deprecating smiles. I then accosted them successively in the French, German, Italian, Spanish, Dutch, and Portuguese tongues, but with no better results. I began to be very much puzzled as to what could possibly be the nationality of a white and evidently civilized race to which no one of the tongues of the great seafaring nations was intelligible. The oddest thing of all was the unbroken silence with which they contemplated my efforts to open communication with them. It was as if they were agreed not to give me a clue to their language by even a whisper; for while they regarded one another with looks of smiling intelligence, they did not once open their lips. But if this behavior suggested that they were amusing themselves at my expense, that presumption was negatived by the unmistakable friendliness and sympathy which their whole bearing expressed.

A most extraordinary conjecture occurred to me. Could it be that these strange people were dumb? Such a freak of nature as an entire race thus afflicted had never indeed been heard of, but who could say what wonders the unexplored vasts of the great Southern Ocean might thus far have hid from human ken? Now, among the scraps of useless information which lumbered my mind was an acquaintance with the deaf-and-dumb alphabet, and forthwith I began to spell out with my fingers some of the phrases I had already uttered to so little effect. My resort to the sign language overcame the last remnant of gravity in the already profusely smiling group. The small boys now rolled on the ground in convulsions of mirth, while the grave and reverend seniors, who had hitherto kept them in check, were fain momentarily to avert their faces, and I could see their bodies shaking with laughter. The greatest clown in the world never received a more flattering tribute to his powers to amuse than had been called forth by mine to make myself understood. Naturally, however, I was not flattered, but on the contrary entirely discomfited. Angry I could not well be, for the deprecating manner in which all, excepting of course the boys, yielded to their perception of the ridiculous, and the distress they showed at their failure in self-control, made me seem the aggressor. It was as if they were very sorry for me, and ready to put themselves wholly at my service, if I would only refrain from reducing them to a state of disability by being so exquisitely absurd. Certainly this evidently amiable race had a very embarrassing way of receiving strangers.

Just at this moment, when my bewilderment was fast verging on exasperation, relief came. The circle opened, and a little elderly man, who had evidently come in haste, confronted me, and, bowing very politely, addressed me in English. His voice was the most pitiable abortion of a voice I had ever heard. While having all the defects in articulation of a child's who is just beginning to talk, it was not even a child's in strength of tone, being in fact a mere alternation of squeaks and whispers inaudible a rod away. With some difficulty I was, however, able to follow him pretty nearly.

"As the official interpreter," he said, "I extend you a cordial welcome to these islands. I was sent for as soon as you were discovered, but being at some distance, I was unable to arrive until this moment. I regret this, as my presence would have saved you embarrassment. My countrymen desire me to intercede with you to pardon the wholly involuntary and uncontrollable mirth provoked by your attempts to communicate with them. You see, they understood you perfectly well, but could not answer you."

"Merciful heavens!" I exclaimed, horrified to find my surmise correct; "can it be that they are all thus afflicted? Is it possible that you are the only man among them who has the power of speech?"

Again it appeared that, quite unintentionally, I had said something excruciatingly funny; for at my speech there arose a sound of gentle laughter from the group, now augmented to quite an assemblage, which drowned the splashing of the waves on the beach at our feet. Even the interpreter smiled.

"Do they think it is so amusing to be dumb?" I asked.

"They find it very amusing," replied the interpreter, "that their inability to speak should be regarded by anyone as an affliction; for it is by the voluntary disuse of the organs of articulation that they have lost the power of speech, and, as a consequence, the ability even to understand speech."

"But," said I, somewhat puzzled by this statement, "didn't you just tell me that they understood me, though they could not reply, and are they not laughing now at what I just said?"

"It is you they understood, not your words," answered the interpreter. "Our speech now is gibberish to them, as unintelligible in itself as the growling of animals; but they know what we are saying, because they know our thoughts. You must know that these are the islands of the mind-readers."

Such were the circumstances of my introduction to this extraordinary people. The official interpreter being charged by virtue of his office with the first entertainment of shipwrecked members of the talking nations, I became his guest, and passed a number of days under his roof before going out to any considerable extent among the people. My first impression had been the somewhat oppressive one that the power to read the thoughts of others could be possessed only by beings of a superior order to man. It was the first effort of the interpreter to disabuse me of this notion. It appeared from his account that the experience of the mind-readers was a case simply of a slight acceleration, from special causes, of the course of universal human evolution, which in time was destined to lead to the disuse of speech and the substitution of direct mental vision on the part of all races. This rapid evolution of these islanders was accounted for by their peculiar origin and circumstances.

Some three centuries before Christ, one of the Parthian kings of Persia, of the dynasty of the Arsacidae, undertook a persecution of the soothsayers and magicians in his realms. These people were credited with supernatural powers by popular prejudice, but in fact were merely persons of special gifts in the way of hypnotizing, mind-reading, thought transference, and such arts, which they exercised for their own gain.

Too much in awe of the soothsayers to do them outright violence, the king resolved to banish them, and to this end put them, with their families, on ships and sent them to Ceylon. When, however, the fleet was in the neighborhood of that island, a great storm scattered it, and one of the ships, after being driven for many days before the tempest, was wrecked upon one of an archipelago of uninhabited islands far to the south, where the survivors settled. Naturally, the posterity of the parents possessed of such peculiar gifts had developed extraordinary physical powers.

Having set before them the end of evolving a new and advanced order of humanity, they had aided the development of these powers by a rigid system of stirpiculture. The result was that, after a few centuries, mind-reading became so general that language fell into disuse as a means of communicating ideas. For many generations the power of speech still remained voluntary, but gradually the vocal organs had become atrophied, and for several hundred years the power of articulation had been wholly lost. Infants for a few months after birth did, indeed, still emit inarticulate cries, but at an age when in less advanced races these cries began to be articulate, the children of the mind-readers developed the power of direct vision, and ceased to attempt to use the voice.

The fact that the existence of the mind-readers had never been found out by the rest of the world was explained by two considerations. In the first place, the group of islands was small, and occupied a corner of the Indian Ocean quite out of the ordinary track of ships. In the second place, the approach to the islands was rendered so desperately perilous by terrible currents, and the maze of outlying rocks and shoals, that it was next to impossible for any ship to touch their shores save as a wreck. No ship at least had ever done so in the two thousand years since the mind-readers' own arrival, and the Adelaide had made the one hundred and twenty-third such wreck.

Apart from motives of humanity, the mind-readers made strenuous efforts to rescue shipwrecked persons, for from them alone, through the interpreters, could they obtain information of the outside world. Little enough this proved when, as often happened, the sole survivor of the shipwreck was some ignorant sailor, who had no news to communicate beyond the latest varieties of forecastle blasphemy. My hosts gratefully assured me that, as a person of some little education, they considered me a veritable godsend. No less a task was mine than to relate to them the history of the world for the past two centuries, and often did I wish, for their sakes, that I had made a more exact study of it.

It is solely for the purpose of communicating with shipwrecked strangers of the talking nations that the office of the interpreters exists. When, as from time to time happens, a child is born with some powers of articulation, he is set apart, and trained to talk in the interpreters' college. Of course the partial atrophy of the vocal organs, from which even the best interpreters suffer, renders many of the sounds of language impossible for them. None, for instance, can pronounce v, f, or s; and as to the sound represented by th, it is five generations since the last interpreter lived who could utter it. But for the occasional intermarriage of shipwrecked strangers with the islanders, it is probable that the supply of interpreters would have long ere this quite failed.

I imagine that the very unpleasant sensations which followed the realization that I was among people who, while inscrutable to me, knew my every thought, were very much what anyone would have experienced in the same case. They were very comparable to the panic which accidental nudity causes a person among races whose custom it is to

227

conceal the figure with drapery. I wanted to run away and hide myself. If I analyzed my feeling, it did not seem to arise so much from the consciousness of any particularly heinous secrets, as from the knowledge of a swarm of fatuous, ill-natured, and unseemly thoughts and half-thoughts concerning those around me, and concerning myself, which it was insufferable that any person should peruse in however benevolent a spirit. But while my chagrin and distress on this account were at first intense, they were also very short-lived, for almost immediately I discovered that the very knowledge that my mind was overlooked by others operated to check thoughts that might be painful to them, and that, too, without more effort of the will than a kindly person exerts to check the utterance of disagreeable remarks. As a very few lessons in the elements of courtesy cures a decent person of inconsiderate speaking, so a brief experience among the mind-readers went far in my case to check inconsiderate thinking. It must not be supposed, however, that courtesy among the mind-readers prevents them from thinking pointedly and freely concerning one another upon serious occasions, any more than the finest courtesy among the talking races restrains them from speaking to one another with entire plainness when it is desirable to do so. Indeed, among the mind-readers, politeness never can extend to the point of insincerity, as among talking nations, seeing that it is always one another's real and inmost thought that they read. I may fitly mention here, though it was not till later that I fully understood why it must necessarily be so, that one need feel far less chagrin at the complete revelation of his weaknesses to a mind-reader than at the slightest betrayal of them to one of another race. For the very reason that the mind-reader reads all your thoughts, particular thoughts are judged with reference to the general tenor of thought. Your characteristic and habitual frame of mind is what he takes account of. No one need fear being misjudged by a mind-reader on account of sentiments or emotions which are not representative of the real character or general attitude. Justice may, indeed, be said to be a necessary consequence of mind-reading.

As regards the interpreter himself, the instinct of courtesy was not long needed to check wanton or offensive thoughts. In all my life before, I had been very slow to form friendships, but before I had been three days in the company of this stranger of a strange race, I had become enthusiastically devoted to him. It was impossible not to be. The peculiar joy of friendship is the sense of being understood by our friend as we are not by others, and yet of being loved in spite of the understanding. Now here was one whose every word testified to a knowledge of my secret thoughts and motives which the oldest and nearest of my former friends had never, and could never, have approximated. Had such a knowledge bred in him contempt of me, I should neither have blamed him nor been at all surprised. Judge, then, whether the cordial friendliness which he showed was likely to leave me indifferent.

Imagine my incredulity when he informed me that our friendship was not based upon more than ordinary mutual suitability of temperaments. The faculty of mind-reading, he explained, brought minds so close together, and so heightened sympathy, that the lowest order of friendship between mind-readers implied a mutual delight such as only rare friends enjoyed among other races. He assured me that later on, when I came to know others of his race, I should find, by the far greater intensity of sympathy and affection I should conceive for some of them, how true this saying was.

It may be inquired how, on beginning to mingle with the mind-readers in general, I managed to communicate with them, seeing that, while they could read my thoughts, they could not, like the interpreter, respond to them by speech. I must here explain that, while these people have no use for a spoken language, a written language is needful for purposes of record. They consequently all know how to write. Do they, then, write in Persian? Luckily for me, no. It appears that, for a long period after mind-reading was fully developed, not only was spoken language disused, but also written, no records whatever having been kept during this period. The delight of the people in the newly found power of direct mind-to-mind vision, whereby pictures of the total mental state were communicated, instead of the imperfect descriptions of single thoughts which words at best could give, induced an invincible distaste for the laborious impotence of language.

When, however, the first intellectual intoxication had, after several generations, somewhat sobered down, it was recognized that records of the past were desirable, and that the despised medium of words was needful to preserve it. Persian had meanwhile been wholly forgotten. In order to avoid the prodigious task of inventing a complete new language, the institution of the interpreters was now set up, with the idea of acquiring through them a knowledge of some of the languages of the outside world from the mariners wrecked on the islands.

Owing to the fact that most of the castaway ships were English, a better knowledge of that tongue was acquired than of any other, and it was adopted as the written language of the people. As a rule, my acquaintances wrote slowly and laboriously, and yet the fact that they knew exactly what was in my mind rendered their responses so apt that, in my conversations with the slowest speller of them all, the interchange of thought was as rapid and incomparably more accurate and satisfactory than the fastest talkers attain to.

It was but a very short time after I had begun to extend my acquaintance among the mind-readers before I discovered how truly the interpreter had told me that I should find others to whom, on account of greater natural congeniality, I should become more strongly attached than I had been to him. This was no wise, however, because I loved him less, but them more. I would fain write particularly of some of these beloved friends, comrades of my heart, from whom I first learned the undreamed-of possibilities of human friendship, and how ravishing the satisfactions of sympathy may be. Who, among those who may read this, has not known that sense of a gulf fixed between soul and soul which mocks love! Who has not felt that loneliness which oppresses the heart that loves it best! Think no longer that this gulf is eternally fixed, or is any necessity of human nature. It has no existence for the race of our fellowmen which I describe, and by that fact we may be assured that eventually it will be bridged also for us. Like the touch of shoulder to shoulder, like the clasping of hands, is the contact of their minds and their sensation of sympathy.

I say that I would fain speak more particularly of some of my friends, but waning strength forbids, and moreover, now that I think of it, another consideration would render any comparison of their characters rather confusing than instructive to a reader. This is the fact that, in common with the rest of the mind-readers, they had no names. Every one had, indeed, an arbitrary sign for his designation in records, but it has no sound value. A register of these names is kept, so they can at any time be ascertained, but it is very common to meet persons who have forgotten titles which are used solely for biographical and official purposes. For social intercourse names are of course superfluous, for these people accost one another merely by a mental act of attention, and refer to third persons by transferring their mental pictures—something as dumb persons might by means of photographs. Something so, I say, for in the pictures of one another's personalities which the mind-readers conceive, the physical aspect, as might be expected with people who directly contemplate each other's minds and hearts, is a subordinate element.

I have already told how my first qualms of morbid self-consciousness at knowing that my mind was an open book to all around me disappeared as I learned that the very completeness of the disclosure of my thoughts and motives was a guarantee that I would be judged with a fairness and a sympathy such as even self-judgment cannot pretend to, affected as that is by so many subtle reactions. The assurance of being so judged by everyone might well seem an inestimable privilege to one accustomed to a world in which not even the tenderest love is any pledge of comprehension, and yet I soon discovered that open-mindedness had a still greater profit than this. How shall I describe the delightful exhilaration of moral health and cleanness, the breezy oxygenated mental condition, which resulted from the consciousness that I had absolutely nothing concealed! Truly I may say that I enjoyed myself. I think surely that no one needs to have had my marvelous experience to sympathize with this portion of it. Are we not all ready to agree that this having a curtained chamber where we may go to grovel, out of the sight of our fellows, troubled only by a vague apprehension that God may look over the top, is the most demoralizing incident in the human condition? It is the existence within the soul of this secure refuge of lies which has always been the despair of the saint and the exultation of the knave. It is the foul cellar which taints the whole house above, be it never so fine.

What stronger testimony could there be to the instinctive consciousness that concealment is debauching, and openness our only cure, than the world-old conviction of the virtue of confesson for the soul, and that the uttermost exposing of one's worst and foulest is the first step toward moral health? The wickedest man, if he could but somehow attain to writhe himself inside out as to his soul, so that its full sickness could be seen, would feel ready for a new life. Nevertheless, owing to the utter impotence of the words to convey mental conditions in their totality, or to give other than mere distortions of them, confession is, we must needs admit, but a mockery of that longing for self-revelation to which it testifies. But think what health and soundness there must be for souls among a people who see in every face a conscience which, unlike their own, they cannot sophisticate, who confess one another with a glance, and shrive with a smile! Ah, friends, let me now predict, though ages may elapse before the slow even shall justify me, that in no way will the mutual vision of minds, when at last it shall be perfected, so enhance the blessedness of mankind as by rending the veil of self, and leaving no spot of darkness in the mind for lies to hide in. Then shall the soul no longer be a coal smoking among ashes, but a star in a crystal sphere.

From what I have said of the delights which friendship among the mind-readers derives from the perfection of the mental rapport, it may be imagined how intoxicating must be the experience when one of the friends is a woman, and the subtle attractions and correspondences of sex touch with passion the intellectual sympathy. With my first venturing into society I had begun, to their extreme amusement, to fall in love with the women right and left. In the perfect frankness which is the condition of all intercourse among this people, these adorable women told me that what I felt was only friendship, which was a very good thing, but wholly different from love, as I should well know if I were beloved. It was difficult to believe that the melting emotions which I had experienced in their company were the result merely of the friendly and kindly attitude of their minds toward mine; but when I found that I was affected in the same way by every gracious woman I met, I had to make up my mind that they must be right about it, and that I should have to adapt myself to a world in which, friendship being a passion, love must needs be nothing less than rapture.

The homely proverb, "Every Jack has his Jill," may, I suppose, be taken to mean that for all men there are certain women expressly suited by mental and moral as well as by physical constitution. It is a thought painful, rather than cheering, that this may be the truth, so altogether do the chances preponderate against the ability of these elect ones to recognize each other even if they meet, seeing that speech is so inadequate and so misleading a medium of self-revelation. But among the mind-readers, the search for one's ideal mate is a quest reasonably sure of being crowned with success, and no one dreams of wedding unless it be; for so to do, they consider, would be to throw away the choicest blessing of life, and not alone to wrong themselves and their unfound mates, but likewise those whom they themselves and those undiscovered mates might wed. Therefore, passionate pilgrims, they go from isle to isle till they find each other, and, as the population of the island is but small, the pilgrimage is not often long.

When I met her first we were in company, and I was struck by the sudden stir and the looks of touched and smiling interest with which all around turned and regarded us, the women with moistened eyes. They had read her thought when she saw me, but this I did not know, neither what was the custom in these matters, till afterward. But I knew, from the moment she first fixed her eyes on me, and I felt her mind brooding upon mine, how truly I had been told by those other women that the feeling with which they had inspired me was not love.

With people who become acquainted at a glance, and old friends in an hour, wooing is naturally not a long process. Indeed, it may be said that between lovers among mind-readers there is no wooing, but merely recognition. The day after we met, she became mine.

Perhaps I cannot better illustrate how subordinate the merely physical element is in the impression which mind-readers form of their friends than by mentioning an incident that occurred some months after our union. This was my discovery, wholly by accident, that my love, in whose society I had almost constantly been, had not the least idea what was the color of my eyes, or whether my hair and complexion were light or dark. Of course, as soon as I asked her the question, she read the answer in my mind, but she admitted that she had previously had no distinct impression on those points. On the other hand, if in the blackest midnight I should come to her, she would not need to ask who the comer was. It is by the mind, not the eye, that these people know one another. It is really only in their relations to soulless and inanimate things that they need eyes at all.

It must not be supposed that their disregard of one another's bodily aspect grows out of any ascetic sentiment. It is merely a necessary consequence of their power of directly apprehending mind, that whenever mind is closely associated with matter the latter is comparatively neglected on account of the greater interest of the former, suffering as lesser things always do when placed in immediate contrast with greater. Art is with them confined to the inanimate, the human form having, for the reason mentioned, ceased to inspire the artist. It will be naturally and quite correctly inferred that among such a race physical beauty is not the important factor in human fortune and felicity that it elsewhere is. The absolute openness of their minds and hearts to one another makes their happiness far more dependent on the moral and mental qualities of their companions than upon their physical. A genial temperament, a wide-grasping, godlike intellect, a poet soul, are incomparably more fascinating to them than the most dazzling combination conceivable of mere bodily graces.

A woman of mind and heart has no more need of beauty to win love in these islands than a beauty elsewhere of mind or heart. I should mention here, perhaps, that this race, which makes so little account of physical beauty, is itself a singularly handsome one. This is owing doubtless in part to the absolute compatibility of temperaments in all the marriages, and partly also to the reaction upon the body of a state of ideal mental and moral health and placidity.

Not being myself a mind-reader, the fact that my love was rarely beautiful in form and face had doubtless no little part in attracting my devotion. This, of course, she knew, as she knew all my thoughts, and, knowing my limitations, tolerated and forgave the element of sensuousness in my passion. But if it must have seemed to her so little worthy in comparison with the high spiritual communion which her race know as love, to me it became, by virtue of her almost superhuman relation to me, an ecstasy more ravishing surely than any lover of my race tasted before. The ache at the heart of the intensest love is the impotence of words to make it perfectly understood to its object. But my passion was without this pang, for my heart was absolutely open to her I loved. Lovers may imagine, but I cannot describe, the ecstatic thrill of communion into which this consciousness transformed every tender emotion. As I considered what mutual love must be where both parties are mind-readers, I realized the high communion which my sweet companion had sacrificed for me. She might indeed comprehend her lover and his love for her, but the higher satisfaction of knowing that she was comprehended by him and her love understood, she had foregone. For that I should ever attain the power of mind-reading was out of the question, the faculty never having been developed in a single lifetime.

Why my inability should move my dear companion to such depths of pity I was not able fully to understand until I learned that mind-reading is chiefly held desirable, not for the knowledge of others which it gives its possessors, but for the self-knowledge which is its reflex effect. Of all they see in the minds of others, that which concerns them most is the reflection of themselves, the photographs of their own characters. The most obvious consequence of the self-knowledge thus forced upon them is to render them alike incapable of self-conceit or self-depreciation. Everyone must needs always think of himself as he is, being no more able to do otherwise than is a man in a hall of mirrors to cherish delusions as to his personal appearance.

But self-knowledge means to the mind-readers much more than this—nothing less, indeed, than a shifting of the sense of identity. When a man sees himself in a mirror, he is compelled to distinguish between the bodily self he sees and his real self, which is within and unseen. When in turn the mind-reader comes to see the mental and moral self reflected in other minds as in mirrors, the same thing happens. He is compelled to distinguish between this mental and moral self which has been made objective to him, and can be contemplated by him as impartially as if it were another's, from the inner ego which still remains subjective, unseen, and indefinable. In this inner ego the mind-readers recognize the essential identity and being, the noumenal self, the core of the soul, and the true hiding of its eternal life, to which the mind as well as the body is but the garment of a day.

The effect of such a philosophy as this—which, indeed, with the mind-readers is rather an instinctive consciousness than a philosophy—must obviously be to impart a sense of wonderful superiority to the vicissitudes of this earthly state, and a singular serenity in the midst of the haps and mishaps which threaten or befall the personality. They did indeed appear to me, as I never dreamed men could attain to be, lords of themselves.

It was because I might not hope to attain this enfranchisement from the false ego of the apparent self, without which life seemed to her race scarcely worth living, that my love so pitied me.

But I must hasten on, leaving a thousand things unsaid, to relate the lamentable catastrophe to which it is owing that, instead of being still a resident of those blessed islands, in the full enjoyment of that intimate and ravishing companionship which by contrast would forever dim the pleasures of all other human society, I recall the bright picture as a memory under other skies.

Among a people who are compelled by the very constitution of their minds to put themselves in the places of others, the sympathy which is the inevitable consequence of perfect comprehension renders envy, hatred, and uncharitableness impossible. But of course there are people less genially constituted than others, and these are necessarily the objects of a certain distaste on the part of associates. Now, owing to the unhindered impact of minds upon one another, the anguish of persons so regarded, despite the tenderest consideration of those about them, is so great they beg the grace of exile, that, being out of the way, people may think less frequently upon them. There are numerous small islets, scarcely more than rocks, lying to the north of the archipelago, and on these the unfortunates are permitted to live. Only one lives on each islet, as they cannot endure each other even as well as the more happily constituted can endure them. From time to time supplies of food are taken to them, and of course, anytime they wish to take the risk, they are permitted to return to society.

Now, as I have said, the fact which, even more than their out-of-the-way location, makes the islands of the mind-readers unapproachable, is the violence with which the great antarctic current, owing probably to some configuration of the ocean bed, together with the innumerable rocks and shoals, flows through and about the archipelago.

Ships making the islands from the southward are caught by this current and drawn among the rocks, to their almost certain destruction; while owing to the violence with which the current sets to the north, it is not possible to approach at all from that direction, or at least it has never been accomplished. Indeed, so powerful are the currents that even the boats which cross the narrow straits between the main islands and the islets of the unfortunate, to carry the latter their supplies, are ferried over by cables, not trusting to oar or sail.

The brother of my love had charge of one of the boats engaged in this transportation, and, being desirous of visiting the islets, I accepted an invitation to accompany him on one of his trips. I know nothing of how the accident happened, but in the fiercest part of the current of one of the straits we parted from the cable and were swept out to sea. There was no question of stemming the boiling current, our utmost endeavors barely sufficing to avoid being dashed to pieces on the rocks. From the first, there was no hope of our winning back to the land, and so swiftly did we drift that by noon—the accident having befallen in the morning—the islands, which are low-lying, had sunk beneath the southwestern horizon.

Among these mind-readers, distance is not an insuperable obstacle to the transfer of thought. My companion was in communication with our friends, and from time to time conveyed to me messages of anguish from my dear love; for, being well aware of the nature of the currents and the unapproachableness of the islands, those we had left behind, as well as we ourselves, knew well we should see each other's faces no more. For five days we continued to drift to the northwest, in no danger of starvation, owing to our lading of provisions, but constrained to unintermitting watch and ward by the roughness of the weather. On the fifth day my companion died from exposure and exhaustion. He died very quietly—indeed, with great appearance of relief. The life of the mind-readers while yet they are in the body is so largely spiritual that the idea of an existence wholly so, which seems vague and chill to us, suggests to them a state only slightly more refined than they already know on earth.

After that I suppose I must have fallen into an unconscious state, from which I roused to find myself on an American ship bound for New York, surrounded by people whose only means of communicating with one another is to keep up while together a constant clatter of hissing, gutteral, and explosive noises, eked out by all manner of facial contortions and bodily gestures. I frequently find myself staring openmouthed at those who address me, too much struck by their grotesque appearance to bethink myself of replying.

I find that I shall not live out the voyage, and I do not care to. From my experience of the people on the ship, I can judge how I should fare on land amid the stunning Babel of a nation of talkers. And my friends— God bless them!—how lonely I should feel in their very presence! Nay, what satisfaction or consolation, what but bitter mockery, could I ever more find in such human sympathy and companionship as suffice others and once sufficed me—I who have seen and known what I have seen and known! Ah, yes, doubtless it is far better I should die; but the knowledge of the things that I have seen I feel should not perish with me. For hope's sake, men should not miss the glimpse of the higher, sunbathed reaches of the upward path they plod. So thinking, I have written out some account of my wonderful experience, though briefer far, by reason of my weakness, than fits the greatness of the matter. The captain seems an honest, well-meaning man, and to him I shall confide the narrative, charging him, on touching shore, to see it safely in the hands of someone who will bring it to the world's ear.

NOTE—The extent of my own connection with the foregoing document is sufficiently indicated by the author himself in the final paragraph—E. B.

Sir Arthur Conan Doyle (1859–1930)

The creator of the world's most famous detective, Sir Arthur Conan Doyle was also a prolific writer of science-fiction and fantasy stories. Born in Edinburgh, Scotland, the descendant of an old aristocratic Irish family, he began writing in 1879 while studying medicine at the University of Edinburgh. By his graduation in 1881 he had made a few sales, including his first science-fiction story, ''The American's Tale'' (1879). He obtained his advanced degree by 1885, but had difficulty in building a successful practice, so he signed on as ship's doctor for an arctic whaler and then an African steamer while continuing to supplement his income through writing.

Doyle was a strange blend of rationalist, idealist, romantic, and mystic. And although the rationalist is most apparent to his mystery fans, it is clear that he had a lifelong interest in the supernatural and bizarre. Some speculate that his fascination demonstrated a need to find, because of an early rejection of religion, some alternative belief system. But in any case, he produced a number of excellent fantasies throughout his entire career, many of which are contained in *The Great Supernatural Stories of Arthur Conan Doyle* (1979).

In 1891, however, Doyle's career was profoundly changed by the editors of the *Strand* magazine. They were so impressed by his first Sherlock Holmes novel, *A Study in Scarlet* (1887), that they commissioned him to write a series of Holmes short stories. The public went wild over these and Doyle was shortly able to gain financial security by escalating his prices. Now he was free to divert more of his energies into participating in current affairs and writing historical romances.

During this period, however, he continued to write a few science-fiction short stories, and from these we have selected his most popular, "The Great Keinplatz Experiment" (1894), a slightly daffy tale of hypnotically induced personality transfer.

By 1910 he began devoting more time to writing science fiction. He produced three novels, including *The Lost World* (1912), a classic account of a scientific expedition's discovery of prehistoric life on a giant South American mesa, and a number of outstanding shorter works such as "The Terror of Blue John Gap" (1910), "The Poison Belt" (1913), and "When the World Screamed" (1929).

The Science Fiction of Sir Arthur Coynan Doyle (1981), a recent collection of all of his shorter science-fiction stories, demonstrates his great potential in this field. But, unfortunately, by 1915 he had become an avid spiritualist because of the war-related death of his son Kingsley. Thereafter, much of Doyle's remaining life was devoted to embarrassing attempts to prove the existence of an afterlife.

THE GREAT KEINPLATZ EXPERIMENT

O f all the sciences which have puzzled the sons of men, none had
such an attraction for the learned Professor von Baumgarten as
those which relate to psychology and the ill-defined relations between
mind and matter. A celebrated anatomist, a profound chemist, and one
of the first physiologists in Europe, it was a relief for him to turn from
these subjects and to bring his varied knowledge to bear upon the study of
the soul and the mysterious relationship of spirits. At first, when as a
young man he began to dip into the secrets of mesmerism, his mind
seemed to be wandering in a strange land where all was chaos and
darkness, save that here and there some great unexplainable and disconnected fact loomed out in front of him. As the years passed, however,
and the worthy Professor's stock of knowledge increased, for knowledge
begets knowledge as money bears interest, much which had seemed
strange and unaccountable began to take another shape in his eyes. New
trains of reasoning became familiar to him, and he perceived connecting
links where all had been incomprehensible and startling. By experiments
which extended over twenty years, he obtained a basis of facts upon
which it was his ambition to build up a new exact science which should
embrace mesmerism, spiritualism, and all cognate subjects. In this he
was much helped by his intimate knowledge of the more intricate parts of
animal physiology which treat of nerve currents and the working of the
brain; for Alexis von Baumgarten was Regius Professor of Physiology at
the University of Keinplatz, and had all the resources of the laboratory to
aid him in his profound researches.

Professor von Baumgarten was tall and thin, with a hatchet face and
steel-grey eyes, which were singularly bright and penetrating. Much

thought had furrowed his forehead and contracted his heavy eyebrows, so that he appeared to wear a perpetual frown, which often misled people as to his character, for though austere he was tenderhearted. He was popular among the students, who would gather round him after his lectures and listen eagerly to his strange theories. Often he would call for volunteers from amongst them in order to conduct some experiment, so that eventually there was hardly a lad in the class who had not, at one time or another, been thrown into a mesmeric trance by his Professor.

Of all these young devotees of science there was none who equaled in enthusiasm Fritz von Hartmann. It had often seemed strange to his fellow-students that wild, reckless Fritz, as dashing a young fellow as ever hailed from the Rhinelands, should devote the time and trouble which he did in reading up abstruse works and in assisting the Professor in his strange experiments. The fact was, however, that Fritz was a knowing and longheaded fellow. Months before he had lost his heart to young Elise, the blue-eyed, yellow-haired daughter of the lecturer. Although he had succeeded in learning from her lips that she was not indifferent to his suit, he had never dared announce himself to her family as a formal suitor. Hence he would have found it a difficult matter to see his young lady had he not adopted the expedient of making himself useful to the Professor. By this means he frequently was asked to the old man's house, where he willingly submitted to be experimented upon in any way as long as there was a chance of his receiving one bright glance from the eyes of Elise or one touch of her little hand.

Young Fritz von Hartmann was a handsome enough lad. There were broad acres, too, which would descend to him when his father died. To many he would have seemed an eligible suitor; but Madame frowned upon his presence in the house, and lectured the Professor at times on his allowing such a wolf to prowl around their lamb. To tell the truth, Fritz had an evil name in Keinplatz. Never was there a riot or a duel, or any other mischief afoot, but the young Rhinelander figured as a ringleader in it. No one used more free and violent language, no one drank more, no one played cards more habitually, no one was more idle, save in the one solitary subject. No wonder, then that the good Frau Professorin gathered her Fräulin under her wing, and resented the attentions of such a *mauvais sujet*. As to the worthy lecturer, he was too much engrossed by his strange studies to form an opinion upon the subject one way or the other.

For many years there was one question which had continually obtruded itself upon his thoughts. All his experiments and his theories turned upon a single point. A hundred times a day the Professor asked himself whether it was possible for the human spirit to exist apart from the body for a time and then to return to it once again. When the possibility first suggested itself to him his scientific mind had revolted from it. It clashed too violently with preconceived ideas and the prejudices of his early training. Gradually, however, as he proceeded farther and farther along the pathway of original research, his mind shook off its old fetters and became ready to face any conclusion which could reconcile the facts. There were many things which made him believe that it was possible for mind to exist apart from matter. At last it occurred to him that by a daring and original experiment the question might be definitely decided.

"It is evident," he remarked in his celebrated article upon invisible entities, which appeared in the *Keinplatz wochenliche Medicalschrift* about this time, and which surprised the whole scientific world—"it is evident that under certain conditions the soul or mind does separate itself from the body. In the case of a mesmerized person, the body lies in a cataleptic condition, but the spirit has left it. Perhaps you reply that the soul is there, but in a dormant condition. I answer that this is not so, otherwise how can one account for the condition of clairvoyance, which has fallen into disrepute through the knavery of certain scoundrels, but which can easily be shown to be an undoubted fact. I have been able myself, with a sensitive subject, to obtain an accurate description of what was going on in another room or another house. How can such knowledge be accounted for on any hypothesis save that the soul of the subject has left the body and is wandering through space? For a moment it is recalled by the voice of the operator and says what it has seen, and then wings its way once more through the air. Since the spirit is by its very nature invisible, we cannot see these comings and goings, but we see their effect in the body of the subject, now rigid and inert, now struggling to narrate impressions which could never have come to it by natural means. There is only one way which I can see by which the fact can be demonstrated. Although we in the flesh are unable to see these spirits, yet our own spirits, could we separate them from the body, would be conscious of the presence of others. It is my intention, therefore, shortly to mesmerize one of my pupils. I shall then mesmerize myself in a manner which has become easy to me. After that, if my theory holds good, my spirit will have no difficulty in meeting and communing with the spirit of my pupil, both being separated from the body. I hope to be able to communicate the result of this interesting experiment in an early number of the *Keinplatz wochenliche Medicalschrift*.''

When the good Professor finally fulfilled his promise, and published an account of what occurred, the narrative was so extraordinary that it was received with general incredulity. The tone of some of the papers was so offensive in their comments upon the matter that the angry savant declared that he would never open his mouth again, or refer to the subject in any way—a promise which he has faithfully kept. This narrative has been compiled, however, from the most authentic sources, and the events cited in it may be relied upon as substantially correct.

It happened, then, that shortly after the time when Professor von Baumgarten conceived the idea of the above-mentioned experiment, he was walking thoughtfully homewards after a long day in the laboratory, when he met a crowd of roistering students who had just streamed out from a beer-house. At the head of them, half-intoxicated and very noisy, was young Fritz von Hartmann. The Professor would have passed them, but his pupil ran across and intercepted him.

"Heh! My worthy master," he said, taking the old man by the sleeve, and leading him down the road with him. "There is something that I have to say to you, and it is easier for me to say it now, when the good beer is humming in my head, than at another time."

"What is it, then, Fritz?" the physiologist asked, looking at him in mild surprise.

"I hear, mein Herr, that you are about to do some wondrous experiment, in which you hope to take a man's soul out of his body, and then to put it back again. Is it not?"

"It is true, Fritz."

"And have you considered, my dear sir, that you may have some difficulty in finding someone on whom to try this? *Potztausend!* Suppose that the soul went out and would not come back? That would be a bad business. Who is to take the risk?"

"But, Fritz," the Professor cried, very much startled by this view of the matter, "I had relied upon your assistance in the attempt. Surely you would not desert me. Consider the honorous glory."

"Consider the fiddlesticks!" the student cried angrily. "Am I to be paid always thus? Did I not stand two hours upon a glass insulator while you poured electricity into my body? Have you not stimulated my phrenic nerves, besides ruining my digestion with a galvanic current round my stomach? Four-and-thirty times you have mesmerized me, and what have I got from all this? Nothing. And now you wish to take my soul out, as you would take the works from a watch. It is more than flesh and blood can stand."

"Dear, dear!" the Professor cried in great distress. "That is very true, Fritz. I never thought of it before. If you can but suggest how I can compensate you, you will find me ready and willing."

"Then listen," said Fritz solemnly. "If you will pledge that after this experiment I may have the hand of your daughter, then I am willing to assist you; but if not, I shall have nothing to do with it. These are my only terms."

"And what would my daughter say to this?" the Professor exclaimed, after a pause of astonishment.

"Elise would welcome it," the young man replied. "We have loved each other long."

"Then she shall be yours," the physiologist said with decision, "for you are a good-hearted young man, and one of the best neurotic subjects that I have ever known—that is when you are not under the influence of alcohol. My experiment is to be performed upon the fourth of next month. You will attend at the physiological laboratory at twelve o'clock. It will be a great occasion, Fritz. Von Gruben is coming from Jena, and Hinterstein from Basle. The chief men of science of all South Germany will be there."

"I shall be punctual," the student said briefly; and so the two parted. The Professor plodded homeward, thinking of the great coming event, while the young man staggered along after his noisy companions, with his mind full of the blue-eyed Elise, and of the bargain which he had concluded with her father.

The Professor did not exaggerate when he spoke of the widespread interest excited by his novel psychological experiment. Long before the hour had arrived the room was filled by a galaxy of talent. Besides the celebrities whom he had mentioned, there had come from London the great Professor Lurcher, who had just established his reputation by a remarkable treatise upon cerebral centers. Several great lights of the Spiritualistic body had also come a long distance to be present, as had a Swedenborgian minister, who considered that the proceedings might throw some light upon the doctrines of the Rosy Cross.

There was considerable applause from this eminent assembly upon the appearance of Professor von Baumgarten and his subject upon the platform. The lecturer, in a few well-chosen words, explained what his views were, and how he proposed to test them. "I hold," he said, "that when a person is under the influence of mesmerism, his spirit is for the time released from his body, and I challenge anyone to put forward any other hypothesis which will account for the fact of clairvoyance. I therefore hope that upon mesmerizing my young friend here, and then putting myself into a trance, our spirits may be able to commune together, though our bodies lie still and inert. After a time nature will resume her sway, our spirits will return into our respective bodies, and all will be as before. With your kind permission, we shall now proceed to attempt the experiment."

The applause was renewed at this speech, and the audience settled down in expectant silence. With a few rapid passes the Professor mesmerized the young man, who sank back in his chair, pale and rigid. He then took a bright globe of glass from his pocket, and by concentrating his gaze upon it and making a strong mental effort, he succeeded in throwing himself into the same condition. It was a strange and impressive sight to see the old man and the young sitting together in the same cataleptic condition. Whither, then, had their souls fled? That was the question which presented itself to each and every one of the spectators.

Five minutes passed, and then ten, and then fifteen, and then fifteen more, while the Professor and his pupil sat stiff and stark upon the platform. During that time not a sound was heard from the assembled savants, but every eye was bent upon the two pale faces, in search of the first signs of returning consciousness. Nearly an hour had elapsed before the patient watchers were rewarded. A faint flush came back to the cheeks of Professor von Baumgarten. The soul was coming back once more to its earthly tenement. Suddenly he stretched out his long thin arms, as one awaking from sleep, and rubbing his eyes, stood up from his chair and gazed about him as though he hardly realized where he was. *"Tausend Teufel!"* he exclaimed, rapping out a tremendous South German oath, to the great astonishment of his audience and to the disgust of the Swedenborgian. "Where the Henker am I then, and what in thunder has occurred? Oh yes I remember now. One of these nonsensical mesmeric experiments. There is no result this time, for I remember nothing at all since I became unconscious; so you have had all your long journeys for nothing, my learned friends, and a very good joke too"; at which the Regius Professor of Physiology burst into a roar of laughter and slapped his thigh in a highly indecorous fashion. The audience was so enraged at this unseemly behaviour on the part of their host, that there might have been a considerable disturbance had it not been for the judicious interference of young Fritz von Hartmann, who had now recovered from his lethargy. Stepping to the front of the platform, the young man apologized for the conduct of his companion. "I am sorry to say," he said, "that he is a harum-scarum sort of fellow, although he appeared so grave at the commencement of this experiment. He is still suffering from mesmeric reaction, and is hardly accountable for his words. As to the experiment itself, I do not consider it to be a failure. It is very possible that our spirits may have been communing in space during this hour; but, unfortunately, our gross bodily memory is distinct from our spirit, and we cannot recall what has occurred. My energies shall now be devoted to devising some means by which spirits may be able to recollect what occurs to them in their free state, and I trust that when I have worked this out, I may have the pleasure of meeting you all once again in this hall, and demonstrating to you the result." This address, coming from so young a student, caused considerable astonishment among the audience, and some were inclined to be offended, thinking that he assumed rather too much importance. The majority, however, looked upon him as a young man of great promise, and many comparisons were made as they left the hall between his dignified conduct and the levity of his professor, who during the above remarks was laughing heartily in a corner, by no means abashed at the failure of the experiment.

Now although all these learned men were filing out of the lecture room under the impression that they had seen nothing of note, as a matter of fact one of the most wonderful things in the whole history of the world had just occurred before their very eyes. Professor von Baumgarten had been so far correct in his theory that both his spirit and that of his pupil had been for a time absent from the body. But here a strange and unforeseen complication had occurred. In their return the spirit of Fritz von Hartmann had entered into the body of Alexis von Baumgarten, and that of Alexis von Baumgarten had taken up its abode in the frame of Fritz von Hartmann. Hence the slang and scurrility which issued from the lips of the serious Professor, and hence also the weighty words and grave statements which fell from the careless student. It was an unprecedented event, yet no one knew of it, least of all those whom it concerned.

The body of the Professor, feeling conscious suddenly of a great dryness about the back of the throat, sallied out into the street, still chuckling to himself over the result of the experiment, for the soul of Fritz within was reckless at the thought of the bride whom he had won so easily. His first impulse was to go up to the house and see her, but on second thought he came to the conclusion that it would be best to stay away until Madame Baumgarten should be informed by her husband of the agreement which had been made. He therefore made his way down to the Grüner Mann, which was one of the favorite trysting-places of the wilder students, and ran, boisterously waving his cane in the air, into the little parlor, where sat Spiegel and Müller and half a dozen other boon companions.

"Ha, ha! My boys," he shouted. "I knew I should find you here. Drink up, every one of you, and call for what you like, for I'm going to stand treat today."

Had the green man who is depicted upon the signpost of that well-known inn suddenly marched into the room and called for a bottle of wine, the students could not have been more amazed than they were by this unexpected entry of their revered professor. They were so astonished that for a minute or two they glared at him in utter bewilderment without being able to make any reply to his hearty invitation.

"Donner und Blitzen!" shouted the Professor angrily. "What the deuce is the matter with you, then? You sit there like a set of stuck pigs staring at me. What is it then?"

"It is the unexpected honor," stammered Spiegel, who was in the chair.

"Honor—rubbish!" said the Professor testily. "Do you think that just because I happen to have been exhibiting mesmerism to a parcel of old fossils, I am therefore too proud to associate with dear old friends like you? Come out of that chair, Spiegel, my boy, for I shall preside now. Beer, or wine, or schnapps, my lads—call for what you like, and put it all down to me."

Never was there such an afternoon in the Grüner Mann. The foaming flagons of lager and the green-necked bottles of Rhenish circulated merrily. By degrees the students lost their shyness in the presence of their Professor. As for him, he shouted, he sang, he roared, he balanced a long tobacco pipe upon his nose, and offered to run a hundred yards against any member of the company. The Kellner and the barmaid whispered to each other outside the door their astonishment at such proceedings on the part of a Regius Professor of the ancient University of Keinplatz. They had still more to whisper about afterwards, for the learned man cracked the Kellner's crown, and kissed the barmaid behind the kitchen door.

"Gentlemen," said the Professor, standing up, albeit somewhat totteringly, at the end of the table, and balancing his high old-fashioned wineglass in his bony hand, "I must now explain to you what is the cause of this festivity."

"Hear! Hear!" roared the students, hammering their beer glasses against the table; "A speech, a speech!—silence for a speech!"

"The fact is, my friends," said the Professor, beaming through his spectacles, "I hope very soon to be married."

"Married!" cried a student, bolder than the others. "Is Madame dead, then?"

"Madame who?"

"Why, Madame von Baumgarten, of course."

"Ha, ha!" laughed the Professor; "I can see, then, that you know all about my former difficulties. No, she is not dead, but I have reason to believe she will not oppose my marriage."

"That is very accommodating of her," remarked one of the company.

"In fact," said the Professor, "I hope that she will now be induced to aid me in getting a wife. She and I never took to each other very much; but now I hope all that may be ended, and when I marry she will come and stay with me."

"What a happy family!" exclaimed some wag.

"Yes, indeed; and I hope you will come to my wedding, all of you. I won't mention names, but here is to my little bride!" and the Professor waved his glass in the air.

"Here's to his little bride!" roared the roisterers, with shouts of laughter. "Here's her health. *Sie soll leben—Hoch!*" And so the fun waxed still more fast and furious, while each young fellow followed the Professor's example, and drank a toast to the girl of his heart.

While all this festivity had been going on at the Grüner Mann, a very different scene had been enacted elsewhere. Young Fritz von Hartmann, with a solemn face and a reserved manner, had, after the experiment, consulted and adjusted some mathematical instruments;

after which, with a few peremptory words to the janitor, he had walked out into the street and wended his way slowly in the direction of the house of the Professor. As he walked he saw Von Althaus, the professor of anatomy, in front of him, and quickening his pace he overtook him.

"I say, Von Althaus," he exclaimed, tapping him on the sleeve, "you were asking me for some information the other day concerning the middle coat of the cerebral arteries. Now I find—"

"Donnerwetter!" shouted Von Althaus, who was a peppery old fellow. "What the deuce do you mean by your impertinence! I'll have you up before the Academical Senate for this, sir"; with which threat he turned on his heel and hurried away. Von Hartmann was much surprised at this reception. "It's on account of this failure of my experiment," he said to himself, and continued moodily on his way.

Fresh surprises were in store for him, however. He was hurrying along when he was overtaken by two students. These youths, instead of raising their caps or showing any other sign of respect, gave a wild whoop of delight the instant they saw him, and rushing at him, seized him by each arm and commenced dragging him along with them.

"Gott in Himmel!" roared Von Hartmann. "What is the meaning of this unparalleled insult? Where are you taking me?"

"To crack a bottle of wine with us," said the two students. "Come along! That is an invitation which you have never refused."

"I never heard of such insolence in my life!" cried Von Hartmann. "Let go my arms! I shall certainly have you rusticated for this. Let me go, I say!" and he kicked furiously at his captors.

"Oh, if you choose to turn ill-tempered, you may go where you like," the students said, releasing him. "We can do very well without you."

"I know you. I'll pay you out," said Von Hartmann furiously, and continued in the direction which he imagined to be his own home, much incensed at the two episodes which had occurred to him on the way.

Now, Madame von Baumgarten, who was looking out of the window and wondering why her husband was late for dinner, was considerably astonished to see the young student come stalking down the road. As already remarked, she had a great antipathy to him, and if ever he ventured into the house it was on sufferance, and under the protection of the Professor. Still more astonished was she, therefore, when she beheld him undo the wicket-gate and stride up the garden path with the air of one who is master of the situation. She could hardly believe her eyes, and hastened to the door with all her maternal instincts up in arms. From the upper windows the fair Elise had also observed this daring move upon the part of her lover, and her heart beat quick with mingled pride and consternation.

"Good day, sir," Madame von Baumgarten remarked to the intruder, as she stood in gloomy majesty in the open doorway.

"A very fine day indeed, Martha," returned the other. "Now, don't stand there like a statue of Juno, but bustle about and get the dinner ready, for I am well-nigh starved."

"Martha! Dinner!" ejaculated the lady, falling back in astonishment.

"Yes, dinner, Martha, dinner!" howled Von Hartmann, who was becoming irritable. "Is there anything wonderful in that request when a man has been out all day? I'll wait in the dining room. Anything will do. *Schinken,* and sausage, and prunes—any little thing that happens to be about. There you are, standing staring again. Woman, will you or will you not stir your legs?"

This last address, delivered with a perfect shriek of rage, had the effect of sending good Madame von Baumgarten flying along the passage and through the kitchen, where she locked herself up in the scullery and went into violent hysterics. In the meantime Von Hartmann strode into the room and threw himself down upon the sofa in the worst of tempers.

"Elise!" he shouted. "Confound the girl! Elise!"

Thus roughly summoned, the young lady came timidly downstairs and into the presence of her lover. "Dearest!" she cried, throwing her arms round him, "I know this is all done for my sake. It is a ruse in order to see me."

Von Hartmann's indignation at this fresh attack upon him was so great that he became speechless for a minute from rage, and could only glare and shake his fists, while he struggled in her embrace. When he at last regained his utterance, he indulged in such a bellow of passion that the young lady dropped back, petrified with fear, into an armchair.

"Never have I passed such a day in my life," Von Hartmann cried, stamping upon the floor. "My experiment has failed. Von Althaus has insulted me. Two students have dragged me along the public road. My

251

wife nearly faints when I ask her for dinner, and my daughter flies at me and hugs me like a grizzly bear.''

"You are ill, dear," the young lady cried. "Your mind is wandering. You have not even kissed me once."

"No, and I don't intend to either," Von Hartmann said with decision. "You ought to be ashamed of yourself. Why don't you go and fetch my slippers, and help your mother to dish the dinner?"

"And is it for this," Elise cried, burying her face in her handkerchief—"is it for this that I have loved you passionately for upwards of ten months? Is it for this that I have braved my mother's wrath? Oh, you have broken my heart; I am sure you have!" And she sobbed hysterically.

"I can't stand much more of this," roared Von Hartmann furiously. "What the deuce does the girl mean? What did I do ten months ago which inspired you with such a particular affection for me? If you are really so very fond, you would do better to run away down and find the *Schinken* and some bread, instead of talking all this nonsense."

"Oh, my darling!" cried the unhappy maiden, throwing herself into the arms of what she imagined to be her lover. "You do but joke in order to frighten your little Elise."

Now it chanced that at the moment of this unexpected embrace Von Hartmann was still leaning back against the end of the sofa, which, like much German furniture, was in a somewhat rickety condition. It also chanced that beneath this end of the sofa there stood a tank full of water in which the physiologist was conducting certain experiments upon the ova of fish, and which he kept in his drawing room in order to ensure an equable temperature. The additional weight of the maiden, combined with the impetus with which she hurled herself upon him, caused the precarious piece of furniture to give way, and the body of the unfortunate student was hurled backwards into the tank, in which his head and shoulders were firmly wedged, while his lower extremities flapped helplessly about in the air. This was the last straw. Extricating himself with some difficulty from his unpleasant position, Von Hartmann gave an inarticulate yell of fury, and dashing out of the room, in spite of the entreaties of Elise, he seized his hat and rushed off into the town, all dripping and disheveled, with the intention of seeking in some inn the food and comfort which he could not find at home.

As the spirit of Von Baumgarten encased in the body of Von

252

Hartmann strode down the winding pathway which led down to the little town, brooding angrily over his many wrongs, he became aware that an elderly man was approaching him who appeared to be in an advanced state of intoxication. Von Hartmann waited by the side of the road and watched this individual, who came stumbling along, reeling from one side of the road to the other, and singing a student song in a very husky and drunken voice. At first his interest was merely excited by the fact of seeing a man of so venerable an appearance in such a disgraceful condition, but as he approached nearer, he became convinced that he knew the other well, though he could not recall when or where he had met him. This impression became so strong with him, that when the stranger came abreast of him he stepped in front of him and took a good look at his features.

"Well, sonny," said the drunken man, surveying Von Hartmann and swaying about in front of him, "where the Henker have I seen you before? I know you as well as I know myself. Who the deuce are you?"

"I am Professor von Baumgarten," said the student. "May I ask who you are? I am strangely familiar with your features."

"You should never tell lies, young man," said the other. "You're certainly not the Professor, for he is an ugly snuffy old chap, and you are a big broad-shouldered young fellow. As to myself, I am Fritz von Hartmann at your service."

"That you certainly are not," exclaimed the body of Von Hartmann. "You might very well be his father. But hullo, sir, are you aware that you are wearing my studs and my watchchain?"

"Donnerwetter!" hiccoughed the other. "If those are not the trousers for which my tailor is about to sue me, may I never taste beer again."

Now as Von Hartmann, overwhelmed by the many strange things which had occurred to him that day, passed his hand over his forehead and cast his eyes downwards, he chanced to catch the reflection of his own face in a pool which the rain had left upon the road. To his utter astonishment he perceived that his face was that of a youth, that his dress was that of a fashionable young student, and that in every way he was the antithesis of the grave and scholarly figure in which his mind was wont to dwell. In an instant his active brain ran over the series of events which had occurred and sprang to the conclusion. He fairly reeled under the blow.

"Himmel!" he cried, "I see it all. Our souls are in the wrong bodies. I am you and you are I. My theory is proved—but at what an expense! Is the most scholarly mind in Europe to go about with this frivolous exterior? Oh the labors of a lifetime are ruined!" and he smote his breast in his despair.

"I say," remarked the real Von Hartmann from the body of the professor, "I quite see the force of your remarks, but don't go knocking my body about like that. You received it in an excellent condition, but I perceive that you have wet it and bruised it, and spilled snuff over my ruffled shirtfront."

"It matters little," the other said moodily. "Such as we are, so must we stay. My theory is triumphantly proved, but the cost is terrible."

"If I thought so," said the spirit of the student, "it would be hard indeed. What could I do with these stiff old limbs, and how could I woo Elise and persuade her that I was not her father? No, thank heaven, in spite of the beer which has upset me more than ever it could upset my real self, I can see a way out of it."

"How?" gasped the Professor.

"Why, by repeating the experiment. Liberate our souls once more, and the chances are that they will find their way back into their respective bodies."

No drowning man could clutch more eagerly at a straw than did Von Baumgarten's spirit at this suggestion. In feverish haste he dragged his own frame to the side of the road and threw it into a mesmeric trance; he then extracted the crystal ball from the pocket, and managed to bring himself into the same condition.

Some students and peasants who chanced to pass during the next hour were much astonished to see the worthy Professor of Physiology and his favorite student both sitting upon a very muddy bank and both completely insensible. Before the hour was up quite a crowd had assembled, and they were discussing the advisability of sending for an ambulance to convey the pair to hospital, when the learned savant opened his eyes and gazed vacantly around him. For an instant he seemed to forget how he had come there, but next moment he astonished his audience by waving his skinny arms above his head and crying out in a voice of rapture, *"Gott sei gedankt!* I am myself again. I feel I am!" Nor was the amazement lessened when the student, springing to his feet, burst into the same cry, and the two performed a sort of *pas de joie* in the middle of the road.

For some time after that people had some suspicion of the sanity of both the actors in this strange episode. When the Professor published his experiences in the *Medicalschrift* as he had promised, he was met by an intimation, even from his colleagues,that he would do well to have his mind cared for, and that another such publication would certainly consign him to a madhouse. The student also found by experience that it was the wisest to be silent about the matter.

When the worthy lecturer returned home that night he did not receive the cordial welcome which he might have looked for after his strange adventures. On the contrary, he was roundly upbraided by both his female relatives for smelling of drink and tobacco, and also for being absent while a young scapegrace invaded the house and insulted its occupants. It was long before the domestic atmosphere of the lecturer's house resumed its normal quiet, and longer still before the genial face of Von Hartmann was seen beneath its roof. Perseverance, however, conquers every obstacle, and the student eventually succeeded in pacifying the enraged ladies and in establishing himself upon the old footing. He has now no longer any cause to fear the enmity of Madame, for he is Hauptmann von Hartmann of the Emperor's own Uhlans, and his loving wife Elise has already presented him with two little Uhlans as a visible sign and token of her affection.

H.G. Wells (1866–1946)

An illustrious social critic as well as a writer, Herbert George Wells has been praised by scholars all over the world. Critical books on his work have been written by individuals from several different cultures, including at least one from the Soviet Union, and there is little doubt that Wells was the single most important shaping force in the development of twentieth century science fiction.

Born of "common" parents into a society that was intensely stratified (if not class-conscious), he fought all his life to escape the constraints that birth imposed upon him, and ended up consorting with men like Joseph Stalin and Franklin Delano Roosevelt. He had the great fortune to study under T. H. Huxley, who exercised a major influence on his life. (It is a sobering thought that Wells, who was sixteen when the great Charles Darwin died, lived to witness the use of atomic weapons—testimony to the rapid social and technological changes to which he addressed so much of his fiction and nonfiction.)[1] Although trained in biology, Wells subscribed to the belief that external conditions made people what they were as opposed to the "Great Man" theory of history, which held that talented individuals shaped events. And although he was an intensely political person (he joined the Fabian Society as early as 1903), it is clear from his writings that he favored the "Philosopher King" approach to government and probably would have applied for the job himself. By the time of his death he was disillusioned about the future of the human race.

---

[1]Indeed, Wells, himself, influenced the development of this awesome weapon. His novel *The World Set Free* (1913) predicted the discovery and use of atomic bombs and stimulated Leo Szilard to begin his successful work of self-sustaining chain reactions. See Edward Cornish, *The Study of the Future* (Washington, D.C.: World Future Society, 1977), pp. 76–77.

Unlike the great majority of his fellow "science-fiction" writers (a term not yet in common usage when he wrote the bulk of what he called his "scientific romances"), Wells was educated in science and could bring serious extrapolation to his fiction.[2] He published five of these novels in the nineteenth century: *The Time Machine*, (1895) which employed a piece of technology (as opposed to dreams, extended sleep or other nontechnological methods) to travel in time; *The Island of Dr. Moreau* (1896), which clearly reflected the influence of Huxley and Darwin; *The Invisible Man* (1897), which has been interpreted as a warning against the potential dangers of abusing science; *The War of the Worlds* (1898), perhaps the great prototype of the "Earth invaded" story; and *When the Sleeper Wakes* (1899), the first of his explicitly "social" novels. Almost all of his scientific romances have been filmed, several brilliantly. These works and the books that followed them found a huge and continuing audience, for as Robert Scholes and Eric S. Rabkin have written, "The great strength of Wells as a writer of science fiction, and his great contribution to the tradition, lay in his ability to combine the fantastic with the plausible, the strange with the familiar, the new with the old."

However, his novels have to a large extent overshadowed and obscured his short stories, which contain some of his most creative thinking and effective writing. The best of these shorter works can be found in *Thirty Strange Stories* (1897) and *twenty Eight Science Fiction Stories* (1952).

---

[2]The term "science fiction" first appears to have been used by William Watson in *A Little Earnest Book Upon A Great Old Subject* (Darton & Co., 1851). See Brian W. Aldiss, "On the age of the term science fiction," in *Science Fiction Studies*, July 1976, p. 213. But this term did not become popular until being reintroduced by Hugo Gernsback in 1929. See Sam Moskowitz, *Explorers of the Infinite* (Cleveland: The World Publishing Co., 1963), pp. 313–333.

IN THE ABYSS

The lieutenant stood in front of the steel sphere and gnawed a piece of pine splinter. "What do you think of it, Steevens?" he asked.

"It's an idea," said Steevens, in the tone of one who keeps an open mind.

"I believe it will smash—flat," said the lieutenant.

"He seems to have calculated it all out pretty well," said Steevens, still impartial.

"But think of the pressure," said the lieutenant. "At the surface of the water it's fourteen pounds to the inch, thirty feet down it's double that; sixty, treble; ninety, four times; nine hundred, forty times; five thousand, three hundred—that's a mile—it's two hundred and forty times fourteen pounds; that's—let's see—thirty hundredweight—a ton and a half, Steevens; *a ton and a half* to the square inch. And the ocean where he's going is five miles deep. That's seven and a half—"

"Sounds a lot," said Steevens, "but it's jolly thick steel."

The lieutenant made no answer, but resumed his pine splinter. The object of their conversation was a huge ball of steel, having an exterior diameter of perhaps nine feet. It looked like the shot for some titanic piece of artillery. It was elaborately nested in a monstrous scaffolding built into the framework of the vessel, and the gigantic spars that were presently to sling it overboard gave the stern of the ship an appearance that had raised the curiosity of every decent sailor who had sighted it, from the Pool of London to the Tropic of Capricorn. In two places, one above the other, the steel gave place to a couple of circular windows of enormously thick glass, and one of these, set in a steel frame of great solidity, was now partially unscrewed. Both the men had seen the interior of this globe for the first time that morning. It was elaborately padded with air cushions, with little studs sunk between bulging pillows to work the simple mechanism of the affair. Everything was elaborately padded, even the Myers apparatus which was to absorb carbonic acid and replace the oxygen inspired by its tenant, when he had crept in by the glass manhole, and had been screwed in. It was so elaborately padded that a man might have been fired from a gun in it with perfect safety. And it had need to be, for presently a man was to crawl in through that glass manhole, to be screwed up tightly, and to be flung overboard, and to sink down—down—down, for five miles, even as the lieutenant said. It had taken the strongest hold of his imagination; it made him a bore at mess; and he found Steevens, the new arrival aboard, a godsend to talk to about it, over and over again.

"It's my opinion," said the lieutenant, "that that glass will simply bend in and bulge and smash under a pressure of that sort. Daubrée has made rocks run like water under big pressures—and, you mark my words—"

"If the glass did break in," said Steevens, "what then?"

"The water would shoot in like a jet of iron. Have you ever felt a straight jet of high-pressure water? It would hit as hard as a bullet. It would simply smash him and flatten him. It would tear down his throat, and into his lungs; it would blow in his ears—"

"What a detailed imagination you have!" protested Steevens, who saw things vividly.

"It's a simple statement of the inevitable," said the lieutenant.

"And the globe?"

"Would just give out a few little bubbles, and it would settle down comfortably against the day of judgment, among the oozes and the bottom clay—with poor Elstead spread over his own smashed cushions like butter over bread."

He repeated this sentence as though he liked it very much. "Like butter over bread," he said.

"Having a look at the jigger?" said a voice, and Elstead stood behind them, spick-and-span in white, with a cigarette between his teeth, and his eyes smiling out of the shadow of his ample hat-brim. "What's that about bread and butter, Weybridge? Grumbling as usual about the insufficient pay of naval officers? It won't be more than a day now before

I start. We are to get the slings ready today. This clean sky and gentle swell is just the kind of thing for swinging off a dozen tons of lead and iron, isn't it?''

"It won't affect you much," said Weybridge.

"No. Seventy or eighty feet down, and I shall be there in a dozen seconds, there's not a particle moving, though the wind shriek itself hoarse up above, and the water lifts halfway to the clouds. No. Down there—'' He moved to the side of the ship and the other two followed him. All three leaned forward on their elbows and stared down into the yellow-green water.

"Peace," said Elstead, finishing his thought aloud.

"Are you dead certain that clockwork will act?'' asked Weybridge presently.

"It has worked thirty-five times," said Elstead. ''It's bound to work.''

"But if it doesn't?''

"Why shouldn't it?''

"I wouldn't go down in that confounded thing," said Weybridge, "for twenty thousand pounds.''

"Cheerful chap you are," said Elstead, and spat sociably at a bubble below.

"I don't understand yet how you mean to work the thing," said Steevens.

"In the first place, I'm screwed into the sphere," said Elstead, "and when I've turned the electric light off and on three times to show I'm cheerful, I'm swung out over the stern by that crane, with all those big lead sinkers slung below me. The top lead weight has a roller carrying a hundred fathoms of strong cord rolled up, and that's all that joins the sinkers to the sphere, except the slings that will be cut when the affair is dropped. We use cord rather than wire rope because it's easier to cut and more buoyant—necessary points, as you will see.

"Through each of these lead weights you notice there is a hole, and an iron rod will be run through that and will project six feet on the lower side. If that rod is rammed up from below, it knocks up a lever and sets the clockwork in motion at the side of the cylinder on which the cord winds.

"Very well. The whole affair is lowered gently into the water, and the slings are cut. The sphere floats—with the air in it, it's lighter than water—but the lead weights go down straight and the cord runs out. When the cord is all paid out, the sphere will go down, too, pulled down by the cord.''

''But why the cord?'' asked Steevens. ''Why not fasten the weights directly to the sphere?''

''Because of the smash down below. The whole affair will go rushing down, mile after mile, at a headlong pace at last. It would be knocked to pieces on the bottom if it wasn't for that cord. But the weights will hit the bottom, and directly they do, the buoyancy of the sphere will come into play. It will go on sinking slower and slower; come to a stop at last, and then begin to float upward again.

''That's where the clockwork comes in. Directly the weights smash against the sea bottom, the rod will be knocked through and will kick up the clockwork, and the cord will be rewound on the reel. I shall be lugged down to the sea bottom. There I shall stay for half an hour, with the electric light on, looking about me. Then the clockwork will release a spring knife, the cord will be cut, and up I shall rush again, like a soda-water bubble. The cord itself will help the flotation.''

''And if you should chance to hit a ship?'' said Weybridge.

''I should come up at such a pace, I should go clean through it,'' said Elstead, ''like a cannonball. You needn't worry about that.''

''And suppose some nimble crustacean should wriggle into your clockwork—''

''It would be a pressing sort of invitation for me to stop,'' said Elstead, turning his back on the water and staring at the sphere.

They had swung Elstead overboard by eleven o'clock. The day was serenely bright and calm, with the horizon lost in haze. The electric glare in the little upper compartment beamed cheerfully three times. Then they let him down slowly to the surface of the water, and a sailor in the stern chains hung ready to cut the tackle that held the lead weights and the sphere together. The globe, which had looked so large on deck, looked the smallest thing conceivable under the stern of the ship. It rolled a little, and its two dark windows, which floated uppermost, seemed like eyes turned up in round wonderment at the people who crowded the rail. A voice wondered how Elstead liked the rolling. ''Are you ready?'' sang out the commander. ''Ay, ay, sir!'' ''Then let her go!''

The rope of the tackle tightened against the blade and was cut, and an eddy rolled over the globe in a grotesquely helpless fashion. Someone waved a handkerchief, someone else tried an ineffectual cheer, a middy was counting slowly: "Eight, nine, ten!" Another roll, then with a jerk and a splash the thing righted itself.

It seemed to be stationary for a moment, to grow rapidly smaller, and then the water closed over it, and it became visible, enlarged by refraction and dimmer, below the surface. Before one could count three it had disappeared. There was a flicker of white light far down in the water, that diminished to a speck and vanished. Then there was nothing but a depth of water going down into blackness, through which a shark was swimming.

Then suddenly the screw of the cruiser began to rotate, the water was crickled, the shark disappeared in a wrinkled confusion, and a torrent of foam rushed across the crystalline clearness that had swallowed up Elstead. "What's the idee?" said one A. B. to another.

"We're going to lay off about a couple of miles, 'fear he should hit us when he comes up," said his mate.

The ship steamed slowly to her new position. Aboard her almost everyone who was unoccupied remained watching the breathing swell into which the sphere had sunk. For the next half hour it is doubtful if a word was spoken that did not bear directly or indirectly on Elstead. The December sun was now high in the sky, and the heat very considerable.

"He'll be cold enough down there," said Weybridge. "They say that below a certain depth sea water's always just about freezing."

"Where'll he come up?" asked Steevens. "I've lost my bearings."

"That's the spot," said the commander, who prided himself on his omniscience. He extended a precise finger southeastward. "And this, I reckon, is pretty nearly the moment," he said. "He's been thirty-five minutes."

"How long does it take to reach the bottom of the ocean?" asked Steevens.

"For a depth of five miles, and reckoning—as we did—an acceleration of two feet per second, both ways, is just about three-quarters of a minute."

"Then he's overdue," said Weybridge.

"Pretty nearly," said the commander. "I suppose it takes a few minutes for that cord of his to wind in."

"I forgot that," said Weybridge, evidently relieved.

And then began the suspense. A minute slowly dragged itself out, and no sphere shot out of the water. Another followed, and nothing broke the low oily swell. The sailors explained to one another that little point about the winding-in of the cord. The rigging was dotted with expectant faces. "Come up, Elstead!" called one hairy-chested salt impatiently, and the others caught it up, and shouted as though they were waiting for the curtain of a theatre to rise.

The commander glances irritably at them.

"Of course, if the acceleration's less than two," he said, "he'll be all the longer. We aren't absolutely certain that was the proper figure. I'm no slavish believer in calculations."

Steevens agreed concisely. No one on the quarterdeck spoke for a couple of minutes. Then Steevens' watchcase clicked.

When twenty-one minutes after, the sun reached the zenith, they were still waiting for the globe to reappear, and not a man aboard had dared to whisper that hope was dead. It was Weybridge who first gave expression to that realization. He spoke while the sound of eight bells still hung in the air. "I always distrusted that window," he said quite suddenly to Steevens.

"Good God!" said Steevens; "you don't think—?"

"Well!" said Weybridge, and left the rest to his imagination.

"I'm no great believer in calculations myself," said the commander dubiously, "so that I'm not altogether hopeless yet." And at midnight the gunboat was steaming slowly in a spiral round the spot where the globe had sunk, and the white beam of the electric light fled and halted and swept discontentedly onward again over the waste of phosphorescent waters under the little stars.

"If his window hasn't burst and smashed him," said Weybridge, "then it's a cursed sight worse, for his clockwork has gone wrong, and he's alive now, five miles under our feet, down there in the cold and dark, anchored in that little bubble of his, where never a ray of light has shone or a human being lived, since the waters were gathered together. He's there without food, feeling hungry and thirsty and scared, wondering whether he'll starve or stifle. Which will it be? The Myers apparatus is running out, I suppose. How long do they last?"

"Good heavens!" he exclaimed; "What little things we are! What daring little devils! Down there, miles and miles of water—all water, and all this empty water about us and this sky. Gulfs!'' He threw his hands out, and as he did so, a little white streak swept noiseless up the sky, traveled more slowly, stopped, became a motionless dot, as though a new star had fallen up into the sky. Then it went sliding back again and lost itself amidst the reflections of the stars and the white haze of the sea's phosphorescence.

At the sight he stopped, arm extended and mouth open. He shut his mouth, opened it again, and waved his arms with an impatient gesture. Then he turned, shouted ''El-stead ahoy!'' to the first watch, and went at a run to Lindley and the searchlight. ''I saw him,'' he said. ''Starboard there! His light's on, and he's just shot out of the water. Bring the light round. We ought to see him drifting, when he lifts on the swell.''

But they never picked up the explorer until dawn. Then they almost ran him down. The crane was swung out and a boat's crew hooked the chain to the sphere. When they had shipped the sphere, they unscrewed the manhole and peered into the darkness of the interior (for the electric-light chamber was intended to illuminate the water about the sphere, and was shut off entirely from its general cavity).

The air was very hot within the cavity, and the india rubber at the lip of the manhole was soft. There was no answer to their eager questions and no sound of movement within. Elstead seemed to be lying motion-less, crumpled up in the bottom of the globe. The ship's doctor crawled in and lifted him out to the men outside. For a moment or so they did not know whether Elstead was alive or dead. His face, in the yellow light of the ship's lamps, glistened with perspiration. They carried him down to his own cabin.

He was not dead, they found, but in a state of absolute nervous collapse, and besides cruelly bruised. For some days he had to lie perfectly still. It was a week before he could tell his experiences.

Almost his first words were that he was going down again. The sphere would have to be altered, he said, in order to allow him to throw off the cord if need be, and that was all. He had had the most marvelous experience. ''You thought I should find nothing but ooze,'' he said. ''You laughed at my explorations, and I've discovered a new world!'' He told his story in disconnected fragments, and chiefly from the wrong end, so that it is impossible to retell it in his words. But what follows is the narrative of his experience.

It began atrociously, he said. Before the cord ran out, the thing kept rolling over. He felt like a frog in a football. He could see nothing but the crane and the sky overhead, with an occasional glimpse of the people on the ship's rail. He couldn't tell a bit which way the thing would roll next. Suddenly he would find his feet going up, and try to step, and over he went rolling, head over heels, and just anyhow, on the padding. Any other shape would have been more comfortable, but no other shape was to be relied upon under the huge pressure of the nethermost abyss.

Suddenly the swaying ceased; the globe righted, and when he had picked himself up, he saw the water all about him greeny-blue, with an attenuated light filtering down from above, and a shoal of little floating things went rushing up past him, as it seemed to him, towards the light. And even as he looked, it grew darker and darker, until the water above was as dark as the midnight sky, albeit of a greener shade, and the water below black. And little transparent things in the water developed a faint glint of luminosity, and shot past him in faint greenish streaks.

And the feeling of falling! It was just like the start of a lift, he said, only it kept on. One has to imagine what that means, that keeping on. It was then of all times that Elstead repented of his adventure. He saw the chances against him in an altogether new light. He thought of the big cuttlefish people knew to exist in the middle waters, the kind of things they find half digested in whales at times, or floating dead and rotten and half eaten by fish. Suppose one caught hold and wouldn't let go. And had the clockwork really been sufficiently tested? But whether he wanted to go on or to go back mattered not the slightest now.

In fifty seconds everything was as black as night outside, except where the beam from his light struck through the waters, and picked out every now and then some fish or scrap of sinking matter. They flashed by too fast for him to see what they were. Once he thinks he passed a shark. And then the sphere began to get hot by friction against the water. They had underestimated this, it seems.

The first thing he noticed was that he was perspiring, and then he heard a hissing growing louder under his feet, and saw a lot of little bubbles—very little bubbles they were—rushing upward like a fan through the water outside. Steam! He felt the window, and it was hot. He turned on the minute glow-lamp that lit his own cavity, looked at the padded watch by the studs, and saw he had been traveling now for two minutes. It came into his head that the window would crack through the conflict of temperatures, for he knew the bottom water is very near freezing.

Then suddenly the floor of the sphere seemed to press against his feet, the rush of bubbles outside grew slower and slower, and the hissing diminished. The sphere rolled a little. The window had not cracked, nothing had given, and he knew that the dangers of sinking, at any rate, were over.

In another minute or so he would be on the floor of the abyss. He thought, he said, of Steevens and Weybridge and the rest of them five miles overhead, higher to him than the very highest clouds that ever floated over land are to us, steaming slowly and staring down and wondering what had happened to him.

He peered out of the window. There were no more bubbles now, and the hissing had stopped. Outside there was a heavy blackness—as black as black velvet—except where the electric light pierced the empty water and showed the color of it—a yellow-green. Then three things like shapes of fire swam into sight, following each other through the water. Whether they were little and near or big and far-off he could not tell.

Each was outlined in a bluish light almost as bright as the lights of a fishing smack, a light which seemed to be smoking greatly, and all along the sides of them were specks of this, like the lighter portholes of a ship. Their phosphorescence seemed to go out as they came into the radiance of his lamp, and he saw then that they were little fish of some strange sort, with huge heads, vast eyes, and dwindling bodies and tails. Their eyes were turned towards him, and he judged they were following him down. He supposed they were attracted by his glare.

Presently others of the same sort joined them. As he went on down, he noticed that the water became of a pallid color, and that little specks twinkled in his ray like motes in a sunbeam. This was probably due to the clouds of ooze and mud that the impact of his leaden sinkers had disturbed.

By the time he was drawn down to the lead weights he was in a dense fog of white that his electric light failed altogether to pierce for more than a few yards, and many minutes elapsed before the hanging sheets of sediment subsided to any extent. Then, lit by his light and by the transient phosphorescence of a distant shoal of fishes, he was able to see under the huge blackness of the super-incumbent water an undulating expanse of greyish-white ooze, broken here and there by tangled thickets of a growth of sea lilies, waving hungry tentacles in the air.

Farther away were the graceful, translucent outlines of a group of gigantic sponges. About this floor there were scattered a number of bristling flattish tufts of rich purple and black, which he decided must be some sort of sea urchin, and small, large-eyed or blind things having a curious resemblance, some to woodlice, and others to lobsters, crawled sluggishly across the track of the light and vanished into the obscurity again, leaving furrowed trails behind them.

Then suddenly the hovering swarm of little fishes veered about and came towards him as a flight of starlings might do. They passed over him like a phosphorescent snow, and then he saw behind them some larger creature advancing towards the sphere.

At first he could see it only dimly, a faintly moving figure remotely suggestive of a walking man, and then it came into the spray of light that the lamp shot out. As the glare struck it, it shut its eyes, dazzled. He stared in rigid astonishment.

It was a strange vertebrated animal. Its dark purple head was dimly suggestive of a chameleon, but it had such a high forehead and such a braincase as no reptile ever displayed before; the vertical pitch of its face gave it a most extraordinary resemblance to a human being.

Two large and protruding eyes projected from sockets in chameleon fashion, and it had a broad reptilian mouth with horny lips beneath its little nostrils. In the position of the ears were two huge gill-covers, and out of these floated a branching tree of coralline filaments, almost like the tree-like gills that very young rays and sharks possess.

But the humanity of the face was not the most extraordinary thing about the creature. It was a biped; its almost globular body was poised on a tripod of two frog-like legs and a long thick tail, and its forelimbs, which grotesquely caricatured the human hand, much as a frog's do, carried a long shaft of bone, tipped with copper. The color of the creature was variegated; its head, hands, and legs were purple; but its skin, which hung loosely upon it, even as clothes might do, was a phosphorescent grey. And it stood there blinded by the light.

At last this unknown creature of the abyss blinked its eyes open, and, shading them with its disengaged hand, opened its mouth and gave vent to a shouting noise, articulate almost as speech might be, that penetrated even the steel case and padded jacket of the sphere. How a shouting may be accomplished without lungs Elstead does not profess to explain. It then moved sideways out of the glare into the mystery of shadow that bordered it on either side, and Elstead felt rather than saw that it was coming towards him. Fancying the light had attracted it, he turned the switch that cut off the current. In another moment something soft dabbed upon the steel, and the globe swayed.

Then the shouting was repeated, and it seemed to him that a distant echo answered it. The dabbing recurred, and the globe swayed and ground against the spindle over which the wire was rolled. He stood in the blackness and peered out into the everlasting night of the abyss. And presently he saw, very faint and remote, other phosphorescent quasi-human forms hurrying towards him.

Hardly knowing what he did, he felt about in his swaying prison for the stud of the exterior electric light, and came by accident against his own small glow-lamp in its padded recess. The sphere twisted, and then threw him down; he heard shouts like shouts of surprise, and when he rose to his feet, he saw two pairs of stalked eyes peering into the lower window and reflecting his light.

In another moment hands were dabbing vigorously at his steel casing, and there was a sound, horrible enough in his position, of the metal protection of the clockwork being vigorously hammered. That, indeed, sent his heart into his mouth, for if these strange creatures succeeded in stopping that, his release would never occur. Scarcely had he thought as much when he felt the sphere sway violently, and the floor of it press hard against his feet. He turned off the small glow-lamp that lit the interior, and sent the ray of the large light in the separate compartment out into the water. The seafloor and the man-like creatures had disappeared, and a couple of fish chasing each other dropped suddenly by the window.

He thought at once that these strange denizens of the deep sea had broken the rope, and that he had escaped. He drove up faster and faster, and then stopped with a jerk that sent him flying against the padded roof of his prison. For half a minute, perhaps, he was too astonished to think.

Then he felt that the sphere was spinning slowly, and rocking, and it seemed to him that it was also being drawn through the water. By crouching close to the window, he managed to make his weight effective and roll that part of the sphere downward, but he could see nothing save the pale ray of his light striking down ineffectively into the darkness. It occurred to him that he would see more if he turned the lamp off, and allowed his eyes to grow accustomed to the profound obscurity.

In this he was wise. After some minutes the velvety blackness became a translucent blackness, and then, far away, and as faint as the

269

zodiacal light of an English summer evening, he saw shapes moving below. He judged these creatures had detached his cable, and were towing him along the sea bottom.

And then he saw something faint and remote across the undulations of the submarine plain, a broad horizon of pale luminosity that extended this way and that way as far as the range of his little window permitted him to see. To this he was being towed, as a balloon might be towed by men out of the open country into a town. He approached it very slowly, and very slowly the dim irradiation was gathered together into more definite shapes.

It was nearly five o'clock before he came over this luminous area, and by that time he could make out an arrangement suggestive of streets and houses grouped about a vast roofless erection that was grotesquely suggestive of a ruined abbey. It was spread out like a map below him. The houses were all roofless enclosures of walls, and their substance being, as he afterwards saw, of phosphorescent bones, gave the place an appearance as if it were built of drowned moonshine.

Among the inner caves of the place waving trees of crinoid stretched their tentacles, and tall, slender, glassy sponges shot like shining minarets and lilies of filmy light out of the general glow of the city. In the open spaces of the place he could see a stirring movement as of crowds of people, but he was too many fathoms above them to distinguish the individuals in those crowds.

Then slowly they pulled him down, and as they did so, the details of the place crept slowly upon his apprehension. He saw that the courses of the cloudy buildings were marked out with beaded lines of round objects, and then he perceived that at several points below him, in broad open spaces, were forms like the encrusted shapes of ships.

Slowly and surely he was drawn down, and the forms below him became brighter, clearer, more distinct. He was being pulled down, he perceived, towards the large building in the center of the town, and he could catch a glimpse ever and again of the multitudinous forms that were lugging at his cord. He was astonished to see that the rigging of one of the ships, which formed such a prominent feature of the place, was crowded with a host of gesticulating figures regarding him, and then the walls of the great building rose about him silently, and hid the city from his eyes.

And such walls they were, of waterlogged wood, and twisted

270

wire-rope, and iron spars, and copper, and the bones and skulls of dead men. The skulls ran in zigzag lines and spirals and fantastic curves over the building; and in and out of their eye sockets, and over the whole surface of the place, lurked and played a multitude of silvery little fishes.

Suddenly his ears were filled with a low shouting and a noise like the violent blowing of horns, and this gave place to a fantastic chant. Down the sphere sank, past the huge pointed windows, through which he saw vaguely a great number of these strange, ghostlike people regarding him, and at last he came to rest, as it seemed, on a kind of altar that stood in the center of the place.

And now he was at such a level that he could see these strange people of the abyss plainly once more. To his astonishment, he perceived that they were prostrating themselves before him, all save one, dressed as it seemed in a robe of placoid scales, and crowned with a luminous diadem, who stood with his reptilian mouth opening and shutting, as though he led the chanting of the worshipers.

A curious impulse made Elstead turn on his small glow-lamp again, so that he became visible to these creatures of the abyss, albeit the glare made them disappear forthwith into night. At this sudden sight of him, the chanting gave place to a tumult of exultant shouts; and Elstead, being anxious to watch them, turned his light off again, and vanished from before their eyes. But for a time he was too blind to make out what they were doing, and when at last he could distinguish them, they were kneeling again. And thus they continued worshiping him, without rest or intermission, for a space of three hours.

More circumstantial was Elstead's account of this astounding city and its people, these people of perpetual night, who have never seen sun or moon or stars, green vegetation, nor any living, air-breathing creatures, who know nothing of fire, nor any light but the phosphorescent light of living things.

Startling as is his story, it is yet more startling to find that scientific men, of such eminence as Adams and Jenkins, find nothing incredible in it. They tell me they see no reason why intelligent, water-breathing, vertebrated creatures, inured to a low temperature and enormous pressure, and of such a heavy structure, that neither alive nor dead would they float, might not live upon the bottom of the deep sea, and quite unsuspected by us, descendants like ourselves of the gerat Theriomorpha of the New Red Sandstone age.

271

We should be known to them, however, as strange, meteoric creatures, wont to fall catastrophically dead out of the mysterious blackness of their watery sky. And not only we ourselves, but our ships, our metals, our appliances, would come raining down out of the night. Sometimes sinking things would smite down and crush them, as if it were the judgment of some unseen power above, and sometimes would come things of the utmost rarity or utility, or shapes of inspiring suggestion. One can understand, perhaps, something of their behavior at the descent of a living man, if one thinks what a barbaric people might do, to whom an enhaloed, shining creature came suddenly out of the sky.

At one time or another Elstead probably told the officers of the *Ptarmigan* every detail of his strange twelve hours in the abyss. That he also intended to write them down is certain, but he never did, and so unhappily we have to piece together the discrepant fragments of his story from the reminiscences of Commander Simmons, Weybridge, Steevens, Lindley, and the others.

We see the thing darkly in fragmentary glimpses—the huge ghostly building, the bowing, chanting people, with their dark chameleon-like heads and faintly luminous clothing, and Elstead, with his light turned on again, vainly trying to convey to their minds that the cord by which the sphere was held was to be severed. Minute after minute slipped away, and Elstead, looking at his watch, was horrified to find that he had oxygen only for four hours more. But the chant in his honor kept on as remorselessly as if it was the marching song of his approaching death.

The manner of his release he does not understand, but to judge by the end of the cord that hung from the sphere, it had been cut through by rubbing against the edge of the altar. Abruptly the sphere rolled over, and he swept up, out of their world, as an ethereal creature clothed in a vacuum would sweep through our own atmosphere back to its native ether again. He must have torn out of their sight as a hydrogen bubble hastens upward from our air. A strange ascension it must have seemed to them.

The sphere rushed up with even greater velocity than, when weighted with the lead sinkers, it had rushed down. It became exceedingly hot. It drove up with the windows uppermost, and he remembers the torrent of bubbles frothing against the glass. Every moment he expected this to fly. Then suddenly something like a huge wheel seemed to be released in his head, the padded compartment began spinning about him, and he fainted. His next recollection was of his cabin, and of the doctor's voice.

But that is the substance of the extraordinary story that Elstead related in fragments to the officers of the *Ptarmigan*. He promised to write it all down at a later date. His mind was chiefly occupied with the improvement of his apparatus, which was effected at Rio.

It remains only to tell that on February 2, 1896, he made his second descent into the ocean abyss, with the improvements his first experience suggested. What happened we shall probably never know. He never returned. The *Ptarmigan* beat about over the point of his submersion, seeking him in vain for thirteen days. Then she returned to Rio, and the news was telegraphed to his friends. So the matter remains for the present. But it is hardly probable that no further attempt will be made to verify his strange story of these hitherto unsuspected cities of the deep sea.

Grant Allen (1848–1899)

Philosopher, scientist, teacher, essayist, poet and author, today Grant Allen is best remembered by the mystery field for his humorous stories about Colonel Clay, the first heroic rogue of short crime fiction (*An African Millionaire*, 1897). However, he also wrote a number of popularly received fantastic novels and short stories.

Of Irish and French-Canadian ancestry, he was born near Kingston, Ontario, where his father served as a minister of the Church of Ireland. But then the family moved to the United States and much of Allen's boyhood was spent in New Haven, Connecticut. He was tutored by a Yale instructor, attended College Imperial in France, and graduated with a baccalaureate from Oxford's Merton College in 1871. After teaching for a couple of years in the British communities of Brighton, Cheltenham, and Reading, he was appointed Professor of Mental and Moral Philosophy at an experimental university for blacks in Spanish Town, Jamaica. There he began to develop an evolutionary system of philosophy. When the university collapsed in 1876, he returned to England and used his severance pay to finance the publication of his ideas in *Physiological Esthetics* (1877). The book sold only three hundred copies, but the praise it received from Charles Darwin and Herbert Spencer helped Allen to begin placing articles in important periodicals such as *Cornhill, Belgravia,* and *The Gentleman's Magazine*.

One day while writing an essay about the likelihood that man would not recognize ghosts even if he saw them, Allen ''threw the argument into the form of a narrative.'' He submitted the story to *Belgravia* under the pseudonym of J. Arbuthnot Wilson, and the editor requested more.

Later Allen's shift to fiction was accelerated by two letters he received from another editor—the one addressed to Allen said the magazine was not interested in receiving his articles, the one addressed to Wilson beseeched him to send more stories.

Among his contemporaries, Allen was most noted for *The Woman Who Did* and *The British Barbarians,* two controversial novels of 1895. The first outraged moralists by suggesting justification for a girl's desire to avoid marriage while conducting an affair that resulted in a love child. The second outraged nearly everybody by suggesting that a twenty-fifth century anthropologist would find Victorian customs to be irrational, parochial, and incomprehensible.

Finally, Allen's always-fragile health deteriorated in the fall of 1899 and he died before completing his last novel, *Hilda Wade*. He did, however, give deathbed instructions to good friend Arthur Conan Doyle and the resulting collaboration was published in 1900.

Allen's shorter works of science fiction and fantasy are very well written and though many can be found in *Strange Stories* (1884) and *Twelve Tales* (1899) it is somewhat surprising that they have not yet been assembled into one volume. Certainly, an excellent lead story would be "The Thames Valley Catastrophe" since it is an accurate and gripping account of love and survival in the face of imminent peril.

THE THAMES VALLEY CATASTROPHE

It can scarcely be necessary for me to mention, I suppose, at this time of day, that I was one of the earliest and fullest observers of the sad series of events which finally brought about the transference of the seat of Government of these islands from London to Manchester. Nor need I allude here to the conspicuous position which my narrative naturally occupies in the blue book on the Thames Valley Catastrophe (vol. ii., part vii.), ordered by Parliament in its preliminary session under the new regime at Birmingham. But I think it also incumbent upon me, for the benefit of posterity, to supplement that necessarily dry and formal statement by a more circumstantial account of my personal adventures during the terrible period.

I am aware, of course, that my poor little story can possess little interest for our contemporaries, wearied out as they are with details of the disaster, and surfeited with tedious scientific discussions as to its origin and nature. But in after-years, I venture to believe, when the crowning calamity of the nineteenth century has grown picturesque and, so to speak, ivy-clad, by reason of its remoteness (like the Great Plague or the Great Fire of London with ourselves), the world may possibly desire to hear how this unparalleled convulsion affected the feelings and fortunes of a single family in the middle rank of life, and in a part of London neither squalid nor fashionable.

It is such personal touches of human nature that give reality to history, which without them must become, as a great writer has finely said, nothing more than an old almanac. I shall not apologize, therefore, for being frankly egoistic and domestic in my reminiscences of that appalling day: for I know that those who desire to seek scientific

277

information on the subject will look for it, not in vain, in the eight bulky volumes of the recent blue book. I shall concern myself here with the great event merely as it appeared to myself, a Government servant of the second grade, and in its relations to my own wife, my home, and my children.

On the morning of the twenty-first of August, in the memorable year of the calamity, I happened to be at Cookham, a pleasant and pretty village which then occupied the western bank of the Thames just below the spot where the Lookout Tower of the Earthquake and Eruption Department now dominates the whole wide plain of the Glassy Rock Desert. In place of the black lake of basalt which young people see nowadays winding its solid bays in and out among the grassy downs, most men still living can well remember a gracious and smiling valley, threaded in the midst by a beautiful river.

I had cycled down from London the evening before (thus forestalling my holiday), and had spent the night at a tolerable inn in the village. By a curious coincidence, the only other visitor at the little hotel that night was a fellow-cyclist, an American George W. Ward by name, who had come over with his "wheel," as he called it, for six weeks in England, in order to investigate the geology of our southern counties for himself, and to compare it with that of the far western cretaceous system. I venture to describe this as a curious coincidence, because, as it happened, the mere accident of my meeting him gave me my first inkling of the very existence of that singular phenomenon of which we were all so soon to receive a startling example. I had never so much as heard before of fissure-eruptions; and if I had not heard of them from Ward that evening, I might not have recognized at sight the actuality when it first appeared, and therefore I might have been involved in the general disaster. In which case, of course, this unpretentious narrative would never have been written.

As we sat in the little parlor of the White Hart, however, over our evening pipe, it chanced that the American, who was a pleasant, conversable fellow, began talking to me of his reasons for visiting England. I was at that time a clerk in the General Post Office (of which I am now secretary), and was then no student of science; but his enthusiastic talk about his own country and its vastness amused and interested me. He had been employed for some years on the Geological Survey in the Western states, and he was deeply impressed by the solemnity and the colossal scale of everything American. "Mountains!" he said, when I spoke of Scotland; "why, for mountains, your Alps aren't in it,[1] and as for volcanoes, your Vesuviuses and Etnas just spit fire a bit at infrequent intervals; while ours do things on a scale worthy of a great country, I can tell you. Europe is a circumstance: America is a continent."

"But surely," I objected, "that was a pretty fair eruption that destroyed Pompeii!"

The American rose and surveyed me slowly. I can see him to this day, with his close-shaven face and his contemptuous smile at my European ignorance. "Well," he said, after a long and impressive pause, "the lava-flood that destroyed a few acres about the Bay of Naples was what we call a trickle: it came from a crater; and the crater it came from was nothing more than a small round vent-hole; the lava flowed down from it in a moderate stream over a limited area. But what do you say to the earth opening in a huge crack, forty or fifty miles long—say, as far as from here right away to London, or farther—and lava pouring out from the orifice, not in a little rivulet, as at Etna, or Vesuvius, but in a sea or inundation, which spread at once over a tract as big as England? That's something like volcanic action, isn't it? And *that's* the sort of thing we have out in Colorado."

"You are joking," I replied, "or bragging. You are trying to astonish me with the familiar spread eagle."

He smiled a quiet smile. "Not a bit of it," he answered. "What I tell you is at least as true as gospel. The earth yawns in Montana. There are fissure-eruptions, as we call them, in the Western states, out of which the lava has welled like wine out of a broken skin—welled up in vast roaring floods, molten torrents of basalt, many miles across, and spread like water over whole plains and valleys."

"Not within historical times!" I exclaimed.

"I'm not so sure about that," he answered, musing. "I grant you, not within times which are historical right there—for Colorado is a very new country: but I incline to think some of the most recent fissure-eruptions took place not later than when the Tudors reigned in England. The lava oozed out, red-hot—gushed out—was squeezed out—and spread instantly everywhere; it's so comparatively recent that the surface

---

[1] A slang phrase of the time, equivalent to our modern "Your Alps swob the show," or "fail to eventuate."

279

of the rock is still bare in many parts, unweathered sufficiently to support vegetation. I fancy the stream must have been ejected at a single burst, in a huge white-hot dome, and then flowed down on every side, filling up the valleys to a certain level, in and out among the hills, exactly as water might do. And some of these eruptions, I tell you, by measured survey, would have covered more ground than from Dover to Liverpool, and from York to Cornwall.''

''Let us be thankful,'' I said, carelessly, ''that such things don't happen in our own times.''

He eyed me curiously. *''Haven't* happened, you mean,'' he answered. ''We have no security that they mayn't happen again tomorrow. These fissure-eruptions, though not historically described for us, are common events in geological history—commoner and on a larger scale in America than elsewhere. Still, they have occurred in all lands and at various epochs; there is no reason at all why one shouldn't occur in England at present.''

I laughed, and shook my head. I had the Englishman's firm conviction—so rudely shattered by the subsequent events, but then so universal—that nothing very unusual ever happened in England.

Next morning I rose early, bathed in Odney Weir (a picturesque pool close by), breakfasted with the American, and then wrote a hasty line to my wife, informing her that I should probably sleep that night at Oxford; for I was off on a few days' holiday, and I liked Ethel to know where a letter or telegram would reach me each day, as we were both a little anxious about the baby's teething. Even while I pen these words now, the grim humor of the situation comes back to me vividly. Thousands of fathers and mothers were anxious that morning about similar trifles, whose pettiness was brought home to them with an appalling shock in the all-embracing horror of that day's calamity.

About ten o'clock I inflated my tires and got underway. I meant to ride towards Oxford by a leisurely and circuitous route, along the windings of the river, past Marlow and Henley; so I began by crossing Cookham Bridge, a wooden or iron structure, I scarcely remember which. It spanned the Thames close by the village: the curious will find its exact position marked in the maps of the period.

In the middle of the bridge, I paused and surveyed that charming prospect, which I was the last of living men perhaps to see as it then existed. Close by stood a weir; beside it, the stream divided into three separate branches, exquisitely backed up by the gentle green slopes of Hedsor and Cliveden. I could never pass that typical English view without a glance of admiration; this morning, I pulled up my bicycle for a moment, and cast my eye downstream with more than my usual enjoyment of the smooth blue water and the tall white poplars whose leaves showed their gleaming silver in the breeze beside it. I might have gazed at it too long—and one minute more would have sufficed for my destruction—had not a cry from the towpath a little farther up attracted my attention.

It was a wild, despairing cry, like that of a man being overpowered and murdered.

I am confident this was my first intimation of danger. Two minutes before, it is true, I had heard a faint sound like distant rumbling of thunder; but nothing else. I am one of those who strenuously maintain that the catastrophe was *not* heralded by shocks of earthquake.[1]

I turned my eye upstream. For half a second I was utterly bewildered. Strange to say, I did not perceive at first the great flood of fire that was advancing towards me. I saw only the man who had shouted—a miserable, cowering, terror-stricken wretch, one of the abject creatures who used to earn a dubious livelihood in those days (when the river was a boulevard of pleasure) by towing boats upstream. But now, he was rushing wildly forward, with panic in his face; I could see he looked as if close pursued by some wild beast behind him. "A mad dog!" I said to myself at the outset; "or else a bull in the meadow!"

I glanced back to see what his pursuer might be; and then, in one second the whole horror and terror of the catastrophe burst upon me. Its whole horror and terror, I say, but not yet its magnitude. I was aware at first just of a moving red wall, like dull, red-hot molten metal. Trying to recall at so safe a distance in time and space the feelings of the moment and the way in which they surged and succeeded one another, I think I can recollect that my earliest idea was no more than this: "He must run, or the moving wall will overtake him!" Next instant, a hot wave seemed to strike my face. It was just like the blast of heat that strikes one in a glasshouse when you stand in front of the boiling and seething glass in the furnace. At about the same point in time, I was aware, I believe, that the dull-red wall was really a wall of fire. But it was cooled by contact

---

[1]For an opposite opinion, see Dr. Haigh Withers's evidence in Vol. iii, of the blue book.

with the air and the water. Even as I looked, however, a second wave from behind seemed to rush on and break: it overlaid and outran the first one. This second wave was white, not red—at white heat, I realized. Then, with a burst of recognition, I knew what it all meant. What Ward had spoken of last night—a fissure-eruption!

I looked back. Ward was coming towards me on the bridge, mounted on his Columbia. Too speechless to utter one word, I pointed upstream with my hand. He nodded and shouted back, in a singularly calm voice: "Yes; just what I told you. A fissure-eruption!"

They were the last words I head him speak. Not that he appreciated the danger less than I did, though his manner was cool; but he was wearing no clips to his trousers, and at that crucial moment he caught his leg in his pedals. The accident disconcerted him; he dismounted hurriedly, and then, panic-stricken as I judged, abandoned his machine. He tried to run. The error was fatal. He tripped and fell. What became of him afterward I will mention later.

But for the moment I saw only the poor wretch on the towpath. He was not a hundred yards off, just beyond the little bridge which led over the opening to a private boat-house. But as he rushed forwards and shrieked, the wall of fire overtook him. I do not think it quite caught him. It is hard at such moments to judge what really happens; but I believe I saw him shrivel like a moth in a flame a few seconds before the advancing wall of fire swept over the boat-house. I have seen an insect shrivel just so when flung into the midst of white-hot coals. He seemed to go off in gas, leaving a shower of powdery ash to represent his bones behind him. But of this I do not pretend to be positive; I will allow that my own agitation was far too profound to permit of my observing anything with accuracy.

How high was the wall at that time? This has been much debated. I should guess, thirty feet (though it rose afterwards to more than two hundred), and it advanced rather faster than a man could run down the center of the valley. (Later on, its pace accelerated greatly with subsequent outbursts.) In frantic haste, I saw or felt that only one chance of safety lay before me: I must strike uphill by the field path to Hedsor.

I rose for very life, with grim death behind me. Once well across the bridge and turning up the hill, I saw Ward on the parapet, with his arms flung up, trying wildly to save himself by leaping into the river. Next instant he shriveled I think, as the beggar had shriveled; and it is to this complete combustion before the lava-flood reached them that I attribute the circumstance (so much commented upon in the scientific excavations among the ruins) that no casts of dead bodies, like those at Pompeii, have anywhere been found in the Thames Valley Desert. My own belief is that every human body was reduced to a gaseous condition by the terrific heat several seconds before the molten basalt reached it.

Even at the distance which I had now attained from the central mass, indeed, the heat was intolerable. Yet, strange to say, I saw few or no people flying as yet from the inundation. The fact it, the eruption came upon us so suddenly, so utterly without warning or premonitory symptoms (for I deny the earthquake shocks), that whole towns must have been destroyed before the inhabitants were aware that anything out of the common was happening. It is a sort of alleviation to the general horror to remember that a large proportion of the victims must have died without even knowing it; one second, they were laughing, talking, bargaining; the next, they were asphyxiated or reduced to ashes as you have seen a small fly disappear in an incandescent gas flame.

This, however, is what I learned afterwards. At that moment, I was only aware of a frantic pace uphill, over a rough, stony road, and with my pedals working as I had never before worked them; while behind me, I saw purgatory let loose, striving hard to overtake me. I just knew that a sea of fire was filling the valley from end to end, and that its heat scorched my face as I urged on my bicycle in abject terror.

All this time, I will admit, my panic was purely personal. I was too much engaged in the engrossing sense of my own pressing danger to be vividly alive to the public catastrophe. I did not even think of Ethel and the children. But when I reached the hill by Hedsor Church—a neat, small building, whose shell still stands, though scorched and charred, by the edge of the desert—I was able to pause for half a minute to recover breath, and to look back upon the scene of the first disaster.

It was a terrible and yet I felt even then a beautiful sight—beautiful with the awful and unearthly beauty of a great forest fire, or a mighty conflagration in some crowded city. The whole river valley, up which I looked was one sea of fire. Barriers of red-hot lava formed themselves for a moment now and again where the outer edge or vanguard of the inundation had cooled a little on the surface by exposure: and over these temporary dams, fresh cataracts of white-hot material poured themselves afresh into the valley beyond it. After a while, as the deeper portion of basalt was pushed out, all was white alike. So glorious it looked in the morning sunshine that one could hardly realize the appalling reality of that sea of molten gold; one might almost have imagined a splendid triumph of the scene-painter's art, did one not know that it was actually a river of fire, overwhelming, consuming, and destroying every object before it in its devastating progress.

I tried vaguely to discover the source of the disaster. Looking straight upstream, past Bourne End and Marlow, I descried with bleared and dazzled eyes a whiter mass than any, glowing fiercely in the daylight like an electric light, and filling up the narrow gorge of the river towards Hurley and Henley. I recollected at once that this portion of the valley was not usually visible from Hedsor Hill, and almost without thinking of it I instinctively guessed the reason why it had become so now: it was the center of disturbance—the earth's crust just there had bulged upwards slightly, till it cracked and gaped to emit the basalt.

Looking harder, I could make out (though it was like looking at the sun) that the glowing white dome-shaped mass, as of an electric light, was the molten lava as it gurgled from the mouth of the vast fissure. I say vast, because so it seemed to me, though, as everybody now knows, the actual gap where the earth opened measures no more than eight miles across, from a point near what was once Shiplake Ferry to the site of the old lime-kilns at Marlow. Yet when one saw the eruption actually taking place, the colossal scale of it was what most appalled one. A sea of fire, eight to twelve miles broad, in the familiar Thames Valley, impressed and terrified one a thousand times more than a sea of fire ten times as vast in the nameless wilds of Western America.

I could see dimly, too, that the flood spread in every direction from its central point, both up and down the river. To right and left, indeed, it was soon checked and hemmed in by the hills about Wargrave and Medmenham; but downwards, it had filled the entire valley as far as Cookham and beyond; while upward, it spread in one vast glowing sheet towards Reading and the flats by the confluence of the Kennet. I did not then know, of course, that this gigantic natural dam or barrier was later on to fill up the whole low-lying level, and so block the course of the two rivers as to form those twin expanses of inland water, Lake Newbury and Lake Oxford. Tourists who now look down on still summer evenings where the ruins of Magdalen and of Merton may be dimly descried through the pale-green depths, their broken masonry picturesquely overgrown with tangled water-weeds, can form but little idea of the terrible scene which that peaceful bank presented while the incandescent lava was pouring forth in a scorching white flood towards the doomed district. Merchants who crowd the busy quays of those mushroom cities which have sprung up with greater rapidity than Chicago or Johannesburg on the indented shore where the new lakes abut upon the Berkshire chalk downs have half forgotten the horror of the intermediate time when the waters of the two rivers rose slowly, slowly, day after day, to choke their valleys and overwhelm some of the most glorious architecture in Britain. But though I did not know and could not then foresee the remoter effects of the great fire-flood in that direction, I saw enough to make my heart stand still within me. It was with difficulty that I grasped my bicycle, my hands trembled so fiercely. I realized that I was a spectator of the greatest calamity which had befallen a civilized land within the ken of history.

I looked southwards along the valley in the direction of Maidenhead. As yet it did not occur to me that the catastrophe was anything more than a local flood, though even as such it would have been one of unexampled vastness. My imagination could hardly conceive that London itself was threatened. In those days one could not grasp the idea of the destruction of London. I only thought just at first, "It will go on towards Maidenhead!" Even as I thought it, I saw a fresh and fiercer gush of fire well out from the central gash, and flow still faster than ever down the center of the valley, over the hardening layer already cooling on its edge by contact with the air and soil. This new outburst fell in a mad cataract over the end or van of the last, and instantly spread like water across the level expanse between the Cliveden hills and the opposite range at Pinkneys. I realized with a throb that it was advancing towards Windsor. Then a wild fear thrilled through me. If Windsor, why not Staines and Chertsey and Hounslow, why not London?

In a second I remembered Ethel and the children. Hitherto, the immediate danger of my own position alone had struck me. The fire was so near; the heat of it rose up in my face and daunted me. But now I felt I must make a wild dash to warn—not London—no, frankly, I forgot those millions; but Ethel and my little ones. In that thought, for the first moment, the real vastness of the catastrophe came home to me. The Thames Valley was doomed! I must ride for dear life if I wished to save my wife and children!

I mounted again, but found my shaking feet could hardly work the pedals. My legs were one jelly. With a frantic effort, I struck off inland in the direction of Burnham. I did not think my way out definitely; I hardly knew the topography of the district well enough to form any clear conception of what route I must take in order to keep to the hills and avoid the flood of fire that was deluging the lowlands. But by pure instinct, I believe, I set my face Londonwards along the ridge of the chalk downs. In three minutes I had lost sight of the burning flood, and was deep among green lanes and under shadowy beeches. The very contrast frightened me. I wondered if I was going mad. It was all so quiet. One could not believe that scarce five miles off from that devastating sheet of fire, birds were singing in the sky and men toiling in the fields as if nothing had happened.

Near Lambourne Wood I met a brother cyclist, just about to descend the hill. A curve in the road hid the valley from him. I shouted aloud:

"For heaven's sake, don't go down! There is danger, danger!"

He smiled and looked back at me. "I can take any hill in England," he answered.

"It's not the hill," I burst out. "There has been an eruption—a fissure-eruption at Marlow—great floods of fire—and all the valley is filled with burning lava!"

He stared at me derisively. Then his expression changed of a sudden. I suppose he saw I was white-faced and horror-stricken. He drew away as if alarmed. "Go back to Colney Hatch!" he cried pedaling faster and rode hastily down the hill, as if afraid of me. I have no doubt he must have ridden into the very midst of the flood, and been scorched by its advance, before he could check his machine on so sudden a slope.

Between Lambourne Wood and Burnham I did not see the fire-flood. I rode on at full speed among green fields and meadows. Here and there I passed a laboring man on the road. More than one looked up at me and commented on the oppressive heat, but none of them seemed to be aware of the fate that was overtaking their own homes close by, in the valley. I told one or two, but they laughed and gazed after me as if I were a madman. I grew sick of warning them. They took no heed of my words, but went on upon their way as if nothing out of the common were happening to England.

On the edge of the down, near Burnham, I caught sight of the valley again. Here, people were just waking to what was taking place near them. Half the population was gathered on the slope, looking down with wonder on the flood of fire, which had now just turned the corner of the hills by Taplow. Silent terror was the prevailing type of expression. But when I told them I had seen the lava bursting forth from the earth in a white dome above Marlow, they laughed me to scorn; and when I assured them I was pushing forward in hot haste to London, they answered, "London! It won't never get as far as London!" That was the only place on the hills, as is now well known, where the flood was observed long enough beforehand to telegraph and warn the inhabitants of the great city; but nobody thought of doing it; and I must say, even if they had done so, there is not the slightest probability that the warning would have attracted the least attention in our ancient metropolis. Men of the Stock Exchange would have made jests about the slump, and proceeded to buy and sell as usual.

I measured with my eye the level plain between Burnham and Slough, calculating roughly with myself whether I should have time to descend upon the well-known road from Maidenhead to London by Colnbrook and Hounslow. (I advise those who are unacquainted with the topography of this district before the eruption to follow out my route on a good map of the period.) But I recognized in a moment that this course would be impossible. At the rate that the flood had taken to progress from Cookham Bridge to Taplow, I felt sure it would be upon me before I reached Upton, or Ditton park at the outside. It is true the speed of the advance might slacken somewhat as the lava cooled; and strange to say, so rapidly do realities come to be accepted in one's mind, that I caught myself thinking this thought in the most natural manner, as if I had all my life long been accustomed to the ways of fissure-eruptions. But on the other hand, the lava might well out faster and hotter than before, as I had already seen it do more than once, and I had no certainty even that it would not rise to the level of the hills on which I was standing. You who read this narrative nowadays take it for granted, of course, that the extent and height of the inundation was bound to be exactly what you know it to have been, we at the time could not guess how high it might rise and how large an area of the country it might overwhelm and devastate. Was it to stop at the Chilterns, or to go north to Birmingham, York, and Scotland?

Still, in my trembling anxiety to warn my wife and children, I debated with myself whether I should venture down into the valley, and hurry along the main road with a wild burst for London. I thought of

Ethel, alone in our little home at Bayswater, and almost made up my mind to risk it. At that moment, I became aware that the road to London was already crowded with carriages, carts, and cycles, all dashing at a mad pace unanimously towards London. Suddenly a fresh wave turned the corner by Taplow and Maidenhead Bridge, and began to gain upon them visibly. It was an awful sight. I cannot pretend to describe it. The poor creatures on the road, men and animals alike, rushed wildly, despairingly on; the fire took them from behind, and, one by one, before the actual sea reached them, I saw them shrivel and melt away in the fierce white heat of the advancing inundation. I could not look at it any longer. I certainly could not descend and court instant death. I felt that my one chance was to strike across the downs, by Stoke Poges and Uxbridge, and then try the line of northern heights to London.

Oh, how fiercely I pedaled! At Farnham Royal (where again nobody seemed to be aware what had happened) a rural policeman tried to stop me, for frantic riding. I tripped him up, and rode on. Experience had taught me it was no use telling those who had not seen it of the disaster. A little beyond, at the entrance to a fine park, a gatekeeper attempted to shut a gate in my face, exclaiming that the road was private. I saw it was the only practicable way without descending to the valley, and I made up my mind this was no time for trifling. I am a man of peace, but I lifted my fist and planted it between his eyes. Then, before he could recover from his astonishment, I had mounted again and ridden on across the park, while he ran after me in vain, screaming to the men in the pleasure-grounds to stop me. But I would not be stopped; and I emerged on the road once more at Stoke Poges.

Near Galley Hill, after a long and furious ride, I reached the descent to Uxbridge. Was it possible to descend? I glanced across, once more by pure instinct, for I had never visited the spot before, towards where I felt the Thames must run. A great white cloud hung over it. I saw what that cloud must mean: it was the steam of the river, where the lava sucked it up and made it seethe and boil suddenly. I had not noticed this white fleece of steam at Cookham, though I did not guess why till afterwards. In the narrow valley where the Thames ran between hills, the lava flowed over it all at once, bottling the steam beneath; and it is this imprisoned steam that gave rise in time to the subsequent series of appalling earthquakes, to supply forecasts of which is now the chief duty of the Seismologer Royal; whereas, in the open plain, the basalt advanced more gradually and in a thinner stream, and therefore turned the whole mass of water into white cloud as soon as it reached each bend of the river.

At the time, however, I had no leisure to think out all this. I only knew by such indirect signs that the flood was still advancing, and, therefore, that it would be impossible for me to proceed towards London by the direct route via Uxbridge and Hanwell. If I meant to reach town (as we called it familiarly), I must descend to the valley at once, pass through Uxbridge streets as fast as I could, make a dash across the plain, by what I afterwards knew to be Hillingdon (I saw it then as a nameless village), and aim at a house-crowned hill, which I only learned later was Harrow, but which I felt sure would enable me to descend upon London by Hampstead or Highgate.

I am no strategist; but in a second, in that extremity, I picked out these points, feeling dimly sure they would lead me home to Ethel and the children.

The town of Uxbridge (whose place you can still find marked on many maps) lay in the valley of a small river, a confluent of the Thames. Up this valley it was certain that the lava-stream must flow; and, indeed, at the present day, the basin around is completely filled by one of the solidest and most forbidding masses of black basalt in the country. Still, I made up my mind to descend and cut across the low-lying ground towards Harrow. If I failed, I felt, after all, I was but one unit more in what I now began to realize as a prodigious national calamity.

I was just coasting down the hill, with Uxbridge lying snug and unconscious in the glen below me, when a slight and unimportant accident occurred which almost rendered impossible my further progress. It was past the middle of August; the hedges were being cut; and this particular lane, bordered by a high thorn fence, was strewn with the mangled branches of the may-bushes. At any other time, I should have remembered the danger and avoided them; that day, hurrying downhill for dear life and for Ethel, I forgot to notice them. The consequence was, I was pulled up suddenly by finding my front wheel deflated[1]; this untimely misfortune almost unmanned me. I dismounted and examined the tire; it had received a bad puncture. I tried inflating again, in hopes

---

[1]The bicycles of that period were fitted with pneumatic tubes of india rubber as tires—a clumsy device, now long superseded.

the hole might be small enough to make that precaution sufficient. But it was quite useless. I found I must submit to stop and doctor up the puncture. Fortunately, I had the necessary apparatus in my wallet.

I think it was the weirdest episode of all that weird ride—this sense of stopping impatiently, while the fiery flood still surged on towards London, in order to go through all the fiddling and troublesome little details of mending a pneumatic tire. The moment and the operation seemed so sadly out of harmony. A countryman passed by on a cart, obviously suspecting nothing; that was another point which added horror to the occasion—that so near the catastrophe, so very few people were even aware what was taking place beside them. Indeed, as is well known, I was one of the few who saw the eruption during its course, and yet managed to escape from it. Elsewhere, those who tried to run before it, either to escape themselves or to warn others of the danger, were overtaken by the lava before they could reach a place of safety. I attribute this mainly to the fact that most of them continued along the high roads in the valley, or fled instinctively for shelter towards their homes, instead of making at once for the heights and the uplands.

The countryman stopped and looked at me.

"The more haste the less speed!" he said, with proverbial wisdom.

I glanced up at him, and hesitated. Should I warn him of his doom, or was it useless? "Keep up on the hills," I said, at last. "An unspeakable calamity is happening in the valley. Flames of fire are flowing down it, as from a great burning mountain. You will be cut off by the eruption."

He stared at me blankly, and burst into a meaningless laugh. "Why, you're one of them Salvation Army fellows," he exclaimed, after a short pause. "You're trying to preach to me. I'm going to Uxbridge." And he continued down the hill towards certain destruction.

It was hours, I felt sure, before I had patched up that puncture, though I did it by the watch in four and a half minutes. As soon as I had blown up my tire again I mounted once more, and rode at a breakneck pace to Uxbridge. I passed down the straggling main street of the suburban town, crying aloud as I went, "Run, run, to the downs! A flood of lava is rushing up the valley! To the hills, for your lives! All the Thames bank is blazing!" Nobody took the slightest heed; they stood still in the street for a minute with open mouths: then they returned to their customary occupations. A quarter of an hour later, there was no such place in the world as Uxbridge.

I followed the main road through the village which I have since identified as Hillingdon; then I diverged to the left, partly by roads and partly by field paths of whose exact course I am still uncertain, towards the hill at Harrow. When I reached the town, I did not strive to rouse the people, partly because my past experience had taught me the futility of the attempt, and partly because I rightly judged that they were safe from the inundation; for as it never quite covered the dome of St. Paul's, part of which still protrudes from the sea of basalt, it did not reach the level of the northern heights of London. I rode on through Harrow without one word to anybody. I did not desire to be stopped or harassed as an escaped lunatic.

From Harrow I made my way tortuously along the rising ground, by the light of nature, through Wembley Park, to Willesden. At Willesden, for the first time, I found to a certainty that London was threatened. Great crowds of people in the profoundest excitement stood watching a dense cloud of smoke and steam that spread rapidly over the direction of Shepherd's Bush and Hammersmith. They were speculating as to its meaning, but laughed increduously when I told them what it portended. A few minutes later, the smoke spread ominously towards Kensington and Paddington. That settled my fate. It was clearly impossible to descend into London; and indeed, the heat now began to be unendurable. It drove us all back, almost physically. I thought I must abandon all hope. I should never even know what had become of Ethel and the chldren.

My first impulse was to lie down and await the fire-flood. Yet the sense of the greatness of the catastrophe seemed somehow to blunt one's own private grief. I was beside myself with fear for my darlings; but I realized that I was but one among hundreds of thousands of fathers in the same position. What was happening at that moment in the great city of five million souls we did not know, we shall never know; but we may conjecture that the end was mercifully too swift to entail much needless suffering. All at once, a gleam of hope struck me. It was my father's birthday. Was it not just possible that Ethel might have taken the children up to Hampstead to wish their grandpapa many happy returns of the day? With a wild determination not to give up all for lost, I turned my front wheel in the direction of Hampstead Hill, still skirting the high ground as far as possible. My heart was on fire within me. A restless anxiety urged me to ride my hardest. As all along the route, I was still just a minute or two in front of the catastrophe. People were beginning to be aware that something was taking place; more than once as I passed they asked me eagerly where the fire was. It was impossible for me to believe by this time that they knew nothing of an event in whose midst I seemed to have been living for months; nor could I realize that all the things which had happened since I started from Cookham Bridge so long ago were really compressed into the space of a single morning—nay, more, of an hour and a half only?

As I approached Windmill Hill, a terrible sinking seized me. I seemed to totter on the brink of a precipice. Could Ethel be safe? Should I ever again see little Bertie and the baby? I pedaled on as if automatically; for all life had gone out of me. I felt my hip joint moving dry in its socket. I held my breath; my heart stood still. It was a ghastly moment.

At my father's door I drew up, and opened the garden gate. I hardly dared to go in. Though each second was precious, I paused and hesitated.

At last I turned the handle. I heard somebody within. My heart came up in my mouth. It was little Bertie's voice: "Do it again, Granpa; do it again; it amooses Bertie!"

I rushed into the room. "Bertie, Bertie!" I cried. "Is Mammy here?"

He flung himself upon me. "Mammy, Mammy, Daddy has comed home." I burst into tears. "And Baby?" I asked, trembling.

"Baby and Ethel are here, George," my father answered, staring at me. "Why, my boy, what's the matter?"

I flung myself into a chair and broke down. In that moment of relief, I felt that London was lost, but I had saved my wife and children.

I did not wait for explanations. A crawling four-wheeler was loitering by. I hailed it, and hurried them in. My father wished to discuss the matter, but I cut him short. I gave the driver three pounds—all the gold I had with me. "Drive on!" I shouted, "Drive on! Towards Hatfield—anywhere!"

He drove as he was bid. We spent that night, while Hampstead flared like a beacon, at an isolated farmhouse on the high ground in Hertfordshire. For, of course, though the flood did not reach so high, it set fire to everything inflammable in its neighbourhood.

Next day, all the world knew the magnitude of the disaster. It can only be summed up in five emphatic words: There was no more London.

I have one other observation alone to make. I noticed at the time how, in my personal relief, I forgot for the moment that London was

292

perishing. I even forgot that my house and property had perished. Exactly the opposite, it seemed to me, happened with most of those survivors who lost wives and children in the eruption. They moved about as in a dream, without a tear, without a complaint, helping others to provide for the needs of the homeless and houseless. The universality of the catastrophe made each man feel as though it were selfishness to attach too great an importance at such a crisis to his own personal losses. Nay, more; the burst of feverish activity and nervous excitement, I might even say enjoyment, which followed the horror, was traceable, I think, to this selfsame cause. Even grave citizens felt they must do their best to dispel the universal gloom; and they plunged accordingly into a round of dissipations which other nations thought both unseemly and un-English. It was one way of expressing the common emotion. We had all lost heart—and we flocked to the theatres to pluck up our courage. That, I believe, must be our national answer to M. Zola's strictures on our untimely levity. "This people," says the great French author, "which took its pleasures sadly while it was rich and prosperous, begins to dance and sing above the ashes of its capital—it makes merry by the open graves of its wives and children. What an enigma! What a puzzle! What chance of an Oedipus!"

C.J. Cutcliffe Hyne (1866–1944)

A popular writer during his time, today C.J. Cutliffe Hyne is little remembered except for *The Lost Continent* (1900) a novel about Atlantis. However, he also produced many science-fiction short stories, a number of which can be found in *The Adventures of a Solicitor* (1898) and *Man's Understanding* (1933).

The son of the Vicar of Bierley, Hyne was born in 1865, and began working part-time in the coal mines when twelve. Apparently this dose of life in the raw was beneficial, because Hyne sped through Cambridge, acquiring both a B.A. and M.A. in natural science.

After graduation he decided to become a writer rather than a minister or teacher, so he began to crank out "pot-boilers, boy's books, and advice to readers as a mythical Aunt Ermyntrude" until coming up with the concept for Captain Kettle: a contentious, red-bearded little Welsh sea captain. The first Kettle book sold well and when, shortly thereafter, Cyril Arthur Pearson started *Pearson's Magazine*, he decided to push Captain Kettle as a strong series character to compete with Sherlock Holmes of the *Strand* magazine. The idea worked and the popular Kettle was to continue his adventures until 1938, by which time he had appeared in a play, filled eleven volumes, and made his creator wealthy.

Hyne traveled all over the world, stopping in places such as the Arctic, Brazil, the Congo, Lapland, Mexico, the Shetlands, and the Spanish Main, often using this experience to increase the verisimilitude of his works. He disliked plotting, usually improvising in an attempt to gain a richer and more ingenuous result. And as a stylist, Hyne strove for a straightforward, impersonal prose that would be easy to read.

While only four of the Captain Kettle adventures contain fantastic elements—*Captain Kettle on the Warpath* (1916), *Ice Age Woman* (1925), *Mr. Kettle, Third Mate* (1931), and *Ivory Valley; An Adventure of Captain Kettle* (1938)—Hyne did write seven other science-fiction and fantasy novels (besides *The Lost Continent*) which explore such diverse themes as diamond-making, a hollow earth, imaginary war, immortality, and magical objects.

Additional details of his life can be found in his autobiography, *My Joyful Life* (1935), which he completed nine years before his death at the age of seventy-eight.

For this anthology, we have selected Hyne's most famous science-fiction short story, "The Lizard," which is a suspenseful account of a battle between man and dinosaur.

THE LIZARD

It is not expected that the general public will believe the statements which will be made in this paper. They are written to catch the eye of Mr. Wilfred Cording (or Cordy) if he still lives, or of his friends and relations. Further details may be had from me (by any of these interested people) at Poste Restante, Wharfedale, Yorkshire. My name is Chesney, and I am sufficiently well known there for letters to be forwarded.

The matters in question happened two years ago on the last day of August. I had a small high-ground shoot near Kettlewell, but that morning dense mist made shooting out of the question. However, I wasn't sorry for an off day, as there was a newly-found cave in the neighborhood which I was anxious to explore—cave-hunting being, after shooting, my main amusement.

I suggested to my keeper that he should come with me to inspect the cave: he made some sort of excuse and I did not press the matter further. The dalesmen up there look on the local caves with more awe than respect. They will not own up to believing in bogles, but I fancy their creed runs that way. I had taken unwilling helpers cave-hunting with me before, and found them such a nuisance that I didn't press for the keeper's society. So I took candles, matches in a bottle, some magnesium wire, a small coil of rope, and a large flask of whiskey, and set off alone.

I hadn't seen the cave for a week or more, and I was a good deal annoyed to find by the bootmarks that quite a lot of people had visited it in the interval. However, I hoped that the larger part were made by shepherds, and trusted that I might find the interior still untampered with.

The cave was easy enough to enter. There was a funnel-shaped slide of peat-earth and mud and clay to start with, well pitted with bootmarks; and then there was a tumbled wall of boulders, slanting inwards, down which I crawled face uppermost till the light behind me dwindled. The way was getting pretty murky, so I lit up a candle to avoid accidents, stepped knee-deep into a lively stream of water, and went briskly ahead. It was an ordinary-enough limestone cave so far, with inferior stalactites, and a good deal of wet everywhere. It did not appear to have been disturbed, and I stepped along cheerfully.

Presently I got a bit of a shock. The roof above began to droop downwards, slowly but relentlessly. It seemed as though my way was soon going to be blocked. However, the water beneath deepened, and so I waded along as far as possible. It was a cold job, the water was up to my chin, and the air was none of the best. I was beginning to think I had got wet through for no adequate result.

But there is no accounting for the freaks of caves. Just when I fancied I was at the end of my tether, I was able to stand erect once more: a dozen yards further on I came out onto dry rock, and was able to have a rest and a drop of whiskey. The roof had quite disappeared to candlelight overhead, so I burned a foot of magnesium wire for a better inspection. It was really a magnificent cave, well furnished with stalactites above and stalagmites below: the candle burned brightly, showing me that the air was healthy enough. And yet the air in this cave did not altogether pass muster: there was something new about it, and anything new in cave smells is always suspicious. It wasn't the smell of peat, or iron, or sandstone, or fungus: it was a faint musky smell, rather sickly. When I inhaled a deeper breath of it, it came very near to making my flesh creep.

Before me stretched a tarn of black water, with a beach of white tumbled limestone on the far side. I pitched a stone into the water, shattering the surface for the first time in a million years. Yes, it's worth doing even a year of cave-hunting to do a thing like that. The stone sank with a luscious plop. The water was clearly very deep. But I was wet to the neck already, and didn't mind a swim. So with a lump of clay I stuck one candle in my cap, set up a couple more on the dry rock as a lighthouse to guide my return, lowered myself into the black water, and struck out. The smell of musk oppressed me, and I fancied it was growing stronger. So I didn't dawdle. Roughly, I guessed the pool to be some five-and-thirty yards across.

I landed amongst the broken limestone with a shiver and a scramble: the smell of musk was strong enough now to make me cough. But when I had stood up, and got the candle into my hand again, a thrill came through me as I thought I guessed the cause. A dozen yards further on was a broken cast where some monstrous uncouth animal had been entombed in the forgotten ages of the past, and mouldered away and left only the outer shell of its form and shape. For ages, this, too, had endured; and indeed, it had been violated only by the eroding touch of the water and some earth tremor within the last few days. A workman with plaster of Paris could have made an exact model of this beast which had been lost to the world's knowledge for so many weary millions of years.

It had been some sort of lizard or crocodile, and in fancy I was beginning to picture its restored shape in the National Museum, when my eye fell on something amongst the rubble which brought me to earth with a jar. I stopped and picked it up. It was a common white-handled penknife, of the variety sold by stationers for a shilling. On one side of it was the name of Wilfred Cording (or Cordy) scratched apparently with a nail. The work was neat enough to start with, but the engraver had wearied with his job, till the surname was too scratchy to be certain about.

On the hot impulse of the moment I threw the knife far from me into the black water, and swore. It is more than a little unpleasant for an explorer to find he has been forestalled. But since then I have more than once regretted the hard things I said against Cording (if that is his name). If the man is alive, I apologize to him. If, as I strongly suspect, he came to a horrible end in that cave, I tender my regrets to his relatives.

I looked upon the cast of the saurian now with the warmth of discovery quite gone. I was conscious of cold, and the musky smell was growing more and more unpleasant. I think I should straightaway have gone back to daylight and a change of clothes if I hadn't thought I could see the outline of another cast. It was hazy, as a thing of the kind would be if seen through the medium of sparsely transparent limestone, and by the light of a solitary paraffin wax candle. I kicked at it petulantly.

Some flakes of stone shelled off, and I distinctly heard a more extensive crack. I kicked harder—with all my might, in fact. More flakes shelled away, and there was a little volley of cracks. It did not feel like kicking against stone. It was like kicking against something that gave. And I could have sworn that the musky smell increased. I felt a curious glow coming over me that was part fright, part excitement, part nausea; but plucked up my courage and kicked again and again. The limestone flew up in tinkling showers. There was no doubt now about there being something springy underneath, and that it was the dead carcass of another lizard I hadn't doubt. Here was luck, here was a find. Here was I the discoverer of the body of a prehistoric beast, preserved in the limestone down through all the ages just as mammoths have been preserved in Siberian ice. As I kicked and battered at the harsh scaly skin of this anachronism, which ought to have perished body and bones ten million years ago, I wondered whether they would make me a baronet for the discovery.

Then of a sudden I got a start. I could have sworn the dead flesh moved beneath me.

But I shouted aloud at myself in contempt. Ten million years: it was impossible. And then I got a further start, a more solid one. While I was raising a boulder for a further blow, a splinter of stone broke away as if pressed up from below, flipped up in the air. My blood chilled, and for a moment the loneliness of that unknown cave oppressed me. But I told myself that I was an old hand: that this was childishness. I continued my battering until a further movement left me in no possible doubt—the beast was actually stirring of its own accord.

Stirring—and alive. It was writhing and straining to leave the rocky bed where it had lain quiet through all those countless cycles of time, and I watched it in a very petrifaction of terror. Its efforts threw up whole basketfuls of splintered stone at a time. I could see the muscles of its back ripple at each effort. I could see the exposed part of its body grow in size every time it wrenched at the walls of that semi-eternal prison.

Then, as I looked, it doubled up its back like a bucking horse, and drew out its stumpy head and long feelers, giving out the while a thin small scream like a hurt child: and then with another effort it pulled out its long tail and stood upon the debris of the limestone panting with a newfound life.

I gazed upon it with a sickly fascination. Its body was about the bigness of two horses. Its head was curiously short, but the mouth opened back almost to the forearm; and sprouting from the nose were two enormous feelers, each at least six feet long, tipped with fleshy tendrils like fingers which opened and shut tremulously. In color it was a bright grass-green. And worst of all was the musky smell.

All this while I had stood motionless, but the beast must have heard some slight movement. I could not see any ears, but it heard me, no doubt of that. Worse, it hobbled round clumsily with its jointless legs, and waved its feelers in my direction. I could not make out any eyes: its sensitiveness seemed to lie in those fathom-long feelers and in the fleshy fingers which twitched at the end of them.

Then it opened its great jaws and yawned cavernously, and came towards me. It seemed to have no trace of fear or hesitation. It hobbled clumsily on, exhibiting its monstrous deformity in every movement, and preceded always by those hateful feelers.

For a while I stayed in my place, too paralyzed with horror at this awful thing I had dragged up from the forgotten dead. But then one of its feelers touched me, and the fleshy fingers pawed my face. I leaped into movement again. The beast was hungry after its fast of ten million years. . . . I turned and ran.

It followed me. In the feeble light of the one solitary candle I could see it hobbling—and hobbling faster and less clumsily now as it worked the rust of ages out of its cankered joints. Presently it was following me with a speed equal to my own.

If the huge beast had shown anger, eagerness, any feelings, it would have been less horrible: but it was absolutely unemotional in its hunt, and this in turn came near to making me feel that I was lost, that I should surrender myself to the inevitable. I wondered dully whether there had been another beast entombed beside it, and whether that had eaten up the man who owned the penknife.

But that thought suggested an idea to me. I had a stout knife in my

301

own pocket. I drew it out and turned to defend myself just as the feelers with their fringe of fumbling fingers were agonizingly close to me. I slashed at them viciously, and felt my knife grate against their armor. I might as well have hacked at an iron rail.

Still, the attempt did me good. There is an animal love of fighting stowed away in the bottom of us all somewhere, and mine woke then. I don't know that I expected to win: but I did intend to do the largest possible amount of damage before I was caught. I made a rush, stepped with one foot on the beast's creeping back, and leaped astern of him: the beast gave its thin small whistling scream, and turned quickly in chase.

We doubled, turned, sprawled, leapt among the slimy boulders: and every time we came to close quarters I stabbed with my knife though without ever finding a joint in its armor. It was clear that this could not go on. The beast grew in strength and activity, and probably in dumb anger though it gave no sign of it; but I meanwhile was growing more blown, more bruised, more exhausted every moment.

At last I tripped and fell. The beast with its clumsy waddle shot past me before it could pull up, and in desperation I threw one arm up to drive the knife with the full force of my body into the underneath part of its body.

That woke it at last. It writhed, and it plunged, and it bucked with a frenzy that I had never seen before, and its scream grew in piercingness till it was as strong as the whistle of a steam engine. Again and again I planted my vicious blows, until it shook itself free in desperation and set off at its hobbling gait directly for the water. It plunged in, swam briskly with its tail, then I saw it dive and disappear for good.

And what next? I took to the water too, and swam as I had never swum before. It was that or nothing—risk the swim, or stay and be eaten. How I got across I do not know. How I landed I do not know. How I got down the windings of that cave is more than I can say, and whether the beast followed me I do not know either. Somehow I got to daylight again, staggering like a drunken man. I struggled as far as the village, noting how the people ran from me. At the inn the landlord cried out as though I had been the plague. It seemed that the musky smell I had brought with me was unendurable, though by this time the mere detail of a smell was far beneath my notice. But I was stripped from my stinking clothes, and washed, and put to bed, and a doctor came and gave me an opiate; and when twelve hours later wakefulness came to me again, I had the sense to hold my tongue. All the village wanted to know where the smell came from: I said I must have fallen into something.

And there the matter ends for the moment. I go no more cave-hunting, and I offer no help to those who do. But if the man who owns that white-handled penknife is alive, I should like to compare experiences with him.

Jack London (1876–1916)

*Born Jack Chaney in San Francisco, Jack London (he took his step-*father's name) was in many ways a tragic figure, despite the fact that he became an immensely popular author before his death at the age of forty. Best known for his adventure novels like *The Call of the Wild, The Sea Wolf,* and *White Fang,* London also made important contributions to science fiction. Many of his most successful novels (but not his s.f., unfortunately) have been turned into movies, some being filmed several times. One of his great themes was the struggle to survive in the wilderness against great odds.

London's mother was a spiritualist, and his natural father deserted the family shortly after his birth. He certainly knew of what he wrote, because he left home at the age of fourteen to seek adventure. He found poverty along with excitement, and held the now-stereotypical list of jobs and activities that writers hold before and while they are writers: he was a sailor who saw a good part of the world; "rode the rails" as a hobo and served time in prison for vagrancy; prospected in the Alaskan gold fields; and worked as a reporter, covering the Russo-Japanese War of 1905. His personal political beliefs combined Marxist socialism with a form of Social Darwinism, a combination that resulted in the ironic position of his supporting the downtrodden, exploited working class while at the same time believing in a virulent form of racism and white supremacy.

He was a pure example of the self-educated man, spending long hours in libraries, and he considered himself to be a working-class intellectual. When he decided to become a writer he approached that profession as a boxer would prepare for an important fight—he trained by writing huge quantities of material in various genres and forms, including poetry. However, success did not come easily at first. He was on the verge of killing himself when his first science-fiction story, "A Thousand Deaths," was purchased by *Black Cat* magazine. By 1913 he had gone from almost abject poverty to being "the highest-paid, best-known, and most popular writer in the world." But old habits die hard, and London more than spent every cent he made. In 1916, after having written nearly fifty books in seventeen years, he died from an overdose of morphine sleeping tablets. Overwork, heavy drinking, and financial difficulties had almost certainly led to suicide.

Four of his novels are science fiction: *Before Adam* (1906), a form of "prehistoric fiction set in the Stone Age that reflected London's aversion to urban life; *The Iron Heel* (1907), an outstanding work that prefigures the Fascist experience; *The Scarlet Plague* (1915), a catastrophe novel that is marred by his acute racism; and *The Star Rover* (1915). In addition, he produced thirteen shorter stories of science fiction, which can be found in *The Science Fiction of Jack London* and *Curious Fragments: Jack London's Tales of Fantasy Fiction* (both 1975).

A THOUSAND DEATHS

I had been in the water about an hour, and cold, exhausted, with a terrible cramp in my right calf, it seemed as though my hour had come. Fruitlessly struggling against the strong ebb tide, I had beheld the maddening procession of the waterfront lights slip by; but now I gave up attempting to breast the stream and contended myself with the bitter thoughts of a wasted career, now drawing to a close.

It had been my luck to come of good, English stock, but of parents whose account with the bankers far exceeded their knowledge of child-nature and the rearing of children. While born with a silver spoon in my mouth, the blessed atmosphere of the home circle was to me unknown. My father, a very learned man and a celebrated antiquarian, gave no thought to his family, being constantly lost in the abstractions of his study; while my mother, noted far more for her good looks than her good sense, sated herself with the adulation of the society in which she was perpetually plunged. I went through the regular school and college routine of a boy of the English bourgeoisie, and as the years brought me increasing strength and passions, my parents, suddenly became aware that I was possessed of an immortal soul, and endeavored to draw the curb. But it was too late; I perpetrated the wildest and most audacious folly, and was disowned by my people; ostracized by the society I had so long outraged, and with the thousand pounds my father gave me, with the declaration that he would neither see me again nor give me more, I took a first-class passage to Australia.

Since then my life had been one long peregrination—from the Orient to the Occident, from the Arctic to the Antarctic—to find myself at last, able seaman at thirty, in the full vigor of my manhood, drowning

307

in San Francisco Bay because of a disastrously successful attempt to desert my ship.

My right leg was drawn up by the cramp, and I was suffering the keenest agony. A slight breeze stirred up a choppy sea, which washed into my mouth and down my throat, nor could I prevent it. Though I still contrived to keep afloat, it was merely mechanical, for I was rapidly becoming unconscious. I have a dim recollection of drifting past the seawall, and of catching a glimpse of an upriver steamer's starboard light; then everything became a blank.

I heard the low hum of insect life, and felt the balmy air of a spring morning fanning my cheek. Gradually it assumed a rhythmic flow, to whose soft pulsations my body seemed to respond. I floated on the gentle bosom of a summer's sea, rising and falling with dreamy pleasure on each crooning wave. But the pulsations grew stronger; the humming, louder; the waves, larger, fiercer—I was dashed about on a stormy sea. A great agony fastened upon me. Brilliant, intermittent sparks of light flashed athwart my inner consciousness; in my ears there was the sound of many waters; then a sudden snapping of an intangible something, and I awoke.

The scene, of which I was protagonist, was a curious one. A glance sufficed to inform me that I lay on the cabin floor of some gentleman's yacht, in a most uncomfortable posture. On either side, grasping my arms and working them up and down like pump handles, were two peculiarly clad, dark-skinned creatures. Though conversant with most aboriginal types, I could not conjecture their nationality. Some attachment had been fastened about my head, which connected my respiratory organs with the machine I shall next describe. My nostrils, however, had been closed, forcing me to breathe through the mouth. Foreshortened by the obliquity of my line of vision, I beheld two tubes, similar to small hosing but of different composition, which emerged from my mouth and went off at an acute angle from each other. The first came to an abrupt termination and lay on the floor beside me; the second traversed the floor in numerous coils, connecting with the apparatus I have promised to describe.

In the days before my life became tangential, I had dabbled not a little in science, and conversant with the appurtenances and general paraphernalia of the laboratory, I appreciated the machine I now beheld.

It was composed chiefly of glass, the construction being of that crude sort which is employed for experimentative purposes. A vessel of water was surrounded by an air chamber, to which was fixed a vertical tube, surmounted by a globe. In the center of this was a vacuum gauge. The water of the tube moved upwards and downwards, creating alternate inhalations and exhalations, which were in turn communicated to me through the hose. With this, and the aid of the men who pumped my arms so vigorously, had the process of breathing been artificially carried on, my chest rising and falling and my lungs expanding and contracting, till nature could be persuaded to again take up her wonted labor.

As I opened my eyes the appliance about my head, nostrils and mouth was removed. Draining a stiff three fingers of brandy, I staggered to my feet to thank my preserver, and confronted—my father. But long years of fellowship with danger had taught me self-control, and I waited to see if he would recognize me. Not so; he saw in me no more than a runaway sailor and treated me accordingly.

Leaving me to the care of the blackies, he fell to revising the notes he had made on my resuscitation. As I ate of the handsome fare served up to me, confusion began on deck, and from the chanteys of the sailors and the rattling of blocks and tackles I surmised that we were getting under way. What a lark! Off on a cruise with my recluse father into the wide Pacific! Little did I realize, as I laughed to myself, which side the joke was to be on. Aye, had I known, I would have plunged overboard and welcomed the dirty fo'c'sle from which I had just escaped.

I was not allowed on deck till we had sunk the Farallones and the last pilot boat. I appreciated this forethought on the part of my father and made it a point to thank him heartily, in my bluff seaman's manner. I could not suspect that he had his own ends in view, in thus keeping my presence secret to all save the crew. He told me briefly of my rescue by his sailors, assuring me that the obligation was on his side, as my appearance had been most opportune. He had constructed the appartus for the vindication of a theory concerning certain biological phenomena, and had been waiting for an opportunity to use it.

"You have proved it beyond all doubt," he said; then added with a sigh, "But only in the small matter of drowning."

But, to take a reef in my yarn—he offered me an advance of two pounds on my previous wages to sail with him, and this I considered handsome, for he really did not need me. Contrary to my expectations, I did not join the sailors; mess, for'ard, being assigned to a comfortable stateroom and eating at the captain's table. He had perceived that I was no common sailor, and I resolved to take this chance for reinstating myself in his good graces. I wove a fictitious past to account for my education and present position, and did my best to come in touch with him. I was not long in disclosing a predilection for scientific pursuits, nor he in appreciating my aptitude. I became his assistant, with a corresponding increase in wages, and before long, as he grew confidential and expounded his theories, I was as enthusiastic as himself.

The days flew quickly by, for I was deeply interested in my new studies, passing my waking hours in his well-stocked library, or listening to his plans and aiding him in his laboratory work. But we were forced to forego many enticing experiments, a rolling ship not being exactly the proper place for delicate or intricate work. He promised me, however, many delightful hours in the magnificent laboratory for which we were bound. He had taken possession of an uncharted South Sea island, as he said, and turned it into a scientific paradise.

We had not been on the island long, before I discovered the horrible mare's nest I had fallen into. But before I describe the strange things which came to pass, I must briefly outline the causes which culminated in as startling an experience as ever fell to the lot of man.

Late in life, my father had abandoned the musty charms of antiquity and succumbed to the more fascinating ones embraced under the general head of biology. Having been thoroughly grounded during his youth in the fundamentals, he rapidly explored all the higher branches as far as the scientific world had gone, and found himself on the no-man's land of the unknowable. It was his intention to preempt some of this unclaimed territory, and it was at this stage of his investigations that we had been thrown together. Having a good brain, though I say it myself, I had mastered his speculations and methods of reasoning, becoming almost as mad as himself. But I should not say this. The marvelous results we afterwards obtained can only go to prove this sanity. I can but say that he was the most abnormal specimen of cold-blooded cruelty I have ever seen.

After having penetrated the dual mysteries of pathology and psychology, his thought had led him to the verge of a great field, for which, the better to explore, he began studies in higher organic chemistry, pathology, toxicology and other sciences and subsciences rendered kindred as accessories to his speculative hypotheses. Starting from the proposition that the direct cause of the temporary and permanent array of vitality was due to the coagulation of certain elements and compounds in the protoplasm, he had isolated and subjected these various substances to innumerable experiments. Since the temporary arrest of vitality in an organism brought coma, and a permanent arrest death, he held that by artificial means this coagulation of the protoplasm could be retarded, prevented, and even overcome in the extreme states of solidification. Or, to do away with the technical nomenclature, he argued that death, when not violent and in which none of the organs had suffered injury, was merely suspended vitality; and that, in such instances, life could be induced to resume its functions by the use of proper methods. This, then, was his idea: To discover the method—and by practical experimentation prove the possibility—of renewing vitality in a structure from which life had seemingly fled. Of course, he recognized the futility of such endeavor after decomposition had set in; he must have organisms which but the moment, the hour, or the day before, had been quick with life. With me, in a crude way, he had proved this theory. I was really drowned, really dead, when picked from the water of San Francisco Bay—but the vital spark had been renewed by means of his aerotherapeutical apparatus, as he called it.

Now to his dark purpose concerning me. He first showed me how completely I was in his power. He had sent the yacht away for a year, retaining only his two blackies, who were utterly devoted to him. He then made an exhaustive review of his theory and outlined the method of proof he had adopted, concluding with the startling announcement that I was to be his subject.

I had faced death and weighed my chances in many a desperate venture, but never in one of this nature. I can swear I am no coward, yet this proposition of journeying back and forth across the borderland of death put the yellow fear in me. I asked for time, which he granted at the same time assuring me that but the one course was open—I must submit. Escape from the island was out of the question; escape by suicide was not to be entertained, though really preferable to what it seemed I must undergo; my only hope was to destroy my captors. But this latter was frustrated through the precautions taken by my father. I was subjected to a constant surveillance, even in my sleep being guarded by one or the other of the blacks.

Having pleaded in vain, I announced and proved that I was his son. It was my last card, and I had placed all my hopes upon it. But he was inexorable; he was not a father but a scientific machine. I wonder yet how it ever came to pass that he married my mother or begat me, for there was not the slightest grain of emotion in his makeup. Reason was all in all to him, nor could he understand such things as love or sympathy in others, except as petty weaknesses which should be overcome. So he informed me that in the beginning he had given me life, and who had better right to take it away than he? Such, he said, was not his desire, however; he merely wished to borrow it occasionally, promising to return it punctually at that appointed time. Of course, there was a liability of mishaps, but I could do no more than take the chances, since the affairs of men were full of such.

The better to insure success, he wished me to be in the best possible condition, so I was dieted and trained like a great athlete before a decisive contest. What could I do? If I had to undergo the peril, it were best to be in good shape. In my intervals of relaxation he allowed me to assist in the arranging of the apparatus and in the various subsidary experiments. The interest I took in all such operations can be imagined. I mastered the work as thoroughly as he, and often had the pleasure of seeing some of my suggestions of alterations put into effect. After such events I would smile grimly, conscious of officiating at my own funeral.

He began by inaugurating a series of experiments in toxicology. When all was ready, I was killed by a stiff dose of strychnine and allowed to lie dead for some twenty hours. During that period my body was dead, absolutely dead. All respiration and circulation ceased; but the frightful part of it was, that while the protoplasmic coagulation proceeded, I retained consciousness and was enabled to study it in all its ghastly details.

The apparatus to bring me back to life was an airtight chamber, fitted to receive my body. The mechanism was simple—a few valves, a rotary shaft and crank, and an electric motor. When in operation, the interior atmosphere was alternately condensed and rarified, thus communicating to my lungs an artificial respiration without the agency of the hosing previously used. Though my body was inert, and, for all I knew, in the first stages of decomposition, I was cognisant of everything that transpired. I knew when they placed me in the chamber, and though all

312

my senses were quiescent, I was aware of hypodermic injections of a compound to react upon the coagulatory process. Then the chamber was closed and the machinery started. My anxiety was terrible; but the circulation became gradually restored, the different organs began to carry on their respective functions, and in an hour's time I was eating a hearty dinner.

It cannot be said that I participated in this series, nor in the subsequent ones, with much verve; but after two ineffectual attempts at escape, I began to take quite an interest. Besides, I was becoming accustomed. My father was beside himself in success, and as the months rolled by his speculations took wilder and yet wilder flights. We ranged through the three great classes of poisons, the neurotics, the gaseous and the irritants, but carefully avoided some of the mineral irritants and passed up the whole group of corrosives. During the poison regime I became quite accustomed to dying, and had but one mishap to shake my growing confidence. Scarifying a number of lesser blood vessels in my arm, he introduced a minute quantity of that most frightful of poisons, the arrow poison, or curare. I lost consciousness at the start, quickly followed by the cessation of respiration and circulation, and so far had the solidification of the protoplasm advanced, that he gave up all hope. But at the last moment he applied a discovery he had been working upon, receiving such encouragement as to redouble his efforts.

In a glass vacuum, similar but not exactly like a Crookes' tube was placed a magnetic field. When penetrated by polarized light, it gave no phenomena of phosphorescence nor of rectilinear projection of atoms, but emitted nonluminous rays, similar to the X ray. While the X ray could reveal opaque objects hidden in dense mediums, this was possessed of far subtler penetration. By this he photographed my body, and found on the negative an infinite number of blurred shadows, due to the chemical and electric motions still going on. This was infallible proof that the rigor mortis in which I lay was not genuine; that is, those mysterious forces, those delicate bonds which held my soul to my body, were still in action. The resultants of all other poisons were unapparent, save those of mercurial compounds, which usually left me languid for several days.

Another series of delightful experiments was with electricity. We verified Tesla's assertion that high currents were utterly harmless by passing 100,000 volts through my body. As this did not affect me, the current was reduced to 2,500, and I was quickly electrocuted. This time he ventured so far as to allow me to remain dead, or in a state of suspended vitality, for three days. It took four hours to bring me back.

Once, he superinduced lockjaw; but the agony of dying was so great that I positively refused to undergo similar experiments. The easiest deaths were by asphyxiation, such as drowning, strangling, and suffocation by gas; while those by morphine, opium, cocaine and chloroform, were not at all hard.

Another time, after being suffocated, he kept me in cold storage for three months, not permitting me to freeze or decay. This was without my knowledge, and I was in a great fright on discovering the lapse of time. I became afraid of what he might do with me when I lay dead, my alarm being increased by the predilection he was beginning to betray towards vivisection. The last time I was resurrected, I discovered that he had been tampering with my breast. Though he had carefully dressed and sewed the incisions up, they were so severe that I had to take to my bed for some time. It was during my convalescence that I evolved the plan by which I ultimately escaped.

While feigning unbounded enthusiasm in the work, I asked and received a vacation from my moribund occupation. During this period I devoted myself to laboratory work, while he was too deep in the vevisection of the many animals captured by the blacks to take notice of my work.

It was on these two propositions that I constructed my theory: First, electrolysis, or the decomposition of water into its constituent gases by means of electricity; and, second, by the hypothetical existence of a force, the converse of gravitation, which Astor has named "apergy." Terrestrial attraction, for instance, merely draws objects together but does not combine them; hence apergy is merely repulsion. Now, atomic or molecular attraction not only draws objects together but intergrates them; and it was the converse of this, or a disintegrative force, which I wished to not only discover and produce, but to direct at will. Thus, the molecules of hydrogen and oxygen reacting on each other, separate and create new molecules, containing both elements and forming water. Electrolysis causes these molecules to split up and resume their original condition, producing the two gases separately. The force I wished to find must not only do this with two, but with all elements, no matter in what

314

compounds they exist. If I could then entice my father within its radius, he would be instantly disintergrated and sent flying to the four quarters, a mass of isolated elements.

It must not be understood that this force, which I finally came to control, annihilated matter; it merely annihilated form. Nor, as I soon discovered, had it any effect on inorganic structure; but to all organic form it was absolutely fatal. This partiality puzzled me at first, though had I stopped to think deeper I would have seen through it. Since the number of atoms in organic molecules is far greater than in the most complex mineral molecules, organic compounds are characterized by their instability and the ease with which they are split up by physical forces and chemical reagents.

By two powerful batteries, connected with magnets constructed specially for this purpose, two tremendous forces were projected. Considered apart from each other, they were perfectly harmless; but they accomplished their purpose by focusing at an invisible point in midair. After practically demonstrating its success, besides narrowly escaping being blown into nothingness, I laid my trap. Concealing the magnets, so that their force made the whole space of my chamber doorway a field of death, and placing by my couch a button by which I could throw on the current from the storage batteries, I climbed into bed.

The blackies still guarded my sleeping quarters, one relieving the other at midnight. I turned on the current as soon as the first man arrived. Hardly had I begun to doze, when I was aroused by a sharp, metallic tinkle. There, on the mid-threshold, lay the collar of Dan, my father's St. Bernard. My keeper ran to pick it up. He disappeared like a gust of wind, his clothes falling to the floor in a heap. There was a slight whiff of ozone in the air, but since the principal gaseous components of his body were hydrogen, oxygen and nitrogen, which are equally colorless and odorless, there was no other manifestation of his departure. Yet when I shut off the current and removed the garments, I found a deposit of carbon in the form of animal charcoal; also other powders, the isolated, solid elements of his organism, such as sulphur, potassium and iron. Resetting the trap, I crawled back to bed. At midnight I got up and removed the remains of the second black, and then slept peacefully till morning.

I was awakened by the strident voice of my father, who was calling to me from across the laboratory. I laughed to myself. There had been no one to call him and he had overslept. I could hear him as he approached my room with the intention of rousing me, and so I sat up in bed, the better to observe his translation—perhaps apotheosis were a better term. He paused a moment at the threshhold, then took the fatal step. Puff! It was like the wind sighing among the pines. He was gone. His clothes fell in a fantastic heap on the floor. Besides ozone, I noticed the faint, garlic-like odor of phosphorous. A little pile of elementary solids lay among his garments. That was all. The wide world lay before me. My captors were no more.